Blood Stripe
The Susanna Marcasi Chronicles

Gina Maria DiNicolo

St. John's Press

Alexandria

GINA MARIA DINICOLO

St. John's Press LLC
Alexandria, Virginia

ISBN: **0966298608**
ISBN-13: **978-0-9662986-0-4**

OTHER BOOKS BY GINA MARIA DINICOLO

The Black Panthers: A Story af Race, War, And Courage. The 761st Tank Battalion in World War II (2014)

DEDICATION

To all the Susanna Marcasi's and those who have overcome.

CONTENTS

ACKNOWLEDGMENTS

I would like to thank the brilliant David White, my editor, artist, and friend. I also thank Rudy Schulz for lending his artistic talents, penning the unforgettable "Bark like a Beagle" as well as "Susanne." He and David also produced a wonderful cover. Proofreader and Marine cohort Robert Hansberry reminded me that we have our respective strengths and proofreading is not one of mine.

And thank you to all the Mike Singletons out there. You keep us sane and make it safe.

FORWARD

"Blood Stripe" began seven years ago as a story of friendship. It is now a wild-ride thriller with a damaged Marine hero. The military and political climate of nearly a decade ago is not so different at this writing, though some of the events in the book, beyond imagination at that time, have since occurred. As an historian and nonfiction author, I have observed that some readers prefer challenging topics when presented in a fictional setting. I have tried to do that here. "Blood Stripe," while rip-roaring and tension-filled, in its broadest context, is a story of good vs. evil. It touches on ugly secrets of the past and present that are not forgotten but, rather, continue obscured from view—by design. It is a layered story that can be read as a gripping and entertaining work of fiction, or for the deeper, metaphorical messages it carries. Regardless, Susanna Marcasi and crew provide excitement as well as hope and renewed perspective.

BLOOD STRIPE

PROLOGUE

Their first day at Quantico enraged him. He would have to compete with "that bitch," as he now referred to Susanna Marcasi, though she still wore the "damn diamond-encrusted slave collar," as she called the engagement ring. Having her at The Basic School that September of 1984 felt like having his mother with him on the first day of kindergarten. Susanna thought the same. Neither let on that they even knew each other, but they did not have to. Their tension permeated the 200-plus officer class, and their Naval Academy classmates dished the details before the end of the first week.

All-out war resumed.

He had long assumed the Marine Corps would stand as his legacy, as it had his father's, in part, as well as his grandfather's. Within days he realized he deplored the Corps as much as the burden of his heritage. In contrast, Susanna, dubious of her choice to shun the Navy, found a home much to her surprise.

Resentment between the two careened out of control.

Susanna seemed unstoppable. She topped the class in academics. In the field, no one could keep pace. The male instructors showered her with attention, though at least half wanted her legs spread for them. Raw desire aside, they found satisfaction in teaching a Marine who understood the nuances of ground tactics. *Female? Tough*, they concluded, as they agonized over what to do with her.

He seethed as he watched Susanna destroy his life—again.

The company trudged out for a week that would break even the most promising. Like her classmates, Susanna fired the M-16 A2 rifle and the .45 caliber pistol, but she did not drop a point, despite a steady and chilly November wind from the north. Onlookers envied her tight groupings. Her accuracy unnerved the range officers.

He took aim at her with his .45, but thought better of pulling the trigger in full view.

"Marcasi, do it again," barked senior firearms instructor, Captain Deke Bigelow.

Susanna and Bigelow had had more than one confrontation in the classroom.

She saw his command as harassment, but fired a second round with the same precision.

The next week, Bigelow trucked her back to the range. She fired every weapon type in the armory, including the sniper rifle, with the same result.

Susanna did not like guns, and the stench of expended rounds made her nauseous.

"We need you on the Corps's rifle team," declared Bigelow.

"Thank you, but I'm not interested," she said trying to contain her disgust.

"But you need to do this for the Marine Corps," he insisted.

"No, I don't, captain. I don't *need* to do this for anyone." She turned to walk away, but stopped and wheeled around to face him. "*You* open up the infantry specialty to me. *You* let me attend the Infantry Officer Course, and then we may have something to talk about."

She pointed at him as she made her demands known.

"So I hit a target. Big deal." She turned away. "I'll meet you at your vehicle ..., *sir,*" she said with intended sarcasm as she stormed off.

Susanna Marcasi stunned the group. One instructor remarked, "Fucking bitch."

Bigelow retorted, "What the fuck do you expect? I hope we're satisfied." He watched Susanna walk away. He knew she had more daring packed in her tiny frame than the hulks formed around him. Without looking at the men he said, "She has a point."

They sat in silence on the ride back. Bigelow cleared his throat, "You're right and I'm sorry. I can't open the 03 specialty, but let me see what else I can do."

Susanna said nothing and stared out the passenger window.

Within hours, word made its way around the company about Annie Oakley and her shooting feat. Her fiancé hid from embarrassment.

He had to stop her.

"Man, it's not a big deal. So she can shoot. It's not like she can do anything with it. She's a … chick," reassured one of his roommates.

It did not help. He sensed the gossip. *Who was the better officer?* floated around the company, but he could not expose the speculation with certainty. She had bested him in every category. He felt trapped by the destiny the men in his family had chosen before him. He would carry the stigma of Susanna Marcasi his entire career—maybe for the rest of his life. He could not let the bitch win. She refused to break off the engagement. For him to end the relationship would make her into a martyr, as would any confrontation with her.

He waited.

Just before graduation, Bigelow called Susanna to the den of infantry instructors. He knew she had chosen intelligence as her specialty. He sat alone at his desk. She walked in with the same dead stare he saw that day at the firing range.

"You have two months before you go to that intel school of yours. I'm inviting you to spend it with the Infantry Officer Class. Two months, but you *do not* get the 03 occupational specialty," he said.

The opportunity presented by Deke Bigelow should have triggered some response, but she felt as blank as a bed sheet.

"Fine. I'll do it," she said.

Susanna had lapsed into a deep depression, not unlike ones she suffered since childhood. Euphoria turned to optimism that switched to hopelessness and profound sadness. The faint promise of feeling better kept her alive. The engagement tore at her. She knew she had to end it with him, but refused to give him the satisfaction.

She figured her choice to accept Bigelow's invitation equated to pointing a loaded .45 at her temple. Susanna slipped into the IOC classroom the first day. Her heart raced. Bigelow had prepped the future infantry officers. They groaned at the news.

Her fiancé glared at her, and she determined she loathed him like no one else, even more than Mick O'Reilly. They continued their game of chicken. Who would blink first? She could bring her betrothed to his knees just by being.

Later that evening, Susanna walked down the left side of a darkened hall toward her room carrying a well-earned can of Tab. As she passed the abandoned men's restroom, two arms reached out and grabbed her. The door closed. He dragged her to the center of the long lavatory as she berated him for another one of his ill-thought plans. Before she could complete a sentence, he cocked his right arm back and landed his fist of the left side of her face. Susanna staggered backward into the white porcelain sinks that lined the wall almost snapping her back at the waist. Her knees buckled and she slumped onto the tile floor hitting her head on the edge of a sink en route. He pulled out his grandfather's .45 and grabbed Susanna by the hair. With her body limp he held her head in the crook of his left arm and forced the pistol in her mouth with his right. When he realized she lay unconscious with no appreciation for what he had planned, he let out an enraged, "No!" and dropped her back on the tile.

"You stupid bitch! Get up!"

He kicked her in the ribs.

"Get the fuck up!"

He stomped on her chest with his right boot. Blood flew from Susanna's mouth. He began to pace.

He determined who lived and who died.

Her life lay in his hands.

"Get up!" He picked her up again by her hair. Blood dripped from her mouth.

He dropped her and flung the pistol.

"Fuck the bullet," he spat.

He grabbed her by the neck of her T-shirt and the waist of her utility trousers and slammed the top of her head against the cold, cinder block wall under the bank of frosted windows. He began to punch her in the face and stomach. He stopped and placed his hands around her neck.

Susanna's eyes opened wide as he strangled her. She reached up and grabbed him by the shoulders and, with what strength she had, kneed him in the groin, forcing him to release his hold on her. As she bolted for the door, the gun caught her attention. She dove for the .45 but he got there first and kicked it from her. She faced him from the tiles. He expected a fearful, quivering girl. He saw a caged fighting dog that had tasted blood and needed to be destroyed. She lost consciousness again after he kicked her on the side of the head. He used his black boots as weapons landing blow after blow. He dragged Susanna into a stall.

"Up for some scuba diving?" he asked, referring to an old academy hazing practice.

He held her head in the toilet and flushed it repeatedly. He wanted to drown her, but pulled her out just short of being rid of Susanna Marcasi for good. He stomped on her head one final time. As he turned to leave, he saw the ring he gave her on her outstretched hand. He pivoted, yanked the engagement ring off her left hand almost taking the finger with it. He pulled out his knife, spread her legs, and sliced through her low-slung camouflage fatigues, cutting her inner thighs in the process. He hesitated, but sliced the pink lace bikini as well as her vagina with a single motion and jammed the one-carat-symbol-of-evil up inside of her with the blade. He started for the sink, but turned and knelt next to her. He pointed the knife at her throat, but sliced a large piece of her white T-shirt, soaked it in the blood pooling between her legs, and drew a red blood stripe down her front.

"You wanna be a fucking Marine? You earned it, bitch," he yelled. He wrapped the cloth in plastic he carried in his cargo pocket, washed her blood from his hands, and left her for dead.

When Susanna did not show up to class the next day, Bigelow looked at the confident and smug young officer and sensed what had happened.

"All of you, get the fuck out of my classroom, now," he bellowed as he stormed out the door.

Bigelow and a collection of infantry instructors went on the hunt. Another two hours passed before they discovered Susanna's beaten body on the cold tile where he had left her. Blood covered the floor and stained the walls where her head had landed. The dark red puddle between her legs had grown. Bigelow found a faint pulse. She had vomited several times.

"Get me a fucking ambulance yesterday," he commanded and posted guard over her motionless body.

"Call the MPs and NIS. Now."

They airlifted Susanna 30 miles to Washington, D.C. Doctors told Bigelow she would not have lasted another hour on that floor. *No, he knew of no one to call*. He felt responsible. He had come to see her as a daughter.

As he sat in the waiting room awaiting further information from the doctors, he tried to piece together what had happened. He surmised the smug bastard had made good on his threats. The vicious attack aside, Bigelow had determined the officer had no business in the infantry and had planned to drop him from the program.

A young doctor came out and saw the tired Marine waiting. He looked much older than a captain should, she thought. Maybe he had been through a lot. Well, at least she had good news.

"Please come with me, captain," said the doctor.

She and Bigelow sat in private. "Lieutenant Marcasi will recover, though her injuries are serious. We stopped the internal bleeding and we don't see any permanent damage, but she will be with us for at least a week, unless we move her to a comparable military facility, like Bethesda.

"I don't know what's going on at Quantico, but we have a sadistic sexual assault here," she said. She explained the injuries in detail.

The doctor's words crushed Bigelow and his ego. He had never felt powerless until that moment. Self-absorbed, he thought he could pull off his IOC experiment, but instead he had put a young woman at risk. Bigelow thanked the doctor, who still had more to discuss, and drove back to Quantico. He made some calls, prepared the paperwork, and had the suspected assailant in his office in less than two hours.

He wanted revenge, but chose the better course.

"Lieutenant, pack your shit. I am dropping you from IOC. NIS will handle the criminal investigation," said Bigelow, seated behind his gray steel desk. The lieutenant showed no emotion. He just stared.

"I don't want you in my infantry. I don't trust you, and your men will never trust you. Now get out!" shouted Bigelow.

The lieutenant smirked looking down at the combat-hardened captain and left.

In less than 30 minutes Bigelow answered his phone.

"The commandant?" he blurted to the TBS commander on the other end of the line. "Colonel, you're telling me that in 20 minutes the Commandant of the Marine Corps has decreed that violent son of a bitch will remain at IOC?"

Bigelow did not mask his outrage.

"That sick bastard will bring nothing but disgrace to the Corps."

CHAPTER ONE

Marine Corps Lieutenant Colonel Joe Earhardt sat motionless on the granite railing staring out at the swift-moving blackness below. His Submariner read 2 a.m. He had worn the Corps's uniform for sixteen years, but at that moment it seemed like decades. What few cars crossed the Arlington Memorial Bridge took little notice of the gargoyle-like figure seated atop the bridge's boundary with legs dangling over the water. Maybe the mist and windshield wipers in motion forced drivers' attention straight ahead. Maybe they found the wisps of fog distracting.

He did not care.

Joe felt snubbed.

"A guy in his shorts and Blues on the Memorial Bridge in the middle of the night? Welcome to Washington, D.C. Pour me another."

Joe toasted this last night of frustration, pain, and gut-ripping guilt and took a gulp from the crystal tumbler in his hand. He lost his balance for a moment, but saved the glass without spilling a drop of the aged whiskey.

The infantry officer's generous collection of medals quivered in the stiff breeze off the Potomac. Passing headlights electrified his gold buttons. He hunched and pulled the uniform's choker collar tighter around his neck to defend against the chill. His makeshift noose almost cut off his airway.

He inched closer to the edge and reached for the pistol.

The Colt model 1911 .45 caliber pistol lay on the stone to his right. His hand bumped the gun—a graduation gift from his grandfather who also had received his diploma and commission from the U.S. Naval Academy. Joe had found the Colt a worthy Marine Corps side arm. He had fired it the prior evening at the National Rifle Association range.

He sat, his bare legs slightly spread as he often did on her love seat.

A faint smile appeared at the double entendre. His mobile phone and an aged, pea green Marine-issue notebook that he favored rested between his thighs. Releasing his collar, he reached into his coat pocket and gripped a computer disk and case between his left thumb and forefinger.

Joe looked around him, but even at 6 feet 2 inches tall, broad-shouldered, and topped with thick, black hair that always pushed the Corps's 3-inch rule, he remained invisible. His rhythmic breathing and the steady pounding in his chest put him in a trance-like state. He pushed the hardcover ledger under his right leg and fumbled with the phone. He opened it. He closed it. He opened it again, shielding the light that stung his bloodshot eyes. He closed it. Tears started down each cheek. He brushed them away with his smooth woolen sleeve. He thought about what he needed to do.

Then he thought of her.

***

She turned to him and whispered something.

"Again?" he asked.

She smiled and nodded. "Again," she confirmed.

No one else heard.

"Does the pope pray this often?" he asked, his lips brushing against her hair.

Joe looked around the conference table at the score of grim men impatient to begin their discussions.

"Gentlemen, forgive me. The senator is more fatigued from her flight than she realized. Will you excuse us? We would appreciate meeting back here in an hour and a half."

He turned 90 degrees and bowed his head in a rare display of respect.

"If that is acceptable with you, Mr. President," Joe said.

Boris Chyngyshev, the murderous and corrupt "elected" president of Kyrgyzstan, had known Lori O'Reilly since she sat in the House of

Representatives and had grown quite fond of her. Any accommodation, however suspect, seemed an honor.

"Of course, Lieutenant Colonel Earhardt," he said in English with a thick accent.

Of course they'll excuse us because of all the fucking money and arms we lavish on them, Joe thought. *But how many more times can I fabricate these transparent excuses? Probably as many times as I want,* he almost blurted out loud.

"Colonel, may we help with anything?" asked a man larger than the former Naval Academy quarterback, startling him with the suddenness of the question.

"Thank you, general. No, no, I can handle things. We'll pick up where we left off soon. If you will excuse us, sir," said Joe, closing further discussion on the matter.

And pick up where *they* left off they did. Joe and Lori made a break for her room at the opulent hotel where the government officials held their sensitive meetings. He would tend to matters important to the senator for the fourth—or maybe fifth?—time that day, and it was only three in the afternoon. He never tired of her during their four years together. Each moment still burst with the joy and intensity of seeing her for the first time.

Joe loved Lori. Her power aroused him. Without notice he would slip his fingers in unspoken places. He would reach under her skirt amidst throngs of strangers. No one could see as he raised her hem ever so slowly, reaching under, caressing her. He would feel her climax in front of everyone. It remained their secret. Joe found himself addicted to the insanity of their unconventional relationship.

But something nagged at him: He often wondered if she felt the same. He envied her ability to detach from him—and everyone for that matter—and had grown resentful of her on some level.

His frustrations faded. An hour-plus together. They wasted no time and started as the elevator door closed. His once-broad frame towered over her as he put his hands beneath her. She pulled herself closer and caressed his body with her thighs as she inched up the muscled fortress. The junior senator from Louisiana had her legs wrapped around him before they reached the 8th floor. He gave her a depth of being, loyalty, and devotion that she found frightening, thrilling, and worrisome. She had a past, well-documented by the media and her rivals, which sometimes included her family. While in the House of Representatives, she moved from senator to senator. Once in the Senate she had more than one House liaison. She only engaged fair game, and her Hill antics stood as nothing more than entertainment for a bored politician—until she met Joe.

Predator. Slut. Whore. She had heard it all and it stung, not that anyone could tell. Much to everyone's surprise none of this had harmed her when the polls opened. In fact, it seemed to endear her to voters. She saw it as a pact—she would watch out for them in Washington, and they would protect her in Louisiana.

"Close the door," she shrieked as he tossed her on the bed.

It had been like this almost every day—every minute—of the ten-day Central Asian junket, thought Joe. As she lay ready for him, he hesitated. Joe never thought of himself as a man with a conscience, but he felt conflicted by his duties as lover and the Corps's point man with the Senate. He pushed the damn Marine Corps out of his mind as he touched Lori. She radiated as he brushed his lips against her flawless skin. Her thick tresses danced with fire as the sun touched them from through the draperies. Fire. She personified fire, he thought, like another woman from his past. Lori drew people to her, as her fire raged within, emanating warmth and light, assuring safety while threatening danger. He tended the fire. He knew he should move with care about the flames, but wanted to live in the excitement she offered. He never shared these thoughts with her. He often thought back to when he first saw her at the dreary headquarters building in New Orleans of all places.

"Of all the gin joints," he said as he knelt over her.

"I chose yours," she laughed.

"But I waited for a proper introduction in Washington."

His mind raced. D.C. stood as his territory, not hers. He had tried to maintain control, but lost that one-sided battle soon after it started. Her laugh disarmed him—again.

Tending the fire.

"At least I've gotten you to keep your shoes on," he said as he removed each one, referring to her penchant for relieving herself of her footwear before a meeting.

On one trip to Spain as the sole female member of the Senate Committee on Armed Services, Joe admonished, "Lori, chiefs of staff of foreign armies prefer that their guests wear shoes when they visit."

She ignored him.

A barefoot Lori with cleavage that would make a porn star envious became front page fodder for a number of major dailies from Spain back to the U.S. After the president called her on the incident, she begrudgingly retired her plunging bustiers and silk camisoles from public life, telling Joe, "They are only for you, dahling."

Her capitulation on the matter of her attire left Capitol Hill staffers and photographers aghast. The move prompted a mock funeral procession complete with miniature casket and custom New Orleans undergarments, including a camisole, finished with purple, green, and gold Mardi Gras-colored beading.

Lori stretched out before Joe, naked and vulnerable. Joe fumbled to remove his uniform, which missed the chair and landed in a pile on the floor. He did not notice—he only saw her. She moaned her pleasure as they knelt on the bed. Her petite silhouette brought memories flooding back.

His thoughts drifted to Susanna Marcasi, as they often did when he lay with Lori. Their relationship came to an unfortunate end, as he termed it, within a year of their Naval Academy graduation, He thought of her often, even when pressed deep inside Lori. Something about Susanna still held him captive. As he caressed Lori, he thought of Quantico. He stood as the last person who should open that life-changing chapter.

"Hey," she whispered, ignoring his distraction. She reached for him pulling him back toward her. "I'm right here."

The damn thoughts had to stop, he chastised himself.

He held Lori. He worshipped her. He satisfied her.

Lori and Joe lay breathing in unison. Her smooth back pressed against his moist chest. His arms enveloped her. Lori's fingers caressed his forearms.

"What?" she asked. She knew his mind had gone elsewhere.

"What, what?" He knew the game. A response of "Nothing" would mean something.

"Where y'at? Whatcha thinking?" she asked.

He hated it when she feigned a dialect local to New Orleans. But it broke the tension as she intended.

"How I want this to always be."

He lied.

"Us?"

"No, me and President Chyngyshev," Joe said.

He pulled back as she lay facing him. He wished he could paint her. Immortalize her.

"We need to get back," he said.

She heard the change in his tone. Flat. Serious.

"Can we just *think* about going back?" she said as she reached for him, half pleading.

"I think physically going to the meeting will get the good president and his thugs out of our lives faster than thinking about it. If we stay here, they'll come looking for us. I think all parties might find that awkward."

"I love you, Joe," Lori said.

He thought of Susanna.

***

Sitting on the rail of the Memorial Bridge, Joe wondered, *What the hell do I know?* He stopped fumbling with the phone and dialed the number. He picked up the loaded pistol next to him. He heard a voice.

"Russell here," the man said.

Silence followed.

"This is Chief Roscoe Russell of the Washington, D.C., Police Department." Russell heard what sounded like traffic. He looked at the caller ID. "Lieutenant Colonel Joe Earhardt, is that you?"

"What the hell do I know except how to fuck things up," Joe mumbled, each word more bitter than the last.

The crystal tumbler shattered on the rail. The shards littered the bridge behind him.

He chambered a round.

CHAPTER TWO

Susanna Marcasi sat on a rickety three-legged stool watching the bedlam below. As smoke whiffed past her second story window, she thought the night seemed like most others. Shots rang out to the east and mamas would soon wail for their "good boys," now fallen soldiers, bleeding on the pavement. "Saints," she murmured, "if you watched enough news reports." Her sarcasm cut through the thick, night air. Sirens pierced the darkness with their mournful cries warning all present. *Why don't bad people ever get shot at 2 a.m.?* she wondered as she looked down upon the wet, blood-stained sidewalk, remnants of an earlier, saintly encounter.

Fourteenth Street had become the reclusive Susanna's window on the world—as well as her penance. Her medicine chest served as an arsenal to combat the past and calm her nightly prowl. Long after sunset as the moon hid from view, she would shop in the trendiest, smoke-filled flesh boutiques. She would scan the room, her drugstore eyelashes and ebony eyeliner masking her lingering gaze. Perchance a boy would catch her eye through the haze. He might look like *him* as he straddled a stool that anchored a long mahogany bar. He might hold himself like someone she wanted—like someone she had known.

She watched.

Topped with wheat-colored hair, this boy stretched to 6-feet 4-inches. His black jeans wrapped tightly around his thighs. She could tell he had *his* hips. She had yet to find the one she sought, but boys like the one with the wheat-colored hair would do. As she made the slow, seductive walk back to her flat with the boy, she reminded herself God would reward her perseverance.

Memories of *him* transformed the scene. She summoned the boy beneath her and she collapsed exhausted, embarrassed by her tears. Another night, another broken dream, a different boy entangled.

But she made love to only one man.

As the boy slept, Susanna might sit for hours, sometimes rocking back and forth, her arms wrapped around her ribcage thinking of *him*, mourning her fleeting grasp of the present, and determined to remember a past that eluded her. At other times, she would lean forward, place her elbows on the peeling paint of the aging window sill, and rest her chin on her hands. She had fallen asleep almost tumbling from the second story more than once—an attempt to end her pain.

The passersby had become her friends old and new. In Washington, D.C., the president of the United States lived in her neighborhood as did those on the run that night. She learned to navigate the troubled waters surrounding her by watching the lives of others play out as she did that night. Other tutorials came courtesy of the ebb and flow of Sal's Pawn and Check Cashing below her flat or stories she would catch as an occasional stringer. Though The Washington Times paid her well for news pieces, she preferred the blistering blog she wrote for the paper.

She safeguarded her anonymity.

After watching the magnificent show from her throne, Susanna started toward her bathroom. At a slight 5 feet 2 inches tall, her voluptuous breasts balanced with grace on her defined torso and 24-inch waist. Her penchant for French undergarments helped her when she seduced the boys now much younger than she. She shook out her waist-length main of espresso-stained hair. She thought her recent highlights made her look like a tramp and swore she would never make that mistake again. The boys seemed to like them, but she thought *he* would disapprove. Not that *he* ever disagreed with anything she did or said, but *he* might reach his breaking point over the highlights. As her mind raced, she thought she may need to cut back on the ammunition from her medical arsenal.

Susanna squinted under the lone bulb that served as her bathroom light. With washcloth in hand she looked in the mirror and decided to leave her false eyelashes, the envy of any 1970s drag queen, and garish eyeliner in place. If she looked like a raccoon by morning, she would clean off the war paint then. Still clad in her undergarments,

Susanna tip-toed across the rough oak planks. She slipped into bed and pulled the covers to her chin. She felt safe shrouded in darkness and shared a kinship with the night. Her circumstance might seem unconventional to some, but she had come to accept her lot.

***

The police cruisers that had rocketed past her minutes earlier made an abrupt course change at Constitution Avenue. Shooting along the wide boulevard, they flew past the Department of State. They screamed toward the Lincoln Memorial and touched down at the base of the Arlington Memorial Bridge, well beyond Susanna's view. The classic North Carolina granite expanse befriended the fleet-footed as well as the infirmed with its wide walkways. The elegant arches of the city's most beloved bridge seemed to kiss the Potomac River. Blue lights bounced their warning off the gilt pair of gargantuan equestrian statues, imposing their might upon all who crossed into Virginia, though some considered the 17-foot tall bronzes a tad too ostentatious for the buttoned-down and understated standards of the uptight federal transplants that made D.C. their cash cow. Many considered the span the most beautiful in the city, linking north to south, the Lincoln Memorial to Robert E. Lee's Arlington House. Symbolism abounded fitting myriad tastes, one aspect Susanna enjoyed about life in the nation's capital. She often sat on the benches that ran the length of the bridge taking in fluids as well as the vista before her, midway through a bone-aching, ten-mile run.

A lone figure stood across the city's moat on what had been Confederate soil.

"What do you mean they haven't found the body?" she whispered, her breathing deep and deliberate to conceal any emotion.

Lori O'Reilly abandoned the safety of the shadows, stumbling as she made her way across the bank. She careened forward, her heels consumed by black ooze. Her phone launched from her leather glove landing on a lone tuft of grass, aglow. "Je-sus!" She sprang toward it as she would at a lightning bug as a child, to capture its power before it went dark. Now barefoot and on her knees, she reclaimed her lifeline to Joe. "Oh, God," she sobbed. "Oh, my God." She pulled the pair of python spikes, footwear Joe preferred over sensible flats or rain boots, from where her feet had left them and gazed at lights dancing on the river's surface.

"I can't believe this," she cried as she steadied herself.

The region had almost a month of spring in its books for 2000, but the seasons did not correspond to predicable weather patterns in Northern Virginia or its neighbor, the District of Columbia. The city enjoyed what many considered its most beautiful period, but Lori shivered in the dampness and chill of mid-April in Washington. She pulled her black trench coat closed at the neck. She looked across the river where she had walked earlier that day. The once-pink cherry blossoms, past their glory, lay lifeless, a hideous mottled brown. Millions, she thought, carpeted the bank to the river's edge. *Was it a sign? An omen?* She gazed along the rippling water as the devoted Potomac lapped its southern mistress. The rains had made the bank treacherous, but Lori saw that only the ground stood between her and Joe. Her lifeless eyes had swollen like the river. But as her tears flowed, her rage welled. She watched as the police made their way across the bridge, cordoned off with yellow "Do Not Cross" tape. Lori had lost her sense of time. Had she arrived an hour ago? Two? She cleaned the mud off her watch. Her twenty minutes there seemed like an eternity.

Lori spotted D.C.'s police chief and rehearsed, "Chief Russell, funny seeing you here." She winced at the hollow greeting. It made perfect sense for him to be there. She knew the real question: What business did a U.S. senator have out there during the investigation of an apparent suicide of a military officer.

She could handle Roscoe Russell.

She looked out over the movement of the river. It cared little that it could have become Joe's watery tomb. The soft ground continued to pull her deeper, yet she made no effort to resist. She considered this their happy place. She laughed to herself as tears began to push a path across her pale cheeks. They had made love more than once near this spot, and not always under night's veil. Maybe he chose this location as some sort of cryptic message for her.

Though she loved Joe, Lori came alive with the attention of the boys and men whom she had bedded and those that wanted to press deep inside her. She stood 5 feet 4 inches tall, but had long, graceful arms with legs to match. Some called her Black Irish, favoring an ancestor born to an Irish beauty who found love with a Spanish invader. Elections electrified her. With her wavy, raven hair, moist black eyes, and milky skin she beamed as she took in the chants and applause that chimed in another term. She acted with the grace befitting her family's status in New Orleans society. Yet she would thrust her arms in victory, something the people loved to see. As she performed for the crowds, she pushed those responsible for her win out of her mind and enjoyed a few moments of liberation before returning to her secret servitude. Everyone got what they bargained for. Some days she could not decide which life she preferred, but tonight on the chilly Virginia bank, the elected-official-as-siren and sleuth beckoned to Joe who could be feet from her or a world away for all she knew.

Her sudden presence at the scene and her palpable panic testified to her fear and regret. Lori had watched as Joe grew mired in turmoil. He had become erratic and careless. A broken man had replaced him. He had hinted at his plan more than once, but she ignored her dark and desperate lover. While reading in bed the previous night she noticed Joe lay in silence, signaling some decision. She started to inquire, but held back, hoping the worst of his melancholy had passed.

***

Earlier, alone in her apartment, her hands vibrated without warning. Lori lifted the phone to her ear. She hoped to hear Joe's voice.

"Lori, it's Bob … Mixon," the caller sighed with some disgust.

Lori's chief of staff never called her after hours. She had nicknamed him "Plausible Deniability," given his fear of discovering Lori in a less-than-ideal situation, meaning her legs around Joe. He would shake his head muttering what he would have to explain to the press—or worse—testify to under oath. She heard his voice and longed for his predecessor.

"Lori," he said.

She fumed.

"Lori, he called," Mixon whispered.

"Who called?" she asked.

He had Lori's attention for the first time since Susanna Marcasi stormed off the job.

"He wants me to keep you out of the ... wait, I wrote it down," Mixon said with some hesitation.

Lori could hear Mixon rustling through his note pad. Always in pencil. Never pen. No electronic notes. Susanna had hired him from the Justice Department, without Lori's approval, which Susanna knew she would not get. What an annoying little weasel Lori thought as she demanded, "Who?"

"... OK. I quote, 'the rumors that might start over the next few days,'" he read.

She hesitated. She knew. At that moment, Lori stood drowning in the business of Washington. She heard a warning as well as a threat.

She did not trust the limp rag of a chief Susanna left her.

"Who called, Bob?"

"Lieutenant Colonel Earhardt," he said.

For Lori, Joe's call confirmed the worst: The moment had arrived to end a life of "hopeless servitude," as he termed it. Something they had in common, she thought. Lori, never quite certain what he meant, thought he referred to their arrangement. She never asked. She had her own challenges and had secured what she wanted from him. She did not care for details—until now.

She hung up without a word and rushed to the bridge as had the rest of Washington, it seemed. The river's banks bustled. She adjusted her trench coat again and smoothed her hair.

As Lori made her way, she watched what seemed like a gathering of the clans. She had hoped to look for Joe, alone, but the area had become a sprawling crime scene. A search-and-rescue helicopter hovered overhead illuminating the bridge like a Hollywood movie set.

"Senator, you really didn't need to come out here," said Russell, shaking his head in disbelief at the site of the Lori O'Reilly.

The words and his disapproval carved through her with their intended jagged edge. She knew her presence only raised Russell's suspicion. She figured the chief had murder on his mind and she just entered his suspect pool. Even after all these years, Russell just never understood how her world worked.

She ignored his dismissive statement.

"What's going on, Roscoe?"

"Senator, I really don't know. My men got reports of a man sitting on the railing of the Memorial Bridge. Someone said he saw a Marine in a dress blue blouse and biking shorts. We don't know much more from there."

He lied.

"So, you don't know, but it looks to me that you think he went off the bridge and … is … in there." She motioned at the Potomac.

Russell had told her too much. "Ma'am, I don't know."

She did not believed him.

Russell watched her shiver.

"Senator, nothing against the great state of Louisiana, but why the hell are you here? This bank is rough terrain for you New Orleans types. And I say that with the utmost respect, ma'am."

Lori and Russell had what some call "history."

Russell, a tall, thin Gonzaga High School basketball star, grew up two miles from where they stood. Even with his Gonzaga pedigree—with grades to match his athletic promise, Russell joined the Marines. He had a plan. After six years as a military policeman he came home and joined the District's police force. The small town boy made good: Russell became the youngest police chief in the District of Columbia. But the timing could not have been worse. Crime careened out of control and the case closure rate by Russell's officers plummeted to the lowest the city had seen in decades. His fights with the city council made front-page news. He would bellow his needs to a ruling body that had other budgetary priorities. Finally, every media outlet reported what had long been feared: D.C.'s murder rate topped the nation. At the same time rumors swirled that investigators found Russell on Mayor Marion Stone's second set of city books. New Orleans jumped when it heard Washington's chief of police might leave the District. A dejected Russell took the New Orleans post and resigned his D.C. dream.

Russell found the New Orleans Police Department more corrupt than its reputation. He also found Lori O'Reilly, who, despite her election to the U.S. House of Representatives, spent a lot of time in her district and hometown. More than once she interfered with his investigations stopping his force cold, though the criminals' lots improved as a result. Russell went to Lori's father, former city mayor Stephen Michael O'Reilly, "Mick" to his strap-hanging cronies, as well as Louisiana U.S. Senator Manfred Stahl, to get her to back out of his department's affairs. In a short period, he fired his corrupt officers and re-created his force with new hires from around the country. The city's leaders backed him with a department-wide pay hike.

Roscoe Russell had risen to the top again. The misunderstanding in D.C. seemed a blessing. But one Wednesday afternoon around 2 p.m., his pregnant wife and three-year-old daughter idled at a stoplight on Claiborne Avenue. They dragged Lucy Russell out from behind the wheel, shot her in the face, and left her in the street like garbage. They called it a carjacking. A couple of miles further out Claiborne, the 15-year-old who shot Lucy tossed Melanie Russell out the door of the moving sports utility vehicle strapped in her car seat. Roscoe and Melanie buried Lucy at home in Washington. New Orleans lavished its support for its favorite chief of police. But Russell sought solace elsewhere. Locals spotted him on the river boats and at Danny and

Clyde's eating shrimp Po' boys and playing the slots. He soon added heavy drinking to his list of pastimes. Despite his complete rehabilitation of the NOPD, the city let him go. His demons remained a secret. He ended up back in the D.C. chief slot by way of Atlanta. His first go around with Washington almost killed him. New Orleans took his family. He could not guess what this match-up would do, and he did not care.

Russell appreciated how Lori kept his New Orleans loss and subsequent disgrace a secret. He turned toward her. She still shook from the cold.

***

"Ma'am, we got a call," Russell deadpanned.

"What? From some semi-sober, visually challenged foreign-born cab driver who happened to be crossing the Memorial Bridge when good people are asleep in their beds?"

She crushed the phone in her hand.

"No. From Colonel Earhardt himself," he said.

The blood drained from her face. Her knees buckled. She felt as if her very soul left her to find him. She searched for words.

"I see," she said.

She could speculate the rest and had no interest in hearing it from Russell. Lori clung to the privacy of her images of Joe.

"Thank you, chief. Please excuse me for a moment."

Lori stumbled again as she made her way further across the embankment and out of earshot. As she opened her phone the light from the screen illuminated her face catching her off guard. Her eyes hurt from the sudden glow and the latest flood of tears. As she stared at the screen, a different sorrow engulfed her. She peeled the wet leather glove from her hand and began pressing the numbers on the keypad. She hesitated, reciting the digits several different ways as if deciphering a winning lottery combination, settling on her own Pick 10. She waited to the sound of her own breathing and the incessant ring on the other end. The back of her trench coat faced the water at whose edge now gathered the top law enforcement brass from the District of Columbia as well as the National Park Police and Arlington County, Virginia.

"I have jurisdiction, Roscoe," said Sam Schmidt, chief of the Park Police.

"Wait, I'm not so sure about that, Sam," added Chief Dana Longman of Arlington County.

Depending on where the incident had occurred responsibility would fall to one of the three.

"Boys, hands off my case," she stated beneath her breath while the triumvirate bickered below. She turned and gazed out into the void before her.

"Where are you?" Lori asked, trembling, as she brought the phone closer to her ear.

CHAPTER THREE

The empty bottle shattered on the floor as she awakened to what sounded like a fire alarm. Susanna, engaged in a death match with her bed clothing, struggled to open her eyes. She felt the grogginess brought on by intemperance found at the bottom of the shattered bottle but fixated on the phone that rarely rang, let alone at 3 a.m. The clang of the 1927 vintage Western Electric grated as much as it reassured.

R-R-R—I-I-I-I-N-N-N-G-G-G.

"Geeez-zus," she said as she broke free from the covers, eyes still closed, clad in her plunging black lace bra and matching thong that clung low to where her thigh joined her hip.

"Christ! Where's the damn phone?"

The sound sent unfathomable pain shooting up from the scars visible at the base of her skull. They told her there had been an accident, but revealed little more.

Susanna muttered, "God damn phone," as her bare feet scuffed across the worn wood floor.

A lone street lamp shown through the front window catching the hollows of her sculpted thighs and abdomen. She headed toward one corner of the cavernous flat and began to disassemble the careless collection of piled outer- and undergarments along with one cat asleep atop the chaos. Clean, dirty, it mattered little to the thick-coated calico, Calliope, occasional other strays, or Susanna, the one fulltime human in what some considered quite the side show. Despite the disorder, the room's sumptuous decor seemed befitting of Marie Antoinette.

"Where are you, Susanna?" pleaded Lori as she waited on the other end.

Susanna pulled the receiver like a rabbit out of a hat. "What do you want?" she barked at the caller as she plopped on the pile of clothes now in disarray on the floor.

"It's Lori," she said. Her downcast tone shook as she spoke.

An extended silence followed. Lori could feel the tension through the line.

Susanna ran through possible responses, all awkward, but none as uncomfortable as hearing Lori's voice again. A sense of loss swept over her. She had no idea of what to say.

Finally, "Why are you calling me?" slipped. She cringed as the words pushed their way through the phone.

"Five Weeks. Now," pleaded Lori.

"Five Weeks?" Susanna clarified. Her mood darkened. "No. You know where to find me," Susanna retorted in a harsh tone and started to slam down the receiver.

"Wait. It's about Joe," Lori said with such force it sounded like a single word, "Joe."

Susanna could hear her desperation.

"Five Weeks. One hour," said Lori before she ended the call.

She exited with the abruptness she had reentered Susanna's life.

"That was a long time ago," she sighed to the prostrating Calliope.

"Oh, God. Five Weeks!" she said realizing she needed to hurry. She moved like she did four years earlier.

Now very much awake, she shook off the final effects of a misspent evening. Susanna reached under the beaded lamp shade and turned on a tall candle stick lamp. She darted onto the cold, black-and-white tile and winced as she caught a glimpse of herself in the bathroom's mirror.

She pulled back her hair in a sloppy chignon at the base of her skull. It helped hide the scars. She sprinted back across the room to an oak rocking chair by her bed and pulled out black leggings and a matching turtle neck. The darkness would hide the wrinkles, she hoped. Susanna knelt by the bed as if she planned to pray and pressed herself halfway under the rail. One at a time, she pulled out her boots like prizes from a box of Cracker Jacks. She made a run for the door as she laced the last one. Susanna grabbed her leather jacket, helmet, and the pack she kept ready for emergencies—like fire and police raids. She froze when she heard the rustling from across the room.

"Damn it," she whispered.

"Hey. Where ya goin'? Come back to bed, baby. Let's do that thing again," said the deep, graveled voice from the bed.

He stretched his smooth torso across the mass of down pillows reaching for her.

"You're really hot for an old chick. What are you, 30?" he asked.

Susanna had forgotten about this boy with wheat-colored hair and what act she had performed.

She looked at him with disgust.

No more, she resolved.

"Get out," she yelled. "You need to leave now."

"Well, I, I thought ..." he stammered.

"No, no thinking. Put on your clothes and leave," she demanded.

"Can I get a ride on that bike?" he seduced.

She threw a $20 at him.

"Get a fucking cab."

She watched from her window as the cab he flagged drove away.

"And I'm almost 37, little boy. No more."

Susanna locked the door behind her. She ran down the long, narrow staircase. It seemed darker than usual. She had never known a handrail so she skimmed the wall with her shoulder as her feet struck the loose tiles on each step. She smelled the faintest scent of urine, as she glimpsed her bike through the bullet-proof glass.

Unlike New York or Los Angeles, Washington, D.C., remained a city that slept—save for those unnoticed and forgotten by the beautiful that teamed its streets and flooded its restaurants by day. They had filled her world. The clothes. The shoes. Oh, the shoes. And the hair. Those well-heeled and well-coiffed days stood as an almost forgotten dream, but the collection of oddities who appeared and exploded in number as the night grew older had become her people. They formed their own social order. Not only did they welcome Susanna, they paid homage to her as their queen.

The sound of the idling old Moto Guzzi filled the air. After she dried the night's rain from the seat and tank, Susanna extended her right leg and mounted the bike. Her hips and thighs ached in the dampness. The doctors said the pain from the double dislocation would fade with time, but after almost ten years her physical and mental anguish seemed to worsen. Susanna battled the occasional blackout, which presented a challenge to riding the bike. She could not get a license to drive, and she could only afford the fickle bike as she lived large in her forgotten kingdom. Susanna had seen some medical files that suggested more to this "accident" than people told her. As she tossed the teenage boy from her bed minutes earlier, she decided she needed to learn the details about this ever-present past. She saw it as another solitary quest: She had learned long ago that self-reliance stood as her only option.

She made the turn and flew down Fourteenth Street. Police cruisers sat spaced every few blocks, but had no interest in her and her outstanding warrant. She made the right on Constitution Avenue. She loved the wide boulevard and thought what a grand name for the impressive thoroughfare. She liked the pairing of Independence and Constitution avenues. She thought everyone should claim politics and history among their vices.

She peeled off to the left. She would take the Memorial Bridge straight into Arlington. In the distance she could see lights against the overcast night sky, a sight not out of the ordinary. As she curved around to the Lincoln Memorial, the scene startled and transported her. She gasped and skidded to avoid the police barricade. Pain shot up her back. Her hips screamed at the suddenness of her move. Susanna surveyed the cruisers, fire engines, search lights, and rescue boats in the water as she restarted the bike and sped off toward the

Theodore Roosevelt Bridge. "Teddy!" she hollered, now at full throttle. He had never let her down. As she crossed the TR, the name fans as well as commuters called the unremarkable span, she had a better vantage of the scene.

Must be a jumper, she reasoned.

For those who ignored the guards—as well as federal law—and embraced sacrilege, Arlington National Cemetery equated the Garden of Eden. As Susanna arrived along desolate Highway 110, she cruised behind a stand of shrubs past the Marine Corps War Memorial, illuminated in all its patriotic, warfighting splendor. Felix de Weldon had done a magnificent job capturing the Iwo Jima flag raising in his massive bronze, three-dimensional rendition. *God damn Marines don't deserve this wonder,* she thought. She turned off the lights and the engine, rolled up on the grass, and concealed the bike as well as possible. With her helmet in one hand and her leather pack in the other she passed over the perimeter wall in seconds.

Arlington Cemetery rose to a commanding ridge above the Potomac. At the top stood magnificent Arlington House, the home Lee and his family had to abandon because of his choice to fight with the Confederacy at the beginning of the Civil War. Susanna continued her hike, extending her legs with each step. Weeks lay just ahead. Section 5 of the cemetery had an unobstructed view down onto the Memorial Bridge.

As she rounded the bend in the road, there lay "Rich Bastard," as Susanna called him. Lori hated the nickname. John Wingate Weeks had more than a grave marker, more than a headstone. The large curved memorial of unpolished granite with benches carved right in could seat a dozen large people with ease. Weeks graduated with Naval Academy Class of '81—1881, that is, just as many in Section 5 had. The school bonded Susanna with Rich Bastard as well as his deceased classmates, though she hated to admit it. Weeks also had served in the U.S. House of Representatives, 1905-1913, and the U.S. Senate, 1913-1919, endearing him to Lori. He served as Secretary of War 1921-1925. Susanna always liked that he "kicked" in 1926.

"That's how it goes in Washington," she would say with some satisfaction.

"Susanna, over here," called Lori as she motioned in the darkness crouched behind the massive monument. The lights from the bridge illuminated the ridge where they stood. Susanna concealed her surprise as well as her sadness at seeing her old friend. She tried to calculate how long it had been since they had spoken.

"Thank you," Lori sighed, relieved to see Susanna.

"Thank you? Lori ...?" started Susanna, annoyed she had agreed to this meeting.

Lori's large eyes met Susanna's dark gaze. A spring mist enveloped them. They looked down at the bridge lit up like a fire ball.

"They say Joe called from the bridge. They say they heard a gunshot," said Lori, looking away, her anxiety unmistakable.

"Lori, who are 'they' and what about this gunshot? Gun fire? This is D.C. It's the same way back home."

Susanna's stern tone shook Lori.

"The District police said Joe called talking about, well, I guess they never told me what he said to them." She looked at Susanna. "They said he was on the Memorial Bridge and they heard a gunshot. They lost contact after that." Lori grew sullen as she shared the information with Susanna. She began to weep.

Susanna reached for Lori's wrists and held them like she did as children, though she hated coddling a senator.

"Joe blowing his brains out? Not possible," she said trying to reassure her, though her choice of words startled Lori. "What else can you tell me? Did someone see him?"

She refrained from asking the obvious: *What had Joe done this time?*

"Susanna, it's all my fault," confessed a tearful Lori. She hung her head, shoulders heaving.

"But how? How is this your fault?" asked Susanna. She could feel that Lori's grief extended beyond Joe.

Lori feared telling Susanna that Joe had flirted with taking his life for some time. She refused to divulge her legislative activities. Accepting the blame would suffice, she thought.

Susanna pressed.

"And Joe? What did you hear from him tonight?"

"Nothing!" pleaded an exasperated Lori. Joe had made his final plans without her. She did not want this to lapse into an interrogation. Lori had witnessed the tension between Susanna and Joe. Watching her chief of staff guard against her lover made her relationship with both almost unbearable. It baffled her that the two could not get along.

Years had passed, but to Lori, little had changed.

The women glared at one another. Susanna's nails bore down on Lori's forearms. Neither noticed. They hovered somewhere between that moment and their past.

"Nothing? Nothing from Joe?" Susanna's tone rose with an air of suspicion. She released her grasp on Lori and began to walk toward the headstones behind Weeks. She ran her hand across the granite marking the resting places of Supreme Court Justice Thurgood Marshall and Chief Justice Warren Burger. She stood in front of Naval Academy graduate Admiral Hyman G. Rickover, the father of the nuclear Navy and the man who caused midshipmen to wet themselves when they would interview with him for entry to the nuclear power program. Aside from the famous men beneath her, an irony not lost on Susanna, in some way these fellow alumnae had become her family, one reason why she had chosen this spot so many years before.

"Nothing" stood as one reason Susanna stormed off the Hill.

"You believe narcissist Joe Earhardt shot himself because of a relationship between a Louisiana senator and a Marine lieutenant colonel?" Susanna asked. She tried not to laugh at the absurdity.

Lori looked down.

"I don't know what to do or think," Lori said flustered and with the slightest whine. She paused and turned to face Susanna, "Which is why I called you."

"Lori, it's been four years," Susanna reminded as her suspicion rose.

Lori did not like the way things had gone with Susanna and dreaded asking this favor.

"I just need to know … I want to know what happened to Joe." Her voice trailed off as she looked away.

All of a sudden Lori's head snapped back at Susanna. "You can move around the city like no one else I know. You get answers. You find answers. People give you answers. Answers appear. I've seen you go after Justice and DoD and even the CIA. Damn the cost. You're fearless and relentless, and you have qualities we know I don't possess. You will find the answer," said Lori with conviction.

Susanna took a step back, struck by Lori's words. She had lost Lori years ago, but longed to have her back. She already had taken two steps forward that night by breaking her last bottle of liquor, though she looked at that as an unintentional sin, and kicking the teenage beefcake out of her bed. Maybe this call from Lori made sense.

Maybe she had a chance at redemption.

Or was it a set-up?

Few had more motive than Susanna Marcasi to see Joe Earhardt dead.

Lori broke the uncomfortable silence, "You know him better than anyone. You can find the truth, Susanna."

The women stood, still suspended in time. Susanna thought about the risks, which made the untidy situation attractive to her. She responded, her phrasing short and staccato as if she reigned back on the Hill.

"Fine. I'll help you, but I need the whole story. The one you've told me doesn't make much sense."

Resigned, Lori let out a heavy sigh. It seemed she carried the world's sins at that moment.

"This could be very bad for me, Susanna," she confessed.

Susanna paused and looked at Lori. "You're telling me Joe's missing and this could be bad for *you*. So, this is about you," said Susanna as she ascended her throne in judgment. "That may be the first honest thing you've told me."

"I need him, Susanna," Lori whispered, pleading her case.

Susanna knew Lori cared for Joe, but her need for him stopped at the satisfaction of her sexual appetite. But Susanna would have to let further inquires rest, at least for the night.

The two women stared at one another concealed by granite monuments and early spring foliage.

"Is that all?" asked Susanna.

"Isn't that enough?" said Lori, surprised.

Susanna turned away. Lori had asked her for past favors that Susanna resented, but she thought she could never repay Lori. Joe Earhardt of all people would make them even.

"Susanna, I ..."

"I'll see what I can find but we need to get out of here now." She nodded toward the cavalry of headlights slowly winding its way through the cemetery.

The women parted and disappeared among the head stones.

Susanna mounted her bike thinking, *Joe didn't kill himself. Any suicidal would know that.*

CHAPTER FOUR

Mike Singleton paced between the narrow rows of computers and top-secret surveillance equipment. Around 2 a.m. his analysts picked up local police chatter they thought he needed to hear. A 28-year-old civilian with four years on the job, Roxie Fay Adams, put together a quick brief for him.

"Commander Singleton, we've picked up some information we think you and the admiral may find interesting," she said standing close enough to make him step back.

Mike heard the urgency in her tone. She handed him the report. "First, please listen to this, sir. We've been monitoring cell phone and radio traffic," she said. Mike strained to listen. Twelve years as a Navy SEAL had not been kind to his hearing, and he kept his handicap from the Navy.

"Can you turn it up?"

Adams handed him a set of headphones.

"Thank you," he said.

She could hear the relief in his voice.

The conversation sounded clear, but just on one end.

"This is Roscoe Russell, chief of police for the District of Columbia." A pause followed, but Singleton could hear Russell's breathing. "Who did you say? Colonel Joe Earhardt?"

Mike heard a muffled response.

"Lieutenant Colonel Earhardt, why are you calling me and at this hour?" The diligent analysts worked to clean up the two minutes that followed, with little success.

"Joe, I'm only two miles from you. Hold on. Hold on."

Mike could hear the strain in Russell's voice.

"Damn," Russell muttered to himself. "I'm almost there, colonel. You wait, Joe, and I'll help you."

More silence followed.

"Joe? Joe! OK. Stay with me." Five seconds of silence. Mike heard an unmistakable gun shot.

"Joe. Lieutenant Colonel Earhardt. Can you hear me? I am almost to your location." Russell put the phone in a cup holder in the center console and switched to his car radio to reach one of his lieutenants. "Get on the God damn Memorial Bridge. I think we have a man down. A Marine officer."

The recording continued with distant muttering from Russell. "He dates that damn senator bitch and then shoots himself."

Russell pulled up to the bridge past the Lincoln Memorial as ten of his men scoured the area. The fire engine's wail grew louder.

"Chief, he's not here," said Sergeant John Castillo as he leaned into Russell's cruiser.

"Did you check all around the bridge?" Russell asked with disbelief.

Castillo had ten years on the force and knew the drill. "We're searching the bridge and surrounding area and have called Arlington County and the Park Police for their help with the Virginia side. Divers are on the way. We've found some broken glass, maybe crystal, on one of the benches. Chief, what is this? A suicide?"

"I'm not sure," said Russell, baffled. "Castillo, did you find ..."

"A shell casing? The men are combing the area right now. We're rerouting traffic over the Roosevelt and the Fourteenth Street bridges. Key Bridge if they want the scenic drive through Georgetown," reported the efficient Castillo.

"Good. Very good, sergeant. Thank you. Good job."

Mike heard Russell mumble, "He's crazy for dating that senator but not this crazy."

Russell left his phone on as he scrambled out of the vehicle. Mike continued to listen to the rest of the back and forth between Russell and his officers.

Castillo alerted Russell, "Captain, it appears Senator Lori O'Reilly is here."

Russell groaned, "You've got to be kidding me. Where is she?"

"Over on the Virginia side, sir," Castillo motioned.

"This should suck the life out of me," Russell remarked.

Mike knew Russell and laughed out loud. The rows of intelligence analysts looked up from their screens and stared at him. Mike scanned the vast windowless room and the 60 or so mix of military and civilians. The analysts considered him reserved, but he had a wicked sense of humor he saved for hairy missions or training evolutions that brought misery to all involved. In an uncharacteristic booming voice he called out to the room with eyes fixed on him, "Am I that good looking? I didn't think so." He turned and grinned satisfied he had stunned everyone in the brainy bullpen of the Defense Intelligence Agency's Pentagon site.

"Roscoe, you poor bastard," he said, though the police chief could not hear him.

Roxie Fay stood a few feet from him, as shocked as her coworkers. Mike saw her and smiled.

"Thank you. I'll take this to the admiral," he said.

She tossed a coy glance his way and sauntered back to her cubicle. Mike had become the top choice for the women around DIA. Some used the term "handsome." The younger ones referred to him as "hot." Some sent e-mails back and forth with explicit sexual fantasies involving the 6-foot 4-inch officer. The admiral enjoyed intercepting sex traffic, as he called it, and sharing the notes with a crimson-faced Mike Singleton.

"Hey, Ralphie," he whispered to his deputy director, Lieutenant Commander Ralph Brooks.

"Yeah, Norton." The two single officers liked to call themselves "The Honeymooners."

"What happened with the Earhardt thing? Why didn't you tell me?" asked Mike, sounding worried.

"Mike, we processed it as soon as we got it. I guess I could have gotten it to you five minutes sooner."

"Ralphie, sometimes I need those five minutes," Mike said.

"Got it, boss," his deputy said eager to please.

Mike knew with better hearing, he would have heard as soon as the analysts did. The admiral would know it, too.

Mike knocked and entered the darkened room. An eerie haze filled the space. A bare bulb jutting from an old desk lamp provided the sole source of light in the office. Four, 20-inch monitors lined the back wall of the tight space and dominated the room. Mike could just make out the admiral's signature vintage Camel cigarette poster that hung above the monitors and the odd framed piece of red-stained cloth that displayed above it.

Blood? A trophy? wondered Mike.

Something about it turned his stomach.

Rear Admiral Ken Bartholomew fell in the "geek" chapter in Mike's sophomoric book. He gave up a life in naval aviation to chase a nuclear power dream and later carved out a successful career in intelligence. Mike came to DIA as an intel interloper. He envied Bartholomew who had invited him as a guest on his superstructure. Few SEALs got this opportunity. In Mike's special operations world, desk duty equated a death sentence. But Mike knew this experience would help him on future missions as well as larger commands. He felt indebted to the admiral.

"Admiral, gotta minute? I have something I think you should see," Mike said from the admiral's hatch, the term he preferred to "door."

Bartholomew felt a kinship to Mike Singleton and had since he first saw him as an incoming plebe at the Naval Academy. When the Navy banished Bartholomew to the Annapolis, it marked the end of his career. His reputation as a renegade had caught up with him when the cunning captain of his submarine pinned a near-fatal mishap on an innocent Bartholomew. He fumed the day he first entered the land-based Second Company office, sentenced to three years of babysitting a bunch of privileged college kids, though he had been one of them less than a decade earlier.

Bartholomew toyed with resigning his commission. He closed the local bars in town each night as he mulled his options. He would enter Bancroft Hall, home to the 4,500-member brigade of midshipmen, looking and smelling like he had slept in the urinal of some local dive. As Bartholomew sat hung over at his desk, Mike Singleton knocked on his door. The slight Bartholomew looked up and saw the company's Saint Bernard puppy. The young lieutenant studied his new charge for no fewer than five minutes while the man-boy stood at attention in the doorway. He motioned him in.

"Jesus, Singleton, where in the hell did you come from?" asked Bartholomew.

Mike froze. Bartholomew waved him in again.

"Sit down. Sit down. Do you have anywhere you need to be? Fuck it. I'll cover for you. Tell me about yourself. Where're you from? Why are you here, as in at the academy?" Bartholomew asked.

The affable 18-year-old reminded Bartholomew of his dreams just nine years earlier. Without knowing it, Mike

Singleton rescued Ken Bartholomew, who fought his way back from his certain professional grave. The enlightened lieutenant replaced his flag-level drinking with AA meetings, tobacco, and Jesus Christ.

Being born-again did not mean he had to upgrade his vocabulary. In his mind, his colorful word choices brought him closer to the Lord.

Bartholomew became the hard, but kind flag officer with whom Mike needed to talk. The two men's paths crossed over the years. Ken kept a close eye on Mike's career. But Bartholomew safeguarded his secret. He did not want Mike to know what he had done for him and risk losing his personal miracle.

"Jesus, Mike, call me fuckin' Ken when we're alone," he said waiving Mike in with one hand and a cigarette in another. Mike thought Ken Bartholomew gracious, language and chain-smoking aside.

"It's Joe Earhardt. There are indications he's killed himself, but the police arrived on site pretty quickly and found no body, no shell casing. Not much of anything. They are processing the scene now, and divers are in the water," Mike announced.

Bartholomew sat thinking. Mike watched as the admiral played the possible scenarios. He looked at Mike.

"What do you think?" he asked.

"Straight up? Even if he wanted to, he wouldn't do it." Mike added, "I'd bet my career on it."

"Mike, it is possible," said a calm Ken Bartholomew.

Mike became agitated, rare as far as Bartholomew knew. "Anything is possible. In fact, there is more evidence that Jimmy Hoffa is buried in the end zone of Giants Stadium than suggesting Earhardt shot himself. Joe? Blow his head off on a bridge? No way. I have known him 20 years. I lived with him for four. He may be a Marine lieutenant colonel, but he is as vain as Miss America."

He watched as the admiral lit his third cigarette during the course of their conversation. The federal government had banned tobacco products in its buildings, a minor inconvenience that Ken Bartholomew ignored.

Bartholomew's office had watched Joe Earhardt for more than two years. His name came up in dealings with foreign governments of interest, so Bartholomew's people turned their attention to him. Joe, though full of bravado, lacked common sense. He saw himself as untouchable, but he had become careless—to the Defense Intelligence Agency's delight.

"This is a fucking shame. Mike, we were getting so close," baited the admiral showing a millimeter between his thumb and forefinger.

"Got it, Ken. I am outta here," said Mike.

"Gee, Singleton, as if I can't guess, but where the hell are you going?" Bartholomew asked in his sardonic way.

"Admiral, my shift ends in five minutes. I have a day off, plus another 48 hours until my next shift. That's 72 hours and 5 minutes, if you don't mind my stealing the five from the taxpayer. I'll see what I can find," responded Mike.

The two men looked at each other. Bartholomew took a slow drag on his cigarette and set it on his coffee mug. With legs crossed he sat back and nodded.

"OK. Short leash, Singleton," he said.

Mike nodded and called from the doorway, "Hey Ralphie, you got it, right?"

"Got it, Norton," assured a disinterested Ralph Brooks, flipping through a women's lingerie catalog.

"Seventy-two hours, Ralphie," said Mike as he walked past Brooks to his own desk.

"Got it, boss."

Mike shoved some papers and a disk drive into a dark brown Filson case, the same one he often took in the field, and grabbed the keys to the Land Rover from his desk. He slipped on his Hugo Boss suit jacket. The officers and analysts did not wear uniforms in the office most nights. As he opened the secure hatch worthy of a Pentagon intelligence thriller, he looked back at Ralph and winked.

***

Mike Singleton hailed from the cradle forming the southernmost part of New Jersey. Bridgeton Township sat 50 miles southeast of Philly and 40 miles west of Atlantic City. Bridgeton dated to the 18th century and several colonial-era structures remained—complete with buckled brick chimneys. But the area stood forgotten. Bleakness screamed from the ramshackle homes that once stood as proud painted ladies of the early 20th century. "Too poor to stay, too poor to leave," had become the locals' motto.

Mike's family seemed better off than most. He and his two brothers grew up in one of the town's grandest residences, if one looked past the peeling paint, rotted wood, and sagging roof. His father owned the local grocery store. His mother ran a rooming house. With 14 bedrooms the money brought welcome relief from Allen Singleton's mounting gambling debts. He managed his habit as best he could, but he found more than one backroom betting parlor that would take his money.

Generosity proved the greatest threat to the family. Allen lost untold thousands forgiving debts at the store, and Elaine Singleton would take in boarders with no means to pay for their room. The solution seemed too simple to Mike, the eldest of the three boys, but his parents explained because of their good fortune, it fell to them to help those in need.

Mike never believed a word of it.

Mike Singleton poured his energy into school. As a star lacrosse player, he made All-American three years in a row. Scouts for Johns Hopkins, University of Maryland, and Princeton showed interest. But the head coach from the Naval Academy made the journey himself to see Mike play, surprising Mike with the gesture.

Allen Singleton owed his "backers" more than he could earn over six months. Elaine relaxed her screening standards. As boarders checked in one night, a redheaded young man, with a pressed cotton shirt and a quick smile, not much older than Mike, charmed Elaine, though his lack of a past and future made her uneasy. But his thick wad of cash swayed her and she pushed aside her concerns.

Friday night the redheaded man invited the other seven lodgers out for a few drinks and a night of billiards. After taking them for a few hundred dollars, he slipped out the back of the bar and headed to the boarding house.

Elaine moved about the kitchen. Certain his luck had changed, her husband paid a visit to a local bookie. Allen smelled a win coming that would change his family's life.

Mike walked in the door at 10 p.m., ignoring his mother's usual interrogation. "Having sex in the back of Dad's car with him driving," stood as the same, flippant response to her questions about his activities.

He stomped straight to his room and stretched out on his bed. He liked listening to a popular local singer, Bruce Springsteen, and felt the depth, pain, and hope of his music. Mike did not understand the concept of class at the time, but dependence on others for survival stopped that night for him.

Mike heard a crash in the kitchen, not unusual in the boarding house, and looked out of his room to see what had happened. He heard his mother pleading and crying, "Don't touch him. Take it all, but please leave him alone. Please!" Mike sprinted down the stairs. From the hallway he could see his mother and younger brother, Mark, tied to the oven door handle. The redheaded man struck her across the face with the back of his hand, snapping her bifocals in two. He turned and laughed as he dragged Matt, the youngest Singleton, into the dining room. Mike caught the redheaded man by surprise and he dropped the child like a sack of flour. The boy lay stunned.

"Matt! Run! Get out of here! Now!" yelled Mike, as surprised as his brother.

Already 6 feet 2 inches tall at just 17 years old, Mike with his thick muscles looked more than his 200 pounds. In a rage, he attacked the redheaded man like a football dummy. They struggled. The man's switchblade pierced Mike's abdomen. He continued to fight and then fell limp. The man saw Mike's blood dripping onto the worn, wooden floor. He wiped the blood from his hands on his white button-down shirt, grabbed the trash bag with the family's few, pawn-worthy possessions, and fled into the darkness. A neighbor's quick action saved Mike's life that night, but the boys lost their innocence and the family remained shattered forever.

Mike accepted the offer made by the Naval Academy lacrosse coach the next week. He moved in with the coach's family across the creek from Annapolis in a quaint hamlet called Eastport. Under the coach's watchful eye he attended a prep school a few miles away.

He had never felt freer—or lonelier.

***

Mike always had a plan whether in the office or out with the teams, but he had no idea of where to begin with the admiral's latest directive. Mike knew Joe well. *Had known* seemed more accurate. It was true: Two guys did not get much closer than when rooming at the Naval Academy. But these young men had grown apart during their second class or junior year. They had stopped speaking by the time graduation rolled around, though they had remained roommates.

Mike exited the Pentagon to a deserted North Parking lot, acres of asphalt that spread from the five-sided building like a national park. He waited in the shadows of the old athletic center entrance.

A second man, shorter and in a charcoal suit and holding a cigarette, joined him. They stood, side-by-side, invisible except for the glow of the tip of the filterless Camel.

"You want me to what?" Mike asked with surprise.

"Mike, I may not have been clear on this Earhardt mess. We need answers. Actually, we may need you to create answers before the police or anyone else does. Earhardt has his hands in more than one pot. We think this could look bad for the Corps as well as DoD. Damn poor timing by your roommate. We had the key in the lock to this thing and now he goes missing. This is not a coincidence," said Bartholomew.

Mike would die for Bartholomew. He felt he owed him more than he could ever repay the admiral. But he had no intention entering into any sort of cover-up.

"Admiral, cover-ups don't work. Someone always takes the fall."

Mike did not want it to be him.

"No. No. Jesus, I'm not talkin' cover-up. I need for you to find him, if he's alive, and invite him back to our pig push. You're a persuasive guy. All that charm with muscle to match," he said.

Mike had not heard the derogatory term for academy dances since he was a plebe.

"OK, what's my cover?"

"This is a little sudden even for us. Sorry, but you're on your own this time. Here in D.C., no one knows you, so why not a journalist?" said Bartholomew.

"Journalist. That's it? With whom?" Mike asked.

"Geez, Singleton, why so clingy tonight? Just find him," demanded the admiral.

"OK. Got it. I'll figure it out. I don't know about you D.C. types." Mike shook his head.

"Keep an eye on the police and that God damn senator girl friend of his. Someone will know something," Bartholomew said. "And Mike, I still say this Earhardt matter is far from what it seems. I need answers."

The admiral's voice lowered and his tone turned serious as he reached up and pulled the towering Singleton closer.

"Mike, I need for you to check in with me regularly."

"I said, I've got it." Mike turned to walk away.

"No doubt. Check in. Short leash, Singleton. Short leash," warned Bartholomew lighting his fifth cigarette.

"Hey, and, uh, Mike, you got that ceremony at the White House for me this morning, right?" asked the admiral almost embarrassed.

"Yeah, yeah. I hate that crap, but yeah, you're covered," Mike said.

"I hear this Stahl is a real bastard so watch out," Bartholomew warned.

CHAPTER FIVE

At 4 a.m., smoke billowed in the halls of the Pentagon's E-ring several levels above nicotine-addicted Bartholomew's office, but the men showed no signs of slowing down.

"Well, boys, my guess is a royal flush has the same cache here as it does on the Hill as well as in New Orleans," said Manfred Stahl with a deep laugh of satisfaction.

For Stahl, a pair of threes would carry the same weight.

He stood up to stretch and walked to the entrance of the office. He looked at his aging profile in the gilt mirror by the door. As the men took much-needed turns in Stahl's lavish bath, he observed the room filled with his French antiques and rare American and German military artifacts. This marked his first day in his new position, or would after the White House ceremony, but he had his personal items moved in weeks before the approval of his Senate colleagues.

Stahl left the Senate to take the job of Defense Secretary, a post he had eyed for several years. His predecessor died in late January when his car skidded off an icy road in rural Maryland. Calvert County police ruled it an accident, though the lead investigator found sufficient evidence of foul play. Stahl left Congress having alienated almost everyone from either side of the aisle. His relationship with the men that night differed from those he suffered on Capitol Hill.

Despite his unenviable reputation, most knew Manfred Stahl as one of the most powerful and unstable men ever to serve in the U.S. Senate. He used that power to improve the lot of the people of Louisiana and asked no forgiveness for the outrageous measures he took on their behalf. His constituents never questioned that he stood to gain in most of the bills he sponsored, but his on-the-line impropriety had become a matter of great debate in Washington.

"Screw the bastards. A bunch of fucking, frightened school girls," he would say.

His nomination by the president for the most lucrative position in the cabinet shocked everyone except Stahl. He would control unprecedented and what seemed limitless budgeting and contracting opportunities. He would have oversight of the nation's military, a fact that frightened most. Rumors swirled that his family served as staunch Nazis during the Second World War. While some rose as leaders in the party, his uncles fought for Germany as had their fathers during the First World War. His mother had been a renowned German spy in Great Britain.

The White House chief of staff and his national security team pleaded with the president offering a dozen more likeable, though less-qualified candidates. The president wanted Stahl. When he accepted the position, Stahl surprised Senate colleagues who considered it a step down for a man with an unrivaled ego and hands deep in the pockets of his home state. His unanimous confirmation by a group that would rather see him dead than on the other side of defense negotiations at the Pentagon added to the drama. "At least we're rid of him," deadpanned one relieved senator.

Stahl stood where he had planned. He picked up his swagger stick from his desk and strode across the room, again admiring himself in a full-length pier mirror.

"Yeah, Fred, real nice furniture," said Billy Herbert, eyeing the nearly naked young women strewn across a settee that would make top antiques dealers salivate.

Fred, as Stahl permitted his friends to call him, overlooked his boorish guest's transgression, "I brought it all from the houses in New Orleans. I thought the Pentagon needed some French artistry instead of this particle board shit they pass off as furniture." He admired one embellished arm chair and muttered, "God damn French."

As the men filled in the mahogany chairs around the table, the room's side door flew open. Stahl's personal security detail leaped into action, but froze while airborne. A man strode into the room uninvited, resplendent in Navy Blue, each sleeve of his blouse ringed in what glimmered like 24-karat gold and topped with the coveted line officer's star.

"Fred, y'old bastard. Never thought I'd see you in the Pentagon, but real estate has taken a beating lately hasn't it?" he said.

The man approached Stahl who stood under a 19th century painting of Napoleon at Austerlitz unfazed by the visitor.

"Since you are not quite Mr. Secretary yet, let me share something with you." The chairman of the Joint Chiefs leaned toward Stahl's ear and in a low growl warned, "Stay the fuck out of my business, and I'll stay away from yours." He stepped back as if he had not uttered a cross word.

"Fred, Christ, congratulations. I'll stop back when it's all official."

Stahl glared at the chairman. The men in the room could feel the chill between the two. Stahl walked back to the game and sat down with his best poker persona.

"Boys, I'm feelin' lucky. What the hell time is it anyway?" Stahl squinted at the English brass ship's clock on the wall to his right. "Jesus Christ, it's just after 4 a.m. Ladies, the night's still young. Deal another hand. All in, girls?"

Stahl looked around the table at men he had known for decades from Louisiana, Capitol Hill, and the chief executive suites of defense giants. They realized Stahl had them trapped, destined to fill his personal coffer. Stahl enjoyed his version of chicken, a game in which he would piss off even those he called friend to his benefit. The men glanced at each other as if they waited for one to make a run for it. No one moved. Billy began to sweat.

"Somethin' wrong, Billy?" hissed Stahl in his, "I-have-got-you-by-the-balls" tone.

"What d'ya mean, Fred? Wit' me? Nothing."

His local New Orleans accent confessed otherwise.

"Hell, I'm just plannin' to take you and the other boys down," Billy said. His voice broke as he looked at the $70,000 pot on the table.

"Just checking. Don't worry, boys," laughed Stahl.

The men began to fidget.

Stahl did not give a God damn about Billy or anyone else, and his guests knew they provided funding as well as entertainment for their twisted host. Stahl cared about one person: Manfred Stahl. The Cuban cigar smoke, top-shelf whiskey, and young women-for-hire helped turn the Secretary of Defense's office into his personal game room, a further display of Stahl's audacious power.

A large figure dressed in black with a .45 caliber holstered at his side approached Stahl and whispered something the other men could not hear. Stahl made no hint of the secret message's contents. Though he would have his own government-funded security team once sworn in, Stahl hired a squad of five personal protection specialists from a Louisiana-based private security firm, "Shoot to Kill," considered by most as the best in the world. Stahl enthusiastically supported what "Shoot to Kill" and others like it could offer him.

"Fred, shouldn't you get ready for the White House ceremony?" asked the urbane Vic Dumaine. His lapel bore his Medal of Honor.

"It can wait, general. Boys, we got business here. And you know this office is always open to each of you. There is a small matter of a badge, but I will handle that nuisance," said Stahl.

As the men continued to play, the smoke from the Cubans set off the smoke alarm in the Defense Secretary's office. Though spared the sprinklers, the fire department arrived. Stahl's black-clad protectors with weapons drawn explained the situation. The firefighters caught a glimpse of the topless women, smoldering cigars, and Stahl's armed wall of protection. They left as quickly as they had arrived.

A pretty girl, a fraction of Stahl's age, wrapped her right leg around him from behind spreading his thighs with her black stiletto. She rubbed her large, uneven breasts against his shoulders in the middle of a high-stakes poker hand.

Stahl placed down his cards. "Calli, I understand this attention, but how fucking stupid are you?" he asked as the force of his powerful arm against her face sent her airborne. She landed on one of his prized silk carpets, her mouth bleeding. All could see a history of bruising on her body.

"Robert, get her off the rug and get her and her whores the fuck out of here," Stahl roared.

Robert Boudreaux had worked for Stahl just a brief time as his assistant since Stahl's last Senate campaign, but he proved loyal and discreet.

Stahl motioned for Boudreaux, who leaned into his boss, "Give her a few hundred dollars."

The girls scurried to gather up the sobbing Calli. Those at the table had not forgotten the brutality of Manfred Stahl.

The men played until 6 a.m. Manfred Stahl became a rich man that evening by most standards.

"Chump change," he muttered.

By 8 a.m., almost handsome in a charcoal Versace suit, crisp white shirt, and a precise regimental-striped tie, Stahl prepared to storm the White House. He wore a small bar pin on his lapel representing his Navy Cross, a consolation prize for his Medal of Honor illicitly approved for his company commander, Vic Dumaine, three decades earlier, something Stahl never got over.

"Robert, where's my wife?" he asked.

"Senator, oh, I mean, Mr. Secretary, she's unable to attend. I believe she has gone to your home in New Orleans to escape the spring chill. The weather here in the north has never agreed with her."

Boudreaux liked Margaret Stahl. Though she had flown to California to visit a male friend, Boudreaux reveled in the role of her protector. Feeding Stahl's mammoth ego with, "Mr. Secretary," could only help Boudreaux survive his unpredictable boss.

"Fucking bitch. She's probably in California with that old pit bull she's banging. Get her on the phone," he said, then gave it a few seconds' thought. "No, forget it. I'll deal with her later," he growled like a junkyard dog. "Just get this blood up before I return and make sure that slut doesn't enter this building. The call girl, not my wife."

Stahl headed for the door.

"Mr. Secretary, your weapon ..." Boudreaux called to him, worried how Stahl might react.

"Geez-us!"

Stahl wheeled around and tore open his jacket revealing a shoulder holster and his H&K USP .45 pistol. He handed the weapon to Boudreaux.

"School girls!" he said referring to White House security, which frowned upon personal firearms.

Stahl strode through the corridors with his security detail. His car waited at the Pentagon's picturesque River Entrance.

"Gentlemen, let's do this," he commanded.

***

As Manfred Stahl picked pockets at his poker table, Susanna Marcasi pulled her bike behind the pawn shop. She skidded in the alley slick from the mist. The stench of human waste hit her like a baseball bat as she arrived. She made her way toward the rear metal door, giving the knob one jerk as she always did, followed by a gentle pull. As the metal screeched, Susanna let out a series of "Shhh, SHHH, Shhhh," which only served to make more noise. Still begging the door to move in silence, she stepped inside. The back entrance made her uneasy. She had heard tales about what went on at that very spot. Fights, abductions, rapes, and a few murders all seemed possible in her opinion. But human sacrifice and witchcraft left her dubious. City officials often pointed to Fourteenth Street as a part of city's rejuvenation.

Are they talking about the same street on which I live? she would wonder.

The building always had lacked the peace she enjoyed living across the river in Arlington. Still imploring silence, she pulled the screaming hunk of metal closed behind her. She stood alone in the dark stairwell.

"Where do you go so early, my darling girl," asked Frau Ellie Schiller, startling Susanna.

Ellie, or Ilse, as they called her during the war, worked behind Russian lines for the Abwehr, the German Military Intelligence Service. As a loyal party member, she believed in the goals of the Third Reich. As a favorite of the Reich's intelligence director, Admiral Wilhelm Franz Canaris, their alliance helped her career despite her young age. Her command of Russian art and literature, as well as the nuances of the language, gained her entry into the inner circle of several of Josef Stalin's most influential confidantes.

Ilse took up with scientist Alexi Orlov to enhance her cover. She did not know the Princeton graduate spied on the motherland for the Americans.

She also did not know the attractive physicist had a penchant for vodka and violence.

The Soviets learned of the pair's spying activities. Stalin ordered their execution. Ilse knew she had to flee. Alone. She would leave nothing more for Stalin's men than a blood-soaked floor in their Moscow apartment.

Amidst the chaos of early 1945 Russia, Ilse waited on a torn sofa stained with her blood from Alexi's blows. He stumbled through the door as he often did at just after 2 a.m.

"What the fuck are you doing up, bitch?" he slurred.

"I wait for you, Alexi," she said in perfect Russian.

As he raised his arm to strike her, she pointed the Luger and placed two rounds into his heart. It was the first time she had fired the Abwehr-issued pistol.

She used the silencer.

She pocketed his gold watch and other valuables. She disposed of his dismembered corpse in the river, the sack weighted by rocks she had staged. She had prepaid three months' rent on their opulent flat to aid her escape.

Ilse returned to a Germany she did not recognize. The Soviets demanded she stand trial, not as a spy, but for murder—a crime for which they had no witnesses and no body.

She stowed away on a troop ship bound for the United States. Ilse von Manteuffel, a favorite cousin of General Hasso von Manteuffel—and possibly his lover—stepped off the ship in Baltimore as Ellie Schiller.

Susanna kept Ellie's secrets.

Ellie blinked and looked at the Italian girl who reminded her of young Ilse.

"Mrs. Schiller, don't worry about me. I just went to meet a friend," Susanna said.

"But you have a friend upstairs tonight," said Mrs. Schiller, who missed nothing in their building.

"Yes. Well, no. I'm not doing that any more. I met a girlfriend," she stammered.

"Susanna, I ask too many questions. You are young and you should have fun. I shall not pry again." Mrs. Schiller did not feign disinterest well.

Ellie's moist eyes met Susanna's.

"You are such a sweet girl. You have been so kind to me. I have something for you."

The aging German spy put her crooked arm around Susanna and drew her closer. Susanna felt her wrinkled skin with its rose-petal softness. Mrs. Schiller stood with her back straight as a board. Susanna assumed her fitness came from her German training in the years leading up to the war. Ellie Schiller pressed the soft cloth into Susanna's arms.

"This will keep you safe," she said.

Susanna opened the aged, discolored pillow case and saw the Luger in the shadows. The gift did not come as a surprise. She understood her old friend.

"Thank you, but why don't we call it a loan?" said Susanna.

Susanna ran her expert hands over the flawless weapon, the envy of many collectors. She raised it sans silencer and put the burned out light bulb in her darkened sights. The deafening sound of a single shot filled the stairwell. The light bulb shattered.

"Excellent shot, my dear," clapped a girlish Ellie.

"Mrs. Schiller, this was loaded!" gasped Susanna at the beginning of an adrenaline high.

"Of course, my dear. One never knows."

CHAPTER SIX

"Don't worry about my damn vote," the senator shouted into the phone. She paused, listening. "Of course I understand what you're saying." Lori hurled the phone across the room. "I loathe him. He thinks he is Lord of the Senate. Thank God we are rid of Manfred Stahl."

Lori huffed, seated at her dressing table wearing an eggshell satin dressing gown. Her hair, just washed and styled, cascaded down her back. Phone episode aside, she appeared resplendent. As her manicurist retrieved the phone, it rang again. Lori placed it on speaker and, after listening to the caller, she let out a slow, deliberate query.

"Mr. Whitman, are you trying to take advantage of a lady and squeeze out of our agreement, sir?" she said pegging her charm-o-meter, as her staff referred to it. "I understand you may not trust some in Washington, but I am as good as my word."

A manicured middle finger disconnected the annoyance.

"Bastards," she hissed through clenched teeth. She glanced at the mantle clock. "Kelly, *please* hurry," she whined as she held out her left hand and admired the painted nails on her right. Crimson. She loved the sound, "Crim...suhn." She drew out the second syllable as she recalled Joe massaging her feet. He liked to paint her toes, too. It aroused them both. When he would finish the top coat on her little left toe, she would rise from her chair and press herself against him, forcing him into the loveseat. Any seat qualified as a loveseat for Lori and Joe. She found undergarments bothersome and would kneel astride him, her natural beauty visible for him to caress. Satiated, she would collapse on him, her legs spreading wider than a contortionist's, all the while ensuring her fresh manicure extended beyond the loveseat's edge.

"Faster, Kelly. Please." Lori pressed speed dial on the speaker phone.

"Yes, mum," said the voice on the other end.

"Is my car ready?" she asked.

An Iranian man with an Oxford Ph.D. and an impeccable accent to match responded, "There are no more cars, mum. I will have to call a taxi cab for the senator when she is ready." Ali's stunning beauty matched his persona. He could not yet work as a chemist in the United States.

"Thank you, Ali. Please make sure it's clean, and the driver speaks English," responded a frustrated Lori. She liked Ali, but a cab? Unacceptable.

Susanna would never have missed a detail as simple as a vehicle when she ran things, Lori thought. For Lori, Susanna played many roles aside from chief of staff including sister, confidante, and the one person she trusted in Washington.

They had taken Capitol Hill by storm, first the House and two years later, the Senate. Susanna catapulted Lori near the top of the political heap, a fact Lori pondered several times a day. Without the steady and brilliant Susanna, she felt her control slip. Damn. Losing Susanna remained Lori's fault. Four years. Their circles rotated a few miles from each other, but Susanna made sure they never intersected. The silence between the two went unbroken until a few hours earlier.

Lori checked the time again. She had learned to keep some semblance of a schedule. She pulled three suits from a walk-in closet the size of a child's nursery, extending her still-tacky nails.

"Black, red, or purple? Each appropriate for the occasion. What do you think, Kelly?" she asked.

Kelly had no interest in Lori's wardrobe and less interest in Lori.

"Am I mourning Joe's death and Fred's ascension to Defense Secretary? Maybe I am the party girl of the Hill? Or is it a day for royal purple?"

Lori loved clothes almost as much as she enjoyed sex.

"Hmmm, which one will piss Fred off the most at his little White House coronation?" She pretended to ponder her choices, but knew the answer all along. "I have to say, I think red will have him seeing scarlet."

Sarcastic and calculating in her tone, she laughed at her little joke. She turned and looked for Kelly's approval.

Kelly had left the room.

***

After she showered and dried her hair that extended down her back near her waist, Susanna opened the door to her cramped closet and pulled out one of her favorites—a sleeveless knit couture sheath with a matching three-quarter sleeve jacket in navy accented with cream. The dress had a narrow bow that stretched the width of Susanna's chest, just above her ample breasts. Her meager salary on the Hill provided enough money to buy a one-of-a-kind like this dating to the early 1960s for $50. Susanna liked to buy vintage. While in high school, she learned guarded secrets from Lori's mother. Though Kathleen O'Reilly could afford every article offered by New Orleans's top clothiers, she preferred vintage designer finds. Susanna's training served her well. This dress hung unnoticed in a corner of a Frederick, Maryland, antique shop, much to Susanna's astonishment.

Susanna thought about her years with Lori and the O'Reillys. A "mixed blessing" seemed a polite way to term it.

After her father's death, it fell to his only child to find a place for her and her mother, Elisabetta, to sleep each night. Faced with her mother's bitterness, Susanna found school her sanctuary. Wise to the ways of the streets as well as the privileged who reigned over the city, she hesitated to accept an invitation to study at the academic powerhouse, St. Theresa's.

She relented.

One dank December afternoon, Susanna walked into the long black-and-white tiled lavatory that served the school's east wing. The day's classes had ended more than an hour earlier, but she delayed her departure. Tonight the Marcasi women would stay at the Catholic mission. The center's coordinator had showered her mother with attention. As he propositioned Betta, the name her mother preferred, his eyes bypassed her and strangled Susanna. She knew his advances would soon follow—as did Betta. Though mother resented daughter, providing the child for a harmless grope assured her preferred treatment on and off the streets.

Susanna changed out of her uniform, folded it, and grabbed her book bag. She checked it for dead animals, unwelcome liquids, or other pranks. As she reached for the door handle, she stopped. Quiet sobbing came from the last stall closest to the windows. Susanna turned to leave, but the crying followed her. She hesitated, but the pain she heard sounded genuine. She walked the length of the room and stopped in front of the marble door. She knocked with care, like she would rap on the lid of a coffin.

The door creaked open. Astonished, Susanna saw Lori O'Reilly, a popular child at the all-girls' Catholic school. Lori leapt out of the stall and threw her arms around Susanna and continued to cry.

Susanna put her arms around Lori.

"Can I trust you?" asked a tearful Lori.

"Of course. Yuh can always trust me, Lori," Susanna said. Her accent seeped its way into the room, a welcome old friend for Lori.

Lori regained her composure. She stepped back and looked at Susanna.

"I'm half adopted!" Lori blurted and began to cry again.

"What do you mean?" asked a perplexed Susanna.

"I heard Daddy on the phone last night. Mama was in the study with him," she said.

Lori took a deep breath.

"My mama's not my real mother." Lori turned frantic. Susanna reached for the girl's wrists and pulled her close.

"Lori. LORI," she repeated, trying to get the girl's attention. "LORI, listen to me. If you hadn't heard your daddy on the phone, would yuh be cryin' now?" she asked.

Lori looked at Susanna and moved her head an inch side to side.

Or talkin' to me, Susanna surmised to herself.

"I guess not, Susanna. But I'm so scared," cried Lori.

"But you don't know anything for sure, do yuh?" Susanna asked.

Lori became calmer and looked at Susanna.

"How do you do it?"

"Do what?" Susanna asked with surprise.

"Your daddy's dead and you don't have a home or a family." Susanna's plight captivated Lori. She stated what Susanna thought remained as little-known facts about her life. Lori had not intended to hurt her.

Susanna did not know what to say to the pretty girl with whom she had never spoken until this crisis.

"I'll walk home with you, if you'd like," said Susanna.

"Susanna, promise you will never tell anyone about my mama," Lori said. Her tearful eyes pleaded.

"I won't tell," Susanna reassured.

Lori put her arms around Susanna. The two girls looked at each other giggling. Susanna wiped Lori's tear-stained cheeks and then dried her own.

While the other girls never accepted Susanna, they envied the bond she shared with Lori. The comments and cruel pranks ceased. Instead of the library, Susanna studied at the O'Reillys' home.

After two terms as mayor, with one hand in most aspects of New Orleans life and the other in the pockets of locals, Mick O'Reilly thought Susanna ideal for Lori, like the sister or puppy she never had. He felt close to the dark-haired child, a sentiment he kept to himself, though his children noticed a difference in the man they loathed when Susanna entered their home.

***

Susanna pinned her hair back in an elegant chignon just as Kathleen O'Reilly had taught her and changed from diamond to pearl earrings. She always wore her academy ring on her right hand and an elegant diamond and platinum dinner ring on her left. She strapped on a large men's 1930s tank watch with its Bordeaux alligator band. She did a double take on the time, but remained ahead of schedule. She applied her makeup like an artist working on her canvas, adding some extra eyeliner and blush for the occasion. She lined her lips in "Raisin" and filled in the outline with a rich, neutral hue further enhancing her already full pout.

She checked her bag one final time—press credentials, wallet, camera, voice recorders, water, keys. Batteries. Batteries. Batteries. She placed her pumps into the bag and slipped on a pair of worn flats. She had decided to take advantage of the clearing weather and walk to the White House. She grabbed a spring coat as an afterthought and made her way down the long front staircase.

At 8 a.m., the traffic on Fourteenth Street seemed unusually light. The sun began to share its warmth. She tilted her neck back and turned in a circle. She had seen the move on an old television show. Was the actress Marlo Thomas or Mary Tyler Moore? It did not matter. Instead of feeling the sun and its power, pain shot up the back of her head like someone had torn open her skull with an axe. She stumbled.

"God damn it," she said under her breath. Remembering the details of the accident, once a frustration, now consumed her. She regained her footing, shook her head, and felt ready to take the White House.

***

She approached the White House filling the role of journalist. The Times's managing editor, Bill Warren, understood her interest in moving into print news. The old-school newsman gambled and gave her the coveted White House assignment in part because he lacked a solid political-defense writer. But she had earned this shot. Aside from developing a robust online following, the paper sold enough advertising on Susanna's "blog" to make a tidy profit for itself.

Susanna looked at the entrance. *Manfred Stahl sworn in as*

Defense Secretary at a White House ceremony? she thought.

Sounded more like tabloid fodder.

She swallowed hard.

CHAPTER SEVEN

The head of White House security watched as a line longer than that for the annual Easter Egg Hunt wound down from the White House southeast gate. A handful of guests arrived early on foot. More abandoned their hired cars as the crowd swelled.

"Hey, chief, this is Ruberg. I am at the southeast gate," said the senior officer for the day's event. "This crowd is a hell of a lot larger than we had planned for given the RSVPs. We need to call in additional men." He waited for a reaction, but the man on the other end was silent.

"What do you want me to do?" Paul Ruberg asked.

The White House chief of staff could not conceal his frustration.

"God damn it. Manfred Stahl is a son of a bitch and the most loathed man in Washington, if not the nation, Paul. Geez. Go figure on the crowd. I didn't think this bastard's family would show." Ron Taylor hesitated. "Jesus, we're being recorded, aren't we? I do this all the damn time. Oh well. Do what you can. Sure, yeah, call in who you need."

Taylor collected his thoughts. "Paul, keep an eye out for Stahl. I think I gave you a photo. I shoulda put a freakin' target on it. This guy was a Marine, but I think he looks like fucking Truman Capote. Regardless, make sure 'Truman' doesn't get caught in this mess. Shit, I know this is on tape."

Paul Ruberg wanted to laugh out loud. The White House chief of staff had never been quite so animated or blunt.

Lori stretched her legs out of the cab and touched down in her 5-inch heels. Susanna approached from the east on foot. Mike Singleton chose the seven-minute ride between the Arlington National Cemetery and Farragut West on the D.C. Metro's Blue Line. The brevity suited him fine. Riding underground in those human cattle cars made him nervous. Mike exited and stepped into the District's bustle. Even at Govie Ground Zero—the White House—people stared at Mike.

This must be why most SEALS are … compact, he thought to himself.

Just a few hours earlier he walked into his hovel of an apartment behind the Marine Corps War Memorial, changed out of the suit he had worn for the night shift, and hung it to the side of his collection of Armanis, the fruits of a lengthy mission in Italy. He slipped on a pair of black jeans that hugged his hips and thighs and a pair of ebony western boots. He looked more like a pin-up than a naval officer. He dreaded the ceremony as much as he abhorred seeing Manfred Stahl again. He would wear his service dress blue uniform with ribbons and his 14-karat gold SEAL pin, a gift from his parents, displayed on the well-defined chest he had sported since his days playing lacrosse at the academy. He slipped on his Naval Academy ring, something he only did for special occasions. The president seemed to rate a glimpse of his well-earned hunk of gold.

As Mike approached the White House, he thought about his last encounter with the incoming secretary. His ties to Manfred Stahl went back a number of years. Mike had gotten to know then-Brigadier General Stahl, a reservist, when he served as the deputy commander at the Marine Reserve Headquarters in New Orleans. Mike worked as the aide to the admiral heading the Naval Reserve, but spent most of his time in his boss's Washington office.

Mike Singleton stood speechless two months earlier when Stahl asked to see him in his Senate office.

"Mike, I want you as my senior military aide when I take over as defense secretary. I need a lethal and kick-ass intel man," stated Stahl as if Mike had already accepted the position.

"Senator, I appreciate the offer, but I don't think I am right for the job. There are skills an aide needs, and I don't have that necessary finesse," he said.

Mike knew he stood as one of the most versatile O-5s in the Navy. He could perform any job as if created for the position. He figured Stahl knew his talents and recalled their time in New Orleans, which brought them to this moment, but he prayed this punt would go his way.

Stahl fumed, "Boy, I understand a lot of things. I know your mama is just getting by in that big old house since your daddy's sudden death, and you're looking at taking her in. I know your youngest brother is trying to get into Johns Hopkins Medical School. I understand your first ex-wife still has a love for the horses. Funny, a lot like your daddy. Her gambling habit has her living in a broken down row house in Dundalk on the fringe of Baltimore—in more ways than one, if we understand each other."

Stahl continued the attack, "She's bleeding you dry, but has some order barring you from seeing that son of yours. Your other two exes are not worth my breath."

Manfred Stahl paused and turned his back to Mike giving him time to consider his offer.

He went in for the kill.

"You can't get custody because of allegations of spousal abuse and regular drunkenness, which we both know are shit." Stahl turned and faced Mike. "There is the matter of your deployment schedule. You've been away quite a bit, son. SEALs don't spend much time at home." He looked Mike in the eye. "While you'd travel with me, this job would assure you sole custody of that little one. My, he has his father's good looks."

He handed Mike a photo taken the previous day. Stahl was as persuasive as he was seductive.

Mike had more family issues than he would admit, but he would not prostitute himself.

"Senator, I know who you are. I know what you do. I understand what you're saying to me," Mike said as he took a step toward Stahl. "Again, thank you for the offer, *sir*, but I must decline. If there is nothing else, senator, I must excuse myself."

Stahl glowed purple with rage.

"I took you as smarter, Singleton. Very well. We will speak again.

This isn't over, commander."

Mike already had left Stahl's office.

***

Susanna caught a glimpse of Lori as she walked by and felt compelled to mention Joe. "I'll begin work on Joe Earhardt as soon as I file my stories," she called. Though true, she knew she sounded desperate. Susanna sought redemption and pleasing Lori would appease whatever powers had pushed her into the darkness. But Lori's attention seemed elsewhere. She did not notice Susanna.

But Mike Singleton stood just a few feet away.

Singleton's head snapped, attracting unwanted attention. *Geez, tone it down, man*, he admonished himself. He made one hell of a Navy blue target trimmed in gold with a Silver Star on his chest shining like a beacon. He looked through the sea of dark suits and spotted the stylish girl. *That has to be her*. He eyed her like he had just hooked the catch of the day.

"Susanna Marcasi, where have you been?" he murmured under his breath.

Mike walked to the left side of the line. He watched the girl who walked out of his life at the Naval Academy 16 years earlier. As Susanna approached security he reached for her arm but thought better of it. Instinct told him she might not be happy to see him. Mike stepped back into the line and stared.

She had become more beautiful with time.

The process of attending a White House function seemed daunting to Mike. He took objectives; he did not wait in line. *Patience*, he cautioned himself, but he had lost sight of Susanna and needed to make his move. Mike Singleton walked to the front of the line. He explained that the DIA director had sent him and the Marcasi woman had become a person of interest, though she did not pose a direct threat to the president or anyone there for the ceremony. An inundated White House security team moved him through.

"That crap never gets old," Mike laughed to himself.

Once through the door he stepped along side of her. Susanna did not notice him as she navigated her way through the White House corridor. Mike crouched and whispered, "Susanna." She did not respond. He made a second attempt. Nothing. He did not know her hearing had been affected when her assailant bashed in her skull. He let her move ahead of him and called, "Susanna Marcasi." She froze. Was someone after her? Had *he* found her? She did not want to draw attention to herself and she did not want to know the identity of her potential attacker. She needed to get this story for Bill. Screw this up and she would spend her time babysitting her useless blog. She saw an opportunity and turned a corner pressing her back up against the wall. Mike strode around the same corner with his 40-inch steps and shot past Susanna.

She stepped out and challenged him to his back, "What do you want? Who the hell are you anyway?"

She yearned for her Luger.

He turned and responded, "Susanna, it's Mike. Mike Singleton."

They stood in the wide corridor. She looked up at the boy. He gave a faint smile and resisted the urge to wave. Her mood changed. He sensed her anger. *Sixteen years*, she thought. *Fucking bastard*, she added. She fought back the tears as she turned and walked away.

Surprised she left him without a word, he could tell he faced a challenge and possible opportunity he had not expected.

He felt unprepared, rare for Mike Singleton.

"Susanna, stop," he said.

"Leave me alone. Go back to your rock with the rest of your SEAL boys. We have nothing to say." Susanna spat the words. She did not realize she bordered on hysteria. Her double dose of black mascara ran down her blushed cheeks.

She looked like a circus clown.

The years vanished. They again became two midshipmen standing in a passageway in Bancroft Hall. Maybe in her room, he thought. Mike froze for a moment, but he had business relating to Joe

Earhardt and the lovely Ms. Marcasi might have information.

"Think what you want. I heard you mention something about Joe Earhardt."

"I don't see how this is any of your concern," said a distrustful Susanna. A sharp pain shot up the back of her head. She winced.

Mike sensed another change. He held out his hand as a sign of peace. "Susanna, I am looking for Joe. He's missing. Possibly dead. You mentioned his name to someone with whom he has a close relationship. I thought you could assist me. Maybe I am mistaken."

He drew a deep breath and held it.

Susanna saw him as brazen. "You show up after 16 years to use me again? I've got work to do here. Good luck."

Susanna crossed past Mike and into the safety of the women's rest room. The ladies' lounge had several overstuffed club chairs and a down settee. She nestled into one of the chairs, collecting her thoughts. She needed to report on Manfred Stahl, not Mike Singleton. The thought of his name sparked more tears. She grasped the thick, rolled arms of the chair and let out a low primal scream, then a second, and a third. She slowed her breathing and stepped into the bright, mirrored lavatory. She looked worse than she felt. She had 15 minutes until seating for the ceremony began. With a makeup war chest in her bag she transformed her sagging eyes and stained cheeks and headed back into the hallway. She saw no sign of Mike Singleton.

She ached at the thought of losing him again.

The White House staff kept the event on schedule, despite a pile up at the security check point. Susanna had her credentials around her neck like other members of the media. Journalists and photographers sat in a section off to the right. She slipped up to the stage and left one of her recorders. Susanna felt both a sense of triumph and embarrassment when she took her seat with the media. She saw how the New York Times and National Public Radio reporters glared at her, an interloper. *Screw them!* Susanna railed. She had lurked as a spectator on the fringe, and now sat smack in the middle of the action. Susanna surmised they knew nothing about issues outside D.C. *How about a real story instead of your meal tickets to feed at the president's trough?* she wanted to shout as she glared at the lot. *You've never been outside the Beltway and don't know a God damn thing about your purported audience!* She continued to chide her colleagues in her mind.

Susanna's thoughts veered toward corruption. The people in the room had no inkling of how money seemed to evaporate as a city's rich seemed to get wealthier. They had no idea of a major finance issue in New Orleans. Government money had found its way into many pockets over the decades, but the matter of federal money to hold back the Mississippi and the water that filled its countless canals stood on its own. New Orleans had more manmade waterways than Venice and trusting residents wanted them sturdy and intact.

More than $20 billion sat for a long-term levee restoration project, but not one person had worked to bolster the complex system in more than 30 years

The New Orleans levees faced numerous challenges. When the South American fugitive nutria population exploded around the Crescent City, the creatures became a pestilence in Orleans and Jefferson parishes. These orange-toothed rodents began to dig into the levees with such ferocity that they compromised the parishes' front line of defense against flood waters. This fur trading scheme from the 1930s that introduced the nutria to southern Louisiana now endangered an entire culture. Officials placed a bounty on their pelts, five dollars per, but not a dent resulted.

The situation took a turn for the absurd. Rumors swirled that during the 1970s, the governor appointed two nutria to the powerful Levee Board, underscoring the board's reputation for corruption. In 1975, the Jefferson Parish sheriff took action. One night he positioned his sharpshooters on the levees around the parish. The body count the next morning stood at 54 dead nutria. To the sheriff's surprise, the slaughter outraged locals.

Levee rescue efforts shifted to Washington, and then-

Representative Manfred Stahl led the charge to increase already generous funding for the Army Corps of Engineers' levee projects. The head of the Corps testified before House and Senate committees. The message: "Fix the levees or all is lost." Stahl paraded the mayor, residents—rich, poor, black, and white—before his colleagues. Money flooded into the state.

Years passed. Funds increased but work never started. The well-fed, rat-like creatures had to go, but somehow they found their way onto the endangered species list. After their recategorization, rabid environmentalists clamored for environmental impact statements. Soon scientists found a fish, thought to be extinct, in the 17th Street Canal, calling for further study. But the circus in New Orleans did not slow the money from Washington, which remained under the sole control New Orleans Levee Board.

The Louisiana governor appointed six of the eight board members. Of the last three governors, two sat in jail, convicted of fraud and the third had committed suicide before he went to trial. No one, not even Senator Manfred Stahl, made a sound about the board. Susanna assumed business as usual—that board members and other city leaders continued to take their God-given cut. But $20 billion proved quite the kitty even for a city used to gauge corruption in other parts of the country.

Take that, Mr. New York Times, she glared.

As they waited, she pulled out her Canon, judged the lenses she would need to capture the president's and new secretary's entrance, handshaking, remarks, and more assorted gripping and grinning, as they say, and maybe a few hugs thrown in. She could see the Navy commander, Mike Singleton, on the other side of the room. She saw Lori toward the front just off center from the podium. She loved Lori, but what a sycophant, she thought. And she wore that horrific red suit. Susanna had told her more than once that suit made her look cheap, but Lori would have none of it.

"Joe likes it," Lori defended.

"Well, Joe cavorts with tarts," Susanna harpooned back.

And, as if she had been wounded, Susanna would wince, "Not the red lipstick and nails." She corrected, "I'm sorry. Crim-suhn."

Lori still needed her in more ways than deciphering Joe's disappearance.

Everyone stood when the president entered; Susanna could not see around the walrus in front of her.

Oh, he's from one of the majors. That makes it OK, she fumed.

She slipped around him with her camera and began to shoot. Pain shot up the back of her neck and the sound in the room became muffled. She heard distorted applause, the title of "Secretary of Defense" and the name "Manfred Stahl." She brought Stahl in close for the photo. She closed her eyes. She opened them again, and looked through the camera. She tried to hide her confusion. She had known him too well on the Hill as he terrorized Lori and her staff, but she always felt they had shared more. She shuddered. Susanna snapped a great photo of the new secretary shoving the president off the podium.

Stahl took center stage as if he retook Iwo Jima.

"Ladies and gentlemen, esteemed colleagues, and friends. I am honored by how many of you took time to come share this important day with me," said Stahl.

He spoke uncomfortably long. Susanna kept checking her back-up recorder. *Yeah, it's still going*, she said to herself. *And so is he.*

"After nearly 30 years with the Marine Corps, a career that ended too soon ..." The crowd erupted with applause. Susanna did not know if they applauded his service or the fact he may have been forced to leave the Corps earlier than he would have liked.

She felt she had run afoul of the Corps, but she did not recall Stahl as a Marine. She would have known. She did time with the Boy's Gun Club, too. *Misogynist Freaks,* as she called them.

"I have looked for other meaningful ways to serve the people of our nation. As many of you know, I served in the House of Representatives and, until today, the U.S. Senate representing the people of the great state of Louisiana."

More applause.

Susanna gasped. Though her memory remained fuzzy, she felt she knew this bombastic man well, before their shootouts on the Hill. She could see Lori looking over at her. Her eyes blinked their Morse Code, "Keep quiet."

"Today, I stand before you ready to serve our men and women in uniform again as their leader." The crowd whispered. The president, a gracious man, did not let on he heard the slight.

"Today we get leadership back in the Pentagon. ... And, finally, Mr. President," all present held their breath, "thank you for your trust in affording me this opportunity. God bless America and God bless the United States Marine Corps and all the other services, too."

The guests jumped to their feet. From Susanna's vantage the action moved in slow motion. Lori cheered. Mike looked concerned. The president appeared underwhelmed and regretful. Stahl stood basking. *Smug bastard*, she thought. Her certainty strengthened. She had known him outside of Congress, but could not place him.

She felt ill.

The White House staff had said no questions from the media, but Stahl balked, "Hell, I represent the Defense Department, and I still represent my people in Louisiana. Of course I'm taking questions."

Stahl called on those around Susanna one by one.

Then Manfred Stahl noticed Susanna Marcasi. They locked eyes. A long pause followed. Any pleasure he experienced that day vanished, but he felt confident she did not recognize him beyond Senator Stahl. *Smart girl*, he recalled. *Too smart. Instinctive*, Stahl thought.

He broke the silence.

"Ms. Marcasi, do you have a question?"

She neither inhaled nor exhaled.

Her mind raced. Susanna scrambled to place him beyond their years on the Hill. Since the accident she went by instinct and feel. She felt she should not allow anyone to know she had a distant memory of him. Manfred Stahl seemed dangerous. She had felt the slightest tremble when she saw him greet Lori before the ceremony.

As the guests waited for her to speak, Susanna looked around the room filled beyond capacity. She knew these people. She had known them well. A larger number had come from Louisiana. She caught sight of Jimmy Dupuy and Billy Herbert. She saw few defense people, but she spotted Vic Dumaine. *General* Dumaine. Far from a typical D.C. crowd, she scanned the room for more New Orleanians.

General Dumaine? Why Dumaine?

Fine. Let's do it, she told herself.

"Yes, Mr. Secretary, Susanna Marcasi with the Washington Times. Mr. Secretary, the $20 billion that has gone from the federal government to Louisiana, to Orleans Parish in particular, to overhaul and strengthen the vast levee system," she slowed her speech, "has not reached the Army Corps of Engineers, leaving the region at profound risk." She had made the statement now she had to come up with a question. "Mr. Secretary, how will your office correct a situation that imperils hundreds of thousands and smacks of systemic corruption at every level."

Silence followed. She knew she lost the gamble, but *Go big or stay home*, she thought. *Flapping in the breeze*, came to mind. Susanna stood there very much alone. She could feel the guests wanting out of the room. She saw Lori out of the corner of her eye mouthing, "No."

Mike, certain of her insanity, nodded approval. *Balls,* he thought, though he remained uncertain if he had witnessed a train wreck or a young woman throwing her body on a grenade. Either way, Susanna had committed professional suicide. The silence continued. Stahl, angered by the challenge, refused to reveal himself to this crowd. He thought to himself, *Still smart. Too fucking smart.*

"Little lady, you tell the Washington Times there is no corruption and our levees are sound." Susanna noticed his face redden as he growled at the gallery. Of course this did not answer where the billions had gone, but the door stood ajar.

She would blow it open later.

"Thank you, Mr. Secretary," she said.

CHAPTER EIGHT

As the ceremony disbanded, most in the room moved toward Manfred Stahl to congratulate him and prove they had attended the coronation. Such effort could result in a future favor granted. Susanna's head ached and she staved off a full panic attack in the aftermath of her exchange with Stahl. She gave up on her other recorder lost in the crowd that now enveloped him. She snapped two more photos, grabbed her bag, and broke for the exit.

"Hi. Yes, well, excuse me. I am trying to leave," Susanna said as she spoke into the chest of the White House linebacker blocking her way.

"Secretary Stahl would like to answer any additional questions you might have for him," said the blocker.

She nicknamed him "Thag."

"That's very gracious, (*Thag*)," she breathed with a half laugh. "I'll contact his staff."

"He wants a word with you now," said the football player turned gangster. She felt like she had fallen in with the mob as her father had.

"May I at least go to the restroom? I need some water," she said.

"I'll have it brought to you," he insisted.

Susanna stood there with her left leg thrust out to the side and her left fist planted on the hip bone. Given the 1960s outfit, she looked like an irate Audrey Hepburn.

"Fine. We'll do this your way—this time," she huffed.

She elongated each word hoping to ruin his day. Not a chink, though, that she could detect. She dug through her bag for the Clonazepam vial. The aide saw she was not going any farther until she had water. A glass appeared. After she took the pill she smiled, "Thank you. Lead the way."

As Susanna followed her captor, Mike appeared, baffled, while Lori stared in anger. Susanna felt like a bobcat with a leg in Stahl's coil-spring trap and looked for a means to escape. As she approached the secretary, she found her opportunity and aimed for a small pool of water in the aisle, slipped and fell backwards striking her head on the floor.

She lost consciousness for a moment, alarming onlookers. Success, she thought, expecting Thag to help her out of the gallery. But Manfred Stahl himself rushed to her aid as cameras flashed. His face filled her field of vision.

She gasped.

Stahl purred like a python. "We're all friends here," a comment he directed at the remaining crowd watching the Stahl-Marcasi tango. He forced a smile as he helped her to a chair. "Sit with me," he said.

"I'm sorry. This is so embarrassing," she gestured to where she had been on the floor. Susanna poured on the innocent girl routine to see where Stahl would go. She worked her tiny waist from his grasp.

Stahl looked at the guests crowded around them, "Please give us a few moments." No one moved. "In private," he demanded.

The crowd dispersed.

"You asked a question about a vicious rumor that has plagued our state for some time. I find it odd that you'd ask it the day I'm sworn in as Defense Secretary," he said. Stahl seemed straightforward, but Susanna felt he fished for answers.

"It is not strange at all, Mr. Secretary. The levee funding belongs to the Corp of Engineers and thus stands as DoD money. It has everything to do with your office as well as the people of New Orleans," she stated.

Stahl could tell she would try his patience. "Ms. Marcasi, these rumors are fabrications by my enemies, and I trust you will write on the topic as the responsible journalist they say you are."

"Thank you. I am sure you are quite busy. I'll be on my way," she said as she reached behind him and slipped the other recorder into her bag. She never took her eyes off of him.

"Of course. Please show Ms. Marcasi out," Stahl hissed.

Susanna felt a bit unsteady from the fall. The four-inch heels she had slipped on before the ceremony made matters worse. She maneuvered her way around the crowds into the open hallway. She breathed a sigh of relief.

"So, Ms. Marcasi has the attention of the new defense secretary."

Susanna turned around. Mike leaned against the wall, arms folded, impressed with his attempt at humor.

She stared at him with no emotion. Without a word she wheeled around to her left and made her way toward the exit.

"Hey. Wait. We still need to talk," he called to her.

Susanna stopped short and turned toward him with such sudden force her shoulder bag swung around her back and hit her in the stomach. She looked at him with fists clenched. "We don't need to do anything. Yeah, we're both looking for Joe Earhardt. Good luck, big guy."

Susanna dismissed him like she would anyone else not worth her time. That list was long. He stayed back and watched as she dodged the growing corridor crowd, changed her shoes without losing a step, and exited outside.

It seemed cooler than when she arrived, and she wrapped the light coat around her. She paused to put on sunglasses even though clouds had obscured the earlier magnificent spring sun. She walked past where she had entered fewer than two hours earlier. Mike surveyed the area and noted a change in personnel at the entrance. He found the rearranged site suspect. He moved toward Susanna and called his office.

Susanna knew she needed to go home. Her phone rang. She ignored it. It rang again.

"What?" Susanna sighed into the phone, knowing the magnitude of Lori's displeasure.

"What were you thinking?" demanded Lori in a loud whisper.

"Nothing. Apparently I wasn't thinking, judging from your tone.

Lori, I know that man, Manfred Stahl, from some time ago," she said. "Lori, we've known something funny has been going on with that levee money for years. Years! Well before I joined your office. The Corps of Engineers wants to move on the New Orleans levee overhaul, but the Levee Board will not release the money. Correct me if I'm wrong, but your committee has sent countless millions down there." Susanna tried to calm herself. She had little patience on this issue and with Lori's "get-along-with-Fred" shtick.

"C'mon. It's all pretty gosh-darn interesting, if you ask me. It was a laugh a minute when I would go down to New Orleans on your behalf to be told there was no money. Something's up. Are we helping people with that money? Oh. That's right. This is Washington. We don't help people," Susanna pontificated in her old chief of staff mode.

"Susanna, leave this the hell alone," demanded Lori.

"This is exactly why I left," said Susanna as she began to walk, increasing her pace with each step.

Lori panicked. "You have to drop this," she pleaded.

Susanna could hear her fear.

"I don't have to do anything except hang up. I'll help you with Joe, but then that's it. I'm out."

Susanna disconnected the call.

***

Once beyond the White House security area, Mike walked several yards behind Susanna. She ignored the activity that surrounded her and turned her thoughts to Joe. She recalled she and Joe had been together much of their time at the academy, even if it had become begrudging for both. She thought about Mike. He and Joe grew close like brothers for a time. She should never have gotten mixed up in a relationship that almost destroyed all of them. While she had forgotten so much, erasing Mike Singleton from her memory proved a fruitless effort. She remembered even the smallest detail about him. As she walked away from the White House, she determined he needed to go. Maybe rescue more doctors in South America.

Regardless, Mike needed to stay away from her. She thought about Lori and recalled the day she walked out of the Russell Senate Office Building for the last time. But Manfred Stahl, senator, defense secretary, and man about Washington, frightened her like blurred memories of a horrific dream.

She shuddered.

She walked a little farther and stopped. She shouted, "I know Manfred Stahl." The revelation made her feel like she had regained a place in society. "I know Manfred ..." she started to call out a second time. But before Susanna could finish her declaration, an explosion catapulted her in the air and forward 15 feet. She had walked straight in the bomb's murderous path. Mike had moved to the side to talk to the admiral on the phone. The explosion knocked him to his knees. Admiral Ken Bartholomew heard the blast through Mike's mobile. Mike processed the scene and guessed the explosion originated at the ceremony entrance triggered by some sort of command-detonated device. The explosive may have been C-4. Maybe PETN, or pentaerythritol trinitrate as his scientist friends preferred to call it.

Mike looked around him. No one moved in any direction as far as he could see. Bodies littered the walkways. He could not shake the ringing in his ears and fell over as he tried to stand. Bartholomew kept talking.

He scanned for some sort of follow-up attack, but he could not get a read as to what form it might take. The admiral pushed for answers.

"Christ, Ken, it could be anything," he shouted to the muffled Bartholomew. "Off the top of my head, I'm thinking another explosion—and soon. Maybe another command-detonated device, but packing more punch. Maybe a vest bomber. Right now I'm worried about possible snipers. I'll let you know when I have more. Out."

He had not taken his eyes off Susanna and saw her ahead of him to the left lying face down. He sprinted toward her through the lingering cloud of dust keeping his head down as he finished his call with the admiral. The dust turned his nearly black uniform gray. An object had ripped through the left arm of his uniform, slicing his bicep. He lost his cover, but his SEAL pin remained in place. He forced a faint smile as he thought of his parents. They met Susanna once, he recalled, as he reached for her.

"I'm fine. I'm fine," Susanna said, deafened by the explosion, swatting Mike away. He grabbed her arm. She pulled away. She had been hit by debris and suffered a number of cuts. Dust also covered her.

The explosion had ripped her from her shoes.

"We have to get out of here. You need a doctor. You're bleeding," said Mike.

"Wait. What about Lori?" Susanna shouted.

"Who?" he yelled back.

"Louisiana Senator Lori O'Reilly. Was she ..." With that Susanna began to feel the effects of the explosion. Aside from the cuts, she had reinjured the back of her head in the fall in front of Stahl. "Mike, we have to check."

She called him "Mike" for the first time.

"Susanna, she's probably in the White House, and they're not letting anyone near the place," he said.

He put his hand on her arm. She jerked it away, "Don't touch me," she growled like a wounded raccoon.

"Whoa!" Mike exclaimed throwing his arms in the air. "OK. I won't touch you, but we need to leave now."

As he continued to shout, Susanna grabbed her camera and began shooting the carnage around her. She staggered toward where the gate had stood—an area that now reminded her of a surreal World War II Germany in ruins. She saw a severed hand here and a leg there. The White House in the haze made an ideal backdrop. Susanna fell to her knees by a headless torso. Tears mixed with the dirt encasing her face. She took it all in with her camera that survived the explosion like a fellow warrior. She photographed a young couple she recalled from the ceremony. They had seemed very much in love. Now they lay twisted, grotesque in death. She still wore her diamond solitaire.

"Lori!" Susanna screamed.

As Mike had believed, a second explosion followed, larger than the first though on the opposite side of the White House.

Susanna fell silent.

Mike grabbed her hand, "Come on! This is no coincidence with Manfred Stahl leechin' on the White House today."

The explosions had shaken the White House to its foundation. A battalion of secret service agents hustled the president out of the room where the ceremony had just concluded. Guests scattered in the chaos. Manfred Stahl stood his hard-won ground. One of his personal security guards received a report of the damage outside the building. Brian Poche, a former Army Special Forces first sergeant, looked at Stahl and nodded. Stahl motioned for him to come closer.

"What are we looking at, Poche?" he asked under his breath.

"A quick survey from Fossier puts the estimate at 25 dead and another 40 wounded, sir."

Stahl nodded, expressionless.

"Marcasi?" Stahl asked with one eyebrow raised and a knowing glance.

Poche shook his head, "She survived with a few cuts."

Manfred Stahl continued to nod, "We have some work to do."

A handful of reporters had returned to get the new defense secretary's take on the apparent bombing when the second explosion shook the White House. This was April 2000, and the nation had teetered on the edge not long before. The doom predicted with Y2K never materialized and people had begun to let their guard down.

Stahl called for calm.

"Ladies and gentlemen, we are in a new century. It is the beginning of the third millennium. We have new enemies, and some disgruntled old ones, who may require expanded Defense Department attention. I don't want to speculate on the explosions. It is too soon to draw any conclusions. But Manfred Stahl's Defense Department stands ready to defend as I've sworn."

Stahl's security detail surrounded him as he spoke. The photographers swarmed like paparazzi for the best image of the day's star.

"Senator O'Reilly, do you have anything to add?" shouted one reporter.

Lori had stood back watching Stahl. He packed more danger than a truckload of dynamite.

"I think Secretary Stahl seems to have the matter covered." Her eyes burned into Stahl's back as she spoke. Her brief statement dripped in sarcasm, apparent only to the departing Stahl.

Pandemonium continued outside the White House. "Of course I can walk," Susanna stated with certainty as she collapsed on Mike. He scooped her into his arms and did his best not to draw attention. Blood covered both of them. Concerned about another attack, he headed for the stand of trees across the walkway. The scene grew more frenetic. Every possible police department, national law enforcement agency, and fire department moved toward 1600 Pennsylvania Avenue. Some emergency vehicles already had arrived.

He looked at Susanna's wide eyes. He propped her against a blooming dogwood tree, its pink flowers matched the polish on her toes. She slid to the ground. Mike started for the crumpled girl, but she looked up at him, "Call Tom. My place. Fourteenth." She pushed her torn purse toward him as her eyes closed. Mike looked at her. He checked her breathing and found a strong pulse. Relieved, he rummaged through the bag. No Toms. He rifled through her wallet and found a coffee-stained, wrinkled shred of yellow paper, "Suzy – Call me when you need me. Tom." There was a number. "OK, Tom it is," consented a doubting Mike. He dialed the number, surprised he still had reception.

"Speedy Courier. This is Tom."

"Tom. You don't …" Mike started.

"Man, can you talk louder? There's a lot of background noise. Are you at a construction site?" Tom asked.

"Not exactly. Tom, I'm with Susanna Marcasi and …" Mike did not get past her name.

"I love my Suzy. How is she?" he asked.

Mike explained the situation at the White House, still not knowing if this Tom could be trusted. Susanna needed a doctor, and they needed to get out fast.

Tom turned cautious. "*Who* are you?" he asked. "Never mind," he said. "Are the roads blocked yet?" It really did not matter for Tom. "Never mind. I am just a few blocks from you. Can you get her to 17th and H? You are on the east side, right?"

"Yeah, Yeah." Though impressed, Mike remained concerned.

"Go down the alley on the side of the building, mid-block between 17th and Connecticut. I'll be coming in from the other direction."

"OK," said Mike with some hesitation, still unsure about Tom. *There are reasons people are couriers,* he thought.

"Tom, we're pretty dirty," Mike warned.

"You haven't seen my truck!" A brief silence followed. "Hey, Mike, stay on the phone with me so we don't screw this up," said Tom.

Mike shouted as he coughed, "I can't move fast enough with this miserable phone. I need to hang up. Call me back in 10. We'll find each other."

"Roger," barked Tom.

"Out," yelled Mike.

Oh, OK. A military courier. Maybe he'll be in a HUMVEE, hoped Mike, unsure if he had become more comfortable with the arrangement or if he had just made a pact with the devil.

Mike placed a limp Susanna back on her feet. He walked, dragging her a few yards. "Susanna, this is NOT working, so don't hold this against me." He lifted her into his arms and dashed toward the rally point.

"Hey. Naw. I can do this. Put me down now," she said, her voice weak, but adamant.

With her feet back on the ground, Susanna came back to life. Adrenaline helped her stay even with Mike as a score of emergency vehicles whizzed past them in the opposite direction. They sprinted like two fugitives on the run. When one police officer tried to stop them, Mike in his dusty, disheveled uniform embellished his credentials and the officer let them pass.

As they ran into the alley, Susanna spotted Tom in his beat-up, copper spray-painted Mazda pickup with a front cab that fit three toddlers on a lucky day. Tom jumped out from behind the wheel with the engine running. Tom "The Rocket" Rodgers stood 5 feet 6 inches tall with a graying, dark chocolate mullet that hung just past his shoulders. He had not washed in weeks. The Coke-bottle glasses gave the Department of Motor Vehicles fits, but there he idled, true to his word. His nickname seemed well-deserved.

"Let's sit her in the middle," instructed Tom. "What the hell happened again?"

Mike sighed. He knew he would have to explain this sequence of events a number of times. He gave the Cliffs Notes version, "There was an explosion as we left a White House ceremony. Debris caught Susanna."

He did not mention that the debris included eye glasses, jewelry, shoes, and body parts.

After Tom pulled forward and saw the barricades on 17th Street, he turned the truck around in the narrow alley and flew between the buildings like driving through a hostile ravine. Tom looked at Susanna. Her skin had turned pale and the bleeding had not slowed.

"We need to get to Georgetown or the Washington Hospital Center or even the VA," Tom said, alarmed.

Mike looked at the hopeless snarl of cars. "Tom, I have some medical training. Let's take her to her place. I don't know where it is, though. I think she said Fourteenth Street."

"Commander, I know it. I live there, too," Tom said.

Great, thought Mike. "Both of you live on Fourteenth Street?" Mike had troubling connecting his model midshipman cohort with Rocket Rodgers.

"She has a place above the pawn shop. I'm out back," explained Tom.

Tom maneuvered his Mazda like a fighter jet. He crisscrossed through alleys like a man on the lam when he saw any sign of law enforcement.

"I was a Cav guy in the 82nd. Their best HUMVEE driver," boasted Tom of his time as a member of the Army's Alpha Troop, 1-17 Calvary with the 82nd Airborne Division. "They tossed me on a general. Too much booze and I took a boatload of pills for my knees back then."

Mike nodded, "Really?"

"Hey, but I'm clean now. Happier than I've ever been." Tom looked ahead. "Hold on, this is going to be tight."

Tom made a sharp turn into another alley and came to an abrupt stop. All three came to rest piled atop one another on the vinyl bench seat in the front of the cab.

They had reached the back of the building. Mike thought he found himself in a scene from a bad cop show. He saw trash strewn about next to used condoms of various colors. A 1970s conversion van with a custom mythical Native American ceremony paint job sat on blocks. He stood on gray-brown dirt carpeted with shards of broken glass.

Susanna and Mike looked like they had been plucked alive from the ashes of Pompeii. Black soot spotted their skin and brow-gray ash still covered their hair and clothing. Susanna had varying shades of red running down her arms, legs, and chest. Mike saw her neck pulsing blood and needed to get her inside.

Mike and Tom nodded at one another as Mike disappeared through the door with Susanna.

He looked at the unending chain of stairs and shook his head, "No." Susanna waived him off and started up the stairs. They walked up the three flights to Susanna's flat. She opened the door.

"Singleton, you were right."

She fainted.

CHAPTER NINE

Mike scooped up the unconscious Susanna. Her pulse had grown weaker. *I've seen worse,* he reminded himself. He laid his custom uniform on the bed to help soak up her blood. He placed Susanna on the size 48 jacket. Her blood consumed the lining.

He did not claim to be Dr. Kildare, but Mike had received detailed medical instruction during his early days as a SEAL. *Some training you don't forget,* he thought. While Mike did not have plasma in the medical bag he always carried, he had a suture kit.

The slash to her neck had worsened since he found her on the White House grounds. A jagged piece of metal had sliced though the skin and lodged close to her jugular. He watched the blood pulse at the rate of her heart beat. Mike considered it life-threatening. He could not fix this, but had a friend who owed him a favor.

He grabbed his phone. "Hey, Doc, I've got a problem."

"Hello, Mike. How the hell are you?" asked the man on the end of the call.

"Fine, Fine. Listen, Doc, sorry to call like this."

Mike explained Susanna's injuries. Mike and his team had rescued Dean Coleman, now John Hopkins Hospital's chief of surgery, after FARC rebels kidnapped three Americans from a Doctors Without Borders mission in Colombia. In the harrowing rescue, Mike's men and the physicians made it out alive, but not without the rebels shooting up all three doctors. Coleman clung to life. Mike never left Dean's side and kept him breathing until Special Forces helicopters airlifted him out a day later.

"Mike, I think you're fine. Remove it, and let's see what you've got," said Coleman.

"Ok. If I kill her, I'm screwed," Mike said.

"Just take the God damn thing out, Singleton. You've treated worse," Coleman reminded him.

Not with someone I loved, Mike thought. He extracted the metal shard and braced himself for the waves of blood. They never came.

"Doc, you're brilliant. The bleeding's slowed," Mike sighed, relieved.

Coleman knew Mike's patient lay in better shape than he realized. Though Mike had seen and treated unspeakable carnage in Colombia, he needed to lead another successful rescue.

"Mike, you owe me a beer," Coleman joked.

"I owe you a lot more, Dean. Thank you."

Mike cleaned Susanna's neck and pieced together the torn skin. He stitched and bandaged it, impressing himself with his suturing skills.

He closed the gash to her head next. He worked his way down her battered body rinsing the cloth and repeating his scan of her wounds. With no sign of further bleeding, he patted her dry.

With the blood and dust removed she looked peaceful. Serene. She appeared very different from the crazed journalist he met at the White House. He lifted the flesh-colored bandages on her wrists. He recognized the marks and for some reason, her cutting did not surprise him. He replaced the bloodied strips with fresh, clean dressings. Any discussion of self-destruction could wait for another day, if they talked about it at all.

When he finished, he admired his work as a painter would his canvas. As he gazed upon the girl in the painting, Susanna opened her eyes and looked back at Mike.

She looked down and saw she wore just her lavender bra and matching thong. She nodded and gave him a knowing grin.

"Dare I ask?" she said.

Susanna sat up in the middle of her bed on Mike's uniform. A wince of pain flashed across her face. He watched as she pulled her thighs into her chest. Her sliced arms grasped her scraped legs. She rested her chin on her knees. Her vacant stare shot off the end of the bed.

She recalled what had happened. "There was an explosion?"

Mike stood a few feet from her, the remainder of his uniform tossed over a chair. His Navy T-shirt and black Calvin Klein knee-length boxer-briefs dripped from bathing Susanna. She looked at him and remembered how alike they were, but from different worlds.

"I think I am beginning to feel it," she said as she hunched over clutching her smooth, white rib cage. Oh, God, I ache," Susanna whimpered. She curled up in a ball lying on her side.

Mike slipped his hands on her shoulders. "Susanna, sit up a little longer." He arranged a collection of pillows to support her back. He wanted to keep her alert and watch for signs of other damage.

An awkward silence followed. Sixteen years separated that moment from the day she walked away. A few weeks before that farewell they shared an intimacy for which she continued to search. She did not know he had not found it again either. Mike paced the area around her bed. He knew he would appear harsh, but what did it matter? He had made too many mistakes with Susanna at school and found himself as inept a lifetime later.

"Why are you looking for Joe?" Mike blurted.

"Must we start in so soon on the well-worn topic of Joe Earhardt?" she groaned. "Why don't you grab me a robe or sum'ting?" She knew Mike Singleton would do anything for her.

Anything.

"Fair enough," he said. He thought for a moment. He heard the accent. Wishful memories. He tossed her a maroon comforter.

"Why are *you* looking for Joe?" Susanna retorted, pulling the comforter around her. Her distrust of Mike seemed apparent. "Didn't you get enough living with him for four years?" she asked, dubious of his intentions.

"I just plucked you from the destruction at the White House, washed the blood from your motionless body, pull a hunk of metal out of your ungrateful neck, and you don't trust me?" he said, incredulous.

"That's right. I don't trust anyone," she said. She would not look at him.

"I could see that from your wrists," Mike commented. He wished he had not played that card so soon.

She ignored him.

"Fine. I tell and you tell. I am looking for Joe because Lori O'Reilly asked me to," she said.

"The senator?" asked Mike.

"Yeah. Do you know another?" Susanna responded.

"Uh, I don't know her. How do you …"

"We were best friends as kids. I worked on a few campaigns, and I was her chief of staff until … until I left to do other things," Susanna said, rushing her life's summary.

Mike looked around and marveled at the space. For a dump of a building outside what he saw inside appeared off the pages of some top haute-décor magazine. Not that he read them, but sometimes Roxie Fay would leave one lying around the office. The vintage and antique furnishings belonged to someone who knew period pieces. Rich hues splashed across the pricey fabrics. It amazed him.

He noticed the mounds of clothes. The kitchen sink sat obscured by a week's worth of dishes. He saw a large collection of old newspapers, but nothing tying her to the academy or Marine Corps. Sixty seconds of observation told him a lot, but, nothing made sense.

"What happened?" he asked changing subjects.

"Nothing. I told you. Lori called me," Susanna said.

"No. What happened to you?" he pushed.

"Well, I don't really recall." Susanna found herself surprised by the question.

"How can you not …?" Mike knew to drop it.

A guarded Susanna opened the topic for a rare moment. She took a deep breath. "I'll say this once. There was an accident when I was the intelligence officer in New Orleans. I have some memory issues."

Mike had heard the rumors, but worked in the Pentagon office of the Navy Reserve Force admiral's aide that month. The command also had offices in the same rundown warehouse as the Marines. Mike knew where Susanna worked at the time, but it seemed better for him to stay away for once. With another failed marriage, he could not stomach the drama of Marcasi, Earhardt, and Singleton.

Susanna started, "I think Lori knows." Her tone changed. "When I asked my question to Stahl today, I felt he knew some secret about me, too. Maybe I'm paranoid." Her voice trailed off.

Mike stared at her not knowing what to say. Susanna had been so full of life, but now seemed adrift. No past, no future. Nothing but the present.

"Is it so bad for Stahl to know something about your past?" asked Mike.

"I don't know. Maybe not. I had this overwhelming feeling of panic when he looked at me. Maybe I've been alone too long," Susanna said with more energy. She seemed lucid and confident, giving Mike hope.

"How long has it been?" he asked, reluctant to press her.

"Since ... what?" She did not want to tell him about the boys in her bed.

"Since you've been here, alone?" he asked.

"Maybe four years," she calculated. She seemed downcast and defeated. She looked up and caught his look of surprise and sorrow.

"Don't do it, Mike. Do NOT feel sorry for me."

She looked into Mike's eyes for the first time since leaving the White House. "Thank you. You didn't have to help me," she said. She looked away. "But it doesn't change anything. I've done fine all these years, and you ... appear." She tossed back the comforter revealing a bruised body clad in rich lace. She looked at him. "Yeah, and I am pissed," she stated, eyes brimming. "Why don't we just go back to who we were before the White House event?"

He held in the sorrow that just turned to grief.

"Sure. Understand," Mike said, his eyes stinging. "But Susanna, I could use your expertise for this Earhardt suicide."

He lied. Mike Singleton could track criminals and innocents alone, but he wanted to keep Susanna close. Maybe he could make good on a tangled past.

He refused to say, "Good-bye," again.

Not yet, at least.

Susanna thought about what Mike had said. She did not want to lose this chance to settle things with Lori, and she did not want Mike Singleton gone for good.

Yet.

"I'll think about it," she said, though she knew she would help him with Joe Earhardt or any other vexing issue he might name. But she needed more from the reserved man who saved her more than once.

"Now you tell, Singleton," decreed a humorless Susanna. She leaned forward.

"I can't, Susanna," Mike's voice crackled.

She huffed, "You bastard. I figured as much," feeling she had been conned.

She felt angrier knowing she would tell him the smallest detail in short order with no effort on his part. She counted it as a weakness when it came to him.

Mike knew she felt betrayed. "Soon. I will explain everything soon."

He held his breath and let it out saying, "You could call me Mike again."

Susanna grew more irate at the suggestion. "Don't. All these years and I hear nothing from you." She began to mutter, "First name? Have you ever known me to be someone easily placated?"

Yes, he thought. He never had to placate her. The understanding and cooperative Susanna had disappeared. Now he faced an angry mountain lion. Mike could tell something had gone very wrong since graduation.

He needed to learn what happened to her.

"You know, whatever, *Mike.* I am not up for games. We need to find out what happened to Joe," Susanna said.

But her interest in the man just beyond her reach had replaced her drive to find Joe Earhardt. She looked over at the marble mantle clock. "It's noon. He went missing about 10 hours ago. Lori says from the Memorial Bridge, where, according to D.C. police, if you can believe that crew, he had a gun and may have killed himself."

She looked at Mike as if ready to reveal an important clue. "I can't believe I was with that jerk those years at school and almost a year in the Marine Corps. What was I thinking?" stated Susanna, sounding mystified.

Mike's version of events differed from Susanna's. Despite his many questions, he could tell this discussion topic would have to wait.

"Is my past with Joe an issue for you?" Susanna asked with mixture of faux desperation and regret.

"Uh ... no. No. It's fine," he said unsure of what she meant. Her comment brought many questions to the forefront, though. He already had lived it and could not imagine it any worse now. He had witnessed more than his share of mayhem.

Susanna could not let the topic of her past with Joe rest. "Don't ask me why we got engaged," she said as she climbed off the bed.

"Months after graduation the relationship moved into its final phase that I label simply as 'Hell,' and we ended it without formally breaking it off."

"I'm thankful we never consummated that unholy union," she added.

"Really?" Mike said with relief as well as disbelief.

"Apparently this surprises you, Singleton," she said.

"Uh, yeah, Marcasi. I guess it floors me," Mike confessed.

"Well, I know I don't have to explain my choices," she snipped. She looked at Mike and pointed. "*You* lived with him. *You* saw what went on at school. *You* know what happened, Mike." Her voice softened and she reached for the comforter.

Mike recalled his unenviable position. He loved Susanna and thought her mess with Joe would just take care of itself. He remembered the pain and resentment. He had questions, but tucked them away.

"Then one day as Lori's Senate chief, I got this call from a Marine major—*Joe Earhardt*, if you can believe it. Senate liaison officer for the Corps, he says. He pushed past me and wanted to meet with Lori to discuss some issues the Marines had been pushing hard on the Hill. I told him to tread lightly during the first encounter and get her in a second meeting. We agreed not to tell her about our past relationship," she recalled.

Susanna felt compelled to continue. "They became smitten with one another that first meeting. I may be the only one who knew. I left her office sometime later," she said as if she sat on a witness stand.

"You left over the senator and Joe?" Mike asked, baffled by the idea.

"I don't know why I'm answering your questions. No. Lori and I fell out over another matter," she said.

Mike nodded knowing much went unsaid.

Before either could speak, Susanna answered her cell phone.

Mike watched as she paced the room in her undergarments. He found her a mix of sexual allure and super hero determination.

"Hello, Bill," she said with false sweetness. "Bill, I know. Yes, I know. Bill, I was in the explosion. It took me a while to gather up my notes. Bill, I could have died."

She looked over at Mike and rolled her eyes.

"Yes, I have photos and will send them. Yes, as soon as I hang up. I will send you two stories on the explosion, one straight news piece and the other a first-person account. Yes, I'll include cut lines with the photos." She bounced her head from side to side as she spoke.

"Nice of you to ask. I'm fine."

Susanna eyed Mike. "A handsome Navy commander came to my rescue and got me home safely. Yes, Bill, there was blood. I think I mentioned there was an explosion. No, I'm not on anything."

She lost interest in Bill at that moment.

She found her silk leopard-print robe and wrapped it around her as she paced.

"Let me go so I can write."

She slipped her feet into her teal heeled boudoir slippers with fluttering matching feathers.

Mike thought she just needed a scotch and a cigarette to complete the look.

"Jesus, Bill. I know. Good-bye. Yes, I love you, too. Good-bye."

Mike did not know what to make of the conversation. *Handsome?* He had never handled compliments or Susanna Marcasi well.

"Are you and Bill, uh, you know?" he asked, looking into her eyes for his answer.

"Oh God, no." She looked away. "Bill took a gamble and gave me a chance. I owe him a lot."

Susanna's voice and eyes softened, "Singleton, I owe you my life. I'll help you with 'Joe Earhardt: Wanted Dead or Alive.'" She howled at her joke. "I wish I could take this seriously, but that prima donna deserves whatever has happened to him."

"So you don't think he killed himself?" asked Mike.

"Do you?" she said.

She knew the answer.

"Joe? Are you kidding? Way too vain," Mike said.

Susanna laughed at the idea of a Joe Earhardt suicide. But she felt nervous with Mike so close again. She ducked into her bath and popped two Clonazepam to dull the anxiety.

She kicked off her heels and let the robe drop as she paced.

"Mike, I need two hours to file photos and two stories. You're welcome to stay, but I will ignore you. Calliope would love the company and can be needy. It's up to you," she said. Susanna's offer seemed sincere. Mike listened, but eyed her almost bare body, albeit cut and bruised.

She felt no pain so why should he?

Mike did not want to leave her alone, but he needed to meet with the admiral. He slipped on his torn, blood-stained trousers and figured the trip back to his place should prove interesting.

"I need to clean up. It's noon now, so I'll call you around 2, Marcasi?"

"I'll be here," she said already working on her story.

He reached out to touch her arm. She moved it beyond his reach by instinct and continued to work.

What has happened to her? he wondered.

CHAPTER TEN

Susanna moved like a woman on fire. She had underestimated the time she needed to file her stories and photos, but she had more pressing issues requiring her attention. She salivated at the thought of delving into Joe Earhardt's suicide. Find the answer and she might unravel other vexing mysteries. Levee money for one, she thought. Yeah, yeah, Lori had demanded she leave the levee matter alone, which screamed, "Dig deeper!" in Susanna Marcasi's parlance.

With no time to spare, Susanna downloaded her photographs and picked the best of each shot. She numbered them and sent Bill the photos with corresponding captions. The Times gravitated toward the ghoulish and grotesque, like the dead couple, as did she.

Forty-five minutes. Damn.

She realized she had *three* stories to craft—two on the bombing and one on the ceremony. She worked faster. She called the White House press secretary's personal cell for the latest casualty figures and looked for White House and law enforcement press releases. Nothing. The lack of a TV in her apartment meant no 'round-the-clock news. She heard Mike's estimate of 25 dead and 40 wounded. She pounded on her keyboard:

Bill, Bombing, news:

At least 20 lay slain and dozens wounded following an explosion at the southeast gate of the White House. The powerful blast rocked the entrance and sent scores scrambling for cover. The area around the heavily guarded entry was destroyed as guests were leaving the swearing-in ceremony for incoming Defense Secretary, Louisiana Senator Manfred Stahl. ...

Bill, Bombing, first-person:

Shortly after Manfred Stahl took his oath as the new Secretary of Defense, I left the White House ceremony. Like a number of guests, I was caught in the day's first horrific explosion at the southeast gate, but I was fortunate and walked away with a few cuts. Though I prefer not to speculate, it seemed like a bomb had been planted at the security screening area. It amazes me that something like this can happen here in Washington. I am not frightened by the incident—I am angered. I photographed the carnage and debris-strewn scene outside the home of the U.S. president. Do we lock down the city? Do we live in fear? Is there a system to deal with purveyors of terror? It seems not. ...

Bill, Ceremony. News (final story):

Long-time Louisiana Senator Manfred Stahl took his oath as Secretary of Defense in a heavily attended—though rare—White House ceremony. Stahl, who also served in the House of Representatives for a number of years, stated, "Today, I stand before you ready to serve our men and women in uniform again as their leader. ... Today we get leadership back in the Pentagon." ...

She stopped short of replacing any reference to "swearing-in" or "ceremony" with "coronation," though she believed that stood as Stahl's goal, or maybe a step to achieve some goal. Manfred Stahl had more talent and daring than Susanna cared to admit.

She played back her recording of the ceremony from the Olympus she had left at the podium and rolled her eyes when the old blow hard spoke. *What a pompous son of a bitch*, she thought. She started to type. "Blah, blah, blah. You freak," she muttered at the recorder. She listened to questions from the other journalists and shook her head. *Have they no imagination?* She stopped typing and continued to listen.

An utterance after the ceremony piqued her interest. Susanna tried to separate the layered voices. She stared at the silver recorder. She played back a five-minute segment. Then two. She paused the recording and retrieved her notebook from her bag encrusted with dried blood. She scribbled her notes.

Susanna shrugged off her displeasure with the three stories and sent them to Bill with an, "I'm better than you deserve!" reminder. Freed from her obligation, she replayed the recording. She saved the voice file on her laptop as well as her new gadget, a USB flash drive.

She burned three CDs. One copy went in with her thongs. She boxed up another CD and slipped it behind cleaning supplies. She wrapped the third in plastic and slid it deep inside a 10-pound cat food bag.

She grabbed her phone, "Singleton, call me. I've got something. We're going to New Orleans."

"We?" asked Mike filling the void as Susanna opened the door to her flat minutes after calling him.

"My, you made it here fast," she commented walking toward her bed that now supported an open suit case. "I see you check your messages often."

He had not yet entered the room. "We?" he asked again leaning against the peeling door frame. He looked taller wearing his black 501s, ebony cowboy boots, a black-and-multi-striped cotton, long-sleeve collared shirt and smoky leather jacket. Mike's enviable head of thick, wheat-colored hair brightened the dark outfit. He kept the sides shorn close, tighter than Navy regulations required. He had sported a well-trimmed moustache that matched his locks, but shaved before returning to Susanna's. He had forgotten nothing about his dark-haired beauty and recalled facial hair stood as grounds for execution in her world. Susanna's standards aside, did her sudden New Orleans announcement stem from the day's trauma? Mike did not want to go on this roller coaster again strapped in next to her.

"Gotta car?" she asked like a gold-digging vamp.

"Yeah, I have a car," he said.

He figured he could handle her. Hell, the Navy had made him its Silver Star-sporting, United States Navy SEAL poster boy. Facing Susanna Marcasi, he trusted his first instinct: trouble.

"Great, because my motorcycle won't get us there. Mrs. Schiller will watch Calliope. Pick me up at 2." Susanna spoke in short, quick, and slurred sentences. Mike felt himself getting dragged back into her world, yet he found beauty in the impending doom.

She did it every time.

"That's in 15 minutes," he said with surprise.

"No. *Two a.m.* We'll get there 6 p.m., tomorrow. It's perfect. Trust me. I have done this trip more times than I care to remember," she said.

Her mind raced.

Mike walked in the room. A click of his boot heel closed the door behind him. He clung to what patience remained. White House explosions. Susanna Marcasi. An energized Susanna rushed from closet to bed to kitchen to window and back to the closet. The faster she moved, the more Mike longed to be in the field.

"Marcasi, stop. Put the clothes down and look at me," he said.

Susanna shot him a menacing look.

"I didn't drive here for your declaration on our next step. Joe went missing here in Washington. Our work is here. I will operate from Washington regardless where you choose to go," Mike said.

Susanna did not like being challenged unless it promised a metaphorical fight to the death, not something she envisioned with Mike Singleton. The two stood there in a silent stand-off. Neither would look away.

Neither could be intimidated.

"OK, I'll bite. Why New Orleans?" he asked.

She turned and walked toward her computer perched on the cluttered dining table.

"Listen to this recording from the ceremony. Joe's suicide extends beyond the Memorial Bridge," she said.

"It's difficult to make out so I'll play it a few times." She played the five-minute segment. Mike hunched over with his hands on the back of her chair. He looked at Susanna shaking his head.

"That was the president and Stahl followed by Lori and Stahl. Listen to this." Susanna played a portion of the two-minute clip. Mike stood up straight behind Susanna nodding his head. He folded his arms. One hand covered his face.

Susanna turned and looked right at Mike's hips. She leaned her head back and could see he stood deep in thought or maybe in pain.

"What is it?" she asked.

"Nothing," he said a little too quickly.

"This is the final segment," she said facing the keyboard.

Mike sat down on the chair on the long side of the table and listened.

"That's Stahl talking to one of the guests. He's a Levee Board member," she revealed.

Susanna waited for Mike's reaction.

He sat in silence looking down at the table. He looked at Susanna.

"Joe's name is mentioned along with the Levee Board in each conversation. And they tie him to pending legislation. We have him in suspicious conversations with foreign governments but not the New Orleans Levee Board. *Who* was that guy?" asked Mike referring to final segment. He hoped Susanna had not caught his revelation about DIA's Joe Earhardt probe.

"That was the Levee Board president, Vic Dumaine," she said.

Mike thought the name sounded familiar. "I know that name, but how do you know all this?"

She had claimed her memory had become spotty. Was it an act? A scam? Was she as damaged as rumored? he wondered.

"These are my people and the levee project has kept me guessing since I was with Lori, except I felt Lori and I worked toward different ends."

She shifted. "Ah, Vic Dumaine is his own tale of show. He's a retired Marine two-star who commanded when I was in New Orleans. You may know him as a Medal of Honor recipient from Vietnam, but rumors have swirled about his award.

"Vic Dumaine served as Manfred Stahl's company commander in Vietnam. It's believed Stahl masterminded the rescue of a stranded Marine company. Some purport Dumaine and his buddies wrote the action otherwise and tweaked the eyewitness accounts giving Vic the medal and leaving Stahl with the Navy Cross. Stahl's a bastard but has used this shameful sequence to his advantage," she explained.

Susanna started to pace and gesture as she recounted the story. "The other Medal of Honor recipients, and the Marine Corps for that matter, never accepted Dumaine into the top-tier club of heroes. They tossed him a first star out of pity and a second to keep him quiet. He is weak, corrupt, and in everyone's pocket because he can't make it on his own. Stahl continues to milk his overwhelming but unspoken vote of sympathy. He owns Dumaine and both men know it. Stahl and his boys from the platoon can come forward at any time and disgrace Vic Dumaine."

She turned and looked at Mike.

"But they haven't. Dumaine provides more value as Stahl's pawn than the truth of Stahl's heroism," she concluded.

Susanna sat on the edge of the bed, as if afraid of tipping her fragile safe haven. She liked the hapless but kind Dumaine. She appreciated his good nature the way she detested the vile Manfred Stahl. Her heart raced. *Dumaine, Stahl, Marcasi? New Orleans? All the more reason to gas up the car,* she thought.

"OK. We can go," Mike said. "It's a two-hour flight and I don't think the board moves at a fast pace. Not much is going to change down there. First I have work to do at the bridge and in the District. My guess is you have some prep, maybe at the Senate? Lori's office?" he said.

Susanna nodded and said, "Not bad, Singleton. Not bad. Fine. Let's split up here and keep in contact." She slipped in, "Then we can drive to New Orleans."

They sat wargaming at Susanna's French parquet table and agreed upon a strategy, but they continued to disagree on New Orleans transportation.

"Fly," insisted Mike.

"Drive," she countered.

CHAPTER ELEVEN

As Mike left Fourteenth Street, he barked into his phone, "Meet me at the base of the Memorial Bridge. Virginia side. ASAP. Bring all your gear. Yeah, yeah. Earhardt's possible suicide. Yeah, I know it's been a few hours. Yeah, I'm looking for any God damn thing." Mike threw up his arms exasperated, "We'll discuss this at the bridge."

He knuckleballed his phone against a brick wall, "God damn Marcasi."

He knelt to pick up the pieces.

Susanna also felt a mix of anger and nostalgia. She wanted Mike to hurt as much as she did.

"Bastard!" she screamed in her apartment.

She suppressed her rage toward Mike Singleton and tossed on a favorite Pucci ensemble that covered her wounds. She wrapped a silk Pucci scarf around her neck, transformed her eyes, cheeks, lips, and hair in less than five minutes, and stormed out the door.

Susanna talked into her mobile as she walked to the Metro for the short ride. "Chris, it's Susanna Marcasi. I need to talk to you about the Joe Earhardt story. I'm on my way over." Susanna paused. "I know. I'll explain in person."

Susanna called Chris Gilchrest again when she stood a block from The Washington Post's Fifteenth Street headquarters. The stop at the paper seemed unworthy of a mention to Mike.

"Chris, meet me at the entrance. I don't think I'm welcome. The last time I was here they threw me out, but you know that," she said. Susanna listened. "Got it. I'll see you in a few minutes."

Gilchrest remained a friend despite her persona non grata status at the Post. He escorted her up to his desk in the Metro Section. He bounced between the Capitol Hill beat and Metro.

"Susanna, this is rather unexpected," Gilchrest said. His all-business tone had an air of indignation. Susanna knew she had a narrow window, if it opened at all.

"I am looking at writing an online entry on the Earhardt suicide," she said, matter-of-fact.

"I assume you read my article," said Gilchrest as he eyed Susanna with suspicion.

"Of course. Who didn't? That's why I'm here. What else do you have on this?" she asked. She laid out her cards for him to see.

Gilchrest had long trusted Susanna. When he reported on the Hill, she proved his best source and better as a companion at the occasional late-night strip club.

He owed her.

With a heavy sigh he looked at her and handed her his files. "OK, but you cannot, I repeat, CANNOT, run this until after we do. Agreed?" he conceded.

Susanna took the 3 ½ inch floppy disk and flipped through the folder he handed her. "Chris, it looks like you have copies of all the police records here," she noted. "Not bad." She nodded her approval.

"OK, I have become a print whore and all-around criminal," he admitted with some relief as Susanna continued to nod. "I'm waiting for some additional information from my source in the department. We may be The Washington Post, but we don't want to get this guy killed, if he isn't dead already," he confessed.

"Chris, if Joe Earhardt is still alive, I'm sure he's well, so I wouldn't worry about his situation," she lied.

Susanna wanted Joe Earhardt to suffer more than any man had ever suffered. She started to turn away, but wheeled around to face Gilchrest again.

"I may have information that will pull this story out of Metro and make it national news for you. I don't know yet, but I'll give it all to you. I won't run anything until your story is out."

Susanna needed Joe Earhardt, not the story. She hurried out of the Post and headed to Capitol Hill.

***

Mike had wanted to talk to the head of the dive team since he first heard of Joe's disappearance. He checked his Rolex. "Fifteen minutes late," he fumed as the team arrived. Mike stood like a granite monument in camouflage utilities that he kept in his office. He watched as four men in wet suits pushed off the bank in their Zodiac. The group looked to Mike who gave them a thumbs-up. Two divers entered the water. The other two waited. The team had the advantage of daylight, unlike Russell's divers. Mike stood watching with his arms folded.

When the divers re-entered the boat, he radioed the team, "Anything?" he asked in a hopeful tone.

"Negative, sir. We're taking more lights and equipment on this next descent. I can tell you there's no body down there, and I don't think one ever made it to the bottom," said the diver.

The second team went in with lights and tools. One diver held the light while the other took photographs. They sifted through leaves and other debris that lay on the bottom. One saw what he thought looked like a watch, but he grabbed the bottom of an old soda bottle instead. The divers found it remarkable how many pieces of wood looked like fire arms and skeletal remains.

After the first team reentered the water and combed down river given the Potomac's swift current, the four divers met Mike on the muddy bank.

"Commander, there ain't nothin' relating to Lieutenant Colonel Joe Earhardt that we could find," reported a confident though frustrated team leader.

Mike's head throbbed. He ground his teeth until his jaw ached. He wanted to find Joe Earhardt bloated, unrecognizable, and very dead at the bottom of the Potomac. A bullet through the brain would have given Mike one less "to do" item. But he sighed containing his frustration.

"Thanks, guys. Beer's on me," he said.

Mike had done more than his share of dives. He would have

plumbed any depth to find Earhardt's corpse. *No evidence of Joe? Humph.* Though unsure where this would lead, he needed the information for his next move.

He did not know the bridge had told a different story.

Mike Singleton made the short walk back to his office and changed into his Navy service dress uniform. He glanced at his watch. He still had no call from Susanna on his cracked phone. He made his way to D.C. police headquarters. Russell met him at the entrance.

"I hate the fucking Navy," greeted a testy Russell.

"I am no fan of the D.C. police force either, chief," returned Mike.

Both laughed and shook hands. "C'mon in. Let's go to my office," said the chief, happy to see a friendly face from the past.

Mike stopped in the men's rest room to blot the mist from his jacket. The rain had let up. Mike never wore the Navy's cheap and putrid-smelling rain coat and refused to carry an effeminate umbrella.

"Mike, it's been a long time," Russell said.

"Not long enough, Roscoe," laughed Mike.

"Let's see. The last time our paths to Hell crossed, you were at NAVRESFOR for some conference, and my guys picked you up in the French Quarter for ..." Russell figured he would give Mike the honor.

"Yeah, pissing in one of your filthy alleys," recalled Mike with some embarrassment.

"You're a classy guy, Singleton."

Russell turned serious. "You want to know about that God damn colonel boy, don't you?"

"Is it that obvious?" asked Mike impressed with how quickly Russell delved into business.

"We saw your boys out on the Potomac redoing our work. Jesus, we may be corrupt, but we're not incompetent," challenged Roscoe without a hint of humor. "Mike, I'd rather talk to you than that crazy senator bitch O'Reilly. Boy, does she piss me off. But that ol' chief-of-staff gal of hers—Marcasi? Now I can work with her."

Roscoe stood up shaking his head as he paced his office.

"Horrible, just horrible what happened to her in New Orleans at that pretty-boy command of hers," Russell said. "I was a Marine. An MP for six years. But if you ask me, the Corps could not give a fuck about Susanna or anyone. They let that bright, young officer get ripped apart by rabid dogs. It happened on my turf, but their heavies pushed my boys out of the investigation."

Russell stopped and snatched a file from his desk. Mike's eyes widened at what Russell revealed. He inched toward the edge of his chair holding his breath.

"I had my suspicions, though," Russell continued. "It was someone at that goat fest of a command. And that fucking Major General Vic Dumaine. Jesus. A Medal of Honor should only go so far. Give me a day with the evidence, and I'll Mirandize the guilty party before dark. Given the level of violence, my guess is the attacker was one pissed off mother and had savaged other people. Women, men, but probably more women."

Russell gestured like a professor as he started to pace again. He looked at Mike as his student on major points of his presentation.

"The girl remembered nothing after coming out of that coma. I don't think anyone has ever told her the truth about how some dirt bag coward nearly beat her to death and tried to burn the evidence," Russell said.

Mike's lips parted. He repeated the chief's words. *Nearly beaten to death?*

The disclosure choked him.

Russell's sources revealed Mike Singleton and Susanna Marcasi appeared to work as a team on pretty boy Earhardt. The attack on Susanna and the Marine Corps's mishandling of the case never sat right with Russell. He thought Mike deserved to know the truth and figured the Navy SEAL might seek justice for the wronged Marine. She deserved a shot at redemption, even if revenge had eluded her.

"Commander, I don't want this Earhardt case and would do back flips to hand it over to the Department of Defense, if I could. Better yet, I'd pass it off to the God damn Marine Corps. Never did like those boys prancing at 8th and I. I'm sorry to come across like such a son of a bitch. The Corps was not exactly welcoming to the 'dark green' Marines, as they called us. Yeah, I'm fucking bitter," Russell said.

The chief stood up and towered over his visitor.

"Mike, yes, your lieutenant colonel is missing, but he left that bridge very much alive," Russell said as he again paced the room. "We found blood on the bridge and some powder residue, but not enough to indicate he fired his weapon. It appears someone dragged him from the railing to a vehicle waiting behind him. Did that person provide the source of the gunfire? We can't prove it—yet. We have tread marks from when the vehicle sped off and are trying to figure out the model of the tire. You know the drill." Russell sat across from Mike. "He could be in Anacostia; he could be in Montana. I don't know where he is. We've gotten his photo and other information out to police departments around the country, but nothing yet. I'm sorry."

He looked to Mike for some reaction.

Russell held up the disk in its gnarled plastic cover. "I found this on the bridge. It has some damage. My people are trying to retrieve information. We know it has a lot of numbers and files under the name of 'Hercules.' Hercules? God damn Marine prancers. I think Earhardt dropped it when they forced him off the rail. My guess is he did not leave it behind by accident," surmised Russell. He handed copy to Mike. "Looks like you and the girl will be busy. Let me know what you find."

Mike gripped the copy like the Holy Grail he hoped it would be.

"Thanks, chief. Will do," he said.

Mike knew this was no small gesture for Chief Russell. He figured Russell handed the disk over for Susanna's sake, but he appreciated his trust.

"Could you e-mail me what you've sent out, chief?" he said handing him his card.

Russell looked at him and snatched the card.

"You bet, Mike, but I'm not sure what good it will do you," said Russell, figuring Mike had his own suspicions.

"Maybe nothing, but I'd like to take a stab at it. Thanks," said Mike, with his mind on Susanna.

Mike Singleton left Russell's office and walked downstairs, dazed. *Nearly beaten to death?* He pushed the doors open with extra force and headed to the Metro. Mike swiped his security badge to reenter his office. With a small gasp, Roxie Fay blurted, "What in heavens happened to you?" Mike looked through her and went back to his cubicle. He used his office phone to make a call. It went into the cell phone's voice mail.

"Short leash, Singleton."

Bartholomew seemed all-knowing.

CHAPTER TWELVE

Susanna left The Washington Post at 3 p.m., sharp. Getting to the Hill a little later than planned might work to her advantage. She would have preferred making her way in the darkness, but not everyone favored her schedule. Susanna decided to walk to Capitol Hill. The temperature neared 60 degrees and the sky had cleared. The walk would give her time to think. Maybe shop.

Her thoughts vectored to Joe Earhardt. He deserved every misfortune God could spiral at the former Navy quarterback.

Susanna piqued Joe's interest early that first year at the Naval Academy. But accepting female midshipmen as peers or paramours stood verboten, a capital crime, warned watchful upper classmen. Inmates ran the asylum. The sentence for befriending a female seemed unthinkable: complete ostracism and repeated humiliation. Senior company bullies stoked the fires of animosity against the women that misfortune—or Satan himself—had thrown their way.

For Homecoming 1980, Joe and Susanna donned their elegant dinner dress uniforms. Resplendent in black and white, the attractive couple accented the look with their gold satin cummerbunds. A generous slit ran up each side of Susanna's formfitting, floor-length skirt.

Had they not been the envy of most at the historic armory ball, they may have survived the evening unnoticed. But at 2 a.m. a group of juniors dragged Joe from his room and pummeled him in the men's rest room. They slammed his skull against the urinal and almost drowned him in a toilet. Mike Singleton rushed to his roommate's aid and pulled the offenders off one-by-one. Nose bloodied and eye swollen, Mike dragged a semi-conscious Joe back to their room.

Times grew darker as Plebe Year progressed. Each morning Susanna found a red stripe painted down her door. She washed it before anyone else saw it. She never reported it. One Sunday she awoke and found the stripe painted the length of her body. Mike Singleton called it a blood stripe, after the name given to the stripe on the Marines' blue trousers. How accurate she thought. Whoever painted her blood stripe did so in pig's blood every time.

Though Susanna veered away from Joe, a ring appeared as Susanna prepared to leave on an academic exchange program with the Coast Guard Academy at the end of their sophomore year. The pair had performed their sexually charged rendition of "Paradise by the Dashboard Light" each week. But engagement? Even the term "boyfriend," did not fit their situation.

Susanna saw Joe's proposal as a means of control. She wanted the brass ring of graduation, not the white gold one bearing a 1 carat brilliant-cut diamond. But desperate and insecure, she accepted his proposal. The two settled in for a long engagement more akin to trench warfare than young people betrothed. But neither would break the engagement.

The stalemate continued.

Their war of attrition replaced a post-graduation wedding. Joe and Susanna met for their next round at Quantico that September.

Susanna approached the Capitol and shuddered at what she recalled. Her life with Joe in those moments seemed as vivid and violent as a Tarantino film. She lifted her chin with pride and pressed her shoulder blades together as Mrs. Schiller had taught her. She made her call.

"Frank, it's Susanna Marcasi. I am on my way over and need to talk to you."

***

Susanna approached the Russell Senate Office Building with a snarl of feelings. She ached for the camaraderie the staff members shared, even during the darkest days of their stand against Senator Manfred Stahl. But her nostalgia turned to revulsion as she recalled legislating for dollars and amassing large sums of money for the "people." Some people did benefit, but not Louisiana voters.

And why am I walking in here after a four-year exile? I must be a masochist! thought Susanna.

She strode toward the main entrance. The Russell Building oozed early 20th century elegance, while its brothers, Hart and Dirksen, reminded her of Stalin's Russia. The House offices cornered the market on charm. How the Senate ended up with plain, mid-century structures remained a mystery, though they possessed more space. Entering any of the office buildings meant passing from one world into a secret society characterized by graft and greed.

She felt like "Susanna through the Looking Glass."

As she stepped inside, she tossed a casual glance behind her. Across the street she saw Lori with a man in a dark suit, but the angle of the sun obscured his identity. The scheduler had Lori out of her office for the day, which meant nowhere near the Hill. Susanna could not pull off the visit with Lori present. She would work like a dervish and planned to exit with Lori none the wiser.

Susanna slipped through the entry to the surprised greetings of those who knew her a lifetime ago. She smiled her toothless smile and gave an uneasy nod. Her eyes darted. Her head snapped in every direction. She felt back with friends, yet she wanted to run. Susanna labored with the weight of her memories like a recreational hiker on Mount Everest. Any feeling of accomplishment escaped her. *What happened to the cavalier Susanna chief of staff?* she wondered. Had she become the distrusting, embittered woman she knew better at that moment? It did not matter. She figured Lori would make her way to the Russell entrance. If caught rummaging through Senate offices, she had no explanation to give her.

Susanna looked at the mobile in her hand. *Just call him, Susanna,* she chided knowing she had little time.

"Frank, it's Susanna. I'm here. Great, I will wait for you," she schmoozed.

Frank Cabot served as Lori's brilliant but annoying legislative assistant. He had many gifts. While he could write a flawless bill, he would alienate everyone he needed for passage in the process. Frank, a former U.S. Army Corps of Engineers officer, had just celebrated his 42nd birthday. He and Susanna toiled together, but he failed to learn to work with all sides with genuine respect.

"Susanna, I admire you. I understand what you're telling me, but this is who I am," explained Frank, while crafting a major bill. Frank worked in concert with the Committee on Environment and Public Works staff on the levee legislation. His language helped ensure Orleans Parish won its billions. The City that Time and God Forgot— or its Levee Board to be exact—had Frank Cabot to thank.

Frank startled Susanna.

"Frank," she exclaimed with feigned enthusiasm, throwing her arms around his morbidly thin neck. He smelled of cooking oil—used oil from a deep fat fryer to be exact. His hair had thinned and grayed and Susanna could not guess when he last washed it. She found him to be one of the least attractive men in government. He looked like hell and would have no place in her office. But the staff belonged to someone else.

She needed Frank Cabot.

"Frankie. God, it's good to see you." She half lied; he knew it, but would take what the Dark Minx, as he called her in his fantasies, would give him. Frank wrapped his long, skeletal arms around her as a sign of affection. She clutched her vintage Chanel bag that held her recording equipment, camera, and three disks and wiggled from his grasp.

"I remember how much you like stairs," Frank said. His enthusiasm at that moment seemed repugnant. He had draped his wretched frame in a wrinkled brown polyester suit.

She swallowed hard. "I'm so eager to see the old office!"

She held her cards close.

Susanna hooked her arm around his and guided him up the stairs. Dragged, really. She jabbered nonstop, something she knew the introvert abhorred. She told Frank about her writing, the Times, her apartment, and even Calliope, describing each in mind-numbing detail. He shook loose from her. Susanna glanced back and noted the horror on his face, which only encouraged her further. He stood in the middle of the grand corridor.

"You know, Susanna, that's great. Oops, I forgot something. Why don't you head to Lori's office?" he offered, desperate to escape. He had forgotten how overbearing the Dark Minx could be.

"Are you sure, Frank?" she asked.

"Positive," he said with the wave of a hand. "I'm sorry, but I have to get this, uh, thing I forgot. You know. Papers at Armed Services."

Susanna turned, interested. With eyebrows raised, her look said, "Really?"

Frank pressed his lips together and shifted his weight.

"Just the usual Title 10 items?" she asked.

"No, it has something to do with a major bill we're working on. We are looking at additional money going to New Orleans for levee work. Somehow the Corps of Engineers hasn't seen a penny. You know those investigations—just government-funded black holes. But you understand all that. This was your issue," he said.

She could hear the mix of aggravation and relief in his voice.

"Of course. I do have some knowledge on the topic that I'd be happy to share. I'd like to know more about the bills you've written to date to appropriate the current funding," she said.

"You know that money still goes to the Levee Board and is supposed to pass to the Army Corps of Engineers. It hasn't changed since you left." A calmer Frank took comfort in discussing legislation. "I craft these bills that are rubber stamped and the money heads south. The Corps has been screaming, but we cannot get the laws changed regarding procedures and oversight. I have rewritten the current bill three times and it hasn't gotten past Lori since she took over the committee. She won't introduce it. The overpowering interest from Armed Services has had a lot to do with Manfred Stahl in his new capacity as defense secretary. But I don't understand Defense weighing in at this point on the well-worn topic of levee funding."

Frank brought both hands to his unshaven face.

"I can't believe some of the crap that goes on," he said, the frustration clear in the strain of his voice.

"What about Joe Earhardt?" Susanna asked.

"You mean Colonel Lori O'Reilly? Well, Joe's been all over this thing, banging his fist about the large Marine presence in Orleans Parish and its vulnerability to the levees. Marine Forces Reserve occupies three warehouses on the Industrial Canal where it meets the Mississippi, and granted, sits on a crucial levee. There are Marines at the Lakefront where Lake Pontchartrain's levees are important. The case for Marines at the Naval Station and Belle Chasse is weak. I would think the Marine Corps commandant has bigger fish to fry on the Hill than a couple of levees," he said

Frank thought for a moment. "And Joe has arranged several congressional visits to New Orleans. He seems to go down often."

"Thank you, Frank. Please stay in touch." Susanna had gotten much of what she needed from Frank Cabot. She turned and moved out of sight, worried about Lori's return.

She looked up and down the quiet corridor. She stepped back into the hall as she slipped off her shoes. Her target: Lori's computer. But she first pulled her recorder for a sound check and inserted fresh batteries into her camera. Susanna had no idea what she might find, but figured she would pull Lori's version of the levee funding and maybe some odd references to other programs.

Once inside, she accessed Lori's files with her list of standard passwords and protocols. As she copied the hard drive, Susanna rifled around Lori's desk for stray disks, file folders, and anything about the levees and Joe. She heard voices and checked the doorway.

She could not leave fast enough.

After the files downloaded, Susanna tiptoed in her bare feet past the meeting room where Lori greeted her visitors, be they constituents, lobbyists, or members. Susanna caught herself as she walked by the often darkened conference area. She noticed Lori's back to the open entry—hair, gathered, knotted, cascading the length of her jacket. She stood almost at attention in her red patent slingback pumps. Manfred Stahl towered over her threatening her like a black bear in the wild. Susanna's eyes widened. She listened for a levee mention or Earhardt clue. Susanna stepped back and positioned herself out of Stahl's field of vision with her back against the opposite wall. As she pressed her shoulders into the plaster, her heart raced. Her head ached. Her moist palms left their imprint on the wall. "Listen to them, listen," she told herself. She fumbled for her recorder. It slipped, tumbling near the doorway separating her from Lori and Stahl. Manfred Stahl looked past Lori. Susanna squeezed her fists and knees in an effort to make herself invisible. But at that moment, she feared for Lori more than herself. Stahl bellowed in the office of evil, as Susanna had dubbed any room under Manfred Stahl's control.

She glanced at the recorder. Its red light signaled "on."

How far Lori had risen, but how far would she fall? Susanna loved her, admired her, and pitied her. Mick O'Reilly had determined his daughter would carry on the family's political tradition. Now it had come to major shoot out with Manfred Stahl. She could feel Stahl's fury. She wanted to call to Lori, but stood mute.

At that moment, Stahl resembled Lori's father. Mick O'Reilly stood as a pillar in the community, but ruled as a ruthless taskmaster at home. The eight O'Reilly children stood as less than Mick's legacy and more as his property. They existed for him to employ as he wished. He lavished them for acts that held the family in high regard. They suffered if they disappointed him.

All feared him.

"You stupid, stupid bitch!" Stahl yelled.

Susanna held her breath as she listened from her notch in the wall.

"And you call yourself senator? You call yourself a woman? You would never have been elected had we not ... Let's see. You ran for New Orleans City Council, the state house and senate, and the U.S. House and lost. You ran for fucking governor against that Ku Klux Klan Grand Wizard. Even he had a higher percentage of the black vote than you did. You could not beat the most hated man in the

South. Face it, O'Reilly, you are fucking nothing without me," growled Manfred Stahl.

He grabbed Lori's upper arm and yanked her toward him. She wrestled from his vice-like grip and backed away from him. Though Lori did not flinch, Susanna thought it time for the Lori to leave. She waited for her to speak.

Instead, Stahl continued his tirade, "First you bring in that bitch Marcasi on as your chief of staff. I hate to fucking admit this, but that whore is smarter than you will ever be."

He pointed at Lori, "She's your God damn chief of staff and starts to look at levee money because she cares about her home town. Because it was her job!"

Stahl threw both arms in the air.

"Jesus, what the fuck were you thinking?" Stahl screeched and stomped like Godzilla.

Susanna froze with terror.

Stahl raised his right arm high behind his head. The blow landed with such force across Lori's face it knocked her off her heels and onto the carpet.

"Well, it's my home town, too, and I say fuck every stupid bastard living in that cesspool," he screamed.

Susanna snatched her recorder and her shoes and ran down the long marble corridor. She took the stairs two at a time and exited the building. She thought of hailing a cab, but sensed Manfred Stahl had men everywhere. Despite the pain from the morning's bruises and a neck wound she felt seeping through her favorite scarf, she ran back to her flat on Fourteenth Street. The vision of Mike leaning under the pawn sign brought welcome relief.

She collapsed at his feet.

CHAPTER THIRTEEN

Susanna would not allow exhaustion to interfere this trip. They had missed the previous day's last flight but could catch the first, a 6 a.m., non-stop. As she shoved clothes into a large suitcase, Mike shook his head. He looked at his black vinyl duffle to get him through what remained an insertion and extraction mission.

"We get in and we get out," he reminded her.

"Yeah, yeah, I know," she said waving him off.

Mike arranged for a 4 a.m., cab pick-up. They waited in the cool spring air. She had a wheeled carrier for her steamer trunks, so their weight did not prove an issue. In minutes the taxi arrived, crossed the Fourteenth Street Bridge, and deposited its fares at Washington's Reagan National Airport. Mike looked at his watch. "God damn it." He did not want to miss this flight, too.

Curbside, Susanna handed over the larger of the two luggage pieces with the Luger locked inside. Neither Susanna nor Mike knew what firepower the other carried, nor did they care. They assumed they could handle any situation even as a couple of carpetbaggers.

While moving toward the gate, Mike studied the early-morning travelers, most with coffee in hand. He thought he caught a glimpse of a member of Stahl's goon squad in their queue. The man appeared in his late 20s, blond, and stood less than 6 feet tall. He carried a small black case but no other luggage. He saw Mike and his silent stare lingered. Mike accepted the unspoken challenge. As Susanna heaved her smaller case on the X-ray belt on her way to the gate, the security official who insisted on rifling through her belongings looked a lot like a Stahl storm trooper she had seen at the White House. The 30-something, 5-foot 8-inch fireplug studied Susanna instead of the bras, sundresses, and shampoo he spilled. He eyed her chain holding her medals of St. Jude and St. Christopher.

"Maybe you should wear these," said the ghoulish messenger.

She grabbed the chain from him and placed the medals around her neck. He smiled as if he had her in his trap. The man piled her belongings back in her case and sent her on her way.

Mike and Susanna reached the gate as the attendant opened the door to the gangway

As they stood in the boarding area, Mike turned to Susanna, "I think I saw a Stahl guy in line."

"I think one is working the X-ray machine," she reported. They both turned together and the latter man in question had vanished. "I think we have a problem," she concluded.

"*You* wanted to fly!" joked Mike. He watched Susanna laugh like the girl he remembered.

"I think Stahl's creeps have taken over National," she said.

"I don't think it's that bad," Mike said, who could not understand the large number of Stahl's men.

"It's like watching rats in an alley after dark and about as useful," she said of the men she believed to work for Manfred Stahl.

They heard the final boarding call.

Susanna and Mike looked at each other, prepared to leap off the rail of a sinking tanker. Each forced a smile as they boarded the plane.

***

"The recording from Stahl's ceremony confirms his involvement," Susanna said. She chatted non-stop after they nestled into their seats. Mike's knees pushed up past his chest and his head rose well above the backrest. Even the aisle seat did not make air travel beyond a tactical helo comfortable for the SEAL.

"How long did I say this flight was?" he moaned as he hung over into the aisle.

"About two hours," she said, pushed against the window.

He shook his head. The folly of going along with her scheme hit him.

She had not changed.

Susanna peered around the seats to see if anyone could hear her. She lowered her voice and continued, "I saw Lori and Stahl in one of the conference rooms."

"What? When?" he asked.

"At the Russell Building. Stahl ranted and bellowed. I didn't think someone could turn purple. He's pissed we're asking questions." Susanna seemed eager for a fight, though she did not tell Mike about Stahl's assault on Lori.

"We?" interrupted Mike.

"Well, me," she admitted.

"He labeled Joe as the fall guy for their scheme. He blew at the fact that Lori sleeps with Joe, though I'm not sure why. Joe and Lori's relationship has become the worst-kept secret in Washington. I certainly told no one. Lori would go on these waste-of-money congressional delegation visits. Normally House members went, but once Joe showed up, Lori turned senatorial globetrotter. Joe arranged trips and traveled with her. Rome, Athens, Paris. Geez, it was 'damn the taxpayer, full speed ahead,'" she said, full of energy.

Mike thought back to his days as Joe's academy roommate and sat unfazed by what he heard. He rolled his eyes and prayed she would stop talking.

"I know this is not that big a deal in D.C., and it's de rigueur in certain circles in my home town. Lori used Joe differently than her colleagues had," she said.

Mike opened one eye.

"The arrangement suited Lori's needs. She got a military aide who crafted defense legislation, with his insider knowledge, and satisfied her sexual appetite at the same time. Despite Joe's, let's call them, 'efforts,' Lori voted against every piece of legislation that stood to benefit the Marine Corps. I won't call her actions vengeful in my defense, but New Orleans relationships run deep, *mon cher*.

"When no one wanted any part of the Committee on Environment and Public Works, Lori became one of the committee's senior senators. She served on the Armed Services Committee at the time, too. *Lori* approved the levee funding because it involved her state. She dispatched Joe to Louisiana after every vote. With Marine Forces Reserve headquartered there, the trips drew no suspicion. Lori had woven an elaborate scheme worth billions and dragged a sap like Joe into her web," she said.

Mike opened his other eye and looked at Susanna.

"You did nothing?" he asked.

"It unfolded in front of me, but I didn't believe what seemed to transpire. So much money. I did not see the motive until Stahl entered the picture. No one could turn back. Even if I had proof, I would not have turned on Lori. I considered reporting Joe, but that would have brought down Lori. I thought my state benefited from billions of dollars, but it hadn't. When she and Joe returned from a trip sailing the Greek isles, courtesy of a constituent and Levee Board member, I had already boxed up what few items I kept in the office and said a simple 'good-bye.' I hugged her told her I loved her. The end," she said

Mike looked at her.

"You gave it all up?" he asked.

"What? Working like a dog for a senator who used everyone within reach, even her best friend? I lost Lori long before I left. Lori had become my drug of choice," said Susanna.

But loss consumed her.

Mike turned to Susanna, "But what about this Levee Board."

"We have plenty of time for that," said Susanna lapsing into the local *laissez les bontemps rouler* tradition and feeling some apprehension about facing her past.

Did Mike Singleton deserve her trust again?

"I need more or I'll turn around and take the next plane back to D.C. Game off," he threatened.

Susanna shook her head sensing his next move. She raised the armrest and slipped her right leg over his left side and slid her left thigh to his right. As she faced him she squeezed his black denim-clad thighs between hers. They seemed larger than she remembered. By instinct, his thumbs caressed her inner thighs. She closed her eyes and smiled.

"Singleton, nicely played. I owe you this much for now," she said pressing her hips closer to his. "I'll give more as, you Americans say, we 'insert and extract,' something I'd pay money to do with you," she purred.

He determined it unwise to fly back to Washington.

With the plane a quarter full and flight attendants buried in the celebrity magazines, she continued to straddle him like she did long ago.

How she loved Mike Singleton.

"As Lori's chief of staff in the House, I would go to New Orleans with the House and Senate chiefs of the Committee on Environment and Public Works and sometimes staffers from Armed Services. Environment and Public Works drove the funding for the levee restoration project, and Lori pushed hard to keep the money flowing—to the Levee Board," Susanna said.

Mike studied her. He only knew her as a girl at the academy, a college kid like himself. Putting her into an adult congressional setting proved difficult. Her voice intoxicated him.

He loved her.

Some things would not change, no matter how much he wanted them to.

He heard little of what followed.

"Well, how do you link Joe's disappearance to New Orleans levees?" asked Mike still concentrating on Susanna. He could feel the tension of her arousal and its slow release on his lap. She slid onto his chest and sighed.

Before the pilot completed his landing instructions over the loudspeaker, Susanna sat buckled in her seat as if nothing had happened. The aircraft bounced hard on landing. "Must be a carrier pilot." surmised Mike. Susanna laughed. He loved to hear her laugh. He hoped to hear more laughter, but he wanted to kiss her.

Susanna had reserved a subcompact. The car rental agent looked at Mike. "How about I upgrade yuh to a full-size?" she offered.

Mike tossed Susanna the keys.

She looked at him.

"Hey, this is your turf," he said.

She spun around toward the row of cars and stood by the driver's door.

"Let's go," she called. Her lack of driver's license and occasional blackouts did not matter in New Orleans.

They turned and looked at one another, each with a slight smirk, and sped off.

She drove down the long airport road to Interstate 10 exiting at the French Quarter ramp.

"Where are we going?" he asked.

"Don't worry," she said.

"I thought we were here to work. Insertion? Extraction?" he reminded her. He looked at her dreading the response.

She broke into a slow, seductive grin. "You were right. My turf, my rules, commander, doll."

They crossed Rampart onto Conti Street. She grabbed a garage door opener from her bag and pulled into a long, low-hung parking area.

"Ready?" she asked, putting the Luger in her purse.

He felt like her hostage, but smiled at the Susanna he remembered.

CHAPTER FOURTEEN

The French Quarter exploded with brilliance in the warm, bright Louisiana sun. Springtime temperatures in New Orleans excited locals as well as out-of-town visitors. The oppressive heat remained a few weeks away.

Susanna started a quick costume change. She moved behind the car with the trunk popped to full, military attention shielding her as she disrobed and scattered her collection of summer dresses on the gray, industrial carpet that had retained its "new-car" smell.

She had serious decisions strewn before her. After much thought, Susanna chose a tiny rayon sundress with a fitted bodice and flirty skirt that covered less than half her thigh. A bright, lemon cardigan covered her shoulders. Mike decided to retain the man-in-black look but abandoned the leather jacket to the trunk of their rental. He wore his boots; she wore strappy sandals with a slight heel. Though captivated by Susanna's sensual strip tease, he noticed that her bruising from the explosion had turned a brilliant red and purple. She had concealed the Luger. Mike looked at Susanna and then looked away.

"What is it?" she asked.

"Susanna, do you have a scarf? Some make-up?" he asked, embarrassed.

She let out a slight gasp. "I forgot." The sweater did not cover her injuries.

As flesh-tone foundation dried on her skin, she wrapped a billowy floral scarf around her neck. Mike's smile suggested she had hidden much of the trauma. She took hold of his arm.

They stood on Conti Street just after 10 a.m. Mike had forgotten the sweet decadence of the Quarter. Susanna looked up at the sun, letting its warmth soak into her battered body. Mike saw that it recharged her. She had not complained since he met her at the White

House. She never complained, yet she seemed different than he remembered, but he could not define how.

Mike spotted "Da Three-Legged Dawg" on the opposite corner. Even in its state of advanced decay, he figured it had a stool waiting for him.

"Are they really open 24 hours?" asked a hopeful Mike Singleton.

"Yep. With booze, food, sports, and more booze. The health department has nearly shut it down once or twice, but it's got your name splashed all over it," she said with a knowing smirk.

Mike, a big drinker at school, spent most weekends drunk. He would sneak his friend, Jack Daniels, into his room in Bancroft Hall and bring women back on the Yard, or campus, for sex. Susanna would rant about Mike's increasing assortment of infractions and his drunken promiscuity. Mike saw it as no one's business how he chose to distance himself from the boy who stopped the rape of his brother. He never wanted to be that vulnerable teen again. Susanna's concern alone should have gotten him to swear off alcohol, but it took a drunken Army-Navy prank that killed an elderly "jimmy legs" gate guard to sober him up.

Their company officer, a frocked Lieutenant Commander Ken Bartholomew, fought to retain the boys, except for Joe Earhardt, lined up on the superintendent's chopping block, though he swore he would kill them all himself if they survived the misguided joke-gone-bad. The crime stood as Joe's first wreck on the wrong side of academy regulations, but the offense promised automatic dismissal. A mysterious figure interceded on behalf of the five classmates involved in the carjacking of the base police cruiser. The matter disappeared.

"I thought you stopped drinking after you guys killed that poor old man," she said. She could not help but chuckle at the incident, but turned serious about Mike's drinking.

"I did stop. Then I started again," he said.

The Doctors Without Borders rescue resumed the flow of spirits through his veins. Mike blamed himself for the gun battle that nearly killed each doctor. His boyhood feelings of helplessness returned. To his disgust, the Special Operations community hailed him as a hero and awarded him the Silver Star. A fleeting tinge of guilt reminded him he let Susanna down, too.

He looked at her.

She interrupted his thoughts.

"Oh. By the way, we're being followed," she said under her breath.

"Now you tell me?" Mike said in a forceful whisper.

"You're the SEAL," she said.

Decay surrounded them as they walked down Dauphine Street. Peeling paint. Cracked windows. Sagging balconies. Entrances sported out-of-season decorations, garish masks, and tarnished beads in purple, green, and gold. Mike dared not say a negative word in the presence of the Queen of the Quarter. Susanna glanced at Mike and figured he had judged their surroundings.

At the end of the next block sat an entrance that bisected the corner. Black and white tile graced the slab under the copper-trimmed awning. Mike took another look around. It seemed the men following them had found other interests. On cue the pair stepped inside a place of contrasts. "Rough 'n' Raw" appeared bright, but deserted, save for the lone figure behind the bar. As Mike sat on the bar stool and contemplated his beverage choice, he noticed the bartender wore a leather vest and leather chaps and little more.

Strange, but maybe it's a part of the theme, he thought.

"Susanna Marcasi. How yuh doing, doll?" The bartender declared with unbridled excitement. They embraced across the shiny mahogany that separated them.

"Jake, I'm good. This is my friend, Mike," she said.

"Mike, Susanna's friends are always welcome here. It was a big loss when she left Lori's office," Jake said.

"Jaaaake." She drew out his name to caution him.

"No, Susanna, our representation in Washington has never been the same without you. I won't say another word about it," he said.

"Beer? Can you recommend a good local brew?" interrupted Mike, uncomfortable with the tribal talk.

"I've got Abita Springs," Jake offered.

"Then that's what I'll have," he said.

"Jake, my usual," Susanna flirted.

As Jake fixed their drinks, she surveyed the stark room. Susanna glanced at the entrance. She and Mike exchanged knowing looks.

"Mike, when we leave, I think we need go out through that back room," whispered Susanna as she gave the front doors a second look.

Mike never relinquished tactical control but made an exception in bar run by a guy in leather. He did not want to draw unnecessary attention but remained certain Susanna would do that for them.

He gave a simple nod.

No one else entered the bar, alarming Mike. Susanna assured him that even in the Quarter, popular watering holes languished early-afternoon. Rough 'n' Raw did not hit its stride until around midnight and Susanna explained they did not want to stick around. Mike turned to face the Western-style, swinging-door entrance.

Susanna eyed Jake and pursed her lips. "No one wears a set of chaps like you do," she said.

Jake flirted back, "Susanna, If I played for your team you know they'd come off for only you."

She blushed. As Mike got up to take a look outside, he reminded himself he had entered a city of heathens who behaved as such. He spotted one of Stahl's men darting across the street. He caught a glimpse of Susanna as she stretched her legs and slid off bar stool like some prop on her burlesque stage. She sauntered over and pulled herself up against him reminding him, "And we're not heathens, Michael Singleton."

"Do you read minds?" he whispered back his lips brushing her cheek.

"We are guests," she stretched and breathed into his ear.

He pulled away and looked her into her dark, fanciful eyes.

"Got it," he said.

"Where y'at, Jake? So, whatyuh hear'on ..." She straddled her bar stool in another stage-worthy move.

Mike marveled at the stool dancer, as he had dubbed her, and at the accent she commanded to serve her purpose. She yapped like some Bronx refugee. The sunlight streaming in the windows caught the red highlights in her hair. Its waves cascaded midway down her back. He wanted to reach out and stroke her locks but stopped himself. *Business. We have business*, he thought. Despite the bruising, the bandaged neck, and the matter with the wrists, she chirped away as if in perfect health.

"Jake, what do yuh hear on the Levee Board?" she asked.

"Sus, you know they are a bunch of crooks. Dey's worse than the insurance commissioners."

Susanna translated for Mike who now stood between her and the bar's entrance, "The last six insurance commissioners are in prison. Fraud," she said.

"We wait for the levee work. We hear there's no money from them bastards in Washington. John Murphy contracts with da Corps and has crews ready to go, but nothing. Jobs are hard to come by here, doll, unless you know da right people. You know what I mean?" Jake paused and looked at Mike by the entrance.

"Are you sure you can trust him?" he asked gesturing over to Mike. "He's big and sorda uptight."

"He's fine, Jake," assured Susanna.

"So, nothin' from the commission. Who's president these days, and who's runnin' the show?" she queried.

"Need y'ask? Susanna, the president is still ol' Vic Dumaine. Same man as always runnin' the Levee Board like he does every other board with Washington money. That medal is that man's meal ticket," stated Jake.

"Still at the Lakefront?" asked Susanna.

"Still on the second floor of the old mausoleum. Doll, you know things don't change here," Jake said.

Mike made eye contact with Stahl's men, the three that he could see. As if on cue, they reached for their concealed weapons and made their move. He did not know if they planned to storm the front or surround the corner bar. His head whipped around to Susanna.

She knew the look.

Mike grabbed Susanna's arm before Jake could ask about her interest in the Levee Board.

"Jake, thank you. There seems to be a problem with some men outside. We need to uh…" Mike started.

"Hurry. This way," Jake said, as if he did this every day. The trio made their way through the back room.

"Damn door's blocked. Use da bathroom window," he directed.

A nude painting of a provocative young man hid the bathroom door. Jake kept looking back into the bar. "You be careful, darlin' and call me if you need anything. That's anything. I'll handle dese guys." He pushed them into the bathroom. "I got some firepower, too. With this crowd? Gotta have it. Go!"

Jake closed the door and repositioned the painting.

Susanna climbed atop the commode to work the window open. Mike leaned against the stained, putrid green wall,

"What the hell are you doing?" he asked.

"Isn't this how guys ditch guys when things aren't going as hoped?" she said straining to break through years of paint.

"I think even you can fit your tight ass through here, Singleton," she said.

"We need to get out of here now. Move, Marcasi," Mike said.

Susanna stumbled onto the floor and out of his way. With one foot on the toilet lid he kicked the window and frame with his powerful size 14 boot. "We'll send Jake a check," he commented with sarcasm.

They heard Jake arguing with the men. Glass smashed. Mike looked outside, nodded to Susanna and disappeared. Ten feet below he motioned for her to aim for his chest. With a determined look, Susanna made the leap, knees landing dead on Mike's sternum. Both tumbled to the ground. Mike scrambled to the dumpster behind them and worked to catch his breath from Susanna's unintended throat punch. He thought she had moved with him. Instead, Susanna lay where she fell in the alley.

She had company.

The growling, slobbering mass hovered an inch from her cheek. Susanna froze.

"Well, hey. Nice dog you got," she said, turning on the YAT accent. "What's his name?"

Mike pulled out his 9mm and watched. He aimed center of mass.

"His name is Marcus," said the crackling voice of the teenage boy.

"Really? May I pet him?" she asked.

As she sat up, the dog, balanced on just three legs, collapsed burying his head in Susanna's lap.

"You're just a big baby, you handsome boy," she soothed. She put her arms around him calming both dog and master with her tone. She kissed the Rottweiler. The boy watched with surprise.

"What's your name?" she asked looking at the youth.

"Sam," he stammered. The boy seemed shy, sad. Alone.

"Marcus, I just want to take you home!" She rubbed the dog's ears. "I love your dog," she said, looking up at the boy. She had trouble seeing his face with the afternoon sun in her eyes.

Something seemed familiar to Susanna about the young man and his dog.

"Do you live around here, Sam?" she asked.

"Off of Poland," he said.

Ninth Ward, she thought. She used to work at Dauphine and Poland, but could not place him or the aging dog.

"Do you mind if I stand up?" she asked.

"Naw, it's fine," Sam said.

She knelt in the hard dirt with her hands on Marcus and then stood.

Mike saw Susanna could handle herself and disappeared.

"You look banged up real bad. Y'OK?" he asked.

"Yes, Sam, I am banged up, but I'm going to be fine."

Sam studied Susanna's face. "No one's ever been so nice to Marcus," he said as the panting dog rubbed against a laughing Susanna. "You Susanna Marcasi? There're some men out front lookin' for you, but I won't tell 'em I saw you."

Sam did not want Susanna to leave. She wanted to give the boy her phone number but feared it might fall into the wrong hands.

She eyed the three-legged dog.

"Sam, listen to me. You are a nice young man. Marcus is an incredible dog, and I can tell you love each other very much. Please don't fight him. You'll lose him if he fights again." She continued to look at the boy. Sam looked down when she brought up dog fighting.

"You're Catholic aren't you?" she asked.

The boy nodded.

"So am I. The Virgin Mary interceded for us today." She opened her purse and handed Sam a $20. "Get something good for you and Marcus to eat, OK?"

"Thank you, Miss. I will, and I won't fight Marcus no more." His voice quivered with emotion. Susanna crouched down and gave Marcus a big hug and kiss and he reciprocated with a few face-soaking licks. Susanna laughed.

She felt a strong attachment to the off-kilter canine. They had shared secrets they would take to their graves. Susanna gave Marcus a knowing glance and he gave an awkward bow before her. She hugged Sam and kissed him on the cheek.

Sam walked back toward the street and Marcus made his way as well as his three legs would carry him. Mike stared at Sam.

Huh, that was different, Mike thought and walked back into the alley and joined Susanna who had started in another direction. Neither spoke for a long time. They took a circuitous route back to the garage.

Susanna broke their silence.

"What happened to our welcoming committee back there?" she asked.

"It sounded like Jake had taken care of them, but I had to be sure. I don't think we'll see those guys again," Mike said as he looked straight ahead.

Susanna had heard the gunfire from Mike's weapon. She let it go.

"Let's grab our bags and go inside," she suggested.

Mike knew not to ask questions. They continued their lovers' tango, stepping off from where they left off in 1984.

Susanna unlocked the door and clicked on the first light switch. They stood surrounded by exposed, early 19th century brick walls and 12-foot ceilings awash with light from widows reaching from the floor eight feet toward the ceiling. Furnishings ranged from 18th century French to mid-20th century modern.

"A friend let's me stay here when I'm in town," she said.

He knew she lied.

So, Marcasi's loaded. Interesting, he thought.

She went into the kitchen. "Hey," she barked as she spiraled a beer across the room. She walked back in with a sparkling water. "Would you prefer water? Maybe a soda?" Susanna asked.

Mike still processed the condo. "Uh, no, beer's good." He tripped over his words. Susanna sunk into the down loveseat. Mike sat in the large Eames leather lounge chair off to her left. *Pull it together, Singleton*, he kept telling himself.

Mike had planned for none of this side show. They had agreed on a down-and-back trip. Insert. Extract. S&M bars did not score as contingencies.

"It seems we need to visit the Levee Board, given what you picked up in those recordings," Mike said, pressing with caution.

Susanna sighed, "I know. Let me give you some detailed background on this outfit before we get on the road. They are a little ways from here out at the Lakefront Airport."

To understand the New Orleans Levee Board took a lifetime of learning. Susanna had a few hours to impart more than 30 years of life with the Levee Board on Mike Singleton.

He gave her 5 minutes.

"I wish I had a white board, but here we go. The state created the New Orleans Levee District in 1890 to protect the city from flooding. It maintains over 100 miles of floodwalls and levees, 200 floodgates, and more than 100 flood valves. It has the city by the balls." She sounded like the board's historian.

Mike leaned forward with his legs spread and elbows balanced on his knees. He rested his chin in his hands and remained fixated on his teacher.

"The Levee Board stood as the one ongoing issue when Lori was in the House. They bickered like children. Negotiations fell to me," Susanna said.

She paused, looking at Mike. "I'll stop with the 'All you ever wanted to know about the New Orleans Levee Board.' Sorry," she sighed.

"No, Susanna. It's fascinating. Really. I'm just surprised." Given Mike's years as an operator on Navy and other missions, he did not know anyone's *legislative side*.

Susanna's command of the topic drew him in deeper.

"Aside from the New Orleans District, we have the East Jefferson Levee District and the Lake Borgne Basin Levee District stretching south on the other side of the Mississippi. Orleans funding is the issue. Because of its infrastructure and population, the parish has gotten the most money," she said.

"After the Hurricane Betsy debacle in 1965, the city suffered unprecedented flooding. It didn't take long to find that levee leaders had not maintained a single floodwall or gate. Washington designated the Army Corps of Engineers to maintain the vast system," she explained.

Susanna continued with her Levee Board primer. "The Levee Board refused to give up its power, and it maintained control of the purse strings. The schism has caused an ugly, constant tug-of-war with the Corps asking for money to start a project and the Levee Board dragging its ass to give the Corps what it needs. Since Betsy, Orleans has seen 30 years of inertia. Time, storms, and the damn rodent nutria have further weakened the levees." Susanna started to come alive as she talked about the funding fight and resident rodents.

"Time, tide, and formation wait ..." Mike let it slip.

Susanna grinned at Mike's reference to an academy tradition. "Surprised you remember much of anything from those days, Singleton," she said.

"I remember everything about one Susanna Marcasi." Mike appalled himself with a line better left to the leisure-suited set. He hoped she had not noticed.

"At this point, the board's account should hold $20 billion. The recording from Stahl's ceremony says the $20 billion vanished around the same time Joe Earhardt disappeared." Susanna played the recording. "Manfred Stahl sounds almost jubilant over the missing funds."

She looked at Mike. "Coincidence? Probably not."

Mike listened. While plausible, it made little sense, he thought.

"Why would Joe steal $20 billion and then shoot himself?" he asked aloud.

"I don't know, but I think we will find answers at the Levee Board," she said.

Mike let out a frustrated humph. "OK, but if we veer too far off the

Earhardt matter, I'm reigning you in."

Incredulous, Susanna hated it when Mike felt the need to assert himself. "Reigning *me* in? I am solving *your* Earhardt problem. I work for Lori O'Reilly, not you, big guy," she said.

"You have no power over me, commander," she said, though she had felt bound to him since their days at school.

He unnerved her. She longed for the safety of her D.C. flat, a disadvantage that he had yet to detect. She reminded herself they walked her turf under her control.

"Earhardt is a major defense, shall we say, 'concern,' which, for me, trumps your senator and levee pirate treasure. Anyway, you need me to get this done. Check–mate," he said.

Susanna's mouth opened, but she said nothing. She had walked away once. She could do it again, Mike thought.

"Susanna, we're working together. I need you and I need you to trust me," he said. Mike Singleton figured he could solve the Joe Earhardt mystery on his own. But for the first time since he and Susanna had parted ways, he did not want to work alone or with one of his precious Special Warfare teams.

Susanna looked over at Mike. "Let me call the board. They can hold odd hours. Everything revolves around alcohol here." She reached for the phone on the other side of the chaise. "They're usually there until 5:30. It's early afternoon. This is a good time. Fewer people." She looked Mike over. "Let's go dressed as we are?"

"Hey, I know I look good," Mike stated in his wry way.

Susanna smirked, but he sensed her anxiety over the Levee Board.

***

They pulled out of the garage. Susanna guided Mike as he drove. He took in the sites—bar after bar. Most had doors and windows open turning each joint inside-out. Music flowed from the bar bands. The streets teamed with tourists.

"Take your next right," Susanna pointed to the turn. "Yeah, see all these people. They're drinking. That's what they come here to do.

Next left," she instructed, again pointing. "It's a shame because the city is so much more. It is a shame because ours is a poor city." Susanna stared at the nameless surrounding them.

"Oops, quick right. Quick right!" she called.

Mike maneuvered the white, full-size sedan around throngs of pedestrians as they drove out of the Quarter. He placed his 9mm on the seat between them.

"You'll have plenty of time if we need it," Susanna said. "Much of the city looks more run down than D.C.'s worst neighborhoods. It is most of what I knew until I got to Annapolis."

Mike looked over at Susanna. She had her knees up on her chest and her feet on the dash looking straight ahead as she spoke. A tear rolled down her left cheek. She made no attempt to brush it away. Mike did not know Susanna's childhood circumstances and felt selfish.

"Mike, make your next left. We'll take the interstate," she said.

As they headed east on I-10, Susanna could see Mike peering over either side of the raised roadway.

"Mike, speed limits are not enforced. I think we need to pick it up," she said more upbeat.

"Yeah, yeah, I know. Susanna, tell me more on the board and where we're going," he asked.

She stared straight ahead.

"Many of the same governor-appointed board members have been in place for 16 years, as long as much of the funding in question has come down from the Hill. I call them 'fixtures,'" Susanna chatted on. Mike's head spun with information.

"You know, Mike, despite the $20 billion and the future of the city, whatever is happening is inconsequential to anyone living in this basin. Everyone has an angle, and they need it to survive on some level, be it $20 billion or $20," she said.

"Mike, this levee deal is similar to every other scam over the past century in this city. Lori's involved. Joe's involved. This could be the reason he's dead. Missing. Whatever. Stahl may have the lead," Susanna said.

Mike would not look at her.

"MIKE! This is not unlike your SEAL mission into South America," she said.

She had Mike Singleton's attention.

Surprised, he asked, "How? ..."

"I read the report. Some of our Marines were involved. That's where you got that Silver Star," she said.

"How far into my records did you hack?" he asked both flattered and outraged.

"Not too far, really. I know you've been deep-selected for promotion a couple of times," she said.

She saw his knuckles whiten as he tightened his grip on the steering wheel.

"Be grateful someone's interested in you," Susanna said. "Listen. Going up against the Levee Board is not unlike meeting the heavily armed FARC head on."

Susanna pointed. "Take this exit!" she rushed.

Mike reacted and drove toward a dreary, two-story bomb-shelter of a building.

"Welcome to the infamous New Orleans Levee Board," she said with a mix of pride and trepidation.

CHAPTER FIFTEEN

A typical day at the Lakefront included a menacing Lake Pontchartrain. Waves crashed over the seawall. Whitecaps extended as far as the pair could see. Not a single boat bobbed in its waters. A vast, violent nothingness stretched before them.

The Lakefront Airport had been the city's headquarters for air transportation from the 1930s until the 1950s. Huey P. Long had the area dredged and filled for his airport and it became a breathtaking piece of real estate on shores of the lake. As fate would have it, Long named the airport for Abraham Shushan, a trusted confident and the Levee Board president at the time.

"... if you can believe Levee Board thuggery goes back so far," explained Susanna who loved few things more than exposing New Orleans corruption.

"Locals say the fixtures bore his initials. After the feds indicted him on—get this—income tax charges, it simply became the New Orleans Airport, but most people referred to it as the Lakefront," Susanna explained, again in her historian mode.

"Older residents recall dances in the soaring terminal during the 1940s. Concrete, almost Stalinist, panels have covered the stunning Art Deco brown-pebble façade turning one of New Orleans's most beautiful buildings into a monolithic white bunker. But the board calls it home," she said.

They drove across the large, empty parking lot, pulling close to the building. The Levee Board occupied a suite of offices on the second level. Susanna and Mike walked around the sides and back of the building, hoping to avoid the main entrance.

They checked the doors. All seemed blocked or locked. Mike and Susanna looked at each other. They strode through the front entry into what had been the posh waiting area for air travelers from an earlier and more elegant era. They turned and made their way up the wide staircase.

"Again, get me in Dumaine's office. I'll copy his hard drive and anything else I can find," Mike said so only Susanna could hear.

The magnitude of their plan hit Susanna. "Consider it done," she swallowed. Mike sensed her concern. He did not like this either and hoped for one of her Catholic miracles.

They slipped into the first room on the right at the top of the staircase. The windowless cave held a vintage mahogany desk and black, ergonomic chair. Judging from the dust, no one had used the old desktop computer in weeks, Mike guessed. He saw this as a good sign for him and Susanna. A stack of not-so-dusty file folders sat on the corner of the desk. From where they stood, they could work unseen. Mike and Susanna split up the collection of folders and rifled through them. "Board Members," "Deposits," "Corps," and "Dumaine." "Hercules" caught their interest. They slipped the five folders into her bag.

Lucky number, thought Susanna.

Standing in the hall again, they could see a light marking the end of the passageway. Mike noticed gray acoustic tile concealed the original ceiling. The board could have hidden an array of electronic detection equipment. He grabbed Susanna's arm and motioned above them. Mike's revelation did not help her queasiness as they moved deeper into the building. Mike shared her concern, but had lived through worse.

She approached the room. Mike followed. They stood centered in the wide doorway.

"Miss Theone?" queried Susanna.

"Why yes, doll."

"It's Susanna Marcasi. How yuh doing?"

"Susanna! Doll, it's been so long. Where ya been? Who don't ya come see me no more? You know JT was always sweet on you," Theone said.

"Miss Theone, you know I've been with Lori in Washington,"

Susanna said.

Susanna looked around the deserted space. Theone le Boeuf worked as Vic Dumaine's executive assistant of sorts. Theone, still striking at 89, had no idea how to answer the upgraded phone system. She had never used a computer. She could not type. She did flirt with the male visitors—older men—though decades her junior. Legend had it she had rebuffed the advances of one Huey P. Long and she did little to deter the gossip.

Rich walnut paneling with recessed lighting and sconces finished her office. They stood on a gleaming, wide cypress plank floor. The leather sofas and club chairs sat finished in deep butternut.

"Miss Theone, the office is beautiful. Did you or Jon Paul decorate it?"

Susanna laid it on.

Theone gave a girlish laugh. She blushed, "Thank ya, doll. It was Mr. Paul."

"Miss Theone, I'd love for ya to meet Mike Singleton, my fiancé."

Mike looked down at Susanna. *YAT speak and fiancé. This beats South America.*

Theone had known Susanna since St. Theresa's. She had worked the receptionist job at the Levee Board as far back as Susanna could remember. Her daughter or granddaughter would step into the position when she retired, which did not appear to be any time soon.

Theone showed no signs of slowing down.

"Miss Theone, is the president in?"

For life seemed a fitting antecedent Susanna liked to add on the Hill for those who seemed to have a lifetime appointment to a post. Had Dumaine not grown so wealthy in his current position, Susanna surmised he would have made a run for some office dangling that medal all the way to the top. She could not understand why he never ran for insurance commissioner. It seemed more up his corrupt alley.

"Doll, normally he'd be visitin' a levee, but he and da board are in an emergency meeting over at Tavern on the Avenue," Theone said.

"Everyone's gone?" Susanna asked. She could not believe their luck.

"I'm the only one here," said Theone. She drew Susanna closer and whispered, though loud enough that Mike could hear. "I need to visit the little girls' room. Would you mind watchin' my desk?"

"Of course not. Take as long as you need, and we'll be right here."

After Theone turned her back Susanna looked at Mike and motioned toward the door on the far end of the room. Mike nodded and hurried toward Vic Dumaine's office, unpacking his computer surgeon's kit as he went.

Mike slipped behind Dumaine's desktop computer. He typed. He retyped. His jaw tightened. *One last try*, he thought.

The password is freakin' "levee"? He laughed to himself. He copied everything. Susanna had piqued his curiosity. He opened the board's financial files.

Susanna panicked by Theone's desk. Now *she* needed to use the little girls' room. She looked around the desk and in the drawers to see if she could find any information about the board's banking practices.

Vic Dumaine and the other seven board members sat around a large dining table. Tavern on the Avenue had been in Jimmy Tavoli's family for decades. Rumored to be a mob hangout during the 1930s, the upscale restaurant served overpriced and mediocre Italian fare. Having turtle and alligator on any menu bothered Susanna.

Dumaine had his laptop on the table and went to log in to check the board's financial records to date. He tried a second time. A message flashed.

"What the fuck? Jesus, Mary, and Joseph. Who the fuck is in my account?" He grabbed his cell phone.

Theone's desk phone jumped. It rang like a burglar alarm. Susanna gasped. She looked at the caller ID. Vic Dumaine. She whispered, "Mike. Mike!" He could not hear her. The phone continued to ring and fell silent after what seemed an eternity. Susanna breathed a sigh of relief. Within seconds a red message light flashed. Susanna jumped back two feet. *Damn,* she thought. "Mike. Mike." Still nothing. She looked down the corridor and saw Theone doing her little hallway dance as she made her way back. Susanna stared at the 5-foot-2-inch dynamo as she concocted a story explaining Mike's whereabouts. She stood straight with her breathing rapid and hands clasped together.

Theone reached her desk and with a big smile said, "I thank you both."

Susanna whipped her head around and there stood Mike—as if he had never left. She touched Mike's arm, a cue to back away.

"Miss Theone, we appreciate your hospitality and don't want to take up any more of your time. You tell that JT, 'Hello,' for me."

"When's the wedding?"she asked.

"We haven't set a date yet," responded Mike.

As they hurried down the stairs, Susanna called over her shoulder, "Oh, Miss Theone, the phone rang. I think there may be a message."

They scrambled for the car, Susanna moving with enviable speed in her sandals. They landed back on the interstate in under a minute.

Mike checked in all directions and pulled up onto a restricted levee area.

"Mike, did you really get it all?" asked Susanna as if they pulled a heist.

"You doubt me?" he laughed.

"No, but how?" she asked, still not convinced.

"It's not something I should go into, but I *will* tell you I had a similar situation in a Saudi palace once." His tone changed, "I am not so sure if his computer had the info we're looking for, though."

Susanna had no doubts about the lazy and predictable Vic Dumaine. As she grasped the door handle Mike put his hand on her forearm, almost obscuring it.

"Wait here," he said.

Susanna started out the door but relented, nodding she would wait.

"It's tucked in the wheel well under the spare," she shouted.

"Yeah, geez, Susanna. Maybe some noise discipline here," he said

Mike went to the back and noticed someone had tampered with the trunk.

"Susanna," he called. "Did you have trouble with the trunk lock?"

"No. Why?" she asked from the passenger window.

"Get out of the car now. Run!" Mike backed up.

"What's wrong?" she asked.

"Someone has been in this trunk," Mike called, adrenaline pumping, suppressing the urge to yell.

"Then open it and let's see," reasoned Susanna.

"Susanna, it may blow," he warned.

"Mike, this is New Orleans, not South America," she said losing patience.

He darted a look at her, "Just stay back."

He approached the car and lay on the gravel checking for any other signs of tampering.

He stood up.

He waited.

"Well?" Susanna asked.

Mike held up his hand, still staring at the trunk.

He slipped the key in and heard a click. He waited for what seemed like an eternity to Susanna.

"Geez, will you just open the thing," she huffed.

Mike raised the lid. Susanna watched him as he bent over and rummaged through the sizeable trunk. He found the computer laptop under the spare tire where she left it.

"Huh. Someone has been in here and God knows where else," he said lifting the spare. "But I can't see anything out of place." Mike looked over at her. "Next time we may not be so lucky."

Like two thieves, they basked in the success of their gamble, stretched out on the hood of the car. For Mike, this seemed like such a throwback, something before he and Susanna met. He felt trapped in a time. Stranded in maybe the 1970s. But it sure beat South America, West Africa, Southwest Asia, and the perennial thorn of Saudi Arabia. But his least favorite remained his missions in the "Stans."

Mike inserted the drive into Susanna's computer. They could not see the screen in the bright sun, so they took up their fallback position in the car's front seat. Susanna grabbed for her laptop.

"Let me go through this first," Mike said. "This guy's got a lot of porn saved. Dumaine's pretty sick," he said, giving a running commentary as he scrolled through the files.

"Let me see. Let's find the levee gouge," he said.

Susanna had not heard the term "gouge" in years. She smiled.

He looked at her with a knowing grin. She sat wondering about Mike Singleton and cared little about Joe Earhardt and the Levee Board for a few intoxicating moments.

Mike focused on the screen. "Geez, what a mess," Mike said, frustrated with Dumaine's lack of organization. He searched on the name "Earhardt." In seconds, countless files appeared as if he had opened the gates to the Emerald City.

"Now I just need to look behind the curtain and find the mighty Oz," he murmured to himself, though loud enough for Susanna to hear.

Susanna stretched across the bench seat looked over Mike's shoulder.

"Joe's all over this thing." Mike cataloged the Earhardt files and checked for a few other names like Lori O'Reilly and Manfred Stahl. Nothing.

Interesting, he thought.

"Maybe ..." Susanna said, hoping Lori might have less involvement than she had thought.

"Maybe ..." tossed back Mike, his skepticism on the rise.

"Susanna, aside from Dumaine, can you give me another Levee Board member's name? Someone not, well, not important," queried Mike as he stared at the screen.

"William Wordsworth," she said.

"Are you serious?" he asked.

"Of course, I'm serious. Just try it and see what you find."

Mike entered the name narrowing the files to three. He opened them. Wordsworth did not fill the role of wizard.

Susanna, hanging over his shoulder, exclaimed, "There they are. All the members and Joe." They both saw the numbers next to each name. Mike checked the file name—Whitney.

"Does 'Whitney' mean anything to you?" he asked.

"The ... bank?" she asked, not understanding the possible association. "The Whitney. It's a bank. It is *the* bank. So these may be... account numbers?" she asked leaning over Mike, pointing at the screen. "And these?" She moved her finger across the mysterious line of letters and numbers.

"Passwords, probably, but we need to look at this more carefully," he said deep in thought. Mike considered mining for data and deciphering puzzles his specialties. Though he did not perform his magic on the team, he had more success than the experts.

"Let's work back at your ... *friend's* place. We're too exposed out here. I don't want us dumped in the Mississippi," Mike said as he looked for a reaction to his bad joke.

"It happens," she said, missing Mike's attempt at humor.

***

As they drove back to the Quarter, Susanna cracked her window to feel the warm air. They watched as the sky went from a brilliant blue to a hopeful red.

Susanna turned to Mike, "Red sky at night ..."

He smiled, "Sailor's delight."

"Really?" she flirted.

"Yeah," he said.

She could not see him blushing.

When they arrived at Conti, they trudged up the stairs with aching legs. As Susanna fumbled for her keys, Mike reached for the door knob and stepped inside.

"Didn't you lock the door?" he asked.

"Of course I locked it. You live here long enough you learn unlocked is the same as an invitation to your belongings," she responded.

Once inside the condo, after a cursory look around for signs of theft, she sunk into the love seat. She wanted the Levee Board and Joe Earhardt to disappear for the evening. Mike sprawled next to her tipping the vintage settee. The two D.C. refugees and infamous Naval Academy cohorts exhaled, exhausted.

"Beer?" she asked with her back to him as she dragged herself into the kitchen.

"Water," he said.

"Water," she confirmed as she spiraled two bottles across the room.

"Thanks," he said.

As Mike's eyes closed, Susanna shot up.

"Let's head out into the Quarter!" she said.

"You're insane," Mike declared. He wanted to lie on the floor and sleep for days.

"Yes, 'tis true, but I want to have some fun. The insane have rights, you know."

"Let me look at these account numbers, and then we'll talk about it," he said.

She stood with her arms folded and her hair wild like she had just returned from a Wiccan convention.

"Mike, you are too far gone to do anything with that information. I'm going with you or without you." She had tucked the charming YAT accent back in its box.

"If you talk YAT, I'll go," he goaded.

"I don't know what the big deal is. I talked that way at school," she said.

"Not like this," he said as he sat captivated. The YAT element made her even more alluring. She shook her head in disgust.

She had not forgotten one Mike Singleton detail.

While he waited for her response, Mike opened the laptop as his phone rang. He glanced at it.

"Oh, Jesus," he exclaimed. Mike answered, "Singleton here. ... Yes, admiral."

"Mike, do you know what 'short leash' means? I need you to check in with me. Have you found anything?" asked the admiral.

"Where the hell are you anyway?" he added.

"New Orleans," Mike said with some apprehension.

"Jesus, Mike, I'm sorry. I thought I heard you say you're in fucking New Orleans." The news did not surprise the admiral. He knew Mike Singleton.

"Geez, Mike, Earhardt went off the *Memorial* Bridge not the *Greater New Orleans* Bridge. What the fuck are you thinking?" he asked.

"We think we may know why he went missing, which will help tell us where he is," Mike said.

"We? Tell me this is the royal 'we,' Singleton," the admiral said in his sardonic way. He knew his boy had fallen under the Marcasi spell—again.

Mike sensed a problem and stepped outside with the phone. "Yeah. Uh, I have Susanna Marcasi with me."

"You have your Naval Academy girlfriend with you? Do you know that bitch and her question about the levee money have made all the majors and fucking Stahl is making our lives fucking hell? He hasn't even been on board a day. He's a tyrant who never sleeps." Ken Bartholomew took a deep drag on a cigarette and exhaled the precious smoke. "Fuck, Singleton, keep me posted. I'll keep Stahl away. You fuck this up, and that's it. If you don't end up at mast, in court, or in jail, then you will resign. Got it?" barked Bartholomew.

"Aye, Aye, admiral," said Mike, mortified.

Susanna remained his fatal flaw.

"SHORT LEASH!"

Ken Bartholomew hurled the entire desk phone across the office. He went over to where it came to rest and kicked it back across the room. Mike knew Ken may never allow him back inside his organization. He sat on the top step leaning forward, his head in his hands.

"Who was that?" asked Susanna, unsure if she wanted to know.

"No one important."

Mike looked at Susanna and threw up his hands "You know, fuck it. This shit isn't going anywhere. Beer? Have anything harder?"

"I have an entire bar," she offered.

He knew this was her place. "Let me at it." Mike mixed a Tom Collins, then a second. Susanna switched from Italian to German mineral water.

"Can I wear this?" Mike asked looking down at the black jeans he had been living in. "You know, give me a minute." Mike grabbed his bag and returned in less than two minutes in blue denim 501s; gray-brown boots; and a crisp button down, long sleeve cream-colored shirt, the color of rich rice pudding.

"Where are you going?" bluffed Susanna.

Fuck Bartholomew and Joe Earhardt, he thought.

"We're going in the Quarter. Lead on, beautiful," Mike smiled.

CHAPTER SIXTEEN

It seemed everyone had the same idea. The Quarter lay before them awash in humanity. The crowd seemed subdued, but heads bobbed as far as the eye could see. The warm night air felt moist. The stench of alcohol and vomit surrounded them. The streets and sidewalks had a slick yet sticky film. Mike thought they had found hell. For Susanna, they entered her Promised Land. She had chosen a micro purse for the evening and abandoned her larger bag and the Luger. She figured Mike had his weapon concealed on him. She slipped her hand into his giant grasp. Susanna felt safe, a rarity, but she remained vigilant amidst the crowd.

Susanna looked up at Mike and tugged his arm. "Hungry?" she asked. He nodded eager for food. She dragged him over to what looked like a six-foot plastic hot dog. The reddish-tan wiener sat in the shaded brown and white bun. He found it comical, yet endearing. Its innocence juxtaposed against the adults-only ways of Bourbon Street.

"Wanna Lucky Dog?" asked Susanna.

He stared at her like a local villager in one of the Stans.

"It's a hot dog," she clarified.

A smile appeared. Two fingers shot up. She had chili and cheese put on both of Mike's and had the man behind the classic vending cart dress hers with mustard and relish.

"Lucky Dog," he mumbled, nodding his approval as he took a bite, chili spilling out onto the street.

Susanna had the need to play tour guide. Again. She did it at Annapolis. She did it on the Hill. She had done it on this trip. *Maybe that's why she majored in history*, Mike thought.

"Lucky Dogs started here in New Orleans almost 50 years ago. The carts are permitted, but you will only see them here in the Quarter. A typical New Orleans handshake deal," she said.

She did not tell Mike she thought the health department should have shut them down years ago.

As they walked alone on one desolate thoroughfare near the Quarter's edge they heard a dog barking within a couple of blocks. Mike moved his hand up Susanna's arm and both halted mid-stride. They saw movement ahead in the shadows. Two men pointed their weapons and started toward them. Susanna thought they looked like the Stahl goons from the airport and Rough 'n' Raw. She and Mike turned and sprinted. She slipped off her heels, but the figures gained ground. Susanna grabbed Mike's arm yanking him into a narrow opening that connected to another unknown passageway. They stepped into the lush courtyard of one of the Quarter's finest hotels. No one followed.

The pair found themselves on centuries-old stone. Susanna never tired of the pocked brick walls and worn, uneven pathways. The black iron lion's head fountain, spouting water from its mouth, stood as her favorite feature. Larger than most she had seen, it hung mounted on a wall in an advanced stage of decay. Its elegance awed anyone who passed.

Susanna wanted to stay, but Mike gave her a tug. They made their way through the opulent lobby and left via the gleaming 1930s brass entrance. They exhaled, relieved.

Back out with the crowds, the odd couple drifted from bar to bar. They paused outside of one to listen to the music.

"I love bar bands," Susanna announced to anyone who would listen. The corner establishment had its bank of entrances open to facilitate the flow of patrons and tunes. Music filled the surrounding sidewalk, entertaining the throngs that passed. It seemed Stahl's men liked bar bands, too. They perched opposite Mike and Susanna in the open doorways, weapons holstered but obvious, sending their intended message.

The band had customers on their feet. As Mike enjoyed the strains of the vocalist crooning Tracy Chapman's, "Give Me One Reason," Susanna counted beats of Chapman's seductive cha cha cha. Both hoped the crowds acted as their protection for the evening. Without a thought, Susanna started a basic cha cha, lock-step moving no more than three feet forward and back on the cramped sidewalk. She swayed and rotated her hips, lost in the music. Susanna mesmerized Mike with her rhythmic dance. Her swivels beckoned him closer. She exited her trance and called, "Hey, handsome." He grinned and pointed at himself. She continued to dance and motioned for him to join her. He counted, "Cha cha one, two, three," and stepped in time with her.

She smiled, "You can still dance."

"Yeah, I guess I can," he stated with a mix of defiance and embarrassment. He thought back to the dances she taught him at the academy and flashed a big smile.

He reached out his hands. She took hold. The crowed stepped back and watched. They only knew a few steps, but the onlookers saw the striking Mike Singleton and the radiant Susanna Marcasi. Her hip swivels swooshed her skirt to where it touched the very tops of her thighs, exposing just enough to enthrall the gawkers. After moving side-to-side, he led her back and forth and pulled her in close to him. She pressed her pelvis against him. She tripped on a crack in the sidewalk, but did not miss a beat. She looked at him. On an open break, she danced back and away singing with the band, "Give me one reason to stay here, and I'll turn right back around."

The song carried a message as storied as their past.

Mike responded as the onlookers increased, "Baby, I got your number, oh and I know that you got mine."

Susanna blushed, but her eyes remained fixed on the boy across from her. The irony intensified the dance. She moved toward him. They joined hands again. Mike and Susanna finished the dance pressed, perspiring against one another. The crowd whistled and clapped wanting more, but neither Mike nor Susanna noticed.

Though Stahl's men continued to follow, the pair sampled the evening's musical offerings. They foxtrotted around more than one Quarter block. They bopped a few swing measures, dodging passing cars. They nabbed their dancing royal flush with an onstage Hustle surrounded by drag queens lip-syncing Gloria Gaynor's "I Will Survive."

She would not let him go again. *Damn Joe Earhardt.*

They saw Stahl's gunmen distracted by a couple of ladies for hire and made a run for the condo around 4 a.m. They looked at one another as an awkward silence surrounded them. Susanna flipped a wall switch illuminating the room. She hurried to the kitchen. "Do you want anything to drink?"

"No, I'm good. Thank you," he said with a nod.

"Well, I have two rooms upstairs," she said, businesslike, as she made her way to the landing.

She put Mike in the master bedroom. "Sleep well. I prefer the little room." She could not hide the mix of sadness and fear in her eyes.

"Susanna, we're safe. I'll set the alarm for eight," Mike said in his reassuring way. Susanna nodded, appreciating the gesture.

"It's not that," she confessed, eyes downcast. Mike knew not to press.

Mike Singleton awoke at six surprised to find the bruised and scraped Susanna curled up on top of the covers next to him. She wore a floor-length, sleeveless cream satin gown trimmed in Chantilly lace. He had stripped down to black boxer-briefs. He left a note on his pillow and pulled the comforter over her. Mike leaned over and brushed his lips across Susanna's cheek. He quenched his thirst with her scent. After a final deep breath he stood up and declared a cautionary, "Whoa, Mikey." He left her sleeping and headed out alone.

Mike returned to a silent condo. When he reached the master suite he saw Susanna had not moved. He brushed her cheek again with his lips and whispered, "Hey, breakfast is ready." She looked at him with a faint smile and closed her eyes again.

"Fine." Five minutes later Mike returned with a tray and breakfast for two. "Is this better?" he asked.

"Wow. I feel like I have been hit by a semi," she responded.

They devoured breakfast as they laughed recounting the previous night's activities like they used to each Sunday evening at school. They prepared for the day's events. Susanna exited the lone shower, cinched a silk robe around her waist, and found Mike already downstairs sitting at the glass-top dining table. The computer hummed.

"Any luck?" she asked, cha cha cha-ing behind him.

Mike studied the screen. "That depends on your definition of luck, and I'd rather have solid information on what Joe Earhardt has been doing. I went to the public releases on the board, and there is no Joe Earhardt. But internal to the board, he appears to have equal status to the members, save Dumaine. He is a ninth name on this eight-person roster," Mike said, more for his benefit than Susanna's.

"I pulled up the rules governing the Levee Board. You're right. This board answers to no one. There are no rules, other than those the board makes. The state can't touch them. Nor can the Feds. But the board has mandated in the event of the death of a member, the board president controls his affairs, including his vote, until a new member is appointed. But Joe was not a member," Mike said.

"Regardless, if Joe is dead, Dumaine knows," he surmised.

Susanna nodded.

Mike shook his head, still looking at the screen. "Susanna, this just doesn't make sense to me. This supposed sham board has very real responsibilities."

Mike had worked his way into the board's bank account. "Here's something solid. I am in the Whitney's files and these numbers have encrypted account information as well as any other personal information the bank might need." He turned the laptop toward Susanna.

"Susanna, the levee money isn't missing. Look. Someone has been funneling it into these nameless board trust accounts for years. The members have held equal shares of the federal dollars though no one could place a name with an account except Dumaine and maybe Joe.

The money came from Washington to the state. In less than a day Baton Rouge would forward the funds to Dumaine's account. For some reason he would wait seven days before he deposited equal portions into each member's account, but he never sent money to Joe, whose account remained empty until 72 hours ago."

Susanna's hands covered her mouth. Her eyes widened as she remained fixed on the screen. She knew little of the board's inner workings until now. She had not been granted such access. She lacked the pedigree of old New Orleans society, like those who lorded over the Levee Board that still viewed her as a subclass.

"Dumaine emptied the eight accounts and moved the money to Joe's account. Joe Earhardt now holds $20, no, $18 billion," Mike said as he pushed the computer across the glass table top and faced Susanna.

"It appears Dumaine skimmed 10 percent from each D.C. appropriation and placed it in a separate account for each member. Each of the eight had access to do as he pleased with this new-found wealth. Two placed all of it into ward projects—they call them wards, right? The others pocketed the cash. It appears Dumaine divvied up hush money to keep board members loyal and quiet," he said.

Mike could see Susanna's thoughts had wandered off again. He wished he knew where her mind travelled. He brought up another screen. "Dumaine opened Joe's account when he took on the Senate liaison position. Not a single transaction until three days ago, hours before Stahl's swearing in and the White House bombings."

Susanna tugged the base of the computer and brought the screen closer.

Mike Singleton leaned way back in his chair. He stretched his tree trunk arms high above his head and extended his rock-solid legs under the table. He took up most of the dining area.

"Until a few days ago, we have a combined $20 billion, less 10 percent, in eight accounts without any outside knowledge. Three days ago, all the money was dumped into Joe's account," he said.

"Oh, here!" exclaimed Susanna. "The next day Joe's account went to zero."

Mike grabbed the screen back. "Whoa, with the money going to … Susanna, jot this down."

She searched for her book and pen.

Mike read off the numbers, "It looks like 632-001-9252-7. This has to be some off-shore account number. He left the PIN in the file, too, 9387-43728537. I don't think Dumaine knows much about this account. I'd like to delve a little deeper, though I don't think it will tell us anything more on Joe."

The two fell silent. Mike looked at Susanna awaiting her reaction. A look or sound would have given him some gauge.

Susanna leaned forward.

"What remains unclear are the, 'Why?' and the, 'What the hell?' not to mention, 'Is Joe alive?' These files won't tell us. But …," Mike said as he slapped himself on the forehead.

"Oh, geez, I almost forgot." He tabbed to another banking screen. "Joe has one thing no one else in the group can claim—a safety deposit box at the Whitney. We need to get into that box—today."

CHAPTER SEVENTEEN

A front had blown in during the early morning hours and stalled over the Crescent City. The winds from the south helped send temperatures past 80 degrees by 11 a.m. The sun played its game of hide-and-go-seek through the high clouds. Locals expected a hot one, no matter how one viewed it.

Mike drove around the block a couple of times as he and Susanna finalized the details of crashing their next party. They had left the condo in running clothes. The raucous Quarter of the previous evening lay still in the morning heat. Mike and Susanna made the short drive across Canal Street to the Central Business District.

They stopped at Mother's, a popular CBD eatery and a favorite of Vic Dumaine's. They entered with black gym bags slung over their shoulders. Anyone who saw the couple would have thought they had come from one of the new, upscale fitness centers popular with the moneyed set.

In fewer than 10 minutes, Mike exited the rest room in a dark gray suit and rich blue button down shirt sans tie. Susanna transformed herself, giving new meaning to the term "Old New Orleans." She wore an elegant dark blue frock with a fitted bodice and buttons up the back. She took shallow breaths careful not to pop a button. Her timeless three-quarter sleeves and full skirt completed the look. She rolled her hair and gathered her locks in a reliable, loose chignon. Her stockings matched her skin tone. She slipped on black, calf-skin pumps.

Eyes could mean the difference between success and failure, she thought. Susanna went with pale, natural hues and wet, brown eye liner. Several trips around the track with the mascara finished off her large brown eyes. She smudged her cheeks with a rose blush stick. She ran a scant line of "Raisin" around her lips and applied a clear, colorless gloss to moisten her pout. After running her hands under the cool water, she patted herself dry and slipped on her petal pink mesh gloves. She thought more about the gloves, pulled them from her hands, and shoved them in her bag next to her Luger. She shook her head. "There are limits," she said to herself. She looked around the sink area as if she lost something.

"Ah. The hat's in the car."

Mike stood outside watching for her. He had packed the car for a sudden trip north—if needed. He saw her exit the bathroom and head for their rally point. Susanna milled about the hostess station and looked at the menu for a couple of minutes, smiled at the manager, and left. She found Mike sitting in the car in the alley.

"Wow," he said as she got in the vehicle.

"Wow what?" she asked.

"Just wow. This isn't something I'd imagine you'd wear in D.C.," he offered.

"Again, you're wrong, commander."

"OK, it's kind of weird, but you look like a war bride. Aren't we supposed to blend in?" he asked, dubious of her efforts.

"It's not like we're robbing the place. I assure you, sir, we'll fit in like faithful Whitney depositors," she purred.

"We *are* robbing the place, Susanna," reminded Mike.

Susanna and Mike stood on St. Charles Avenue at the red granite entrance to the Whitney. They walked into the venerable bank as they would a da Vinci exhibition at the National Museum of Art. They looked ahead of them. The Whitney's main branch seemed at least a football field in length. They walked past the russet and cream square pillars along the off-white marble floor. Susanna counted no fewer than 17 tellers in front of them with more to each side. She had slipped her hand in the crook of Mike's arm. His bicep swallowed it. They walked past four security guards, but no one appeared lethal. The Whitney seemed to hire guards either 30 pounds overweight or well past age 60.

Susanna gave a slight tug on Mike's arm and nodded right. They entered a carpeted area of a half dozen desks, a sterile enclave in the

Whitney's headquarters. They walked past a fifth guard to Anne Gaucheau, or so her desk plate said.

"Excuse me," Mike said with a smile. "I'm Lieutenant Colonel Joe Earhardt, and I'd like to access my safety deposit box. This is my wife, Jill."

Susanna smiled her toothless smile and blinked a friendly hello. Anne instinctively looked down at Susanna's left hand. She had moved her academy ring and turned it around to feign a poor substitute for a wedding ring, but it seemed she passed the test.

"Of course, Colonel Earhardt. Please, one moment," said Gaucheau.

Mike put his arm around Susanna's waist and kissed the top of her head.

She looked up him, "You, colonel, are a vile creature. Why ever did I marry you?"

Whitney vice president Thaddeus Delacroix stood near the bank of tellers absorbed in conversation with Anne. He nodded as he leaned in to hear her. He stood straight, nodded again, looked at Mike and Susanna and walked toward them.

"Colonel and Mrs. Earhardt, please have a seat," said Delacroix as he escorted them to his office. Mike and Susanna sat in two, high-back green leather chairs. Delacroix sat behind a gleaming mahogany desk.

Thad, as he liked to be called, glanced at Susanna's left hand, and then at Mike's. He was not wearing a ring, an omission acceptable for men.

"How may I help you?" he asked.

"Mr. Delacroix, I'd like to view the contents of my safety deposit box," said Mike.

"Of course. May I see some form of photo identification? Will Mrs. Earhardt be accompanying you?" he asked.

"Why, yes, of course," said Mike as he smiled at his bride.

"Mrs. Earhardt, if I could please see the same from you," requested Delacroix.

Mike pulled out his wallet and handed Delacroix a Virginia driver's license and a green military identification card. He sat back and waited. Susanna presented a Virginia license as well as her pale peach military family member ID to the man who seemed a little uncomfortable with the couple. Susanna leaned forward awaiting the Delacroix verdict. She looked over at Mike giving a nervous smile.

He knew she worried about the IDs. Earlier he had declared, "Susanna, we need IDs as Lieutenant Colonel and Mrs. Joe Earhardt if we are going to get into that safety deposit box."

"We need to see Jake," recommended Susanna.

Mike took off out the door. Susanna grabbed her bag, keeping pace for the four blocks.

"Jake, I need to use your ID equipment," Mike said.

Jake opened his mouth to speak.

"Jake, camera, paper, laminating machine. Back room?"

Mike had work to do.

"Sure, Mike," Jake stammered. "You're not tellin' anyone are ya?"

"Jake, I need to use it. What do you think?" Mike said.

The relieved bartender took Susanna and Mike back to his little sideline. "This is quite an operation," Mike said, impressed.

"Mike, I make fake IDs every damn day. Business gets slow, ya know. I make military IDs, driver's licenses, passports, you name it. My work has been viewed at the court houses and every bank and police precinct in southern Louisiana. It's a fucking gift," declared Jake with pride.

"If you don't mind, I'd like to make ours. I've done this a few times, but thanks," said Mike with a nod.

Mike surprised Jake. "Sure, sure, Mike. Whatever you need." Jake turned and began to walk away. "I'll be back out at the bar. We get an early morning rush."

As Susanna sat watching Thaddeus Delacroix, she prayed Mike knew his counterfeiting craft.

Delacroix started to hand the cards back to them. He stopped as the phone on his desk rang.

"Hello. Yes. Yes. Not yet. Yes. No. Goodbye."

As he spoke into the phone, Susanna wanted to scream.

"Everything seems to be in order. Please come with me." He handed back the IDs. A security guard with a full mane of white hair that Susanna thought pushed 70 years of age followed the three. A separate building behind the St. Charles headquarters housed the vault. Without noticing, they passed into original 19th century structure. They continued to walk. The large vault appeared on their left. Claustrophobia consumed Susanna in what seemed more a soundproof safe room than a bank vault.

Delacroix saw her go from olive to ashen.

"Is something wrong?" he asked, alarmed.

"May I have some water, please? We're expecting," she smiled.

The bank vice president stood at the entrance and dispatched Anne for the water. Mike inserted the key. Susanna knew that breathing. Rhythmic. Labored. He worried that the key he snatched from Dumaine's desk, that some unknown fool had marked, "Earhardt Whitney Box Key," might not fit, making him the dupe in their hoax. The long exhale relieved the tension. He pulled out the box. They peered inside. "Darling, I am going to rest this on the table," he said. Mike and Susanna angled their bodies so no one else could see. They looked at each other and Mike gave a slight shrug. Susanna bypassed the computer disk and stared at the key with its Art Deco design and guessed it dated to the 1920s. She savored the rich patina that came with age. If the key in the box did not hold profound import, then someone controlled their ruse, she feared.

The contents disappeared, and Mike slipped the drawer back in its place.

"Thank you, Mr. Delacroix," Mike said as he and Susanna exited. His arm rested around her waist. They now had the long walk across the marble gridiron.

The imposters looked out and saw the street lined with police cruisers, lights flashing. *Could this be about us? So soon?* Mike wondered. *Probably not, but better to play it safe.* He asked Susanna about the entrance by the vault. She whispered, "Yes, but ..."

They walked the length of the bank a third time, turned toward where they had met Delacroix and continued around to the right. They passed another guard and smiled. The glass doors waited ten feet ahead.

"Susanna Marcasi," declared Levee Board president Vic Dumaine. "It was so rude of me not to seek you out at Fred's ceremony."

Susanna felt a calm sweep over her, like that before certain calamity. They stood out of Delacroix's earshot. She glanced up at Mike. She had to handle Vic Dumaine. She could only hope Dumaine had not witnessed their deceit minutes earlier.

She and Mike had robbed the Whitney.

"Well, general, I am sure it was not intentional," she said. She paused, looked at Mike again and smiled, "Sir, I'd like for you to meet my fiancé, Mike Singleton."

Dumaine played the perfect gentleman and gracious war hero. "This is wonderful news. Congratulations. What brings you to town? I guess you've heard we're finally moving forward with the levee work." Dumaine knew he was under tremendous scrutiny because of perceived corruption on his Levee Board. He could not oversell the board's plans, be they real or fabricated. The line had blurred for him years earlier. "No more endangered species lists. No more environmental impact statements. No more accusations. We are prepared to move funding to the Corps of Engineers within the week."

Susanna and Mike stood speechless. They looked at one another questioning their research into the levee funding. They turned toward Dumaine and nodded their approval.

"I find your visit quite a surprise. There's a lot going on in

Washington, especially with that old goat Stahl as Sec Def," said Dumaine as he put his arm around her. "Susanna, it used to be just us with you heading the G-2 and Fred as my deputy. We were good. Very good."

Susanna's brow furrowed. *How could this be?* she wondered. It seemed like a dream, but the past's outline became clearer.

Manfred Stahl played deputy commander while Dumaine took first chair. As the gaps in her memory filled, she recalled Stahl as a fixture at the reserve headquarters. The three of them, with her far junior in rank, comprised a tense, but effective triumvirate. She recalled how she loved overseeing the intelligence activities of the force. All-knowing and all-powerful. She decided who lived. She did more than traditional intel. She ran surveillance for Stahl. She bugged the mayor's office. She placed cameras in the homes of those who piqued Stahl's interest. She saw it as her duty and wanted to please Stahl and Dumaine, whom she found to be a kind man. She believed in them, their work, and the whole damn Marine Corps.

At that moment her innocence shattered.

"General, I almost forgot. I guess I think more of the secretary's contributions on the Hill and yours with the board," she covered with a nervous laugh. Susanna processed Dumaine's information and her recollections. She stood horrified.

"You're right. It was a lifetime ago." Dumaine waived it off. "The present is what's important. Why don't you two have dinner with me at Jimmy's tonight, say 7 p.m.? Have you seen that crew yet? I know they'd love to see our local girl."

Susanna looked up at Mike.

"General Dumaine, we'll see you at 7, sir," Mike said, filling the silence.

The shock she suffered rendered Susanna mute.

Mike pointed toward the door and they dashed out. The car sat just across the street near the corner with St. Charles. They turned right and stared at the gathering of police cruisers. They had no interest in a gun fight, and their two pistols could not overtake the dozen officers ahead. They walked as if nothing had happened.

Mike's mind raced. *Shit.* They had just robbed a bank. He wondered how many crimes they had committed in past 30 minutes.

The building on the corner next to the vehicle stood under renovation. Mike and Susanna disappeared behind plastic sheeting and walls of Tyvek to wait out the siege. The police continued to lay in wait in front of the Whitney, when all of a sudden one barked an order and four officers ran down the side street.

Mike watched.

"When they get to the other corner, walk to the car and slip in," he instructed.

"We'll have to drive past them," stated Susanna.

"Yeah, I see that," Mike said.

The officers approached the far corner.

"Hey, they're in the corner building!" exclaimed one of the officers, confirming the show of force targeted them. The remaining officers on St. Charles headed toward the construction site. The fugitives now had weapons drawn and moved deeper into the maze of two-by-fours and plastic sheeting. Susanna slipped on a pile of wood screws and fell on the dusty concrete slab. "Fuck. Geez. I'm fine." Not that Mike had stopped to check on her. She caught up to him as he dodged dangling electrical wire.

They found themselves in a construction jungle.

Not a worker could be found in the building. They both saw a body in the early stages of decomposition to their right, partially concealed with a plastic tarp. The stench struck them, but they needed to find a way to their car. They heard gun fire and the whiz of bullets.

"Are they shooting at us?" asked Susanna who dropped to the ground.

"It looks at that way," said Mike as he worked to find their yellow brick road. "You're not wearing those Ruby Slippers of yours, are you?"

"Mike, I am not dying in New Orleans," declared Susanna.

More shots rang out. Susanna spotted a set of doors, older doors. They ran slamming their bodies' full force against the bronze and tempered glass, but bounced off. "Fuck!" Mike whispered under his breath. He raised his 9mm.

Susanna grabbed his arm. "Wait," she said. She sidestepped the doors. With a powerful front kick she broke through a portion of the Tyvek wall. Mike looked on as shocked as Susanna. *Locked doors and paper walls?* he wondered.

New Orleans, reasoned Susanna.

The rental car waited around the corner. Another shot rang out. Mike and Susanna nodded to one another and walked to the car. They climbed in unnoticed.

Like Bonnie and Clyde, they pulled out and drove toward the officers. Everyone had guns drawn. The pair had moved with such fluidity the police did not notice they had escaped until they sped down Camp Street.

Mike ducked while looking through the rearview mirror, face flushed. Susanna had seen him perspire just one other time since she had known him—their previous night of dancing in the streets of the French Quarter.

"You got everything out?" he snapped

"Yes. You stashed our bags and computers in the trunk?" she asked.

"Yeah, all of it. I don't think we're coming back any time soon. We are now fugitives. Federal ones at that," said Mike.

He thought of the admiral and felt ill.

"Mike, take 10 East and get off at Chef Menteur Highway. No one will look for us there," she directed.

Mike could not see why he took the exit, but this was Susanna's country, not his. They sat on the trash-strewn highway shoulder. Susanna looked to see if anyone had followed as she went to the trunk for a change of clothes.

"Mike, you need to see this," she called, choking up.

In the trunk on top of their bags lay a bleeding Marcus. The note resting on his dark coat read, "Miss, please give him a nice home."

Susanna guessed Sam tried to save his dog, a heroic act of love, one more selfless than she had ever managed in her woeful existence.

Marcus looked peaceful, but blood covered his face. Someone put a bullet into Marcus's head. She had no idea what damage the round had caused. They would have to wait. Susanna worried about Sam. She felt helpless, but she could save Marcus.

Mike scooted her out of the way and looked at the gunshot wound. The bullet had lodged in the bone above the right eye.

"Damn lucky dog. Whoever finds him will know more when he wakes up," he said.

Her moist eyes pleaded, but her tone remained adamant, "Mike, Marcus needs to come with us. We could use someone with some luck, like our three-legged friend."

She thought for a moment, "Give me your jacket."

"You are not making a dog bed from an Armani suit!" Mike stepped back.

"It's all about you, isn't it?" Her eyes turned cold. "Fine. Unbutton me."

"Here?"

"Yes."

Mike unbuttoned the dress that accentuated Susanna's curves. She stepped out of the dress to reveal her lace undergarments. For the trip to the Whitney she added garters with her stockings.

"Jesus, Marcasi. You are fucking killing me," groaned Mike, leaning on trunk rim. The car tipped to the right off the uneven shoulder.

Susanna chose a straight periwinkle blue cotton skirt and a white formfitting tank with half-dollar-sized periwinkle-and-lemon shaded flowers. She pulled them out of her suitcase without regard to the cars whizzing by them. She clicked each tooth on the side zipper all the while staring at Mike. She hiked up her skirt and placed her right foot on the bumper rolling down her stocking. She did the same with the left leg. Mike pegged his arousal scale and took his cue from his racy companion. He stripped off his trousers and shirt and burgundy wing tips. He pulled on a clean, pressed pair of form-fitting black jeans that Susanna seemed to enjoy. Black boots and a crisp, striped button-down shirt responded to her couture.

Susanna did not notice. After she made a bed in the back seat from a Gortex jacket and some of the workout wear she had packed, she walked over to Mike. "I can't lift him myself," she declared. Even missing a leg, the old Rottweiler weighed at least 140 pounds.

"Thank you. Big points with St. Francis," she commented as the dog rested on the vinyl bench seat. She saw from Mike's vacant stare he did not understand the reference. "You know, St. Francis of Assisi? Animals?" she clarified. Mike shrugged. "Never mind. I'll dispense with the Catholic jargon the closer we get to D.C.," she sighed.

Mike looked over at Susanna. "Dr. Doolittle, it's 16 hours back," he said.

"Fourteen if you drive faster. Make a U-turn at the light and take I-10 East."

CHAPTER EIGHTEEN

Mike broke many land speed records and traffic laws during the 16-hour trip, which he shaved to just more than 12 hours. He drove without food, water, or a chance to relieve himself until the white rental gasped for fuel. He and Susanna took advantage of the dim and dirty restrooms at all-night gas stations and stocked up on fat and sugar. Each clung to a jumbo coffee, and they made themselves sick on French Vanilla creamers.

His pistol sat ready on the front seat, the only thing between him and Susanna.

Once in Mississippi, Susanna lifted her head off the passenger window where she had attached it when they left New Orleans. She unrolled her hair. Mike studied her in the shadows cast by the dashboard light as she removed the black bobby pins and placed them in a small case inside her handbag. She shook her head and the self-created curls framed her face. Susanna's chignon had come loose; her tendrils rested on her left shoulder and ran down her back. She settled in for the drive. She looked straight ahead.

"You're quiet," she deadpanned.

"Well, it's not like you're Chatty Cathy. Can you check the radio?" Mike asked.

"NPR is not an option here," she responded with little enthusiasm.

"I heard a rumor they now have music in Mississippi," said Mike impressing himself with his humor.

Susanna sighed at his sarcasm, "I suppose they do."

She made no effort to reach for the dial.

Mike spoke slowly hoping she might understand, "Su-san-na. Do … you … think … you … could … find … us … some … music? I … come … in … peace."

She started to laugh, "God, I hate you. Ugh! Yes, I will find music. I hope you can still sing."

"I wouldn't worry," he winked.

Mike had many talents. He could make the worst joke entertaining and he could rewrite pop song lyrics from the '70s and '80s. With just a few notes, he would create a new opening and then improvise as he went along. He had elevated this to an art form. Next to Susanna, music long stood as Mike's true passion, though the Navy had few opportunities for SEAL singer-lyricists. With his above-average voice, he won more than a few contests in the underworld of the misnamed Spec Ops Choir Boys.

Mike recalled how Susanna would laugh at his musical antics at the academy. She would sit on the large desk he and roommate Joe shared and preview their latest act. She howled herself off the two-person study surface falling to the cold, tile floor more than once.

Tonight, he needed to impress.

Susanna switched on the radio. "Stations fade quickly here."

"Well, I guess you'll be busy," he said.

She hit one. Mike flashed a look of disapproval. She found another song with a stronger signal. She looked at Mike as he bobbed his head. His lips moved but he made no sound.

"Are you singing?" she asked.

He ignored her. His head nodded to the beat; he mouthed something.

Then came the sound.

I want to bark like a beagle through the trees.
I want to bark like a beagle, chase some fox in front of me.
I want to bark like a beagle until I'm free.
That's my grand revelation.

Susanna laughed watching him sing like a wolf howling at the moon. "You are insane," she said, as thrilled with his act now as she was more than a decade before.

Mike smiled and continued.

Chase the foxes
Who think they're very sly.
Chase the raccoons
With the rings round their eyes.
Chase the song birds
Before they take to flight.
Oh, oh, there's a solution.

Susanna doubled over, "Wait, Steve Miller? C'mon. You are going to have to do better than that."

"Marcasi, you need to find a better candidate. It's on you, babe. You find the song, I create the magic," Mike said, throwing down the music gauntlet.

Susanna wrapped her arms around her ribs as she howled. She looked like a wounded animal in the throes of death. As she gasped for air, she managed, "Jesus, Mike, you're a genius!"

She would enjoy the show.

He pointed his chin toward the radio signaling Mademoiselle Station Changer to get back to work. She complied.

"Oh. Oh, yeah! Hold it there. This is great." Mike's enthusiasm filled the vehicle. With his chin up he began to sing in a falsetto.

Susanne, you don't have to stop at the red light.
Those roll days are over
You just have to ride your bike into the night.
Susanne, you don't have to wear that helmet tonight.
Cruise the streets at high speed
You don't care if it's wrong or if it's right.

Susanne, you don't have to stop at the red light.
Susanne, you just have to blow thru the red light.
Blow thru the red light, blow thru the red light.
Blow thru the red light, blow thru the red light.
Blow thru the red light, oh …

Mike continued, eyes off the road, staring at an enchanted Susanna.

I loved you since I knew ya.
I would always bend down to ya.
I have to tell you just how I feel.
I won't share you with your two-wheeled toy.
I know my mind is made up
So put away your peanut.
Told you once I won't tell you again it's a one way.

Susanne, you don't have to stop at the red light.
Susanne, you don't have to stop at the red light.
You don't have to stop at the red light.
Blow thru the red light, Blow thru the red light.

Susanna's jaw dropped in awe. She laughed so hard Mike thought she had stopped breathing. They continued the game another two hours until both settled into the rhythm of the long, dark drive.

The green glow from the dashboard provided the only light in the car. Susanna fixated on it. Mike's one-man concert brought to mind a favorite. Susanna stared at the dash and in her sweet alto voice confessed,

"Though it's cold and lonely in the deep dark night, I can see paradise by the dashboard light."

She looked at Mike and fell silent again. Mike's eyes widened. *Christ,* he thought. *Marcasi and Earhardt used to perform songster Meatloaf's anthem standing on her desk at school, but with roles reversed.* She sang the male part wearing her white-works uniform trousers tied low and tight around her hips. Her signature hot-pink string bikini formed a provocative, fully exposed "V." She wore a ragged, cut-off, blue-rimmed T-shirt, leaving little to the imagination as she would bump and grind. Sometimes she performed barefoot flashing blood-red nails that matched her vamped-up lips. Other times she wore clunky, off-white Keds. Joe, always the boy-toy, feigned virginity and would wear the black classroom uniform with tie and matching Buddy Holly-style glasses. Frenzied girls chanted "WU-BA" when he appeared wearing Working Uniform Blue "A." He chose white socks to go with his black shoes.

Joe looked like a dead-ringer for heart throb Tom Cruise.

Second Company would crowd outside Susanna's door clapping, whistling, and hollering. Soon other companies came to see the captivating, almost X-rated show. The audience grew so large they moved to the Third Wing stairwell. The duo made the "Salty Sam" column in the "Log" underground magazine more than once. Finally the dour, nuclear power battalion officer shut them down. Thinly disguising their names as he always did, magazine smut columnist Salty Sam announced, "Scarsesi and Darehardt too Hot for First Batt; Join Eighth Wing Players."

Jesus, what the hell happened? wondered Mike, more than 15 years removed from the fun and camaraderie.

Susanna sat lost in thought. She could not stop thinking about the song. The light. *What did the light mean?* Her thoughts shifted to Mike Singleton. She wondered what it would be like with him by the glow of this dashboard light.

"Susanna. Hey, 'Sweet Hips.'" Mike had coined her well-deserved nickname.

Startled from her secret world and worried Mike could read her thoughts she blurted, "Geez, what?"

"He's moving," Mike informed her.

She turned around. In the dim, green glow, the slobbering dog resembled a murderous canine. Marcus looked at Susanna, then at Mike, and back at Susanna. His right lip curled exposing a mouth of very large teeth. He continued his low, menacing growl.

Mike shook his head, "He has a bullet in his head and probably needs to piss."

Susanna could tell she had a testy Mike and an angry dog. She put up her hands to reassure him. "I'll handle this," and turned, "Hey, Buddy. Hey, Marcus. Who's the good boy? The big, baby boy?"

Susanna's soothing tones served to further agitate the dog. Marcus began to bark, slinging saliva in every direction. Mike and Susanna cruised at 85 mph with a crazed dog inches from at their backs.

"Try giving him that shrimp Po' boy, but break it up," Mike recommended.

Susanna tossed pieces back and the dog caught and devoured every crumb, licking the dressing that fell to either side. It seemed Marcus liked gas station cuisine. Once the growling stopped, Susanna unbuckled her seat belt and climbed in back seat, her cotton skirt revealing her smooth thighs, further torturing Mike.

"What are you doing?" asked Mike, who already knew the answer.

She placed her arms around the large Rottie holding him like a big stuffed bear.

Susanna and the three-legged dog bonded as survivors. Fighters. They had grown tough, but after years of abuse and rejection just wanted someone to give a God damn whether they lived or died. Though used for personal gain, both wanted to please their master of the moment. Susanna enveloped him with the tenderness she longed for. The two off-kilter refugees both searched for a place of their own. He gave her hope. She and Marcus would triumph. She knew she would owe the beast her life. She hummed and began, "You are my sunshine, my only sunshine. You make me happy when skies are gray."

Mike joined in, "You'll never know dear ..." Susanna became quiet. Mike continued, "... how much I love you." They both sang, "Please don't take my sunshine away."

Susanna sang a refrain.

Mike's mind raced. *Damn, she remembers that silly song.*

Mike took over. He crooned. He remained her Man in Black.

"The other night, dear, as I lay sleeping, I dreamed I held you in my arms. When I awoke, dear, I was mistaken, so I bowed my head and I cried."

Susanna harmonized the soft refrain as she had so many years ago. She sang staring at Mike. He could see her tears from the rearview mirror. He studied her angelic face in the nighttime glow.

"You are my sunshine, my only sunshine. You make me happy

when skies are gray." Together they finished, "You'll never know, dear, how much I love you. Please don't take my sunshine away."

Susanna buried her face in Marcus's thick black coat and sobbed as they drove through the Alabama night. Neither spoke until they reached Virginia.

CHAPTER NINETEEN

Manfred Stahl had settled in for the evening in his pricey townhome across from the Marine Corps War Memorial. As he sat in his library, his mobile rang. He looked at the screen.

"Dumaine, this better be good."

Though the Levee Board president enjoyed his status as a retired general as well as his claims to heroic deeds, he lived with the constant threat of exposure as a fraud. He and Manfred Stahl had known each other more than 30 years, and Stahl knew things about him more damning than the Medal of Honor scam. Vic Dumaine almost wet himself every time he talked to Stahl.

"Fred, uh, Fred. How are you?" Dumaine stuttered.

"Who cares? Give me a God damn report. Are the persistent bitch and her Navy sex toy dead?" growled Stahl.

Dumaine swallowed hard. He liked Susanna, and her companion seemed like a decent man.

"Fred, uh, not exactly."

"I thought you had the entire NOPD on that bank with orders to shoot to kill." Stahl had set his back-up plan in motion. Vic Dumaine's failure came as no surprise.

"Fred, I did. They, they ... got away," Dumaine hyperventilated.

"But all else went as planned. They've seen the accounts and emptied the deposit box."

Stahl knew he would have to handle the matter of Marcasi. He welcomed the rematch.

"Are you sure, Dumaine? She has the key?" asked Stahl.

"I am positive. Joe knew to keep that box solely as a repository for the key. I checked everything myself," Dumaine said unsure of what he knew.

"Where the hell are they now?" demanded Stahl.

"Fred, they're driving back to Washington and should be there in the morning," said Dumaine with some regret over Susanna and Mike.

"Fred, Susanna seems pretty clear on what we've been doing." Dumaine sounded worried, hiding his hope that his nightmare with Stahl might end.

"Stop whining like a fucking school girl, Dumaine. Susanna Marcasi doesn't know shit, and even if she did, it won't matter because she and her trained SEAL will be the only ones who will ever have that information. That minor detail soon will be of no consequence," Stahl roared.

Stahl hung up. "Marcasi, I have been waiting a long time."

CHAPTER TWENTY

Stahl shook his head. While Dumaine had caused him enough problems, the bitch O'Reilly stood to derail him. He should have put an end to her in the Senate conference room when he had the chance.

He slammed his fist as he recalled the encounter.

"I thought you had fixed this mess but, no. Did you not hear me the last time we *chatted*?" Stahl bellowed, "Let me review. You decided to lift your skirt and spread your legs for that poor excuse of a Marine. *My* fall guy. Someone the Marine Corps actually gives a God damn about. And, AND, you call that bitch Marcasi for help. *Help?* What the fuck were you thinking? We are so close. SO very close. Nothing is going to stop this operation. YOU are not stopping this operation. I don't care if you are the senior senator from Louisiana or Jesus Christ himself. Some low-rent Marine and that fucking whore Marcasi? She's your mess. You need to take care of her." Stahl's voice had grown hoarse.

He broke his swagger stick on the conference table.

"I have already done my part to rid us of sweet Captain Susanna Marcasi," hissed a defiant Manfred Stahl.

Lori rose from the floor where she landed from Stahl's blow seconds earlier. She leaned forward on a mahogany conference chair and slapped her hands on the gleaming table top.

"Don't you *ever* touch me again. I am *not* one of your *ladies* who frequent your all-night poker games for the alcohol and valium you provide. I hear the cocaine caused challenges with your backers. *Mais n'important, mon cher.* That's what you ply your pretty militia boys with isn't it, you fucking TRAITOR," shouted Lori.

Stahl took notice of the woman he saw as no better than the stripper with her mismatched breasts he had thrown out of his office the morning of his swearing in. In Lori O'Reilly he saw a scourge upon the world's most capable political body. She inserted the erection of any member of the House or Senate that suited her. But she could not make the claims of Catherine the Great, and Joe Earhardt stood as no Grigory Potemkin. Manfred Stahl saw Lori O'Reilly as a disgrace.

He should have broken her neck.

"Well, Senator O'Reilly, please. You certainly have my attention," said Stahl with a small, patronizing bow to his serf and sparring partner.

Lori felt a strength she lost many years earlier. She had let her family and Susanna carry her through. Though grateful, in military parlance, she would carry her own pack.

Her relationship with Manfred Stahl needed to change.

"Fred, you're right, I'm here in large part because of you. But my dependence stops now. I don't want to appear ungrateful, but no one owns me, Fred, and no one owns my vote," said Lori, teeth clenched.

Stahl tread with care. "Don't let that Marcasi girl influence how you do the people's business."

"The people's business or your horse trading, Fred? Susanna never has been for sale. I should have listened to her a long time ago." She snatched Stahl's backup swagger stick from him. She slammed it on the table mimicking Manfred Stahl's favorite move meant to intimidate. It shattered shooting in six directions. "I am sure you have a replacement," she said feigning sympathy as she flung the piece that remained in her hand at him.

Lori sauntered about the room. She looked at Fred. She knew this man better than she knew herself.

"I know you've been on the Hill rustling up votes for the Monroe Class frigate," she said.

Lori turned and spoke with her back to him. "Thirty-three billion would go a long way to funding an even larger force-for-hire." She twisted her petite waist at "force-for-hire" and glanced at him. She closed her lids and raised them flashing her smoky eyes for emphasis.

Manfred Stahl stood up, his face glowing red. He tried to speak but not a syllable left his gaping mouth.

Lori sashayed up next to him and spoke in a slow, sultry voice, "Fred, I am not the only one who knows about Hercules. Looks like you have supporters out there, but you always have preyed upon the weak and the desperate. They may not be as reliable as your think."

The Monroe bill already had passed the House. Stahl projected it would pass the Senate for the first time despite years since its introduction. The Navy had balked at the project. While the bill funded the 55 vessels in the class, it ignored monies necessary for the staggering maintenance costs that come with any ship. The Navy had staved off the bill until this session. Stahl arm wrestled enough in both chambers once the president announced his appointment as Defense Secretary.

But the bill would squeak by with one vote—that of Senator Lori O'Reilly. The untimely resignation of Matt Edwards for running some Ponzi scheme with education dollars gave Stahl 99 senators. Lori's threat gave him 98, handing him a probable tie. Stahl could count on the vice president's vote against anything that had Manfred Stahl support, no matter the topic.

Without Lori O'Reilly, the Monroe's $33 billion would remain beyond Stahl's reach.

"Fred, I'm done. No more votes on interstates-to-nowhere to fund your pet projects. No more levee roulette. I will *not* be present for the Monroe vote," she said.

"You bitch! You miserable, fucking bitch! We have worked for this," Stahl fumed, pounding the table on each word.

"No, *we* haven't, and the people of Louisiana have no interest in Manfred Stahl's toy soldiers," Lori said. She knew she swam in treacherous waters, but it felt right. She had lost the fear that had long consumed her.

"Good-bye, Fred. You have the levee money. If you need to talk, go tell it to your buddy, the president. You've got his ear and his balls, too, or so I hear."

Lori walked out of the room. She walked out on Manfred Stahl. She felt free and invincible, but exposing the Stahl cabal would fall to someone else. She had done her share.

Lori returned to her office. She noticed her computer screen glowed with her "Fred" files, but gave it little attention. She thought of this new beginning for her and the people of Louisiana. She felt a rush of excitement for the first time since coming to Washington without being sexually aroused.

Lori made one call. "Susanna. Thank you." She spoke to the voice mail as she would talk to her childhood friend and confidante. She remained cautious of prying ears. "I saved something for you, just in case." She hesitated. The words were caught in her throat. "Hey, I love yuh, Susanna. Please call when you get this."

***

Concerned for Susanna's safety, Mike mentioned she might want to stay at his place. For Susanna, the suggestion triggered disturbing memories of her years with the O'Reillys. Events flashed like a silent film. Leaving her mother in the forgotten world at the Catholic mission came at a price, one she only later understood. She thought about Mike's offer, but unlike with Mick O'Reilly, she now had a choice.

"Thank you, but, I'll be fine," she said.

I've lived through worse, she thought.

Susanna looked over at Mike. "But we still have work to do."

She appeared eager.

Mike nodded. He forced a grin as he pressed a couple of buttons on his phone. He motioned to Susanna with his chin, and then to the phone. She would witness a classic Mike Singleton move to lift her spirits.

"Listen to this," he said in a loud whisper as he signaled for her silence.

"Well, Mike Singleton. How nice of you to call me for the first time." Admiral Ken Bartholomew's tone dripped with sarcasm.

"Admiral, we're in …"

"Pentagon North Parking, I know. And I'm on speaker phone so you can impress Ms. Marcasi with her broken down company officer," he said.

Susanna looked puzzled, pointed at the phone and mouthed, "Lieutenant Commander Bartholomew?"

Mike nodded.

"Lieutenant Commander Bartholomew?" asked Susanna holding in her laughter.

"Jesus Christ, Marcasi. You're as brilliant as the big ox next to you," the admiral said.

"Singleton, my office, now." The line went dead, and Mike and Susanna laughed with their memories of then-Lieutenant Commander Ken Bartholomew.

"He'd have invited you, but I can't get you in the spaces. Wait here with Marcus. I'll only be a few minutes," he said, assuring the conflicted young woman next to him. A steady rain had begun to fall. Mike sprinted through the athletic center entrance and disappeared.

Mike strode through the office to the whispers of his colleagues. Before he could knock, Bartholomew motioned for him to come in and shut the door. The admiral looked more like a mob boss in the haze than a man most expected to become the Chief of Naval Operations someday.

He held out his arms to each side and shrugged, "What the fuck, Mike? You still don't check in? It's Marcasi. You wouldn't leave her alone at school either."

Mike ignored him. "Ken, we're back and we have what we need from New Orleans. Eighteen billion dollars was moved from an account Earhardt had to some mystery account I need to research."

"You coulda figured that out from here," Bartholomew said, sounding concerned.

"Not fully, plus we have the contents of his safety deposit box."

Mike stood up to the admiral.

"Big fucking deal. Find him. Short leash, Singleton. Call me at least once a day. Got it?" barked Bartholomew. He leaned back in his chair, puffing a foul-smelling cigar.

"Working for you is like working for the head of a crime family," Mike said, stating what both already knew.

Mike's comment did not amuse Bartholomew. Mike knew the look.

"Yeah, yeah, I got it," said Mike.

He turned to leave, but he had forgotten to mention a few details. "Ken, we may be in some trouble with our work at the bank. I need to know you will cover both Marcasi and me."

The admiral stared at him.

"Well, I guess you can find another highly trained beast of burden to do your bidding," said Mike with a grin. He knew nothing he could say would threaten the chain smoker before him.

"Whatever you need, Mike. I got you *and* Marcasi."

Mike trusted him.

"Get out of here," Bartholomew yelled as he threw a soda can at him. "And leave that Marcasi girl alone."

Mike put up his arm signaling his old friend to drop the subject. He walked out of the building and back to the car.

Bartholomew picked up his secure line, "They're back," he said, void of emotion. He hung up and slammed the phone in the drawer.

Mike returned to an empty car. It sat with the back doors flung open, but no sign of Susanna or Marcus. He froze. He heard the stories. He knew Manfred Stahl wanted Susanna Marcasi the way some men want an eight-point buck for their wall. He had planned to tell her his thoughts on Stahl as well as his feelings for her and now regretted his hesitation. He looked around, his sight blurred by his alarm. He called out, "Sus ..." and then he saw her. Under a black umbrella, his Armani jacket hung below Susanna's knees. Marcus raised a leg leaving his mark at the Pentagon like so many before him. Susanna gave a little waive.

"Watch the jacket!" he called feigning his irritation.

"I am!" she retorted, not at all intimidated by her partner in crime. By the time he joined her under the tree, the rain had soaked the humans and canine, but Marcus looked resplendent in a garter-belt collar and sheer-stocking leash.

Mike felt the vibration of his phone. He glanced at it and shook his head, grateful he had not lost Susanna and the slobbering hound.

CHAPTER TWENTY-ONE

A sound came from the safe Manfred Stahl kept in his new office. He retrieved the latest in mobile technology. He knew the caller.

"Good Morning, Secretary Stahl," said a man with a pitch-perfect British accent.

"Yes, good morning, Fahim."

"I am glad we have caught you. It is early in your country," said Fahim.

"You never have to worry about catching me. I am always available for the prince or his envoys," said a congenial Stahl.

"Thank you, sir. Would you please hold for him?"

Manfred Stahl thought it a damn shame that an eager, savvy young man like Fahim played for an inferior Saudi Arabian team. He sat at his desk waiting for Prince Abdullah Talal, head of Saudi defense, his counterpart in this third-rate, but wealthy nation.

"Mr. Secretary, good morning," said the prince.

"Your highness, it is always my pleasure," returned Stahl.

"Forgive my rudeness, but I'd like to get straight to business. You have our order filled, yes?"

Stahl had known the prince for some time. The Naval Academy hosted Talal as an exchange student during the early 1980s. He grew close with Joe Earhardt and lived two doors down from him most of their four years together.

"I signed off on it yesterday." He did not tell the prince that he still awaited funding from the Monroe Class bill." Stahl growled to himself at the thought of the pending vote.

"Very good, Mr. Secretary. The issue of funding necessitates my call," stated Talal with some reluctance.

A long, tense silence followed. Stahl could not imagine how Talal knew about Lori O'Reilly and the bill.

"Mr. Secretary, we cannot meet your price," said the prince.

Stahl exhaled, relieved his Hill challenges remained a secret. "Well, your highness, I have buyers lined up for services. Either you meet my price, or our deal is off. Judging from our intelligence traffic, you need what I have."

"Fred, we have always been very good to you. We have backed you financially and in other ways over the years," stated Talal, making his case.

"And I have represented your kingdom's interests on many matters on the Hill. We're even. I may even be ahead. I consider us friends, but this product is worth much more than your kingdom has agreed to pay," said Stahl, teeth and fists clenched.

The Saudi deal stood as one of Stahl's largest contracts in this latest venture. He could not afford to lose it, but did not want word to get out that he would negotiate his price.

"I understand, Fred. I will contact you again within 24 hours," said the prince.

"I'll be here, your highness," responded Stahl.

Stahl hung up first and flung the phone across the room.

"Fucking, cheap-ass Arabs," he spat.

***

Mike took the Memorial Bridge into the District. Susanna had decided she and Marcus would stay on Fourteenth Street assuring Mike that Mrs. Schiller and Tom would help her. Mike began to argue, but short of kidnapping her, he had to comply. He had learned long ago dissuading Susanna Marcasi could prove painful.

He did not want to go to that dark place again.

As they drove, they discussed ratcheting up their Earhardt efforts. Susanna planned to go through Levee Board information and delve into the off-shore account. Mike would physically track Joe. They pulled behind Susanna's building. The sight of Tom's van reassured them.

Mike stared at the mural.

"Just help Marcus and me in, please," sighed Susanna. Mike could have his love affair with Tom's vintage Indian princess on his time.

"Sure. C'mon Marcus, you slobbering lover boy," Mike said as a feeling of foreboding came over him.

Ellie Schiller waited on the landing. "My child, where have you been? They came for you." Mrs. Schiller pointed with her crooked finger at Susanna's apartment, as they trudged up the stairs.

Susanna remained silent, but her thoughts went to Manfred Stahl. While she had upset a few people on the Hill, only he had threatened her safety. The Dumaine connection at the Levee Board screamed "Stahl."

Everything seemed to point to Stahl.

They found the apartment door ajar. Before Mike could stop her, Susanna reached in and flipped the light switch by the entry door. Mike came up from behind and grasped her arms. Marcus crouched.

"Don't touch me," she warned. "I'll take it from here." Susanna wanted the New Orleans odyssey finished and stepped through her doorway.

As she started her second step, Mrs. Schiller called out, "No!"

With Susanna's wrath fresh in his mind, Mike grabbed her—and Marcus—and dragged them back through the entry.

"Whoa, whoa. Hold on a second," he cautioned.

Mike pointed at what looked like a fine wire running from the side of her bed to the wall and another line crossed her kitchen area, four inches above the floor. Mike scanned the ceiling and pointed to a new motion sensor. Susanna looked down and shook her head in disgust. She just wanted to go home. She wanted her clothes. She wanted to start a life with Marcus. But she understood someone— probably Manfred Stahl—had made her homeless—again. She understood the whole building could blow if she so much as curled up on the bed that sat just 25 feet from her. They had to leave what had been her sanctuary. She had visions of herself with Marcus on a blanket and plastic cup at the top of an escalator outside a Metro station. A three-legged dog could pull in at least $100 per day in dimes, nickels, quarters, and dollars.

She turned and looked at Mrs. Schiller. "Did you see these people?" she asked her Nazi friend.

"I heard them. They came a few hours after you left with this one." She gestured at Mike.

"But did you see anyone?" pressed Susanna. Her frustration appeared as anger.

"They parked in the alley. When they went to leave, the security lights lit up. I could make out little, but here are my notes and here is the information on their vehicle and license plate." Mrs. Schiller handed over her intelligence just as she had been trained decades earlier.

They turned away from the apartment door.

"I am not sure what's in there, but I know the right guys on the D.C. police force. Let me call them in on this. I can't fix this one," Mike said with genuine regret.

She nodded and gave a faint smile.

Susanna left the building like MacArthur leaving the Philippines. Stahl or no Stahl, why would someone target her apartment? Mike had his pistol drawn and covered them as they climbed into the car. He felt someone watched them and it had everything to do with Joe Earhardt. It seemed he and Susanna had gotten too close to something, and he wished they would let him in on the secret.

The mud-splattered rental car looked like a combat vehicle. Mike sent dirt and glass shards through the air as he employed some effective evasion tactics. If he only had his old Toyota Hilux from Africa. "If you going thin-skin, go Hilux," he believed. Few understood his obsession with a trusted set of wheels and a loaded firearm—the more guns and ammo the better. Susanna watched him drive as he might on a bad day in Islamabad.

She could tell his mind had left D.C.

"Mike, I get this protection scenario, but we're in Washington," she said.

He grunted his understanding but moved like he had just rescued a hostage in a third world country. Mike took the same route Susanna had taken on her motorcycle, but his clumsy, skidding turns paled to her elegant precision on the road.

"Hold on." Mike crossed three lanes of traffic, having almost missed the turn for the bridge. Airborne, they came in sight of the Lincoln Memorial. Both breathed a sigh of relief in Virginia.

"We'll get cleaned up at my place," declared Mike, impressed with his performance.

"Do you think it's safe?" she snipped.

Mike Singleton lived outside the Fort Myer Army post across the street from the Marine Corps War Memorial. His two-story apartment occupied the first and second level of a modest, four-story brick building dating to the 1960s. Less than a quarter-mile toward Rosslyn and to the rear of his building rose new, multimillion-dollar townhomes. They swallowed the middle class charm of the older neighborhood, Mike thought. He had no idea Manfred Stahl lived in one of those town-palaces, as locals called them.

Stahl's choice of residence had come as no accident.

CHAPTER TWENTY-TWO

Joe Earhardt awoke on a torn mattress, his face stuck to the fabric with his own blood and saliva. As he opened his eyes, he felt like someone had just pummeled him in a cage fight. His shoulders throbbed as he felt rope binding his wrists behind him. His hands tingled from a lack of blood flow. He caught a glimpse of the yellow synthetic cord binding his ankles.

Where the hell am I? Is this the U.S.? he wondered. He lay still, scanning the cavernous space.

Another 10 minutes passed with no sign of the men who took him from the bridge. He recalled three thugs, all in black with HK MP-5 sub machine guns and HK USP .45 cal. pistols. Weaponry aside, his assailants did not know how to bind a captive. Joe thought he could work his arms under his legs as he heard two men returning. Straining and almost blacking out from the pain, he pushed his legs through his bound arms and lay back in his bloody slurry.

"Fucking Stahl. What a fucking hard ass. We're not his slaves. We know what the hell we're doing," said Doug Polanski, clad in black to his neck.

"Stahl pays us a shitload of money, so I recommend we put up with his crap and do whatever he wants," said the Alex Frost, who could have passed for Polanski's twin.

"What the fuck?" said Polanski.

Stahl's men looked over at what appeared to be an unconscious Joe urinating on himself.

"Man. Wow," said Frost

"Potent. Geez," winced Polanski.

"Clean him up."

"Clean who up?" asked Polanski.

"Stahl's not going to like his boy passed out in his own piss. Let's get it done before he shits all over himself, too," warned Frost.

"Christ, did you have to bring that up?" protested Polanski.

"Fine." Frost, the more sensible of the two, started toward Joe while Polanski went for towels and spray cleaner. When Frost stooped to get a better look at the immobile Joe Earhardt, he lost his balance. Joe pushed his weight against the man who tumbled to the ground in front of him striking his head on the concrete. Polanski turned when he heard the commotion and raised his weapon to fire.

"Do you really want to shoot your partner here? I mean, you're such a great team and it would be a tragic waste," said Joe.

Joe knelt and used the dazed Frost as a shield. A single shot rang out and they watched Polanski fall to the ground. Frost's jaw dropped open. As he looked in the direction of the gun fire, both he and Joe turned to dive for safety. A second shot echoed. Joe rolled over to find the back of Frost's skull missing.

Joe Earhardt looked at the figure that had just entered the warehouse. His muscles tightened. His jaw jutted forward.

"What the fuck, Dad? Geez, I've been hangin' out with your goon squad, tied up in this fucking cave waitin' for a family reunion with you of all people? I shoulda known," he said.

The man did not respond. Joe watched him as he approached.

Joe Earhardt had lifted himself off the smooth concrete floor. He stood by the urine-and-blood-stained mattress and looked at the man who stood 10 feet from him.

He continued with sarcasm, "Oh, I'm sorry. Where are my manners? I meant 'What the fuck, Mr. Secretary, sir.' Those titles just make you hard, Dad, don't they?"

"We have work to do, Josef," snarled Manfred Stahl.

"What's all this about?" asked Joe, gesturing to the warehouse and his captivity. Despite the blood and bruising, he spoke with confidence; his body remained rigid befitting the true Marine that still eluded him.

"All this?" said Stahl as he surveyed this small piece of his kingdom.

"First, no son of mine is going to kill himself. Second, I had planned for us to run this operation together, but I wonder where your loyalties lie."

Stahl paced, ensnaring Joe in his trap.

"Do you want out, Josef? Be a man and tell me. Would you rather die? I can arrange that. But do *not* expose my work for whatever your reason du jour is. I am glad to have you on board, son, but if you're wavering, stay the fuck out of my way," he said.

Joe could feel his father's simmering rage.

Stahl's son could not believe they had gotten to this point. What the hell had happened? As much of an ass as Manfred Stahl had become, he stood as a legend from a war that most wanted to forget. Four Purple Hearts for combat injuries. Three times the Viet Cong mangled him. A fourth near-fatal incident landed him in the hospital in Saigon. Rumors circulated his own men had shot him.

Apparently, he was an ass then, too.

No one could believe that an American—five to be precise—would turn on Manfred Stahl in a country overrun by foreigners and communists. It mattered little they called the country Vietnam.

During the successful rescue of the Marine company that Stahl planned and led, a mine explosion killed three of his men and left Stahl with a mangled right leg. Not only had he lost his platoon sergeant, who had become one of his most trusted friends, he lost much of his right heel in the incident.

A shattered Manfred Stahl came home to New Orleans and his family a hero, but Stahl saw nothing but failure. It was 1967. He moved in and out of military hospitals. The doctors prescribed a plethora of pills. Stahl did not know what half of them did, but he took what he could get.

Manfred Stahl saw his hard-won control slipping from his grasp. He felt his mind and family crumbling. Young Josef did not understand his father's erratic moods, and he recalled his mother did not allow him to see much of his father, even though they lived under the same roof. Despite the discord, wife and son moved where the

Corps sent Stahl.

By early 1969, after less than eight years of marriage, the pretty sailing champion from Annapolis begged her husband to get help. Judy Stahl called his friends, but they closed ranks around Fred. Stahl had saved a number of Marines and civilians during his combat tours in a series of harrowing and daring incidents. He deserved his career and a life—however he wanted to live it. The booze and the pills? Hell, everyone had to get through the day anyway he could.

One damp October evening, Cindy, Judy's closest confidante, dimmed her lights as she pulled into Judy's concrete driveway in her blue Chevy Nova. Terror-stricken by the situation, she had a bad feeling about Judy's escape. Judy also sensed something amiss that night.

With Joe asleep in the back seat, Cindy balanced the last box against her chest. She put her white patent boot on the front stoop and stepped smack into Manfred Stahl. She screamed, shoved the box at Stahl, and ran inside. Judy and Cindy made a dash for the Nova through the kitchen door, but Stahl had arrived at the vehicle first. Judy stood defiant as she held a trembling Cindy.

"It's OK, Cindy," she said. "Stay by the car with Josef."

Stahl and Judy disappeared into the house closing the door behind them. Thirty minutes passed without a sound.

Cindy began to cry, "Oh my God. Oh my God, he's killed her. What do I do?" She roused poor little Joe to head to a neighbor's for help. After she had the drowsy fellow standing in the driveway, she heard Stahl's voice.

"That won't be necessary. Give me the boy," Stahl said mechanically.

Stahl placed a sleepy Joe in his room. Sounds of his mother's muffled cries prompted the young child to push back his covers and go to his window. He watched as Manfred Stahl dragged his wife out back bound like an animal. She carried their second child, but had told no one. Joe witnessed his father break the bones in his mother's sweet face. He watched as he knocked out four of her teeth and tore out clumps of her long golden hair. With a silencer on his pistol he shot her through both feet. He would have paralyzed her, but thought it too difficult to explain—even for him. Unknown to Stahl, she miscarried a son that night.

Two weeks later authorities escorted Judy and Joe away from the house. She returned to Annapolis. Three years later she married Glynn Earhardt, a professor of military history at the Naval Academy.

Despite Judy's restraining order, Stahl kept an eye on the boy. His interest heightened once Joe entered the Naval Academy. Stahl did not approve of his association with the Marcasi girl, "that fucking whore," as he referred to her. He knew she rose from the poorest of the poor in New Orleans. Stahl wielded tremendous influence because of his place in history as a war hero. He blamed Joe's problems at Annapolis and Quantico on Susanna.

***

"So, Josef, you were sitting on the Memorial Bridge at 2 a.m., because you find it peaceful? The loaded Colt, your grandfather's cap gun, was for protection?" asked Stahl.

Stahl stood with his back to Joe. "We did not recover the files. I'd like them, please."

Joe found his father mesmerizing.

"We found pieces of a 3½ inch case. I believe there is a disk with, let's call it, 'proprietary information' for your current concubine, Lori O'Reilly. I know you would not want that in the wrong hands, son," said Stahl.

"Wrong? Like yours, Fred?" spat Joe. Self-loathing welled as he looked at his father. Joe Earhardt saw himself in Manfred Stahl. He reflected Manfred Stahl at his worst, a genetic fact that drove him to the bridge that night. He could not stand the conflict any longer: Should he embrace life as his ruthless father or kill the demon?

He had chosen the latter.

"No. Not mine, Josef. On the topic of hands, I want you to keep that tarted-up senator happy."

Stahl's tone threatened.

Joe studied the enigma before him. *Saint? Sinner? Patriot? Traitor? An unholy god?* Joe had believed his destiny to be that of his father—as a war hero. The opportunity faced him more than once. He allowed indecision and fear to defeat him. Joe Earhardt knew he stood as a sycophant and coward—and chose to die.

Joe retreated to his most valuable talent: persuasion through refined charm and empty promises. He walked as a dead man among the living. He had nowhere to turn, except to the haven standing over him.

Tell 'em what he wants to hear!

"Fuck it, Fred. You're the ringmaster of the Manfred Stahl Circus. It's gaming and the stakes are high, Dad. You gamble big with public money and people's lives. And guess what? I love the hell out of it. I get off on it. It turns me on even more than Lori does. Yeah, I'm into it." Joe had begun pacing, gesturing.

His eyes danced afire.

"Beating the life outta Marcasi back at Quantico? I had never felt such power. I cannot describe the rush of each blow. And then to watch her suffer? Better than sex. Yeah, I get you, Dad. I AM you, and yeah, I'm in. Way in. I want to ride this wave as long as we can and then catch the next. Bring it on, Mr. Secretary."

Embrace it or kill it? wondered Stahl.

Manfred Stahl grew concerned. Josef stood as many things, but not a zealot. Stahl did not need people at his level doing God's work for its orgasmic effect. Such miscreants proved weak, unreliable, and dangerous. He would have to observe his son a little longer before he made a decision on Josef's future role in his paramilitary empire.

Joe's mood darkened. His head half tilted forward swaying. "But we have a problem. You fucking played me like you play all the other saps, Mr. Secretary," Joe said. He sat in a blood-stained office chair looking up as his father who stood just beyond his grasp. "Why didn't you just let me die?"

"As I said, you know I could not let that happen. I love you, son." Stahl's outward expression of emotion, though meaningless, sickened him. He grew certain his son could not be trusted, but he had placed him in that Senate position for a reason.

"The files, Josef. The disk with the files that you planned to leave behind," demanded Stahl.

Joe held his breath and looked for an escape. *How could he know?* Should he lie? Come clean? Maybe he could take things if a different direction.

"I drew the line beyond family, and I am ashamed," said Joe, eyes downcast. He hoped to leave the statement open for his father's interpretation.

Manfred Stahl decided to follow his son's lead, "You're talking about that whore Marcasi?"

Susanna? Joe expected his father to spit Lori at him. *Why that bitch Susanna?*

"Marcasi, your white-trash piece of ass, is with your old roommate as we are standing here. It's all very touching. They're looking for you, Joe. Lori, your current whore, asked for Marcasi's help in finding you. Even that God damn admiral at DIA wants you found alive."

"The Defense Intelligence Agency?" asked an incredulous Joe. *Fucking Bartholomew? Son of a bitch.*

"Perching yourself on the Memorial Bridge wasn't one of your more discreet moves. We're lucky it's just that troll Bartholomew." Stahl walked away waiving his royal hand. "DIA is of no consequence to me."

Stahl wheeled around pointing at his son as he shook with rage. "Do you think I am stupid, boy? You planned to destroy my work, my life, and take a bullet because you couldn't face me or the prospect of a prison sentence," said Stahl in a booming voice.

His father had stated the facts. Joe knew he had to perform to reach safety behind the Manfred Stahl lines.

"I've kept an eye on Marcasi over the years to keep her out of the way," offered Joe, though he only saw Susanna twice in Lori's office.

Stahl scoffed, "You think this absolves you for your sins against me? Maybe you've been watching her, but you weren't there to stop her."

Manfred Stahl's face burned with rage. Reptilian in nature, Joe never knew his father to perspire, but he noticed Stahl's moist brow.

"Vicious, vicious attack. Poor, fragile thing," Stahl mocked. "The reports say she fought like an animal. She broke her arms beating off her attacker. It's what saved her life. A rape that almost split her in two. Can you imagine such violence?" He paced as he gestured. "A blow to the head that halved her skull? Who does such things? I'm surprised the person didn't just slit her throat like a farm pig at slaughter."

Manfred Stahl felt unstoppable.

"That's the man I want on my team," Stahl said.

Joe felt his face turning scarlet. Beads of sweat formed on his upper lip and blood continued to trickle out the side of his mouth. He appeared calm but sensed where this father-son talk would veer.

"Why? Why are you telling me this?" Joe asked.

"I have kept up with the girl, too," baited Stahl.

"Why?" asked a stunned Joe.

"Let's call her—useful. For some unknown reason, people like her. She played miracle worker for that pathetic O'Reilly. That bitch cannot function without her. The stupid girl walked away from a Louisiana senator to live in some tenement with a collection of ne'er-do-wells," said Stahl.

"Son, slipping into the darkness of a swift-moving current isn't going to change a God damn thing. They'll never allow you at Arlington when they learn of your unspeakable crimes."

Stahl's words struck Joe hard.

"Joe, what you stole from me gets you a full ride at Leavenworth. What you did to Marcasi adds another life sentence, but no one really knows about that yet. She wiped out your box at the Whitney. She has what you stupidly left behind. All will be in a jury's hands soon enough."

Fred's version of the facts gave Joe pause.

"I would never betray you, Dad."

Stahl saw his son's desperation. "Maybe. Maybe not. But Josef, I'm tiring of this charade. I'll be direct. Marcasi long has caused problems for us. Now she stands on the precipice of exposing my work."

Stahl's chest puffed out and his voice deepened.

"Your selfish folly brought Marcasi back from the dead. She's your mess. I want her removed from my business permanently. Do we understand each other?"

Stahl gazed upon his son like a feudal lord.

Joe gave a slow nod, his eyes fixed on his father. "My mess. Got it. Pay to play."

Joe understood the murderous act his father commanded. He had left Susanna for dead once. Now he would finish her. *The sins of the father become those of the son*, thought Joe.

"Good boy. Very good boy," Stahl hissed.

He did not trust his weakened son for a moment.

"No Arlington burial would destroy your mother," Stahl said, sealing the deal.

Manfred Stahl knew he would have to report this latest development, but it would have to wait, he thought, as he watched the police swarm the warehouse.

Chief Russell arrived on the scene with a dozen uniformed police officers and a S.W.A.T. team. Russell's men could not have been older than 25. *Children on the D.C. streets*, thought Stahl. *Clear-skinned boys who could kill at 500 meters or more*. These men made Manfred Stahl salivate. Their skills aroused him. Stahl put down his weapon and raised his arms in the air.

"Easy, Roscoe," he called. "It's Secretary Stahl. I found Lieutenant

Colonel Earhardt. Unfortunately, I had to kill his captors."

Russell rolled his eyes, "Jesus Christ," he muttered as he holstered his weapon. As the officers cleared the area, Stahl felt a rush like from his days with his platoon in Vietnam. Same boys. Some faces. Police or U.S. military, so *unprepared,* he thought.

God save the fucking queen.

CHAPTER TWENTY-THREE

No sooner had Susanna gotten Marcus settled, Mike walked out the door with a grunt and a wave. She assumed Bartholomew had summoned him. Her feelings oscillated.

She rummaged through her vintage purse holding her Luger and their haul from the Whitney. Though drawn to the key, she plucked the computer disk. On her screen, she saw files saved in various formats, but all used the name "Hercules." It took some time, but she determined someone built Hercules as a sprawling paramilitary organization. She found foreign involvement. Many nations appeared as clients. She searched on specific names but could not connect Joe, Stahl, Lori, or the Levee Board to this new player.

The key from the Whitney box intrigued her. It looked important, the way small keys sometimes do. It opened something related either to the levees, Hercules, or maybe the secrets of the missing Joe Earhardt. Maybe it would unlock the missing bits of her memory. She squeezed it in her hand and sighed.

So much effort yet she could prove nothing. She had found no reason for Joe Earhardt to disappear, unless he had tired of his work as the Corps's gigolo. She shook her head at the thought of Joe and the Marine Corps. Susanna knew she stood as more of a warrior than Joe Earhardt could ever claim.

***

Susanna switched to Lori's files. She saw the Monroe Class bill and wondered why that garbage piece of legislative old news had resurfaced. It appeared it had grown to from $20 billion to $33 billion and somehow a vote seemed imminent. It appeared Lori had signed on after Susanna left. Susanna knew the Navy did not want the program. She wondered if Monroe now stood as a scam in the tradition of the levee appropriations. Between Hercules and Monroe lay an answer, maybe *the* answer, but she did not see it.

She felt certain she and Mike squeezed New Orleans for more information than she could have hoped. She thought the same about Lori's office. All clues seemed to lead to Manfred Stahl in some way. She realized she needed to sack Stahl's fortress to find the link. She found his address in a couple of key strokes, but his location shocked her.

Susanna changed into a black turtle neck and tights that hugged her body. She laced up her motorcycle boots. She gathered her camera, a few extra batteries, and her small digital recorder. She placed them in the black pouch and strapped it around her waist. She grabbed Joe's Art Deco key and slipped it in her pouch as well. She felt safer taking the Luger along. She carried her leather riding gloves, the only ones she had given her sudden forced departure from Fourteenth Street.

Halfway down the stairs she exclaimed, "Oh no!" as she spotted Marcus sitting in the small living room surrounded by white polyester clouds of what had served as sofa filling. A satisfied Marcus rushed to meet her at the bottom of the stairs.

"Oh, no! No, no, no! Oh, Marcus, what have you done?"

He looked up at her and sighed. She dropped on one knee, waist deep in the filling that carpeted the room a foot from the eviscerated couch. She put her arms around his muscular neck and gave him a big kiss.

"We'll worry about this later."

He slobbered as she spoke.

"You are one handsome dog," Susanna said.

He panted his approval.

"Marcus, give me a minute." She walked into the kitchen for a drink of water. "Oh, no!" she gasped. Marcus, a counter-surfer, had pulled everything from Mike's Formica countertops to the floor. Anything edible had disappeared. What looked like a box of Cheerios lay limp, soaked in slobber and crushed in the corner. Susanna sat amidst the chaos and howled with laughter. She pulled out her phone to call Mike, but put it away.

"Why tell him now? Let's give the man some peace," she confided to Marcus.

She pulled out the phone again. "Mike, just checking in as requested. I'll see you later. No need to call me back. I'll just think you're checking up on me if you do, and it will piss me off."

She felt confident the call would take care of "Short Leash" Singleton for the next hour or two.

CHAPTER TWENTY-FOUR

Susanna stormed Stahl's fortress from the rear, where she thought him most vulnerable.

Manfred Stahl lived at one of the most enviable addresses in Arlington. The enclave of stately structures loomed, row upon row, like some post-apocalyptic Oz. It appeared Stahl had connected two of the largest townhomes, giving him well over 6,000 square feet of living space on the end with a much sought-after view of the Marine Corps War Memorial. Susanna figured Stahl got hard every time he looked out his window. If it was not booze or women, she recalled, it was his fucking Corps.

Susanna had checked Stahl's schedule with his office, but questioned its accuracy. Between supposed White House meetings that afternoon and evening, Susanna calculated a small window during which she could get in his house and pull the files she needed.

She knew Stahl's organizational habits from their time in Washington.

Her boot slipped as she scaled the wall enclosing his town-palace, but she remained unseen. She had smashed Stahl's army of security cameras with well-placed rocks. She looked like a cat burglar as she swung her other black-clad leg over the stone. Her right boot dropped within a foot of a set of quivering teeth. She gasped as she admired the magnificent creature. The Doberman seemed as taken by the intruder.

Had they reached a brief détente?

"Hey, Buddy. Hey, handsome man," Susanna assured, her voice shaking.

She had no idea of the dog's name or gender, but knew all dogs liked to be called "buddy." She slipped on her motorcycle gloves and dropped down in the yard. The dog leapt back. He again bared his teeth with a low growl, crouched down, and ran off. In a moment he returned clutching his toy. A femur. Hercules, as emblazoned on his collar, appeared the size of an Assateague pony. He dropped the bone at Susanna's feet and prostrated before his new mistress.

"Hercules, no time to play," she said.

He bounded and barked, encouraging her to throw the human pacifier.

"Shhhh."

She motioned for the dog to be quiet and eyed the back door for Stahl's goon whom she had glimpsed through the front entrance snoring under a screen blasting "Court TV." Susanna tossed the well-chewed bone across the charming French Quarter-like courtyard. Hercules bounded back.

"OK, one more," she said.

The dog started and stopped and started again. She threw the bone in the other direction and darted for the French doors.

She watched for movement on the palace's darkened lower level as she pulled down on the door lever. Her smile of satisfaction turned to a grimace of frustration. *Who locks a back door?* She jabbed her black-clad elbow through a single pane and unlocked the door. No alarm. No goon. No Stahl. She understood her run of luck probably reflected her naiveté more than her breaking-and-entering skills.

As her eyes adjusted, she saw she had found Stahl's lair. The lower-level study also served as his Marine Corps vanity room, though any room probably had a Manfred Stahl "I love me" element to it.

As "Court TV" continued to fill the main level above her, she started toward Stahl's desk. Susanna felt a sharp, sudden pain. She crouched down to relieve the cramping in her lower abdomen. She let out a small cry. *Get to work. It will pass.* But the pain intensified with each step. She dropped to her knees clutching her upper thighs. She choked back the nausea and lifted herself into a French leather club chair for a moment's rest. She looked at the desk.

"Ugh," she winced. "Move."

Susanna sensed a presence. She reached for her Luger as a

miniature dachshund appeared, growling at her feet. She hesitated, but reached for the five-pound security system.

"May I pet you?"

The small dog backed away and then ran toward his visitor. He sat with his head high as Susanna ran her trembling hands against his smooth fur. She picked him up and held him. She looked at his tags as he licked her face.

"OK, Zeus," she said talking to his petite snout. "I need to look for something, 'den I gotta go."

Susanna knew she had squandered too much of what little time she had. As she stood, she felt wet. Susanna looked down and noticed her thighs. She shined her flashlight on blood-soaked tights. She looked back at the club chair and held her breath. Blood covered the seat cushion and had seeped into the cracks of the old leather. She worked to soak up the blood using her shirt. She rummaged through the bath off the study and returned with an armful of wet paper towels and tile cleaner. She wiped and scrubbed; her mind raced for an explanation. Why would she hemorrhage? Pregnancy remained impossible.

"That's as good as it's gonna get, Zeus. Can you believe this?" She put everything back in its place and tucked the discarded towels in a plastic trash bag.

She approached Manfred Stahl's hand-carved desk. She looked at the marble clock by his fountain pen. Her eyes darted to her watch. *Time, tide and formation ... certainly wait for no one. Son of a bitch.* She had 15 minutes, tops, to find what she needed and get out. She felt ill. Worse, Mike Singleton called it when she dropped an early hint of her plan: This may have stood as one of her worst ideas. *He had a point*, she begrudged.

The papers on the desk top appeared personal in nature. Assorted statements, bills, *Cheap bastard;* investment information, *Rich bastard;* and a yellowed copy of old divorce papers, *Bastard.* The separation agreement made for interesting reading. She had put it aside to get back to God's work when "Josef Stahl" caught her eye on

Page 2. She froze, horrified. *No*, she thought as she snapped a photo. *Impossible.* But it explained strange comments and events as far back as their time at the academy. Any blood relation between Stahl and Joe changed things. It changed everything, including the past. Susanna scoured the divorce dossier.

She found her answer: Stahl had fathered Joe. Her racing random thoughts that had plagued her since the academy stood suspended. Things made sense. She found solace in a revelation that should have made her run.

Joe Earhardt's lineage should not have mattered.

But it did.

She shuffled through bank statements. "As requested," signed, "Grand Cayman Financial Group. Your Pathway to Financial Security." She snapped a photo; the last four digits of the account number looked familiar.

She looked closer at the statements. His wealth gathered dust in one. The other, with an aka of "Hercules," had large sums of money enter and exit each month. She saw no indication of the $18 billion transaction, but Susanna reasoned Stahl's next statement would show the transfer.

Father and son!

Susanna tugged the top desk drawer. Stahl kept it locked. She noticed the style and patina of the lock. Almost without a second thought, she reached into her pouch and produced the key from Joe's New Orleans safety deposit box. It fit Stahl's private drawer.

Stahl had to have murdered Joe! How biblical! How Shakespearean!

She opened Pandora's Box. A thick, legal-sized envelope marked "Marcasi" topped the pile. "Jerk," she growled as she emptied its contents in the middle of the leather-top desk. Susanna flipped through the sheets, unsure of what she would find. She saw that her life sat in the envelope. New Orleans, the academy, Quantico, the Marine commands, the Hill. She fumbled through to the time of her accident. She found a handwritten letter from the Commandant of the Marine Corps,

Fred,

Though the investigation into the Marcasi attack is inconclusive, you are too close to this matter. I am rescinding your promotion to major general. Submit your retirement papers immediately. We are all very fortunate she survived.

Carl

Susanna froze. "Court TV" had fallen silent. She heard footsteps above her. They passed. She heard a door open, then close. *Did he leave? Would he return with reinforcements?* She still had work to do.

She found a medical report from Tulane Hospital and the Marine Forces Reserve inspector general's notes. She took the time to read them. Her tears stained the original documents in her hands. Some entries stood out: "Raped with long metal object, probably large-gauge pipe;" "Legs dislocated;" "Skull – multiple fractures from repeated blows with metal object;" "Massive internal bleeding."

Her eyes dropped down, "Death imminent."

She found interviews with the Marine Corps inspector general and the DoD IG stating she had reported Manfred Stahl's activities two months earlier, but they had not acted on what they deemed absurd accusations. Susanna read the top page and began to photograph the more than 100-page report faster than her camera could react. *Am I dreaming? Did I die? Was this the accident they told me about? It feels familiar, but ...?* She couldn't recall the details of an attack. But with Manfred Stahl involved, nothing happened by accident.

I want this file.

Susanna's head filled with muted memories of a young Marine intelligence officer on the Marine Forces Reserve staff. Three crumbling cinderblock warehouses between Poland Street and the Industrial Canal housed the New Orleans-based headquarters. Cannonball-sized holes pocked the structure. Lulled by her position of some importance as the second in charge of all force intelligence, she had let down her guard with the charming deputy commander, Brigadier General Manfred Stahl.

The fog that long had enveloped her cleared. Joe may have held the key to the lock, but she held the answers to long-held secrets in her hands.

She remembered.

What else lay in this mother lode? She wanted more answers. What had she and Mike been chasing? A Stahl smokescreen? She almost tore the papers in her zealous pursuit of the truth.

The thickest envelope by far read "Josef." She lifted her chin and pressed her shoulder blades together. She laid the divorce papers by the "Josef" dossier. She found a copy of Josef Stahl's birth certificate, May 2, 1962. Parents: Manfred and Jennifer. She found a copy of a letter Stahl sent to Joe at the academy telling him about her impoverished past. The simple letter back read, "Fuck off, Dad." She chuckled. *Of course*, like *father, like son.*

She found a report from Quantico. The assault read worse than she remembered. She had no idea Joe had shoved the engagement ring deep inside her—with a knife.

Rage replaced her brief regret.

She opened a cloth-covered, water-stained ledger. The smeared scrawl went for pages, penned by someone other than Stahl. She kept the book. She continued to search the desk, but found nothing about Joe's suicide. She uncovered a number of scribbled notes about a bridge.

Abduction? Someone kidnapped that snake?

Susanna's camera clicked.

Though engrossed in the story of Josef Stahl, a slim folder beneath Joe's caught her attention. In bold letters someone had printed, "Poseidon."

"Poseidon?" Susanna looked down at Zeus. "Is this what *Mahn-fred* calls himself?" She drew out his name. "You can trust me," she said with a wink.

The dog whimpered.

"Poseidon" proved a big nothing. She held an empty folder. *Strange. Maybe "Poseidon's" information sits in a computer file.* She discounted the thought. She had to search the rest of the desk.

Her deadline loomed.

Two ragged, pea-green ledgers, the ones the military had issued by the truckload, labeled "Guns and Ammo," attracted her interest. They seemed decades older than the water-stained book in Stahl's center drawer. They sat alone in the upper left-hand drawer. Entries in the first began when Stahl was a Marine captain in Vietnam and ended around the time of Susanna's Marine Forces Reserve "accident." The second picked up two years earlier in 1998. She took both ledgers. She had forgotten about Stahl's gun-running days, but that piece of history seeped back into her memory.

Two envelopes labeled "Hercules I" and "Hercules II" filled the right-hand desk drawer. She looked at each envelope and saw "Poseidon" printed in pencil. For Susanna, "Poseidon" stood as a narcissistic profession by Stahl who self-stroked his mammoth ego.

"Hercules I" contained a thick, jumbled mass of information. Susanna found this out of character for Stahl, but typical of Joe. She found lists of foreign dignitaries, royalty, and top U.S. government officials. It focused on the Middle East and North Africa. *Contacts? To buy guns? No. To sell guns?* "Hercules II" held thicker rosters of several thousand names with corresponding defense installations, military specialties, and contact information. She saw it as a gun-toter Rolodex for the paramilitary organization revealed by Lori's files. She placed the Hercules envelopes back in the drawer. She figured Stahl knew exactly where she stood and would give her enough chain to land herself in jail—or at the bottom of the Potomac.

Did he plant this for me?

She glanced at the clock. Her back tightened. As she tried to arrange the desk as she found it, she changed her plan and grabbed as many choice folders as she could. She hesitated, but grabbed the "Hercules" files and snatched a lone disk. Her mind raced. She thought about Joe as Stahl's son. "Hercules" and the power the name implied concerned her.

If she had to guess, Stahl had built more than a paramilitary outfit.

As she clutched her haul, Susanna heard the door close upstairs. Footsteps approached.

"Zeus? Where are you? Come here, my little Schatzie."

Zeus cowered at her feet. Susanna heard Manfred Stahl's voice calling for his dachshund. She mouthed "Go!" to the dog pointing in Stahl's direction as she heard Stahl make his way to the top of the stairs continuing to call for his dog. Susanna picked up a dull letter opener from the desk and crouched behind the leather sofa angled by the French doors. Zeus followed and trembled against her. A sharp pain radiated from the back of her skull. She swallowed her nausea as she felt the blood seeping on her thighs.

"Oh, God," she breathed and made the sign of the cross. It was the first time she had prayed to a higher being and not sworn since the academy.

Stahl called, "Schatzie," as he made his way toward his office. He had not yet reached the lower level. Susanna kissed the dog, apologized to the little fellow, threw her Hail Mary pass, and took cover. Stahl reached the final step as the dog landed at his feet.

"There you are," he charmed.

Stahl took the dog in his arms. Zeus growled at him. He slapped the dog hard enough to snap his head around. He hurled his tiny body against the French doors. Stahl spat something in German and slammed the bathroom door.

Susanna knew she had left her finger prints throughout the space, not to mention her blood. She had to get out that back door. She shoved the letter opener under the sofa and lunged for the door handle. Inches from freedom, she heard a dazed Zeus whimper and saw him struggle to stand. "No," she mouthed. Susanna reached for the dog, thought better of it, and said, "Sorry, little guy," as she rushed the French doors. She passed Hercules. "I can't take you, either, big guy. Not right now."

In fewer than 10 seconds she scrambled over the wall with the files, her Luger, and a large bag of wet towels.

As she ran, Susanna checked her bloody tights in the sunlight. To her astonishment, the stains had disappeared. She glanced at the bag of the paper towels she used to clean the blood from Stahl's chair. She held a bag of wet, clean, white towels. She clicked through the possibilities.

Was this purgatory or a descent into the safe haven of madness, she wondered.

The latter seemed more plausible, but she needed time. She bargained with God for just a bit of time before she lost her sanity. After all, she had stumbled upon God's work in revealing Stahl's scheme.

The matter of Mike Singleton remained. Maybe not the loftiest of pursuits, but one's worldly needs can cleanse another's soul.

CHAPTER TWENTY-FIVE

"What took you so long?" asked Joe Earhardt in his cynical way that Susanna deplored. He stood with arms folded and one foot on the aging concrete steps leading into Mike Singleton's building. He sported his trademark smirk, an attraction their first week together, but one that now made her seethe. Her pace slowed when she saw him. Stunned, she wondered if this vision of Joe related to her earlier blood-drenched mirage. She never imagined he would appear—just appear—out of nowhere.

Maybe he knew the route back from Hell.

As the breeze pushed her hair off her face, she approached holding the bag that questioned her stability.

"Joe," she sniffed. "I thought third-day resurrections had already been taken."

God damn Stahl.

The torn and blood-soaked Dress Blue blouse atop his black boxer-briefs made Joe look more like a New Orleans gutter punk than the Marine Corps's top Senate liaison. Her displeasure flashed its warning, "Rocky shoals ahead." She likened Joe's presence to being strapped to a mechanical bull. He had come back from the dead to trample what little she had in her life—again. She noticed Mike standing a few yards away. *Had he assisted Joe? Had he used her?* She would play out this pathetic scene starring the bold and once-promising. She figured they could stage a three-way cage fight. Disaster waited no matter what move she made.

Uneasiness engulfed the once-trusted friends turned loathsome rivals.

Susanna, Joe, and Mike stood motionless, eyeing one another, together for the first time in 16 years. Susanna's confidence turned to bitterness. Joe glowered with hate. Mike felt overwhelmed by sorrow and regret. Each concealed his or her interpretation of their tangled past.

Mike recalled when they met their first day at the academy. Three innocents on the taxpayers' dime. Susanna soon fell under the Earhardt spell, but meteors shooting across the night sky burned longer than Susanna's interest in Joe as far as Mike could tell, but neither acknowledged the end of the month-long affair. Mike made his move, but the watchful disapproved. Cavorting with a female midshipman stood as a crime as Joe had learned, but to do so with a roommate's property? As a known athlete, Mike escaped their wrath, but Susanna paid for their transgression.

Mike had betrayed and humiliated Joe. In turn, Joe shackled Susanna to an empty engagement and used it as a declaration of war against her and Mike. Joe had his, "You may fire when ready, Gridley," style. Susanna subscribed to, "Damn the torpedoes. Full speed ahead."

Her semester away at Coast Guard had brought them to this stand-off.

Given what Susanna had seen in Stahl's office, no one rose above suspicion. Her mind churned to process the scene. Mental flashes illuminated a jumble of memories, clues, and fears.

She looked at Mike again, certain he had betrayed her.

"Were you expecting him?" she asked, gesturing at Joe without the courtesy of turning her head toward him. "I get the midshipman roommate boy-bond bit, but you used me, Singleton?"

Mike could feel her anger. He pointed at Joe.

"Expecting *him*? Are you joking?" Mike said, incredulous.

She sensed an elaborate scheme to discredit her in front of Lori, derailing her shot at the elusive redemption she had created.

"You knew! You knew he was alive. Did you plan to catch up on old times and foreign military gunslingers? Split levee dollars?" she accused.

She slipped her fingers around the Luger's grip.

Mike saw her as paranoid and dangerous.

"I don't even know how to answer that."

He and Joe, despite sharing a room for four years, did not speak to one another their final three semesters. They let themselves believe their schedules conflicted and put up a good façade for the company. But Mike had betrayed Joe with Susanna. It tore at him more than the pain he caused his family when he walked away from his imperiled New Jersey home.

Great moves, he thought in retrospect.

Mike's decision to pursue the girl in his boyish fantasy remained unforgivable where one is measured by honor, an absolute state with no qualifiers. His world shunned failures, but somehow no one, except Joe, faulted him, though Mike carried the burden of his sins.

Susanna's fear of being made the fool eclipsed her need for truth. Mike understood her more than she would admit. Joe sensed opportunity. Watching the bitch and his old roommate claw at each other surpassed the satisfaction of great porn or high-grade heroine.

"What's the deal, Mike?" asked Susanna taking a step toward him. She waited.

Joe held Mike's interest. Something seemed very wrong to Mike.

That mother fucker. He's here to kill her.

The three-way standoff fell silent, but decades of anger bubbled to the surface.

"Lori called me a few nights ago. Worried, Joe," she said.

Susanna turned toward him with a cold and menacing look. The wavy ends of her hair fluttered in the breeze as she approached him.

"She worried about your safety and asked for my help to find you—like I'd ever want to find your lying ass again. I half-hoped your rumored suicide matched the truth."

Susanna hurled her barbs. She wanted to crush Joe. She studied his face and felt certain he arrived to finish her off.

But why now? Stahl?

"I agreed to help her. Then I find ..." Susanna almost mentioned the kidnapping, but stopped herself. She would have no way of knowing the details of Joe's disappearance, unless she had gotten the information from Stahl or someone else involved. She did not know if Joe and his father swapped secrets, so she chose her words. "... I find you here in Arlington," she recovered.

He repulsed her.

"You pathetic bastard," she yelled as she launched her phone at Joe's head. "Call Lori *now* and give her the miraculous news."

She trembled with rage.

Joe stood there looking at the phone on the step. A minute passed. He reached down. Another 60 seconds went by. It seemed an eternity. He looked at Susanna.

"I'll do it," said Susanna as she snatched back her phone. Before she could finish dialing Lori, Mike stopped her.

"Not yet, Susanna," he said. She had not heard him but saw him shaking his head.

"What do you propose?" she asked.

Mike sized up Joe. He had seen many kidnapping victims over the years. Even as an assassin, Joe seemed like he had other problems.

"Kidnapped?" asked Mike.

"Is it that obvious? Let's go inside," Joe said. He would tell Mike a rehearsed script of events, which did not include information about his father.

Marcasi can wait, he thought.

Susanna blocked them. "No. I'm not going inside any place alone with either one of you."

With the Luger in her right hand, she directed, "Turn around and walk to Mike's car."

The men looked at one another, then back at Susanna. Without another word they walked to the Land Rover. Susanna sat behind Mike and Joe.

"Drive onto Fort Myer," she instructed.

Susanna hid the gun under her thighs as they drove on the Army post yards from where they had stood.

"Keep going," she said as Mike looked back at her.

They drove the length of the installation and entered the large, crowded commissary parking lot. They sat in silence, but the tension tore at the three of them. Mike and Joe looked at one another.

"Park as close as you can," she said.

Even with the assured security of the Army post, she sensed that the boys conspired to move against her. She slipped the Luger from its hiding place and motioned with the loaded pistol.

"Now get out and stay ahead of me, but keep it close. Each of you grab a cart. I want to see your hands," Susanna instructed.

Joe and Mike shook their heads. She slipped the gun back into her pouch and out of sight. They knew she carried her weapon illegally on post as well as in the District. Both men knew her well enough to know her way trumped any law. They looked up at the threatening sky and back at the menacing woman.

"You've done enough damage for the three of us," said Joe to Mike, unprompted.

"I know," said Mike as they entered the store.

"I'll shop and you talk," she said. "It seems like poor Joe is now a victim of his father's ambition," revealed Susanna.

"What the hell do you know?" jabbed a surprised Joe.

She pointed at the men. "I've been angry at *you* and *you* and the academy and the fucking Marine Corps for almost half my life. I am filled with rage most days, but as much as I resent you, *Josef*, physically harming you won't make any of this right."

Josef Stahl. She could not help but reveal her hard-earned knowledge. But the concept made her angrier.

"Don't push me, Joe, or I will kill you here in the produce section."

Susanna's revelation startled Joe, but he thought it wise to let it go to see what else she might know. Joe looked up at the water-stained acoustic tiles and bright fluorescent lights. "Jesus Christ, Susanna," he said, his arms out stretched.

Susanna moved closer to Joe. Her body shook as she spoke, "I should have died that day at Quantico and again in New Orleans. But I guess you know that. Maybe God saved me for today. But I don't care anymore. Now move!"

Susanna tried to conceal herself in plain view. She hated herself, a prisoner of a life of damage inflicted. She grabbed a five-pound bag of russets and heaved it at Joe's head with a loud grunt.

Vengeance, she thought.

Reeling from Stahl's encounter with Lori, she wondered why she had survived. Betta, Mick O'Reilly, Joe Earhardt, and Manfred Stahl. Had she survived or had they broken her, piece by piece, along the way? She confronted gut-wrenching regret: Mike Singleton, who chose desire over honor, and Joe, a bloodied and broken man. She saw their pain but it did not compensate for her loss. The Naval Academy promised to be the foundation from which they would vault to lofty accomplishments. More lies. She saw no way to resolve this deep-rooted conflict.

They stood mired by the seedless grapes.

She turned without notice and tossed up her arms.

"You know, I'm done. Let the authorities sort this out."

Susanna meant God.

Neither Mike nor Joe wanted anyone outside their combative circle to know that Joe Earhardt lived. The men coaxed Susanna. She relented. She palmed a honeydew like a basketball into Mike's chest. For a moment, she pitied the boys who had provided some relief during those dark academy years.

Joe saw Mike out of the corner of his eye. *Successful, fucking handsome SEAL hero*, he thought. *The stuff you read about in the Post or cheap-ass novels.* Mike stole a legacy that belonged to Joe. He could not comprehend the meaning of a Silver Star, but he had not become a deceitful, disloyal fuck like Mike. He knew the whispers. He stood as the commandant's lackey as well as the Senate gigolo. As Manfred Stahl's only child, he carried an unfathomable burden as well as a probable death sentence.

Joe looked straight ahead. "Funny, we've all known each other forever. You, me, Mike. We're classmates. Company mates. For God's sake, Mike, we were roommates." He cleared his throat. "Susanna, if I recall, you fucked Mike while you were at Coast Guard, but refused to spread them for me, you low-rent whore."

Joe lunged at Susanna. The long-necked bottle of extra virgin olive oil became Susanna's defense. She connected with the left side of Joe's head. The bottle shattered when it hit the tile floor.

To her surprise, Joe staggered, but caught himself against the shelving. Joe's skin turned three shades of scarlet.

"You God damn slut," he yelled.

Heads turned.

"Shut up. Just, shut up," Susanna screamed back.

Mike agreed he had done the unthinkable. He had betrayed both of them, thrusting them into an untenable position. They pretended it did not happen. Though just two inches taller than Joe, Mike stood as a hulk of a man. Joe no longer sported the mass he did as a football player or young Marine officer. This Joe Earhardt had become a pale D.C. denizen, an unfortunate fact obvious to Mike when Joe surfaced. Mike watched Joe's lips tremble and a tear appear in the corner of his eye.

He hated Joe.

All held blame, Mike reasoned. He bit the inside of his right cheek as his hands shook. He reached for his concealed pistol, but knew it would end his career. Whom would he execute? Joe? Susanna?

Himself?

"Christ, Joe, just leave it alone." Mike stood tall like an oak. His breath pushed Joe's straight bangs farther to the side.

"What? You never fucked my fiancée?" he challenged, shouting up at his old roommate. Shoppers slowed and listened.

"Jesus, Joe, no," Mike said in an effort to close the chapter, move on, and appease his pit bull-like admiral.

Susanna watched the two argue.

"Did you visit her there?" Joe refused to let it go. His voice quivered as he fought back his tears.

"Did you spend time with my fiancée? Did you?" Joe screeched.

"It was the greatest day of my life," Mike stated, relieved of the burden he had carried.

***

As memories of Mike's visit to Coast Guard sent the tension between the three into overdrive, Mike reached for his vibrating mobile with an audible sigh of relief. He looked at the screen and smirked. He never thought he would be happy to hear from Ken Bartholomew.

"Singleton," he said, phone to his ear, shoulders relaxed for the first time since Joe appeared.

"Jesus, Singleton. You answered my call. I'm fucking honored. What the hell have you found?" asked the admiral, who paused to take a long drag of his latest cigarette.

"Well, Lieutenant Colonel Joe Earhardt for one thing," declared Mike.

"Christ, Mike. It's about God damn time. I have smoked three packs already today. I'll blame my death from lung cancer on your incompetence," said a sardonic Bartholomew.

Mike felt thankful for their friendship, especially given the armed commissary standoff.

Bartholomew's tone changed. "I'm not on speaker, am I?

"No, sir," responded Mike with some surprise.

"Good. Mike, how is he?"

"Alive. Fine. He says he was abducted from the bridge." Mike disappeared around the end of the cereal aisle. He lowered his voice,

"I think higher powers are involved."

"Well, you're just fucking brilliant, Mikey. My dead grandmother could have told you that," said Bartholomew sporting his combative mood.

"We're sorting things out." Mike knew the three stood unraveling their past together.

"We? Jesus, don't tell me Marcasi is still with you and you *three* are finding your inner selves?" asked Bartholomew.

Mike figured the admiral's summation came close.

"Christ, Mike, It is so God damn obvious. The only come-to-Jesus meeting will be in my office. Ditch Marcasi. Now," ordered the admiral.

Mike felt his face flush. "Uh, admiral, that's not a good idea. My guess is Stahl's involved, and he's got some grudge or something against Marcasi. She is bait for us, and as long as she is with me, she's safe. Trust me, we need her. She doesn't know it, but she needs us."

Bartholomew took a deep, satisfying drag from his filterless Camel.

"I want you and Earhardt in here ASAP. No Marcasi. Got it?" he instructed.

"Uh, yeah. Yes, Ken, I got it." Mike found the admiral's behavior odd and the request out of character.

Susanna's quizzical look met Mike as he rested his hands on this cart.

"Bartholomew. He wants Joe there now," said Mike.

Susanna looked at Mike. His unexpected mention of their time in New London left her ill. The Fort Myer ruse had not forced Joe Earhardt to his knees as she had hoped.

She had a fall-back plan: She prepared to shoot them both.

Mike and Joe looked down at their carts.

"Leave 'em. Walk out," she said as she pulled out her Luger. "Now. Stay a few steps in front of me."

She determined it unwise to kill them now. She needed more information.

"Drop me off at your place," Susanna instructed Mike, with the Luger pressed against his ribs.

"Are you sure? O ... OK."

Despite the pistol pointed at him, he wondered, *what is she planning?*

As Susanna began to exit the vehicle, Joe spoke, "I sat on the rail. It was supposed to be so easy." He swayed his head almost in a dreamlike state. "Just one shot. One. I'd slip unnoticed off the bridge into the river and out to sea. I timed it with the tide."

He looked at Mike. "I had a flawless plan until these two guys grabbed me from behind. I woke up in some warehouse. Tied up. Fuck, Mike, I was supposed to be dead. I need to die," he said as he grabbed Mike's arm, pleading. "It was supposed to be quick and easy." He started to cry and wiped his eyes. "Geez, you gotta rag or something?

"Mikey. Jesus, I'm not going to fucking Leavenworth. Lori can't lose her seat." He regained his composure. "You gotta help me, buddy."

Mike looked at the pitiful heap the handsome, dark-haired boy had become.

Joe's brief account of the bridge triggered more memories Susanna had the good fortune to obscure until that moment. The stench of gasoline and old, lead-painted wood burning around her permeated her senses. A decade later she still awoke each night gasping through the toxic fumes of the fire that almost consumed her. The gut-wrenching details of the rape on Dauphine Street became clearer. The sensation felt fresh, as if it happened that morning. She had no escape and God had no mercy for her.

She had become a prisoner of her own sought-after truth.

CHAPTER TWENTY-SIX

Lori sat in her Russell Building office staring across the room. She started to call Susanna several times, but put the phone down on each attempt. Stahl remained her problem. Her time with Susanna long had passed. No good would come from dragging her deeper into this mess. Her eyes stung as a wave of overwhelming loss washed over her. Bob Mixon knocked on her door and peered in.

"Lori ..." Mixon said.

She turned her head away. Lori did not want him to see her tears or the fresh bruise left by Manfred Stahl's hand during their "meeting" in the conference room.

"Lori, is everything OK?" Mixon asked. He could see the tear-spotted blotter.

"Of course, Bobby," she said.

Her false optimism signaled a problem, he thought, but what could he do? He only let her call him "Bobby," and would do anything she asked.

Lori turned to face him. "It's late. Why don't you and the others call it a day?"

Mixon looked at her again and saw her mottled red and purple cheek. The trickle of blood running from her swollen lip caught his attention. She saw his face. She touched the throbbing split.

She had become a warrior like Susanna. She had eked out a win in her latest battle, but would have to don full armor to win the war.

"Lori," gasped a confused Bob Mixon who almost climbed across her desk in an effort to assist her.

"Just forget about this, please, Bobby, and tell no one," she said as she waived him off. "I need for everyone to leave."

Mixon had never seen a woman battered or witnessed any physical altercation on the Hill.

"Understand, senator. You have my numbers. I'll check in with you in a couple of hours," he said.

He tried to sound confident, but she could see the matter had shaken him.

Lori looked at the space in front of her, uncertain if she had wrestled her life back from Stahl. He had come to her office to remind her that she waded as deep in "patriotic appropriations" as anyone. She had betrayed her own people for what she considered a greater good. Another tear appeared in her right eye. She concluded Stahl still owned her even without her Monroe Class vote. How could she have been so naïve? He could slap her around and she could do nothing to stop him. She sat thinking of a way out when she was startled by her cell phone.

"This is Lori O'Reilly," she said. Her voice caught in her throat as she choked back the tears.

"Lori, I've seen him. Joe's alive," Susanna said, hoping she pleased Lori.

"You've seen him?" Lori's mood lifted.

"Yes, yes. He didn't want me to tell you, but I promised you I'd do my best to find him. Well, he turned up. I didn't really find him," Susanna said.

"How is he? What'd he say?" Lori asked sensing something amiss.

"He's fine. I'll let him explain. I think he's heading over to the Hill now," Susanna said, though she knew he had gone to the Pentagon.

She craved Lori's approval.

Lori hesitated, "Do you believe him, Susanna? Your judgment is much better than mine. What should I do?" Lori's brief joy turned to concern.

Far from the jubilant reaction Susanna had expected, she sensed Lori's suspicions.

"It doesn't matter what I think. He's alive, Lori."

"Susanna, did you get my message?" Lori asked, worried and preoccupied.

"I did, but I doubt I'll have to get into your computer." *Again*, she thought.

"Susanna, listen to me." Lori's voice softened to a whisper. "Those files on the computer are marked 'Hercules.' I have some voice recordings with 'Hercules' included in the file name. You'll see them." A long pause followed. Neither women spoke. "I just want you to know they're there in case I can't get to them. I've told no one else, not even Bobby." She paused. "Please, keep an eye on the Monroe Class frigate vote."

"Oh. OK." said Susanna. If Lori spoke in code, Susanna could not decipher it.

"I love you, Susanna."

Susanna found Lori's voice eager and nervous, very different from her earlier message.

The line fell dead.

Lori stared ahead recalling the night the girl most envied died, only to be reborn moments earlier in her stand-off with Manfred Stahl. *Rebirth followed by eternal life?* the senator wondered.

Sitting alone in her Senate office, Lori began to understand Susanna possessed a strength Lori long resented.

One Saturday, 16-year-old Lori O'Reilly sat behind the wheel of brother Tim's new white Bronco, eager to show off her driving skills. Several hours into an unchaperoned sex-for-booze fest at classmate Mary Sleno's house, at least 15 boys and girls squeezed in the vehicle. Tim jumped on the tailgate when he saw his sister driving away his prize.

Lori sped down river from Audubon Park. She caressed the pearlescent steering wheel with her left hand and took swigs from a vodka bottle with her right.

She had started drinking hours earlier at the basketball game.

The Bronco rolled as a four-wheeled open bar. Bottles of spirits passed from mouth to mouth. After another gulp of her father's top-shelf Russian import, Lori announced, "One hundred dollars says I can hit 100 miles per hour on Tchoupitoulas!" Her friends cheered, chanting, "Go! Go! Go!" The needle passed 80 mph. The live oak canopy and the 140 proof in her veins obscured her vision.

The vehicle rocketed toward the intersection with Napoleon Avenue, and music venue Tipitina's came up fast on the left. She glanced at the speedometer. It approached 110 mph when Peter Mancini, a 21-year-old Marine reservist and up-and-comer on the Zydeco scene, stepped off the curb. The impact with the Bronco amputated his limbs and decapitated him. The drunken students continued to chant. Lori felt a bump and thought she hit a trash bag. John Fogerty and "Bad Moon Rising" deafened her. She already had driven on the sidewalk as well as the grassy neutral ground. Tim also felt the bump, but hovered, preoccupied with unbuttoning Mary's blouse. Lori turned left at Louisiana and took St. Charles back to the party as it broke up, courtesy of the frazzled neighbors and the NOPD. Lori's friends climbed out the windows and she and Tim headed the one-half mile home.

Tim climbed into the passenger seat. Too drunk to drive, he felt grateful Lori handled the evening as she always did. She parked by the curb for about 20 minutes before she turned in the gated driveway. As the garage door opened, she saw her father and younger brother, Paul, standing back by the work bench shielding their eyes from the headlights. Lori stopped. She saw the look on her father's face. Mick O'Reilly motioned her in and closed the door.

The Bronco proved the accuracy of the call he had received. The force of the impact with Mancini crushed the front grille as well as the left-center of the hood. Mancini's blood and tissue fragments covered the front of the Bronco. Mick O'Reilly shook his head. Tim slumped, unconscious from the alcohol. Lori knew something terrible had happened. She met her father in front of the vehicle and muffled her screams as she covered her mouth with both hands. The grief-stricken father opened his arms as his daughter buried herself in his chest.

Susanna heard the noise in the garage and stumbled upon the tragedy. She turned to leave, but Mick motioned for her to stay. Susanna saw it as a family matter, but Mick O'Reilly had lost his princess that night. He needed help.

Lori sat in her darkened office. She forgave her father and Susanna. She took responsibility for her fall.

Mick O'Reilly flung the passenger door open. He grabbed Tim's bicep with his monstrous hands and yanked him onto the garage floor. Paul got him on his feet as he vomited beer and pizza on the door of his mother's Mercedes.

"We gotta take care of this," declared Mick.

"You want me to dump it in the river, Daddy?" asked a groggy Tim, unsure what had happened. He feared the giant of a man, and remained eager to please his father.

"No, I need for you and Paul to scrub this thing down with bleach. Go out River Road across the river way past Marrero out where it's black, pitch black. Scrape off the VIN everywhere it appears. Then torch the son of a bitch," instructed Mick, shoving a gas can into his son's chest. "But take out all your crap. Strip it for the whore it is. I want that thing naked before it burns." He looked at his bewildered boy. "I'll get you another car, God damn it. Tim, just get it done."

Lori turned unsure what to do.

"Lori, go inside with Susanna."

Lori placed her head on her desk and remembered how Susanna lay in her bed with her as she cried. Susanna wiped her tears. She ran her ring finger through her hair. She ignored the Quarter-like stench emanating from her pores. Susanna's touch calmed Lori. The girls did not exchange a word. The time for judgment had passed; the torch moved to Susanna.

The media frenzy over Mancini's death made Joe's disappearance years later seem even more pointless. Few cared. Only the Post ran its brief, flaccid piece on Joe the Jumper, as Susanna began to call him. Joe stood as a nobody. His colleagues viewed him as a sex slave to the over-50 set and a boot licker at best. He did not have the panache of the Gangland wannabes brandishing their stolen pieces beneath Susanna's Fourteenth Street window. The body of a District thug, a good boy, of course, ran as headline fodder. Lori thought of how Joe had longed for combat and medals for battlefield bravery. He never got them, not that it would have mattered.

Lori thought of secrets she never shared. Susanna never knew Joe told Lori he would soon leave active duty to get into something more lucrative. He would scoop up his senatorial charge in his arms and talk of his turn at the money trough. He would buy her that 3-carat emerald-cut she had her eye on and be by her side forever.

CHAPTER TWENTY-SEVEN

Joe settled into his seat and eyed Mike. "So, the bitch is gone. What do you want to know?"

Mike sat with his hands on the steering wheel watching as Susanna walked to his apartment. The three had found no resolution, just pain and regret. His body sat frozen on the Rover's bench. He turned toward Joe, who stared back at him. Mike shook his head, hesitant to take his old friend in like a prisoner. Joe nodded. Mike put the Land Rover into gear, glanced at Joe again and decided on a scenic route to the Pentagon. Maybe through Maryland. It would give them time to talk.

As they drove high along the Potomac, Joe pulled out two surviving Cuban cigars from his soiled uniform jacket. He handed one to Mike and extended his flickering lighter as a peace offering.

Mike noticed Joe slip a phone back into the cigars' hiding place.

"Your phone survived the kidnapping?"

"Yeah, and good thing I have both. These idiots insist I carry two. Mikey, I hate fucking Washington," said Joe, frustrated.

"So, Mike, what the fuck can I tell you? That's how this works, right?" asked Joe in his smug way.

Mike drew his pistol and pressed the accelerator. Joe clung to the passenger door and dash.

"What the hell are you doing, Singleton? Tryin' to get us killed?" yelled Joe.

"Yes," responded Mike as he pointed the gun at Joe.

The vehicle became airborne at 95 mph. Mike glanced in his rearview mirror, slammed the brakes, and skidded across the median heading back toward the Pentagon.

"What the fuck? You're as crazy as she is!"

You will never understand her, Earhardt, Mike thought.

"This is your fault, Mike. You owe me, buddy. Let me out now."

Mike ignored him. He had broken free of their past.

"Ken, we're pulling into North Parking."

***

"Singleton and Earhardt, two of my favorites," Bartholomew said as he motioned the men into the stale-smelling office. The putrid scent of cherry air freshener caught Mike by surprise.

"Christ, Earhardt, sit. Sit. You've had quite a time." He turned to Mike, "Mikey, stand by the hatch, but keep it open."

Bartholomew took a drag from his cigarette and rested it on the crystal ashtray. Another burned behind him on a stack of papers near his bank of computer screens.

"Door's wide open for you, Joe. What can you tell me?" asked Bartholomew.

Joe turned and looked at Mike and then back at the admiral. Bartholomew studied Joe in the haze from behind his desk.

"Hey, Mike. I think I got it from here. Just close the door behind you," said the admiral.

Mike's look of shock changed to realization. *You fucking used me.* Bartholomew could not have shown his hand more clearly, Mike thought. Without a word, he left the admiral and Joe and stormed out of the building.

***

Ken Bartholomew paced as he spoke, "Joe. Joe. Josef, I expected you to be more like Fred when we entered into this arrangement." He slammed his fist on the desk.

Ashes shot at Joe.

"No one jeopardizes this operation. Not you, not Stahl, not the fucking pope."

Joe reached for his Cubans, but the admiral's wrath made him reconsider the move.

***

The dimness of the room set her imagination afire. She felt the aura of a tribal council around the dining table. She met with her trusted advisor, a three-legged-but-lethal Rottweiler as she waited for the chief who had enemies to slay at the five-sided fortress.

The door flung open and the knob dented the wall as it had many times before.

Susanna rose to welcome the chief of the SEAL tribe.

He stopped in the doorway.

"I need you," she said without blinking.

Mike looked at Susanna figuring something had happened. He looked around and saw the war zone he had called a living room. He waded through a sea of white polyfill. His sofa sat reduced to a metal frame with wet, chewed fabric fragments. He walked toward the kitchen fearing what he might find. The sink sat empty and the countertops, bare. Every conceivable cooking implement lay strewn on the linoleum. Dirty dishes appeared licked clean.

His sternness melted.

For the first time in 20 years, he felt at home. He had not enjoyed such abject chaos since his boyhood in New Jersey.

"Marcus?" he asked Susanna as he picked up a punctured soup can and some piece of plastic he no longer recognized.

"Mike, I'm so sorry. I'll replace everything. He is such a good boy," she said.

Marcus heard his name and lumbered his way to his host. Mike genuflected and wrapped his thick arms around the slobbering dog.

God damn dog. He hated it when Susanna was right.

"We need to go through this crap," she said, gesturing at the table top.

"You're not finished yet? I don't get a full report? Geez, I had planned on some heavy drinking," he said.

It must have gone badly with the admiral, she thought.

"Mike, are you OK?" she asked.

Mike had wanted to pose that question to her. He could only imagine what disturbing secrets she uncovered in the files.

He sighed, still surprised, "Ken tossed me for a private lap dance with Joe." He felt Bartholomew had cut him from the team.

She showed no reaction.

Mike watched Susanna as she sat at the dining table surrounded by files. He looked into the paradise he found in her eyes. They had lost so much.

"Hey, are you hungry?" he asked, trying to shake off the admiral's rejection.

"Nah," she grunted, preoccupied.

"Wanna beer?" he asked.

She tilted her chin to her chest with a look that said, "You can't be serious."

"Oh, that's right." Mike had not been with one woman long enough to understand the protocol.

"Can we get to work on this? I don't think we have much time." She had grown impatient.

Mike pulled out two cigars from his utility jacket.

"Cuban?" he asked.

"Ugh!" She grabbed the cigar.

"Bartholomew did what?" she finally exclaimed. Mike's revelation hit her. Hard.

"He wanted to talk to Joe—alone," Mike shrugged.

"Oh, no. No. No. No. Mike," she said.

"I know what you're thinking, but I just can't imagine he's involved," said Mike.

Susanna sighed in frustration. She felt disaster imminent. Still clad in black, she sat and studied the papers on the dining table. An orange Lucite three-bulb fixture dangled over the center of their war room. Susanna glanced at her computer screen. She continued to hover with her fat cigar jammed in the right side of her mouth like Winston Churchill.

"What's churning in that mind of yours?" Mike asked as he dumped his clothes off the matching dining chair. He popped the cap from the warm beer Marcus left for him.

"Aside from the fact that our charming Secretary of Defense is Joe's daddy and the admiral is God-knows-what?" she tossed back.

Mike looked off to one side. "Well, Marcasi," he pursed his lips and sucked in the air like Bartholomew dragged on his Camels. "That's fuckin' brilliant," he barked, doing his worst impression of Ken Bartholomew.

"We've been watching Earhardt at DIA for two years and figured as much. And we pulled Joe's birth certificate to confirm it. They behave more like master and servant in some over-the-top medieval melodrama than father and son. Joe plays hunchback to Stahl's archdeacon."

Mike took a few sips of his beer. "Professor Earhardt always seemed too weak to have spawned Joe. When we were in all that trouble with our Army-Navy joke, the good professor paced wringing his hands worried about his precious tenure—not Joe. Only someone like war-hero nut job Stahl could have saved our asses. I had my suspicions then. Well, good for them. I hope they're happy," he said.

Mike pointed to the Earhardt pile. Susanna pushed it across the table.

"But why would the admiral want to meet with Joe? It just seems he would have other priorities than to meet with the Corps's Senate whore and a disgraced one at that," said Susanna.

"Leavenworth for 50," he said, referring to the federal prison and game show, "Jeopardy."

"Stop, this is serious," she laughed.

"Susanna, this is Joe," deadpanned Mike.

Susanna threw her head back at the thought of the Joe Earhardt-Ken Bartholomew reunion. Then-Midshipman Joe Earhardt engaged in all-out war against Lieutenant Commander Ken Bartholomew. Bartholomew resented Joe as a kid of privilege who played the part to extreme. Their conflicts became legend.

"Bartholomew wanted Joe to himself. I guess I've lost my most-favored boy status," repeated Mike, in disbelief.

"That makes no sense. Do you think it relates?" she asked.

"Of course it relates. It all relates. Bartholomew is using me to some end, but don't ask me how. Yet," he said.

Susanna pushed another stack to Mike and gave him control of the computer. He moved to where he had more room to work. She had slipped the latest Hustler magazine into a folder at the bottom of the stack. She saw the humor.

"I assume you have information from Joe," she said perched on the bottom step.

"No," Mike responded without explanation. He felt embarrassed that he had squandered his opportunity with Joe. He thought the mistake would cost them. *God damn Marcasi*, he thought. Susanna remained at the forefront of his mind.

She thought it better the letter the topic drop.

"I think we can agree 'Hercules' is a paramilitary company," he stated.

Susanna nodded.

Mike continued, "New Orleans diverted our attention to the levees. Though they have provided seed money, the answers are here." Mike gestured at the mass of information strewn before them.

He glared at Susanna still aghast he went along on her New Orleans junket.

She waited on his next thought.

Mike shook his head. "This is Stahl's baby. He jockeyed for position to head the Armed Services Committee and then arranged to be named Defense Secretary to support his business ventures."

Susanna nodded.

Like Moses with the Ten Commandments, Mike held up the thick files Susanna took from Stahl's office.

"It's all here. This is his force." He tossed one stack on the table. "Look. Hercules LLC purchased thousands of acres in central Louisiana, a place where the training of legions of paramilitary would go unnoticed. My guess is his area abuts Fort Polk to camouflage the sounds of tactical engagements, if nothing else. I think my office can find it using the satellite."

He tossed another stack. "Thousands of men await Stahl's command. Read the names." He tossed another stack. "Add tens of thousands more who have the skills he needs. Look. You can see all the personal information on males in the infantry, ordnance, and artillery fields as well as electronics and explosives experts, Special Forces professionals and others—you know the types. Where else is a sniper going to go after he hangs up his uniform?" Mike flipped through the pages. "I see ... hmmm... yeah, supply pros and financial people, too."

He shook his head. "The drawdown of the services in this economy has sent these guys running to Manfred Stahl." He slammed down another list. "But, as you found, this is his recruiting Rolodex. "These guys are on active duty but close to separation.

"Given that money on his off-shore coral reef, 7,000 names appear on the Hercules payroll," he said as he alt-tabbed to another screen. "This report from last week projects that number to jump to 20,000 by July." He alt-tabbed again. "This graph shows almost exponential growth into September 2001," he said.

"That takes a lot of cash," Mike said.

She watched him.

"Susanna, he has the means to build more than an army," Mike stated, but he found it difficult to believe.

Susanna nodded. Stahl's penchant for the unconventional fueled him. Brilliant though dangerous, no one could match him. His methods triggered speculation around the Corps and the Capitol, but found acceptance with those he dazzled. Crushing weak nonbelievers increased his already voracious appetite for power.

Physical, adrenaline-pumping violence made Stahl unstoppable. The company of attractive young males who could commit violent acts without question further heightened his pleasure. Such boys' value extended beyond dollars. A strong Stahl and a virile force of well-muscled males would prove a lethal combination.

"He moved to DoD to grow his business," said Susanna.

"It's more than that." Mike thought about what Susanna said. "He needs the prestige as Defense Secretary, but he has to move as an independent broker—no constituents, no fellow senators, no burden of reelection."

Mike paused.

"But what is his end game?" posed Mike.

He looked at the figures. "We're missing something. A project as immense as Hercules needs more money now, and maybe a continuous infusion of cash," he said.

"Those bills you asked about. Sometimes someone cannot get a bill passed or can't secure White House backing. In those cases someone might pass legislation on one program to fund another," said Susanna.

"A little lawmaker roulette." Mike stated, nodding.

Susanna sat back in a gnawed recliner. "Well, yes. We rob Gaston to pay Thibodaux. It seems this is how Stahl paid for Hercules—the levee money."

Susanna leaned forward, her boots lost in the sea of white.

"We'd introduce legislation and rustle up cosponsors from different interests and from different corners of the political planetarium. We'd tie the bill to as many states as possible adding as many amendments as necessary to secure passage. The cosponsors get the money they've been gunning for, and we get our $500 million."

Mike slouched and folded his arms across his chest.

She gave him a sideways glance. "Casinos don't come cheap, Mike," she said.

She scooted next to him and plopped her feet on the smoky gray glass table. She folded her arms just as he had with some satisfaction.

"Sometimes other people get tied in. It's unintentional. The president comes to mind," she said.

"The president?" asked Mike.

Susanna understood the gravity of the revelation and whispered, "Yes, the president. Stahl has owned him since before the president served in the Senate."

"Here." Mike tossed the torn ledgers at her. "Vietnam, right? Selling arms in country? Maybe why his men shot him? Regardless, he has graduated to selling the services of armed men and possibly entire units." He pointed to the thick, modern books of paper. "Those ledgers? In addition to bodies, he needs fire power. He also wants to sell weapons but cannot get his hands on the guns and missiles from Capitol Hill, but can shop for whatever he and his clients want from the comfort of his Pentagon office."

"What are you saying?" asked Susanna.

"He's providing a service," Mike said.

"You're defending him?" she said.

"No, but paramilitaries make a lot of sense. I don't think I can count the number of times I wished I could have paid for a unit and some additional firepower out of my own pocket."

Mike pulled Susanna in front of the screen. "Look at this. He provides follow-on weapons training to his people. It appears they must fire 'expert' or they're tossed from the program." He continued to scan. "The self-defense and fitness programs are taken right from the Special Forces' latest techniques." Mike continued to read. "In fact, this is copied word-for-word and move-for-move." Mike sat back. "They have an extensive Israeli-style hand-to-hand program, too, something I wish we'd do more of. They also get more explosives training than our top experts.

"But we can prove nothing. Stahl can dodge any allegations on the levee money. He stuck Joe with that mess. No one will care about the levees. They never have. However, any other legislation that vectors money into his paramilitary coffers could send him away," said Mike.

The screen had Mike's attention. "Look at this. Remember how it appeared the levee money went to Joe and then to an unknown account?" Mike pointed at the screen. "The money traveled through a number of gates before it landed in the offshore account. I had expected just one person authorized on the account, but it's not Stahl. I think it is this 'Poseidon,'" said Mike.

He turned to Susanna. "I think you're right. 'Poseidon' is our guy," he said.

"Poseidon may have kept us alive so far. I think he has something on Stahl, but, on a larger scale, poses more of a danger to all of us than Manfred Stahl. Grab up Stahl, Poseidon slips back under the surface. We have to find him before he submerges. Stahl is our best bait. If we're lucky—or smart—we can lure Stahl *and* Poseidon and reel them in before they get away," reasoned Susanna.

"Would Joe know Poseidon's identity?" asked Susanna.

"Maybe, but I doubt it. Anyway, he is in Bartholomew's hands," answered Mike.

She grabbed back her computer. After a few key strokes she pushed it back to Mike.

She tossed a stack of papers that came to rest by his left hand. "Here. The Monroe Class frigate bill. One of the biggest sham pieces of legislation ever."

Mike looked at her. "You ... knew about this?"

"Yeah, it's important enough that Lori told Stahl she would not be present for the vote. He was so angry he knocked her to the floor. Stahl and Poseidon want those funds. I think Poseidon will reveal himself or herself for $33 billion."

"Why didn't you tell me?" he asked.

"I started to on the plane to New Orleans, but I did not see that the bill or altercation related to Joe. I'm trying to make sense of it as well. It wasn't an issue until now."

"Have you ..."

"Contacted her? No."

She lied

"I wouldn't know what to say to her," she said.

"Susanna, if this isn't the answer, it brings us close." Mike said.

Mike thought for a moment. "Wait."

He reached for the disk from Stahl's desk. Mike saw the same files as Susanna had earlier.

"Susanna, hand me Joe's ledger from the bridge."

Water stains smeared a number of pages. Mike knew the author as soon as he saw it. He thought he held the musings of a crazed, dishonored Marine officer. He scanned the pages looking for references to criminal activities. Instead of the bitter and self-centered Joe that he expected, he discovered a thoughtful man that Mike assumed no longer existed.

Joe Earhardt had recounted the history of his father's ventures from the bizarre, like Stahl's penchant for slapping Joe around to working naked in his old Senate office. It seemed Stahl also would recite Robert Duval's lines from "Apocalypse Now." The video played on continuous loop in his home and Hill offices. Lieutenant Colonel Robert Kilgore would declare, "I love the smell of napalm in the morning," while Stahl banged his South American prostitutes or danced an Argentine Tango.

Mike passed the ledger to Susanna as she sat next to him. She read, "Until now, I have called these people 'mercenaries,' but ol' Fred shakes his fist, 'My boys are God damn patriots!' Whatever. Security gigs have kept the easily bored (and mentally challenged) trigger pullers busy, but Fred believes Hercules will revolutionize warfare. Dad's right, and he will cause systems to change, governments to fall, and his world, which is achievable, will render us one nation under a demigod. Thirty-three billion dollars would transform his band into a force of testosterone-hyped, gun-slinging, well-respected shock troops he has trained them to be. He will rent units large and small to those with the deepest pockets. His strongest relationship seems to be with one well-placed Saudi prince with a camel racing habit."

Susanna continued reading, "Fred will supply battalions to the highest bidder and will push a Congress that despises him, but is tethered to him, and a cowering president who dares not cross him, to all but scuttle a bloated Defense Department. Ultimately, with some tweaks to the Constitution, the president would order the men of Hercules to fight the nation's wars and defend its borders—for a price."

Joe knew his father saw him as little more than a loose end. He felt compelled to expose his bastard of a biological father or die in obscurity.

He scrawled his love for Lori and assured she had no involvement in his father's scheme.

Susanna spun around and knelt on the cushion by Mike, grabbing his arm with both hands. Her cherry blossom-colored nails dug into his bicep.

"Mike, in exposing Hercules, Joe thought he could save Lori. He would die for her."

Mike remained dubious of Joe's written confessions and retorted, "Joe's apparent confession proves little. We are closer to a jail cell than Manfred Stahl at this point. And if Stahl's as confident as Joe writes, why the interest in you, Susanna?"

***

"Christ, Mike, he's gone," said Ken Bartholomew as Mike answered his mobile on the last ring.

Mike sat forward.

"Earhardt?" he asked.

"Who else?" said Bartholomew.

"What, what happened?" Mike's suspicions grew. He began to pace.

236

"The fucking Marine Corps got involved and had their people here. Stahl's office sent people, too. It was standing-room only at DIA. They sent some God damn private-hire guys. Don't ask. I don't even know how they made it through security. They took him out," said Bartholomew.

Took him out of the room, or took him out forever? Mike knew this type of interference in his business would upset Bartholomew, but Ken seemed almost calm—for Ken.

Mike said nothing.

"Singleton. He's either coming back to you, his ol' boy toy, or off to hide with his whore on the Hill. I don't think he's running to Daddy," said the admiral.

"OK."

"OK what, Mikey?"

"I got it," said Mike.

"Admiral, by any chance did you notice if Earhardt had his phone on him?" Mike asked.

"Phone? The God damn phone? Fucking Corps had it and handed it to him as they were leaving my office," came Bartholomew's stilted response.

The admiral had lied and Mike knew it.

"Thanks, Ken. Things are clear. I got it," said Mike.

What the hell? Maybe I should just join up with Fred Stahl.

***

"When I met with Lori that night, she seemed panicked about Joe, but the terror in her eyes shot past the subject of Joe Earhardt and the bridge. I felt enveloped by her fear as we spoke in the cemetery." Susanna shuddered. "I had a misted window on the future and left with a sense of dread," she said.

"Like the hammer has been cocked but you can't see the gunman?" offered Mike, beginning to see the connection.

Susanna thought for a second. "Worse. When you find yourself alone and beaten and have lost the will to fight for your life. When he extinguishes all hope."

Mike looked away. He knew she referred to herself.

"But there's always hope. Joe was Lori's hope and he saw her as his salvation," she said.

She fell silent. Susanna's thoughts turned to crack the code of the man next to her. She brushed his thigh allowing her hand to linger. Was he her gate keeper and protector? Did he still love her or had that ship sunk?

Mike turned and saw her slumped on the deflated cushions. He could not count the times she had fallen asleep atop her academy rack, or bed, when he had planted himself in her room. She fell asleep on Joe's rack as a matter of routine. Getting her down from the top bunk always posed a challenge. He only dropped her once. The gash to her head didn't require stitches, though the doctor said she had a mild concussion. Mike blamed Joe, as he always did. Tonight, she slept in his living room. He would have liked something grander for her, but she did not seem to mind.

"C'mon, Marcasi. You take the bed. I'll take what's left of the couch," he whispered as he carried her up the stairs.

Mike pulled back the sheets and placed her on his side of the queen bed. He pulled the covers up to her chest. As he turned, a hand grabbed his thigh. He tried to pull away, but she embedded her nails.

She looked up at him. "Stay." They had played this scene before. He bent over to kiss her cheek as she turned so her lips would meet his. Even with one knee by her side and one leg on the floor she pulled her legs up and hooked her feet around his waist. Her arms clung to his neck as she pulled him closer.

He did not just love her. He had carried her inside of him since the day they met. The hurt. The anger. The perennial flame drew the moth closer. She slipped out of the Lycra that masked her beauty and rolled on her back, knees slightly parted. Susanna tugged at his waist and smiled. Desire overwhelmed him as he touched her hair. He hesitated. He felt ready but embarrassed to reveal his yearning.

Maybe she would reject him. Maybe she would judge him. Mike expected Ken Bartholomew to appear in his room or maybe a raid by Stahl's gun-toters. But all remained quiet. Mike reached behind her and pulled her hips to meet his. The past few days proved irresistible foreplay as had the past years. She realized the stand-in boys and her mental re-creations could not compare to Mike Singleton guiding them through their night as one.

CHAPTER TWENTY-EIGHT

It was not yet 6 a.m. when Susanna awoke alone, bed sheets soaked with passion. Mike Singleton's scent surrounded her. She crept down the stairs in one of his XXL T-shirts from the laundry basket. An old Navy lacrosse shirt. The holes and stains attested to its age.

"What happened?" she queried, grinning and yawning as Mike shoved a mug of steaming coffee in her hands.

"I think I must have fallen asleep, and you gave up on me and went to bed," he said.

"That's what I thought," she said nodding her head. "Well, you probably should be more alert. I know you want to satisfy your guests," she teased.

He nodded, double entendre noted.

Mike stood on the tattered carpet. The room had gone from the aftermath of a Category V hurricane named Marcus to order she could only recall from Mike's room at school. Susanna's eyes examined Mike from his hand-painted mug, over his bicep and well-developed deltoid, across to his perfect pectorals, down to abdominals touched by the hand of God, to the waistband of his boyish pajama bottoms. She had the honor of running her lips across his body map in complete bliss. She looked up at his face. He smiled and she felt sure he read her thoughts and approved.

The silence with him intoxicated her as had consummating their union.

"Gotta TV?" she asked, breaking the tension.

Mike pointed at the 48-inch screen across from her.

"Oh. Remote?" she asked.

He walked toward her. Her feet sat on the smoky, 1980s coffee table, one of the few items that survived the Marcus rampage the day before. He reached for her leg; she closed her eyes. Susanna peeked to see Mike had retrieved the device resting under her feet.

"Oh. Thanks." She stung with embarrassment and he could tell. "Do you mind if I turn on the news?" she asked.

"Do you watch TV in the morning now?" He remembered she railed against it at the academy likening it to a cardinal sin.

"No, not really, but we have been hiding from reality for ... When was Stahl's ceremony?" Susanna shook her head knowing she had fallen behind on entries to the Times, but Bill had not called so, she must be safe—or fired.

She tried station after station. "Where's CNN? How can two places so close have such different cable line-ups? It's infuriating," she huffed.

She pulled her legs under her while watching the screen. She looked away toward the kitchen. Breaking News. "A senator has been found dead ..." flashed across the screen.

"Hey, Mike," she called.

He peered around the kitchen entry with a frying pan in one hand and whisk in another. "More coffee?" he asked eager to please her.

No one had been this nice to her, she thought.

"I'd love some. May I help?" She slinked into the kitchen.

As they spoke in the narrow galley, a picture of a smiling Lori popped up on the screen above footage of police removing what looked like a body bag from Russell Senate Office Building. Susanna looked back at the TV and forgot what she had seen seconds earlier.

"Well, this is cozy," Susanna said as she sashayed behind the chef.

"I know it's small, but it works for me. Omelets?" he offered.

Susanna smiled.

"I'll take that as a, 'Yes,'" he said.

She put her coffee down and worked her way past him a second time. "I saw something interesting on the news and can't recall what it was." Her arm brushed against his. "Singleton, you can be distracting. Maybe it will come up again." Her firm stomach pressed against him as he stood at the stove. She sang, "It was long ago and far away ..." borrowing again from one of their road trip's anthems. Both grinned without the other's knowledge.

"There's always breaking news with these guys," opined Susanna.

Mike heard her gasp.

"Again, Louisiana Senator Lori O'Reilly has died. Her death remains under investigation." Lori's official portrait lingered on the screen.

Susanna and Mike looked at one another. Susanna said nothing, her mind in overdrive.

"I have to call Mr. O'Reilly before hears it from someone else," she rushed and she pulled her book from her case.

"Susanna, ..." started Mike

His phone rang.

"Christ, Singleton. Are you still with Marcasi?" asked Bartholomew.

"Good morning, admiral. What may I do for you today?" Mike asked with intended sarcasm.

"Well we have a new issue, not really our problem, but I think it relates to our topic. Have you seen the news?" asked the admiral.

"Yes. Confirmed?" he asked.

"If I didn't have it confirmed would I waste my breathe talking to a womanizer like you?" Ken Bartholomew harped on Mike's unenviable track record with women.

"Probably not," snapped Mike.

"These guys are into something, Mike. They kill a U.S. senator?" Bartholomew changed tone.

Ken Bartholomew hesitated. "I need Earhardt back, Mikey. He may be a thief and a gun runner, but I doubt he's a killer. Hell, he couldn't manage to kill himself. But, Mike, this one's easy. Earhardt's not going anywhere now that his girlfriend's dead. He's coming to you. Well, unless he finds another bridge. We have most of what we need, but I want it all."

Mike heard the layers of the admiral's demand, but it made little sense. He had no plans of asking Bartholomew for clarification. Mike doubted Joe murdered Lori, but figured he knew something about her death.

It all had to relate.

"Right ... admiral." Mike's hesitation sent its intended message.

Ken Bartholomew knew he had made a mistake in dismissing Mike with Joe in his office, but could not be sure the extent of the damage. He had groomed Mike for this moment and needed him unwavering and loyal. If the SEAL began to question, the intuitive Mike Singleton would uncover secrets like those surrounding the dead senator, something Bartholomew could not allow. Earhardt already ran loose with too much information, but remained the frightened, gutless boy his father rejected. Singleton proved Bartholomew's bigger concern, but saw a two-for-the-price-of-one opportunity.

"You'll see him soon. Grab him up again and I want you both back in my office. I don't care about his father or his Marine Corps." The admiral laughed, "You guys stave off my boredom. Thanks, Singleton."

Mike knew the admiral could be a caustic son of a bitch, but now tried to understand his motives. He hung up the phone and sent it crashing to the floor.

"Who? Wait! No one important, right?" asked a preoccupied Susanna.

Mike watched Susanna. He wondered how alone she felt. She lost a sister in Lori.

"Are you OK, Susanna?" he asked walking toward her.

Susanna looked away from the TV. "Uh, I'm fine. Really."

Mike thought she seemed like a delicate piece of fine china about to shatter.

"So, was that our confirmation?" she asked.

"Yeah, yeah it was." Mike hated to reaffirm her loss.

Susanna grabbed her phone and notebook. She started toward the door, but returned to her place at the dining room table and started to work.

She needed Mike more than she needed to be on site.

***

"Bob, yes. Yes, I know. That's why my first call is to you, Lori's chief of staff."

Susanna looked at Mike.

"Susanna, I'm not sure what to do. You'd think we were an office of lepers. No one will come near us," said a distraught Bob Mixon.

"Let me help you. We need a conference call in 20 minutes with your entire staff." Susanna listed the people needed for the looming telephonic meeting. "Just tell them I am representing the family. Tell them anything. We need to lay this thing out and coordinate our efforts. Twenty minutes." Susanna remained calm but spoke with urgency. She tried to conceal her continued frustration with Mixon. *Limp bastard. Not one of my better recommendations to Lori.*

"OK. Got it." Mixon sounded lost in the suddenness of the tragedy.

"Bob, wait. We need Stahl's chief, too," she said.

"You want to involve Stahl's office? Forget it," he said.

"We can trust his chief," said Susanna.

Mixon sat in silence. He knew Susanna understood the realities of his job better than he did, even after four years.

"OK. Twenty minutes. Thanks, Susanna. I would never have ..." Mixon stumbled on his words.

"It's fine. Go!" she commanded.

Susanna sat at the table, a stream of tears raging down each cheek. Susanna started to make her next call, but she put the phone down, Mike watched. She picked up her mobile again and punched in the ten numbers. Mike saw her shudder.

Susanna's voice remained steady,

"Hey, good morning, Mr. O'Reilly. Yeah, yeah this is your lil'

Susanna." Susanna gulped and shook her head. "I'm fine. Mr. O, I need to talk to you. It's about our Lori." She listened as O'Reilly praised his eldest child whom he had terrorized.

Susanna's thoughts left Lori and moved to the years she suffocated under Mick O'Reilly's roof. Why had the Blessed Virgin abandoned her while Sick Mick climaxed at her feet? Susanna shook, crying harder than Mike had seen. He thought she cried for Lori. Susanna let out with an occasional, "Yeah, that's Lori!" in a quivering voice.

"Susanna, is there somethin' wrong? You can tell me, doll," coaxed Mick.

Susanna wanted to lash out at the man more vile than the street perverts she encountered as a child.

***

Mick O'Reilly knew his sins and understood he needed some sort of insurance to secure his place in heaven. He hated his children for not being Mick O'Reilly. He made Lori available to sloshed political cronies to prepare her for elected office for the sake of the family name. But saving Susanna from the Catholic mission seemed the sign from God for which he hoped. When he looked at Susanna Marcasi he felt certain the Madonna appeared to him. This blessed virgin came as his Golden Ticket to the feet of the Lord.

Mick wasted no time and dressed the child in the traditional blue and white robes soon after her arrival. He had small marble altar on which he placed her. Mick arranged Susanna as the master painters had portrayed the Virgin over the centuries.

Mick O'Reilly prayed to his child Madonna, asking her to intercede on his behalf with Jesus Christ. He would light candles at her feet. Susanna always feared the robes would catch fire. He burned foul-smelling incense that made her gag. She would run to the bathroom after his ritual and vomit.

For 13-year-old Susanna, escape seemed impossible. She had endured his fantasy for two years. She could don the robes or live on the streets, she reasoned. Betta had died, thanks to the drunken uncle-of-the-day plunging his truck into the Mississippi from the heights of the Huey P. Long Bridge. She thought life with her mother had been better than this gruesome ritual.

Susanna wrapped herself in her robes a she did each session and stood by the altar waiting for Mick O'Reilly. Though Mick always placed her on the altar like a doll, she turned and slipped her bare right foot on the cool marble with her hands on the flat surface for balance.

Mick O'Reilly came up behind her without a sound and grabbed her arm yanking her back. She fell to the floor. He stood above her. She looked at him, stunned, unsure what to do or say. She dared not move. She figured her days with the O'Reillys would end soon—if she survived the next few minutes.

In those tense moments with Mr. O'Reilly above her, she learned she had no fear of death. Dying at the hand of the bloated, red-headed oddity before her seemed absurd.

She would survive Mick O'Reilly or they would spend eternity in Hell together.

Mick knelt next to Susanna, his tears falling upon her robes. He reached into his pocket and pulled out a fighting knife, something Susanna had not seen before. Her eyes widened as she crept unnoticed like a crab away from his trap.

Mick O'Reilly fixated on the blade. With the knife in his right hand he raised his left arm and slashed across his wrist and down his forearm. He released a moan of passion as blood appeared and flowed from his wrists to his bicep. His breathing became labored. Susanna watched and backed further away. Placing the knife in his left hand, he raised his right arm and brought the blade across and down again. His loud cry of joy coincided with a thrust of his hips. As he lay on his back moaning, Susanna could see the large moist spot on the front of his trousers. He rolled over and crawled, smearing a path toward her. As blood dripped down his forearms, he touched her knees and lifted the robes, inch-by-inch, over her creamy, youthful skin. He stopped mid-thigh. With arms bathed in crimson, he wiped the blood from the shallow cuts in the smoothness between her thighs, and then down her legs.

Susanna shook, but remained silent.

Mick O'Reilly stopped when he got to Susanna's feet. He kissed the pink polish on her toes and gently picked up his Madonna in his arms and placed her on the altar. He dropped to his knees and began to weep. He begged for God's forgiveness.

She wanted to run.

Over the next several days, Mick O'Reilly confessed a litany of sins. Each session began with the bizarre cutting ritual; each day he climaxed with the second slice. He spoke of the people he had killed, those he had swindled, and the many women he had taken, most of whom came after his marriage to Kathleen.

Mick O'Reilly confessed what most had suspected about Lori's birth mother. Lori knew the truth that day crying in the lavatory. The nun rejected young Lori when she sought a closer relationship with her.

Mick O'Reilly disgusted Susanna. His confession was Lori's to hear.

She knew she had to leave the O'Reilly home and never return.

Susanna turned down the Tulane scholarship pushed on her and announced to the O'Reillys, as close to high school graduation as possible, her decision to attend the U.S. Naval Academy.

***

"Mr. O'Reilly, you know I love Lori, and I want you to hear it from me." Susanna wanted to crush him with the news. She drew a deep breath and paused.

"Something's happened to Lori." Susanna listened to the breathing on the other end. She knew his rhythms and she hated him. She couldn't think of a delicate way to break the news. Maybe that was OK, she thought.

She wanted him to hurt.

Susanna told him the police found Lori slain in her office. Silence followed on both ends of the phone. Mick finally asked a few questions in stunned disbelief. Susanna chose words that could heap the most guilt on him possible. The two fell silent again. She understood that, as the messenger, she would shoulder the burden of this sin. Her call probably signaled the beginning of the end of her relationship with her surrogate family, but that had happened as she posed on his marble altar.

Sick bastard dominated her thoughts.

Oblivious, Mick did not sense the gulf between them. He shared his wishes. Susanna nodded and agreed with the grieving father on the other end of the phone. She took a few notes. As she hung up she said, "I'll take care of it."

She thought, *you fucking freak.*

Mike's interest piqued from the call. He looked at Susanna. He would take a sign, but she looked at him, lips pressed together.

"One more call and I'll explain." She knew she would never give Mike the latitude he had granted her.

He nodded and walked out.

***

Roscoe Russell paced his office, ranting into the speaker phone on his desk when his mobile phone vibrated. He looked at it twice as if he could not believe what he saw. He disconnected the other call and answered in his gruffest voice.

"Chief, it's Susanna Marcasi."

Russell softened like butter on a warm New Orleans day when he talked to Susanna. This call marked one of very few occasions when he had no words.

He felt responsible.

"Susanna, I … I don't know what to say. I don't have anything for you," he said.

"Chief, we both know who did this," said Susanna.

"And the Capitol Hill Police know, too. We are sharing jurisdiction, but until we have more to go on, I have to defer to those prancers on the Hill." Marines. Police. If someone got in Russell's way, he labeled him or her a "prancer."

"If someone gets me something solid, I'll move on it." He hesitated. He had known Susanna in New Orleans. "I can't ask you to do this," he said, his voice downcast.

"You're not asking" assured Susanna, who wanted Russell and his men working the murder, not the Hill's force.

Russell thought of Susanna's beaten body inside the burning structure. "This is too dangerous. We'll find another way."

"Chief, I got it." Susanna fed off the energy of the crisis.

She felt unstoppable.

CHAPTER TWENTY-NINE

A Capitol Hill police officer noticed a light in Lori's office and drops of blood in the hall around 3 a.m. Two hours earlier he noticed nothing unusual. He drew his pistol and crept into what had been Lori's safe haven. He found the senator beaten and awash in her own blood, slumped over her desk with her right cheek on the blotter. Her lifeless eyes stared back at him.

Her warm corpse told the officer he had just missed the killer.

The coroner determined the attacker tortured Lori for some time before killing her. He used a heavy lead pipe to snap her legs so she could not run and her arms so she could not resist. He cut her skirt and lace underwear with a sharp blade. The coroner found slicing of the vaginal wall. Her attacker sodomized her with a large-gauge pipe as well as the blade. He left a trail of rage across her body. He crushed the bones in her face. The excessive bruising on her neck showed he strangled her and revived her to recommence his ritual of execution. Any of the head blows that cracked her skull could have killed her, but Lori drowned in her own blood after the killer slit her throat.

The motive for killing one of the most popular senators on the Hill baffled investigators. They had never heard of "Hercules" or senators playing fast and furious with public money.

Lori's chief left his home a few minutes after 3 a.m. when he got the call. Virginia State Troopers pulled Bob Mixon over on I-95 North. He wore white boxers and a matching, short-sleeved T-shirt, two sizes too small. Police had clocked him at 110 mph. They removed the handcuffs after he explained his position and the situation in Washington. Four squad cars escorted him to the Russell Building. One officer gave him a windbreaker and a worn pair of sweat pants. He identified Lori's body. The O'Reillys kept their lawyers busy. Lori had no will, no directives. She only knew Washington colleagues who happened to have law degrees.

Detectives interviewed Susanna. She never mentioned Manfred Stahl or the myriad motives that could have played a hand in Lori's death. She would solve this puzzle herself. Joe Earhardt appeared to have a motive as Lori's lover, but as far as any law enforcement official in D.C., Virginia, or Maryland knew, his location remained a mystery.

The lead investigator told Susanna, "This guy has done this before." Susanna nodded. She would never reveal what had occurred. Lori's mangled body stood as a warning to Susanna, but she would not give them the satisfaction of smelling her fear. They would never understand she had nothing to lose. When the medical examiner released Lori's remains to Susanna, her wounds brought back memories and solidified her resolve. She contacted a mortician known for his work with accident victims. Before parting, Susanna looked at him, her tone threatening, "Here is a photograph. She was stunning. Please, her family will be here. Spare nothing. Make her beautiful again."

Russell read the autopsy. The injuries appeared almost identical to Marcasi's except Susanna's attacker had not slit her throat.

"Mike, we may be looking at the same guy on O'Reilly and Marcasi," Russell shared. He figured the DIA investigation into Joe Earhardt would now run parallel to the O'Reilly murder.

CHAPTER THIRTY

Without a word, Susanna grabbed her laptop and note book and dashed upstairs. She returned in minutes clad in black, but with more of an urban-hipster flair versus the cat burglar look from the previous day. Susanna reached for the door knob but felt a gentle tug on her left arm.

"Where're you going?" asked Mike, as he packed up for his Joe Earhardt mission. He already had a good idea.

"Lori's office," she said.

"It's a crime scene," said Mike, knowing he chose the wrong approach to use with Susanna.

"I'm going before someone else gets into the files she mentioned." She looked at Mike and smiled. "Don't worry about me. I'll Metro over," she said and turned away.

Mike wanted to take her back to bed.

Within minutes, Susanna gazed on the Potomac from the passenger's seat of the Land Rover. Mike sped across the Memorial Bridge. The Capitol seemed a world away. Three miles could prove a lifetime in D.C.

Susanna's phone rang. She looked at it and shook her head. She answered, gushing with charm, as she flashed Mike her look of displeasure. Bill Warren ranted on the other end. Susanna had not filed a story or blog entry with the Times in several days and had not checked in about stringer assignments.

Bill had left her countless messages.

The call did not go well.

"You sent me some flaccid piece about the Army Corps of Engineers and the work that is NOT being done on the levees? I can't run this crap," he said.

She knew he was right. She didn't care.

"Then ... THEN you send me some bodice-ripper about dancing in the streets of the French Quarter? Now you're asking the blog to go on vacation because of fucking O'Reilly's death?" he shouted.

Bill, a kind and jovial man, caught himself. "Susanna, there's been a hell of a lot of blog fodder here. In fact, we have missed provocative entries since that Marine went off the bridge." Bill's frustration mounted.

"Why don't you just go on sabbatical to some third-world country? I hear Somalia is popular," he blurted.

Susanna sat in silence. She had given Bill her unwavering loyalty. No, fealty. She served as his vassal and he reigned as her lord. She let his out-of-character tirade pass.

"Jesus, Susanna, give me something," pleaded Bill, distancing himself from the ogre on the phone a few moments earlier.

 "I quit," she said.

"What?" he asked in disbelief.

"Bill, I quit. Give my job to someone else."

Bill caught his breath. "Susanna, I'm sorry. Give me something."

"Bill, I promise to have the whole story for you after Lori's funeral."

Susanna had little interest in writing the story, but needed the job. Her savings sputtered. She thought of another way to placate him. "Hey, Bill, you pay me by the piece anyway, so look at this as saving money."

Bill made sounds Susanna could not decipher.

"Bill, you're breaking up. I'll try you later," she said disconnecting the call.

Mike could see her weariness. She sat next to him like a lifeless sack of flour. He had pieced together information from her succession of phone calls in his dining room, her undeclared command post.

Without a prompt she stated, "Mr. O'Reilly asked me to plan Lori's wake and funeral mass. It is very administrative. Boring, really."

Mike knew the high-profile funeral of a murdered senator registered as far from boring and he grew concerned. Other than her call to the Hill staff, she had no plan for this mission and headed into a guerilla camp blind. She knew this, but remained nonchalant.

"Thanks for filling me in," he said, with eyebrows raised.

He loved her.

"Pull up on Delaware. I'll hop out," she said.

She smiled, "Thanks."

"Leave the Luger," cautioned Mike with his right hand out.

"I can slip it through; I may need it," she said.

He looked at her. She handed him the weapon and magazines to him.

"Use it when you find Joe," she smiled.

Susanna strode through the entrance of the Russell Building like McArthur retaking the Philippines. Her straight ebony skirt, black cashmere turtleneck, wide Italian leather belt paired with her studded dominatrix boots did not scream Capitol Hill, but the ensemble underscored her power. She carried a black trench coat and matching collapsible umbrella. She called up to Lori's office. The phone went into voice mail. She tried two more times with the same result. She tried Stahl's former chief of staff, Tony Barré, who agreed to stay on for Charles Gagnet. The governor appointed Gagnet to the Senate seat vacated when Stahl became Defense Secretary. She hung up as soon as someone answered Stahl's old line.

Susanna made her way toward the staircase and ran smack into Barré.

"Susanna Marcasi? I was on the call earlier. Hey, oh, hey, I am so sorry. You and Lori were tight," he said. Barré's genuine expression touched her.

His azure eyes captivated her.

"Thank you," she said.

Glancing down, she tried to move past him. Barré, an Army

veteran, enjoyed an enviable reputation as one of the better looking men on the Hill. Though single, he and Susanna never hit it off in that way. One day in the hall she declared, "I prefer to pick up my men in bars, fuck them, and toss them out before morning." Her profession shocked Barré and killed any chance the two would join romantic forces. But as chiefs of staff they held court like king and queen.

She saw the effect Manfred Stahl had on Barré. He now sported the weight of the world evident from his growing waistline, pasty complexion, and dark circles under his eyes, the envy of any linebacker. He held open his arms, and Susanna leaned into a chest that had lost all tone. When they got upstairs Susanna asked if it had been a rough few years. She regretted it as soon as she said it.

"Does it show?" he asked with the stare of a lost puppy.

"No, no. Not all at. I was just curious," Susanna overcompensated.

The police had cordoned off Lori's office, but Susanna and Tony stepped through barrier tape.

Barré confessed, "Stahl was fucking killing me. Now, this guy the governor appointed has some village missing its idiot. A hand puppet would have been more effective." He looked over her the whole time as he spoke. "Christ. You look fantastic! What is it that you do? I want to work where you do. Geez, Susanna. I should have been all over you when you were with Lori, but working for that fucker Stahl. Well ... you know."

Susanna nodded. She understood Tony's predicament. She turned away in part from embarrassment, but in large part repulsed at the thought of rolling around with Tony Barré in his unfortunate shape.

"I am sure you have some things you want to go through."

He turned to leave.

Susanna, eager to see what he knew, called after him, "Tony, wait. I do have some questions you could help me with."

"Sure, sure. What can I tell you?" Barré would have sold Gagnet into prostitution for a chance to please Susanna.

"Tony, have you heard of Hercules?" asked Susanna with caution.

"As in mythic hero or Stahl's fucking Doberman?" Barré popped two antacids at the thought of Stahl.

"Neither, actually. It may have been a Stahl project," she hinted.

"Hercules might as well have been his chief of staff. In fact, if you find him, I have a job for him," ranted Barré, resentful of his former and current bosses. "No. Never heard of a project with that name. Susanna, do you really think he would have told me? Manfred Stahl's chief of staff—laughing stock and last to know?" Barré shook his head and laughed. "Susanna, I am just so fucking bitter. No, that bastard never told me about Hercules, Zeus, Athena, or Jesus Christ."

Susanna felt certain Tony had told her the truth. "Thanks."

Barré turned to leave.

"Tony, if you ..." she started.

"Don't worry. I won't tell anyone you were here. I loved you and Lori. I hope they catch the psycho," he said.

Finally alone, Susanna went into Lori's dark office and crouched in front of her computer. The screen provided the sole source of light. She had her list of recycled passwords.

Lori's desk phone jumped. A startled Susanna knocked a large pencil holder off the desk as her heart raced faster with each ring. She knew she was running out of time. She gathered up the mess and dove back into Lori's files.

Distant footsteps made her uneasy as she began to copy the "Hercules" documents and audio files Lori had mentioned. The steps' pace increased and halted in the hall in front of Lori's reception area. A pair of Capitol Hill police officers burst into Lori's office with guns drawn. The bright ceiling lights illuminated the darkened room. They searched the deceased senator's closet of an office but found nothing unusual. They walked past the darkened computer several times. Susanna watched from her cubby under the desk as one officer brushed his leg against the desktop's warm CPU.

"This is Moran. O'Reilly's office is secure."

"Copy that. Come on back to base."

"Roger."

Susanna exhaled.

Still folded under the desk, she phoned ahead to her next appointment. "Dr. Houston, this is Susanna Marcasi. I will be there in 20 minutes. This is an extremely important matter."

***

The temperature had dropped 10 degrees during her brief time in the Russell Building and the wind swirled around Susanna. She clasped the neck of her coat closed and lowered her head like the scores of other pedestrians surrounding her. With one hand warm in her pocket and the other losing feeling in the cold, she waited for the heavens to open. She peeked skyward and to her surprise it appeared the sun might claim its rightful place that day over the rain.

How rare, she thought.

Susanna felt safe in the middle of the crowd. But the throngs of government workers concealing her thinned as she approached the brick building. She looked behind her every few seconds. Snap! Her head would whip around challenging anyone who dare approach her. Snap! She would not die on a District street, no matter who tailed her. Snap! She did not envision a double funeral with Lori. Her destination closed in fast. Her pace slowed. She almost genuflected as she entered the masterpiece and surveyed the cavernous space.

Susanna Marcasi had chosen the National Building Museum as the site for Lori's wake, one of few places large enough to hold the crowds she expected. It stood as one of Lori's favorites, next to the Capitol, for business or pleasure. Susanna met with building officials who hesitated but agreed to the wake.

They had little experience with death-related events.

The top museum staff shuddered at the revelation of an open casket, but relented when Susanna informed them she represented the distraught family. She neglected to mention they would host an Irish Wake. She suggested that caterers handle food and drink. Susanna proposed viewing from 10 a.m. to 10 p.m. each day, but she would ensure someone remained with the deceased at all times. She paced out her vision for the onlookers. The casket would sit off toward the wall away from the staircases, but a third of the way into the center of the grand hall. She also would need a separate room for the family. The museum director and his staff nodded in agreement. All took notes.

"Ms. Marcasi, the National Building Museum considers it an honor to support our departed friend, Senator Lori O'Reilly," said Dr. Jack Houston, the museum's director. He had taken on a macabre tone, but it did not matter to Susanna.

She felt she had taken Iwo Jima. The staff did not know what had just hit them and just nodded in agreement.

"Is there anything more we can assist with?" asked Houston.

"Can you get me a piano?"

Susanna excused herself, went into the women's restroom and threw up.

***

Reeling from Lori's death, Susanna needed solitude to collect her thoughts. She glanced at her watch and looked in the ladies' room mirror. "Just hold it together. Your mind has been generous. You have to see this through."

Susanna spoke to the image looking back at her. "Lori, I feel stronger now than I can remember, but my doubts seem to overtake the gains we've made. I don't know ..."

"Susanna, you're fine. We're fine. We'll make it. We always have."

Susanna found Lori's voice reassuring.

"You know, I hate that red suit. And that Crim-suhn lipstick."

Susanna saw Lori in the mirror looking as cheap in red as she always had.

"At the moment, it's unavoidable. Don't worry. You can bury me in black or one of the Chanels. Feel any better?" asked Lori.

Susanna realized her unprecedented opportunity. "Lori, what, what happened? Who ..."

Lori smiled. She appeared serene. "Don't worry. I'm not far." Lori drew her breath and reached for Susanna, pulling her to the surface of the mirror.

"But he is closer," she warned.

Susanna broke from Lori's grasp and pulled away.

"Who, Lori? Stahl?" she shouted at the mirror.

Susanna stared at her own reflection.

"No. No! Don't leave me again, Lori!" Susanna screamed as she reached through the glass to find her. The force of her fist shattered the portal. Blood dripped on the white porcelain.

Susanna stared at the broken mirror and her sliced hand. She crouched down resting her head on the edge of the sink. "No, no, no," she said as she turned her head from side-to-side. She closed her eyes. One tear sat in the corner of her deep, smoky brown eyelid. She thought for a long time and felt ready—again. She stood and saw her reflection. The broken glass had disappeared, as had the blood and the cuts to her hand. She glanced at her watch. No time had passed since she entered the restroom. Lori's magic? God's mercy? Neither, she understood. Susanna already had accepted she soon might lose complete grasp of the present. She had made her peace with that probability long ago. Other than Marcus, she had nothing to lose—except maybe Mike—but she had to move forward.

With her list of demands met by the National Building Museum for Lori's wake, Susanna left to make arrangements for the funeral mass. She had strong-armed a priest or two in the past and would again, if necessary. St. Joseph's, Lori's favorite church, sat across from the Hart Senate Office Building. Its understated brownstone exterior made its soaring interior even more breathtaking. A simple bronze plaque at the entrance noted Robert F. Kennedy chose to worship there, another plus for Lori.

To sit in St. Joseph's, one gazed at the heavens. Gold stars danced against a ceiling of rich, midnight blue. As Susanna stood on the hardwood floor she imagined Lori as one of those stars. She looked at seating capacity and overall size of the church. She found it perfect. The pastor came rushing in and apologized, but he had been across the street. Susanna smiled and reached out her hand.

"I'm Susanna Marcasi. I am making the arrangements for the senator's family."

They waded through the important details. Susanna would have the church from 8 a.m. to noon on Friday. Police would close off surrounding streets. Father John Mulvaney would say a full mass. The family asked that Susanna be the only speaker and give a simple eulogy. The priest walked Susanna through the sequence of the funeral from before the casket arrived to the departure of the last visitor. Susanna presented him with a list of hymns and readings and asked about an organist.

"You seem to carry a tremendous burden, Ms. Marcasi."

"You are very observant, Father," she smiled. "If you only knew." She kept her hand pressed in her pocket.

"Is it anything you care to talk about?" he asked.

"Maybe someday, but not right now," she said.

Susanna felt one with the kind priest. "Thank you, Father. I'll call with more details."

Exhausted, Susanna flagged down a cab driving by the church. As they inched through traffic, it seemed a good time to make a call.

"Short leash, Singleton," she said after Mike came on the line.

"I'm honored. Where the hell are you?" asked Mike.

"I just finished at the Building Museum and church and will be back soon," she fudged.

"Soon?" Mike raised his tone, knowing Susanna.

"Yeah, soon." Susanna did not like being questioned.

"I may have additional information," he said.

She could hear the tension in his voice. Mike had not wanted her going out alone.

"He thinks I'm like a porcelain doll," she announced to her cabbie friend.

Susanna gathered her bag and looked for her wallet. "Can you wait for me?" The driver nodded. The cab idled in front of her building on Fourteenth Street. She looked across the street and saw a black car she thought she recognized. She exited the taxi, ran around to the back of the building, and hiked the stairs to her flat. "Do Not Cross" tape still covered the entry. Mrs. Schiller had left a note, "You are still in danger, my girl."

Susanna let out a grumble of disgust and squeezed past the tape despite the warnings. She headed straight into the bathroom and closed the door. She placed her forehead on the cool porcelain sink. She could have fallen asleep bent over. As she stood up, her knees buckled and her world began to fade to black. She grabbed for the smelling salts that one of her young, one-night suitors had left behind. They became her new best friend. She gathered several outfits, jewelry, and make-up. She chose a dark spring coat and dodged the tape as she slipped back out the door.

Susanna had grown weary of being followed. She placed her clothes in the cab and walked across the street up to the black-windowed town car and made an unpleasant gesture.

"Leave me the hell alone, yah freak," she yelled as she pounded her fist on the windshield.

She hiked up her skirt and tried to smash in the driver's bullet-proof door with the heel of her boot. "Fuck 'em," she muttered as she turned her back in defiance. She assumed they would continue to trail her. While at St. Joseph's she felt that God himself stood on her side. So, if things went as threatened, it seemed she had a spot reserved with the Big Guy himself.

Satan waited on Stahl and Earhardt.

The cab dropped her off at the Metro Center station. "Good luck, Miss. I pray for your safety," said the driver. The statement took Susanna aback, but she dismissed it as coincidence. Susanna tipped him $30. She gave a little waive from the sidewalk.

Susanna stood on the corner as he drove away. His words echoed. She looked up and down the street. She saw two men in well-tailored suits near the black Lincoln she kicked. They tried to blend into the crowed. The sunglasses did not help their effort.

She remained still. *Am I paranoid?* she wondered. *Why would anyone come after some unknown hack?* She could see they had sight of her. They pointed. They locked on their target.

Susanna ran.

She raced down the escalator dodging riders every step. The two men closed behind her. She reached the platform just as a train opened its doors. She walked the length of the train, an inch from each car. She did not board. Susanna glanced back at the men trying to push their way through the sea of riders. Without an unnecessary movement she slipped into a car as the doors closed. The men in pursuit never saw her board. She ducked as the train passed them.

"What train is this?" she asked another passenger.

"Blue Line to Franconia," the young woman responded. Susanna smiled and leaned against the brushed metal bar, heart pounding.

She walked from the Arlington Cemetery station toward Mike's, mindful of every living person within 100 yards.

***

Her watch read almost 3 p.m. She stopped at the War Memorial as she did every time she passed it to pay homage to flag raiser Mike Strank, killed in action on Iwo Jima. She felt certain Strank had returned as Mike Singleton. She kept the secret between her and the massive bronze figure.

As the wind whipped around her, Susanna crouched at the entrance and digging through her bag for the key. Mike opened the door and looked down. Their eyes met. He smiled. She hesitated, then took his outstretch hand.

"You act as if I'll shatter. I'm not yours to save, Mike. I am not your problem."

She saw the hurt on his face.

He had no explanation. He could not help himself.

He did not want to lose her again.

"You're right." Mike stood in the doorway, confused by her unexpected indignation.

"What did you find?" he asked.

"Not much. The police searched the office, I had to move," she stated without emotion.

"That's … it?" Mike asked, surprised.

"Yeah. Sorry if I let you down while risking my life," she huffed.

Mike tried to imagine how Susanna felt. "Susanna, I'm sorry about Lori." He leaned against the door frame. "This is about more than the murder of a U.S. senator, but I think you know that," he said.

She knew everything related.

"What happened with Joe?" she asked, sensing a change.

"Bartholomew is wrong on this. We wait. Joe will come to us. He did before," Mike said. He did not share his increasing concern that the admiral might have an alternate agenda.

"I think we can end this. Me, Stahl, and a single bullet," Mike said unholstering his 9mm.

"Stahl owns everyone, Mike. It won't matter." She did not look at him. A bullet could not eradicate such corruption or evil. Someone would just snatch the battle flag and move forward.

"He doesn't own you, and that enrages him," Mike said

"I am just one …" Susanna started.

Mike interrupted, "You're not. There are cracks. According to what Joe left behind, they've threatened Lori for months on the Monroe bill vote. Stahl planned to kill Lori if she did not vote for the Monroe bill. In fact, he had arranged for Joe to kill her—one reason behind Joe's suicide attempt. He and Lori broke with Stahl some time ago," said Mike.

Susanna shook her head. Taking on Stahl seemed pointless.

Mike shrugged, "Stahl has stepped on it. He has made a very public mess. If there is a top player, this 'Poseidon,' let's say, this guy is pissed. Too many people know about Stahl's activities. How he keeps all of Congress and its legislative camp followers quiet is a mystery. But in less than a week as Defense Secretary he has careened out of control—a bit too reckless for Poseidon."

A part of Mike still craved a position in Stahl's guns-for-hire scheme. But Manfred Stahl stood as a ticking time bomb and Mike bet self-destruction would soon follow.

"Stahl should have let Joe go off the bridge that night. The abduction and Lori's murder have deviated from Poseidon's plan. They have drawn too much attention—the kind Stahl craves and the type his boss sees as detracting from the mission. Susanna, the type of secrecy Poseidon needs is not that different from the needs of a Special Warfare operation," Mike said with certainty.

He had Susanna's attention.

Mike turned and concluded, "Stahl has become a liability to his own operation."

Susanna added, "If you're right, then this ultimate king-of-the-superstructure is strong, decisive but deep behind the scenes. Like Bartholomew?"

"No, but he or she is the last person you'd expect. Hiding in plain sight," said Mike.

They fell silent and eyed one another.

"It's you!" they said at the same time, pointing at one another fumbling for firearms.

"Christ, Marcasi, it's not me," Mike said.

"Well, it isn't me. I've been on Fourteenth Street the past four years living above a pawn shop with a Nazi reliving her glory days with the Führer and a mullet-sporting courier who calls his '70s conversion van sporting an Indian mural home. *You're* the silent warrior type," Susanna accused.

"You have Stahl's personality. You're more his kid than Joe is," Mike said.

They stopped.

"I'm sorry, Susanna, but you are a lot like Stahl." His clarification did not help.

She looked away, but she had to agree.

"Fine. What do you suggest?" asked Susanna.

"We wait. We will put you out as bait and wait. Poseidon will present himself at some point. Maybe at the wake. Maybe at the funeral. I don't think he is a threat to us. Stahl and Joe—they're dangerous.

"With you alive, Susanna, Stahl is waiting for his opportunity," Mike concluded.

CHAPTER THIRTY-ONE

Susanna converted Mike's rescued living room into her personal funeral-planning war room. She had hoped to cajole Dr. Houston into allowing her to work out of the Building Museum, but Mike convinced her she remained a target. Given the day's events, she agreed. Charts and diagrams of the museum and church, plus recommended routes between sites, lined the walls, windows, and covered his refrigerator. She pinned guest lists to the furniture. Susanna broke into Mike's cigar stash and chomped a stogie as she paced reviewing the imminent operation.

Despite her precision, Susanna felt contact with the present elusive. Mike tried to wrestle responsibilities away from her, but she clung to every last vestige of her life with Lori. In two short days she worked to create a wake and funeral befitting royalty, beyond Lori's, the one-time Queen of Rex, wildest expectations. She felt Lori's presence. She had remained with Susanna since their restroom rendezvous at the Building Museum, appropriate given their meeting as children in the St. Theresa's lavatory. God had taken Lori, but had given her back to help, she thought. She probably sat in Mike's living room wearing God-awful Crim-suhn as Susanna worked, laughing about Marcus, Susanna's new charge.

Susanna held fast to her fantasy as the credits rolled on their uneven, lifelong friendship. The often bitter girl affair gasped as the senator drowned in her own blood. Despite proof Lori remained with her even in death, Susanna felt alone. She had had one friend— Lori. Nothing had changed in more than 25 years though their work took them to opposite ends of the metaphorical globe. But then Joe appeared. Susanna had never brought Joe from the academy to New Orleans, so Lori had never met him. She watched Joe and shared she had not planned to tell Lori of their long, tumultuous engagement. She recommended he do the same.

Joe, oblivious to Susanna's olive branch, retorted, "Don't fuck this up for me, Susanna."

"Joe, you are more than capable and need no help from me," she said.

Susanna decided she had to erase Lori's part in the legislative equivalent of the Jesse James Gang, if not for her reputation, then the sake of her family. She already had pored over thousands of documents before she left the Hill and had the staff and Lori's legislative director do the same. As far as the record showed, the cabal of congressional officials had covered its tracks well. Nothing looked out of place. Funds appeared to go to intended recipients. Though Lori voted "yea" on the bills, Susanna felt certain no one could tie these schemes back to her.

Around midnight Susanna closed her eyes on the sofa behind Mike, who sat on the floor studying more pages from Lori's files. She drifted into a dream she had enjoyed hundreds of times before. They headed out for a last Spring Break. Their time at the U.S. Naval Academy would soon end. She hummed as Bruce Springsteen crooned, "Can't start a fire. Can't start a fire without a spark ..."

The phone playing back-up to the E-Street Band seemed out of place. She left the spring of 1984 and reentered the spring of 2000.

Once-brilliant cherry blossoms lay lifeless on the river's edge and Lori lay murdered.

But Susanna would always have her dream.

She would always have the boy.

Susanna awakened, grinning with satisfaction. She answered her phone, breathless as if she and the dream boy had consummated their years-long relationship on that sand-filled, yellow bed spread.

She found no one on the other end.

"Are you OK, Susanna?" Mike thought she looked different. *Was she ill? Was the stress too much?*

"Mike. I have this dream. It's Spring Break First Class Year. I have had it since the accident."

"And ...?" he asked.

"Well ..." she hesitated. "We're together. Bruce Springsteen is playing and I tell you 'I love you.'"

She looked away, mortified.

"Tramps like us, baby we were born to run," he sang in perfect pitch. "Yeah, I have the same dream."

She froze.

"That trip, that evening ... They've gotten me through some pretty bad times," he said.

She looked at him.

"I still love you, Susanna," he said.

She needed to run, but wanted the boy more. Susanna stood up and walked behind the sofa. She put her lips on the top of his head and gave him a long, slow kiss. He reached for her, but she already had started a deliberate walk up the stairs.

He watched her and sang, "Can't start a fire, can't start a fire without a spark ..."

Susanna disappeared at the top of the steps.

Mike sat in the dark humming to himself. "Messages keep gettin' clearer ..." He found their past tragic yet sobering. He thought of Russell's clear description of the attack on Susanna in New Orleans. He could not imagine such violence against her. Worse, he could do nothing. He preferred to think about the Susanna he knew at school. He thought about the promise of that final Spring Break. She seduced him to "Born to Run." As she lay in his arms clad in the scant piece of cloth, he kissed her lips, her neck. He ran his tongue down her stomach and brushed her thighs. She brought his lips back to hers and strapped her legs across his revving engine.

They had never shared such intimacy. Mike summarized, "I love you. Break it off with Joe." She gave him the same vacant look. He held her. They cried together.

The day came when she disappeared from Annapolis without a

word. Mike later blamed himself for not knowing about the attack at Quantico. Word of Susanna's assault had woven its way in and out of class gatherings. Rumor credited Joe Earhardt with the ambush, something Joe did not deny.

Mike thought of the brutal New Orleans attack. As the Navy Reserve admiral's aide, he should have known. Maybe he did not want to know.

You are such a fucking coward, Singleton.

He thought of the red-headed man abducting his little brother. Mike almost gave his life to save the little boy. Now he obsessed on Susanna. He needed to do something for her.

And maybe for him, too.

What is it with this Marine father-son duo? wondered an angry and confused Mike Singleton. Mike walked to the other side of the room and put his large fist through the wall by the TV.

It did not help.

He needed to do more.

He walked out the front door and headed for the Marine Corps War Memorial. It was after midnight. He wore his plaid pajama bottoms, a Plebe-issue Naval Academy sweatshirt that looked four sizes too small, and a pair of worn cowboy boots. He climbed atop the granite base of the illuminated bronze statue.

Tourists thought Mike played a part in some late show at the monument.

Mike stood and looked at the innocent civilians surrounding him. He looked at the imposing bronze, which seemed larger close-up than it appeared from the ground.

Mike Singleton stood ready to take his place in history. He took a deep breath and shouted, "Fuck you, Manfred Stahl," as he wrote the same in urine at the base of the bronze. He took care not to desecrate any of the flag raisers, notably Mike Strank, after whom he had fashioned himself. He almost had enough left to write, "Fuck you, Joe Earhardt," too, but dribbled on the "d."

The Park Police waited on the ground to arrest him, guns drawn, certain they had a homeless psychopath to book. They called ahead to reserve a psych ward bed.

As Mike sat handcuffed in the back of the cruiser, an old friend approached.

"Boys, we are very familiar with Commander Singleton. I am happy to take him off your hands. Here, put these on him," said the man.

Roscoe Russell grabbed the handcuffed SEAL and appeared to take him into custody. Once out of earshot, he doubled over laughing, "Christ, Mike, I wish I had thought of this. I would have pissed on those prancers' precious statue years ago—and I was one of them!" Russell turned serious, "We'll get him. Until then, Mike, you gotta keep it in your pants."

CHAPTER THIRTY-TWO

"Lieutenant Colonel Earhardt, the secretary isn't seeing anyone."

Joe Earhardt, despite donning the Corps's meticulous, green alpha uniform, looked like a 12-stepper on a binge. His collar flapped open. His tie hung askew. His belt loops sat empty and he wore two different black shoes—one leather and one faux patent Corfam. The stench of stale alcohol permeated the outer office. He carried two concealed pistols and his personal favorite—a switchblade.

Joe planned to kill Manfred Stahl in the next 60 seconds.

"Colonel, please …" called Major Dieter Schulz.

Joe Earhardt stormed past his father's junior aide and burst into the Defense Secretary's office. Two men from Stahl's security detail tackled Joe from behind and the three sprawled wrestling on the silk carpet in the center of the office. Almost on cue, Stahl's aide closed the door.

Joe strained to look at his father, "You fucking bastard. She didn't have to die!"

Sergeant Enrique Lopez and Corporal Erik Kuhn took Joe's two pistols, cuffed him, and dragged him on his feet. They fixed their firearms on the intruder.

"Sergeant Lopez, Lieutenant Colonel Earhardt can be a dangerous man and an ingrate, but I think I can handle him," said Manfred Stahl.

Stahl wasted his sarcasm on his unsophisticated body guards. He looked at both young men, who salivated at the thought of killing the Marine Corps officer. "Please release him, but keep your weapons ready, just in case he proves more creative than I credit him."

Lopez looked at his boss, about whom he had already been warned, and the unstable man they had in custody. "Sir, I don't think that's a good idea," he said.

"Thank you. I'll be fine. Trust me, gentlemen. I have been preparing for this family moment with my son. We have a way we take care of these problems in Louisiana, but Josef would know little about the ways of my people, though he appears to understand we exact our revenge with violence when necessary," said a regal Stahl.

Lopez eyed Stahl thinking him a madman. He and Kuhn uncuffed Joe and slipped out the door.

Manfred Stahl stood behind his desk. "Josef," said a red-faced Stahl, his voice shaking as he spoke. "I have been extremely patient. Now get out. This is further proof of your mother's bad influence."

Joe lunged forward, reaching for his father's throat.

"You murderer! I will not be dismissed as some strap hanger. I am Josef Stahl," he yelled.

Joe gathered strength from his grief. He would act as Lori's agent. He would do for her now what he had not done when he had her.

"Then act like Manfred Stahl's son," bellowed Stahl. He faced Joe. "You disgust me," he said teeth gritted. His finger pointed at a devastated Joe Earhardt.

Stahl looked down and shook his head. "Josef, women like your mother, Senator O'Reilly, and Susanna Marcasi stand ready to die for what they think is right. They *think*, but they don't *know*. They represent a great risk to a nation better served obsessing over gullible saps, washed-up rock stars, and the latest diet aid. Others like them will die."

He shifted.

"Our work is what's serious, Josef," Stahl said.

"For once I'm not talking about your outrageous scheme," said Joe. "I am talking about what you've taken. Mom, Lori, Susanna, and who knows how many others? Can't you see what you're doing?" asked Joe with a commanding presence, something Stahl had never seen in his son.

"I recommend you leave your mother out of this. I let her live," cautioned Stahl.

Joe had forgotten his father's brutality until he lost Lori. As he stood before the man he felt certain stood responsible for Lori's murder, he thought of his mother and the terror she endured to keep him safe.

Stahl looked at his disheveled, adult son and slammed his swagger stick on the desk. Joe winced.

"What are you doing here? You have 10 seconds, and then I'll throw you out myself."

Stahl had tired of his son long ago. He could smell Joe's fear returning. He watched his son's new-found strength drain from his soul.

"They're onto us, aren't they?" Joe said.

He had lost his resolve.

The suggestion outraged Stahl. He stood up on his hind legs like an angry bear. "No, God damn it. The power of this country resides with me alone," Stahl bellowed.

His security team came running in, weapons drawn.

"Get out," Stahl shouted, never taking his eyes off Joe.

"The weak must die. Your bitch came to me frantic when you disappeared. I looked past it. Then, she threatened to jeopardize our operation. I cleaned up your mess, Joe."

The son remained silent.

"We have other interests to consider."

Somehow, his father made sense.

"Then she dragged that Marcasi whore back from the dead and into my life. She's worse than your mother. Our operation is flawless. Had O'Reilly exposed our position, she would have ended your career. You would have been charged with larceny at best. A half-wit could make a case for treason. They would have exposed your intimate—and I'm being polite—relationship with a member of Congress. Some state school lawyer would have sold you right into 30 years at Leavenworth, sparing you the death penalty. O'Reilly knew the harm she could do. She had to go," said Stahl, convinced he did God's work.

Joe lost his way again in those few moments. Conflicted about his father, he feared him, yet admired him. Joe dripped with sweat as if he just exited the waters that raged around father and son. He shook, terrified. He knew Stahl had tied everyone of import to him in a way his demise would prove worse for them. Stahl had absconded with the president's metaphorical paddle leaving him in dangerous waters, something only he, a worried commander in chief, and now Susanna Marcasi and Mike Singleton knew, though both had dodged Fred's masterful web.

Neither man said a word. Joe decided he needed to stay close to his father for protection during this crisis. Stahl had rescued his son through numerous past troubles, but doubted he could secure Joe's loyalty. Stahl had planned for this scenario. He noted a hint of urine in the room. Stahl knew the man-child in front of him had just desecrated the Marine Corps uniform by pissing on himself.

"At least O'Reilly and Marcasi have the balls you lost years ago."

CHAPTER THIRTY-THREE

Day One of a three-day public marathon dawned. Both Susanna and Mike sprung up at 4 a.m., stumbling into one another in the darkened hallway. Susanna beat him to the single bathroom. "Son of a bitch!" he yelled at her, in part, as well as at running into the locked bathroom door, jamming his right foot under the wooden barricade. He limped into his bedroom and landed face up on his bed. The only light in the room came from the bedside lamp. He wrapped his arms behind his head propping himself up on the pillow, waiting. The shower gave way to memories of the sound of distant waves crashing on a beach and laughter as they pushed one another out of the bathroom that then served ten. Mike acquiesced as he always did with her. Her final days with Lori had arrived and he feared having to let her go again. He repositioned himself in freshly laundered sheets, now anointed with the hair of a three-legged dog, making a nest of privacy and safety. His mind meandered back in time.

He thought again to that final Spring Break. They drove along the beach. Susanna preferred the Land Rover's driver's seat even when he sat behind the wheel. She would wedge herself between him and the steering column and would spread her legs on either side of Mike. Her knees grasped his hips. They faced one another. With her arms draped over his shoulders she would dodge to block his view. He evaded her efforts. After a few days of tandem driving, Mike maneuvered the vehicle with ease with one hand and drove Susanna to secret pleasure with the other.

Susanna and Mike laughed for days together in the Land Rover. She had come to love his car. She called him "Rovo Man." She found it unoriginal, but he liked it. He dubbed her "Music Maven." It fell to Susanna to find tunes so he could sing an artist's fare or craft his own lyrics.

"Wait, wait," he said, hands off the wheel, palms covering the car's radio. "Here's your Plebe Summer anthem. Turn it up." Susanna had mastered working the radio behind her from Mike's lap. Mike gave her an annoyed look.

"Geez. Crank it, Marcasi."

She reached behind her and turned the knob until it stopped. The car vibrated as Mike sang with the radio blasting.

"Come out Virginia, don't make me wait.
Catholic girls start much too late.
Aw but sooner or later it comes down to fate.
I might as well be the one. ...

You mighta heard I run with a dangerous crowd.
We ain't too pretty; we ain't too proud.
We might be laughin' a bit too loud.
Oh but that never hurt no one.
Only the good die young."

Susanna stopped her lap dance, looked away and smiled. A tear inched down her right cheek.

She vanished. Mike Singleton lay in his room overlooking the dumpsters outside his Arlington bedroom window.

"Hey, Mike." Susanna nudged him. "All yours. Thanks." She went downstairs and fixed him the breakfast they never got a few days ago. Mike's phone rang. He looked down.

Damn.

"Singleton," he said into the mobile.

"You know, Mike, you win," said a perturbed Ken Bartholomew. "Check in with me when you're not quite so busy."

Mike fumed.

"Maybe it's Marcasi, but you gotta come around. Shift your mind to Earhardt. Get it in your head you will get lucky with him and only him," said Bartholomew. "Where the hell is he?"

In silence, Mike mimicked the admiral whose pep talks inspired until he learned back at the school the admiral recycled and regurgitated them to his boy du jour.

"Earhardt's bad news. Find him. Mike, we're almost there." He took a long drag on his filterless cigarette. "Grab up this guy one final time, we get the rest of the information we need, and we can pop a cold one. Or you and Marcasi can do your horizontal victory dance," he said.

Mike remained quiet, planning.

"Singleton, are you fucking there?" Bartholomew had lost patience.

Nailing Earhardt assured the admiral a second star and set the stage for the quick third, thought Mike.

"Yeah, yeah, I'm here," Mike responded.

"Jesus, drink some coffee. Hey, we're wearing suits over the next three days." He worked to bring a rogue Mike back into the Bartholomew fold. "No uniforms."

Mike said nothing. Ken Bartholomew sometimes did not know what to say to the younger officer he considered a brother.

"Mike, one more thing. Go armed. As heavily as possible. I can't give you firepower from here. Earhardt is mad as a hornet over that senator girl dying. He'll show today if you don't find him first," said Bartholomew.

"Got it," sighed Mike, who wanted to be left alone.

"Hey, good luck, and I'll see you back here," said Bartholomew.

Mike found something different in the admiral's tone. Maybe his cadence or rehashed word choice. Maybe he finally succumbed to the Surgeon General's warning on the use of tobacco products. He knew not to ignore a change in a man he considered one of his closest friends who had lied to him for no apparent reason.

Mike sensed they would fight on opposite sides.

Susanna and Mike ate breakfast in silence save for Mike's "Thank you," for the mini feast she had prepared. She smiled as she drank her coffee and passed on the omelet. They went to their respective corners to don their armor for the day. Mike put on another Armani suit. Susanna pulled out a couture black sheath with a three-quarter sleeve knit jacket, circa 1964. The outfit had a matching princess coat.

As he opened the door for Susanna, Mike eyed the ensemble. She caught his disapproving stare, put her arms out to each side, shrugged, and smiled. Her new bag carried two spare pairs of shoes—one pair of flats and the others 4-inch pumps. Together they cradled her Luger.

"You went to the apartment," Mike said knowing the answer.

"A girl's gotta dress," she retorted with a smile.

The skies offered another overcast day. The chance of rain neared 100 percent. The gray sky made Susanna feel even more somber and alone. The burden to which the priest had referred almost suffocated her on what seemed the long drive to nowhere.

Susanna stared out a fogged passenger window. The mist distorted the figures passing by. As they approached the Building Museum, Susanna saw a lone person near the entrance.

"Mike, stop!"

Susanna watched the well-dressed stout man who now had a full head of graying hair with hints of Irish red locks.

It had been 20 years, but she would never forget the depraved Mick O'Reilly.

"Mike, do not let me out of your sight when I am with that man. It's Lori's father," said Susanna.

Mike nodded.

Susanna slipped out of the Land Rover and sprinted in her heels. She soared over the black puddles that dotted the pavement. Mike watched the man hold open his arms and Susanna disappeared as he wrapped them around her. In a second she pushed back and stood beyond the man's grasp.

"Mr. O'Reilly, it's not even 8 a.m. I was picking you up at the train at 10," she said, repressing the years of servitude as his breathing Mother of Christ Barbie.

Mick O'Reilly, though overcome with grief, felt joy as he looked at the Blessed Virgin who had saved his own daughter so many times.

"I want as much time as possible with my girl, Susanna," he said, fighting his tears.

Susanna did not know what had happened between Lori and her father after she ran off to join the circus, as Lori termed Annapolis. Did he miss her, or did Lori's funeral serve as another spectacle for the O'Reilly name? She led him into the building, keeping her distance. Both came to a sudden stop. Across the great main hall stood a fortress of flowers from those mourning the loss of Lori O'Reilly worldwide. The outpouring awed them. In the center sat Lori's solid mahogany casket. The undertaker had just arrived. He looked at Susanna and she nodded.

"Mr. O'Reilly, this gentleman will open the casket," she said. Susanna stayed back until Mick O'Reilly turned and waived her toward him.

"I have put a lot of people into one of these over the years. I guess God thinks it's only right that I have to bury my child." He looked at Susanna. "Stay with me for a few moments," he said, crying, just short of a complete breakdown.

Mick O'Reilly conversed with his daughter as if nothing had happened. Susanna had Lori dressed in her favorite black-and-white wool Chanel suit, the one she wore when she first won her Senate seat. Susanna saw that death could not extinguish her beauty as she lay on the bed of egg shell satin. The mahogany contrasted beautifully with her skin and picked up the highlights in her hair.

While in Chief Russell's custody for his most recent public urination incident, Mike and Roscoe agreed on a 10-officer detail for the two-day wake and eight officers at the church. The chief planned to make an appearance each day. Because of security concerns, the president's staff recommended he not attend. Hill security had gone over the site in detail and gave its approval. They expected all members of the House and Senate as well as most of their staffs. Susanna learned from Mr. O'Reilly that, aside from his sizeable family, he expected a good portion of New Orleans elite.

"Susanna, can we translate this into a number?" asked Mike.

"I could not even guess. It's a lot of people, though," she said.

Mike looked at Susanna and reached for her arm. She stepped back, eluding Mike's grasp.

"Susanna, I'm concerned about Joe and Stahl. Do not engage either one alone. Make sure I'm there," he said.

"I'm not sure if they'll show," said Susanna, somewhat aloof.

"They're sharks and they smell blood. They'll be here. Joe's erratic, but Stahl has this all worked out," stated a certain and ready Mike Singleton.

Susanna knew Stahl wanted her and had delayed the confrontation as long as possible.

Mourners began arriving before 9 a.m. The museum opened an hour early to get visitors out of the cold, steady rain that had begun to fall. Lori's staff arrived first and agreed to help handle the crowds. As Lori's siblings entered, Tim and Paul offered to handle the care and feeding of the New Orleans delegation.

By noon, Susanna felt confident. She slipped on a pair of more comfortable shoes and gave Mike an optimistic nod, to which he shook his head, "Premature, Marcasi."

Jesus, thanks for the vote of confidence, Mike, she thought. *You're just sucking the life out of me.*

A call roused Susanna. "Meet me in the in the north corner of the second level tonight, 10:30. I need to talk to you alone," the familiar voice said.

CHAPTER THIRTY-FOUR

She had expected the call. She could check off one of two problems. She leaned against a far wall to observe. Though the family mourned, Mick O'Reilly had taken over the event, much to Susanna's relief. He set up the flow of visitors so that he could meet with each one. Susanna thought him the consummate politician, but berated herself for being so judgmental at such a difficult time. His children arranged tables and chairs with the piano off to the side. Tim brought his guitar, an addition that pleased Susanna, and sang a tearful dirge followed by a lighter folk song. She figured he saved "Danny Boy" for later. Staffers and members sat with the family eating, drinking, and recounting hilarious Lori stories. Susanna admired them, but did not understand this foreign ritual. But it had gone better than she had hoped, and they would do it again the next day.

"Seems to be going well," said a vigilant and unconvinced Mike.

"He wants to meet at 10:30. Tonight," confessed Susanna in a hushed tone.

"Joe?" Mike asked.

"Yeah. Alone with me," she said.

Susanna and Mike went to the agreed meeting place. Mike looked around. "You can do this. I will cover you."

The rest of the afternoon, Susanna wondered, *What did Joe want? To say he had murdered Lori?* Would he talk about his sex life with Lori, about which Susanna had heard too much already.

Would he talk levee money?

The agreed upon rendezvous arrived after the last of the mourners had gone. Joe Earhardt waited dangling his .45 as he pressed his hips against the second-floor railing. He wore his green Alpha uniform. He saved his Dress Blues for the funeral.

"Joe," Susanna called.

"Leave me alone, Susanna," he warned.

She continued toward him. He crouched at the railing and motioned with the pistol for her to leave.

"Look at her. She was my angel. Susanna, please forgive me. Can Lori forgive me? I loved her, but I have committed some heinous acts."

He waived the loaded pistol like a toy.

Mike, from the shadows, scanned the upper levels and his gaze rested. He walked to the corner stairwell never taking his eyes off his subject. He took the steps two and three at a time.

His fixed his aim.

"Joe, put it down. Slowly. Now," Mike growled.

"Fuck off. This is God's revenge," he called out to Mike, whom he could not see, but whose presence he could feel. "You don't live with a guy four years and not get to know him. Love him."

"Joe, put it down." Mike commanded.

Joe carelessly tossed the pistol on the carpet and wept. "Man, I fucked up. I really screwed things up." Mike took two steps forward. "Turn around, Joe." Joe stood there and made a half-hearted lunge at Mike who pushed him back with the bottom of his shoe.

"Joe, if Bartholomew didn't need you, I would have shot you at my house the other day. What the hell are you doing? Is this what Lori meant to you?" Mike asked.

Joe moved away from the railing and leaned against the opposite wall. Mike kept his weapon aimed at him.

Joe looked resigned but confused.

"Bartholomew? He doesn't need me. Fuck him. He didn't need me two nights ago. He needs me to shut up. He wants me out of his miserable life. He thinks he's the nation's savior. He's lucky to have made flag."

An embittered Joe slurred his speech.

Susanna and Mike looked at each other, eyes widened, wondering.

"Joe, give me the whole story," said Mike.

Susanna reached for her bag and switched on her recorder.

"Mikey, you got it already. I know I'm the fall guy, but I got some respect out of it for a change," Joe said.

"And Lori?" asked Susanna.

Joe began to sob, "Oh my God. This is my fault. She didn't know the details until a few days ago."

Mike interrupted, "Details? What details?"

"Mike, I screwed up. I told her who all the players were. I even told her about Poseidon. Man, I know I screwed up." He gestured down at the casket, "This is all my fault."

A look of horror crossed Joe's face. He moved toward Mike, pleading, "You gotta get her name off everything. I got her involved in some things she never knew about. Please, Mike."

Mike Singleton turned cold looking at his old friend.

Joe turned to Susanna, "Please, Susanna. Help her."

Twenty years of Joe Earhart rushed through her mind like a tidal wave that moment followed by a lifetime with Lori. She denied him the comfort of knowing Lori's name already had been erased.

"Stahl?" asked Mike.

A long pause followed.

"You know, screw him. My father is brutal, but fucking brilliant."

Joe looked down at Lori in silence. He shared none of his father's talents. He turned to Susanna and thought of his mother. All three women had threatened Stahl's quest for his rightful place in history. At least the Viet Cong had ensured his status as a war hero as had the cowards who fought under him. But these women ... All three had the heroic daring that had always eluded Joe. But none could comprehend the gravity of her actions. Susanna stood as the primary threat, snatching Stahl's promotion to major general and forcing him to retire. She had no idea what she had set into motion. Joe embraced his mission that evening and snatched his pistol from the rug. He pointed it at Susanna to exact his father's revenge—again.

"A single misstep by one could ruin everybody personally and professionally, except for Fred. He walks away unscathed. Fear is a brilliant means of control," said Joe. His eyes looked like black ice; his movements, quick, but uneven. Heavy perspiration soaked the jacket of his uniform.

Mike prepared to fire. "Joe, put it down."

"I've reported to my father over the years. Susanna, he knows you're the one who blew the whistle at Guantanamo on the supply scam the Marines ran with the Cubans. Yeah, some righteous female lieutenant scuttled his operation. You can't hide from him. He knows everything about you from information I've provided," Joe embellished.

Joe dropped the gun to his side and paced the balcony with a swagger. He felt proud of his work. Joe Earhardt felt like the hero he never became. He wanted to surpass his father's legend, but he knew he remained somewhere in the shadows. Manfred Stahl avoided claiming Joe Earhardt as his son. He continued to pace. His momentary pride returned to self-doubt and loathing.

Mike stood back. His eyes followed his old friend, his trademark long, black bangs dripping with perspiration. Their commanding position above the main hall brought back memories of the midshipmen who bunked together through four years of elation and disappointment. They hung on through the Susanna affair. Should the credit go to the boys or the magic of historic Bancroft Hall?

Mike shook his head. Things looked bleak.

"Man, fix it. Fix this and be done. We may be able to keep you out of prison, but fix what you and Stahl have been planning," pressed Mike.

"I just wanted his approval, but I knew I'd never really have it." Joe collapsed, sobbing. He wiped his face on an already-soaked green sleeve.

"He admires Susanna more and he fucking raped her," yelped Joe in excruciating emotional pain.

As Mike moved toward Joe, he looked at Susanna. He saw no reaction from the girl in the vintage sheath with all the firepower she needed in her black clutch.

"Vietnam scarred my father's virility. As much as violence arouses him, he still could not violate Susanna or any woman the way he wanted," revealed Joe.

Joe realized he had said too much. He pressed his shoulders back and lifted his chin. He regained his composure. He regretted allowing them seeing him as the broken man he had become. He eyed Susanna.

He resented her as much as he did in that Quantico lavatory.

Joe stood and laughed, "It's not about the money, Mikey. It's the fucking power."

Joe knew he had waited too long. He aimed at Susanna, his mess. She had her hand on her Luger ready to fire through her handbag. Mike took aim at Joe.

"She forced his retirement from the Corps and now she threatens what he has worked to build." The pistol shook as Joe spat the words.

"Then why isn't he here, Joe? Are you his fall guy again? His lackey?" taunted Mike.

Joe let out a guttural scream and turned the gun on himself.

"Yes!" he shouted, tears streaming. "Yes! I'm nothing. He says Susanna and Lori have the balls I never had."

"Joe, put ..." Mike began to repeat.

Joe ran away, screeching like a madman. "He's riiiiight!"

Mike watched.

"Go after him!" urged Susanna.

"No. We wait," assured Mike.

CHAPTER THIRTY-FIVE

Manfred Stahl sensed a problem. He had not heard a single siren, let alone the scores he expected. He heard no reports of more dead senators or a son shot or in police custody. No report of Susanna Marcasi slain at the wake of her dear friend.

Even across the Potomac in Arlington, he would hear the arousing sounds of a mass casualty cacophony.

"Two days. He has had two days. Fuck, do I have to handle everything myself?" he asked as he smashed a rare Weimar vase against the French doors in his home office. He felt disdain for Joe, a weak son of a bitch just like his mother. He would deal with him later.

Stahl's business could not wait. As he left his Arlington home he walked past his Doberman, Hercules. The dog dodged his hand and growled. He slapped the dog and walked out the front door. His driver and bodyguard waited for him at the end of the landscaped slate walk.

"National Building Museum, gentlemen," he said.

Stahl's gleaming black limousine pulled up to the front of the elegant structure.

The clock struck 7 p.m., the second and final day of Lori O'Reilly's wake. Stahl still had several hours to view the deceased Senator O'Reilly and cast his spell on all the like-minded huddled around her.

When Stahl entered the large main hall, it seemed as if he sucked all the warmth out the door. He wore a belted black rain coat, which added at least 20 pounds to his already overweight frame. A black fedora covered his balding head. He never carried an umbrella. He stood at the entrance and removed his hat and his black leather gloves. His security guard helped with his coat. He appeared almost handsome in a charcoal Hugo Boss suit. He looked around and could see no other tragedies had befallen the mourners that day—meaning

Susanna Marcasi remained unharmed. He glanced up at the railing and saw no sign of Josef, despite his instructions to meet him there at 7:00.

"Heinrich, on second thought, I'd like to be alone. Wait with the vehicle," he instructed. Heinrich surmised something distracted his boss: Stahl's kindness raised suspicion. Driver and bodyguard drove off looking to buy liquor and maybe score some turbo love. Stahl would never know.

Manfred Stahl took command of the room, charming everyone he encountered. Bigger than life, he sought out Mick O'Reilly, whom he had known for years on the political circuit, but the two were never close. The titans gave one another a bear hug for the crowd, albeit an icy greeting. Stahl moved on. Members of Congress fawned over the man who had every member's missteps committed to memory. Stahl saw it his duty to hold court before he moved to the line that wrapped around the hall. He waited to view Lori's remains. He would wait as long as needed to see her corpse. As he knelt down in front of the casket, he noticed how peaceful she looked.

Her beauty radiated in death as it did when he slit her throat.

She thought she would challenge him and pull out of their deal?

Another stupid bitch.

Stahl took out a white, monogrammed handkerchief and blotted his eyes. As he left the casket he saw Susanna walk toward the stairs. To the restroom, he guessed. Most of the mourners watched him, but he had waited too long not to make his move.

"I don't like being used as bait," she whispered to Mike, as both stood with their backs against opposing metal partitions in a women's restroom stall.

"Don't worry. Do you have your pistol?" he asked.

Susanna knocked her head against the partition as she nodded.

"We can end this soon. None of us will engage until he brags about his crimes. Or he makes an attempt to harm you," Mike said.

"Great," she deadpanned. "He is not going to spew information.

That's not his style."

Susanna inhaled wondering how many breaths she had left with Manfred Stahl on the prowl. She stepped out of the ladies' room. Stahl gave her a moment then slithered up behind her.

"So, Susanna, it's just the two of us again," he said in a hushed, seductive tone.

Startled, she could feel his warm breath in her hair. He had pressed up against her. It disgusted her. He moved his hand up her arm, brushed her skin every few inches. She waited. Stahl took his fingers and brushed back a few fallen tendrils of her hair.

"You are even more beautiful with your hair back," he whispered.

Susanna held her breath. Stahl moved his hand just below her shoulder muscle and wrapped his fingers around her arm, crushing it. He tugged her back toward him forcing her to balance on his chest.

He began to kiss her neck. Mike, who had slipped out of the restroom and moved up another stairwell, watched, winced, and waited.

Susanna relaxed her body pressing deeper into Manfred Stahl. He became aroused as he often had with the girl over the years. As his lips left her neck he took a breath, inhaling everything Susanna. She knew she had but a brief window. She pushed off the unbalanced Stahl's ribs, wheeled around retreating a few steps. She took on the stance of a seductress, which had served her well as a shooter's stance, and prepared for what she hoped would be their final engagement.

His quiet breathing, the strength of his grasp, and the heat that emanated from him like a wildfire repulsed her. Stahl had not changed. She did not care about his crimes against man. An army? Money laundering? The list of the guilty in Washington grew. No. Manfred Stahl hated women with an intensity that defied explanation. Stahl did not attempt to gender cleanse because he knew it stood as the one act even those most fearful of him would stop. But he could terrorize, abuse, rape, and murder a chosen few.

These women threatened him most and deserved a life of pain or no life at all. His reign of terror could extend indefinitely with no one the wiser.

***

Stahl came to Marine Forces Reserve over a long congressional recess. The Corps had just selected him for his second star. The staff knew of Stahl's quirks. They believed his promotion had more to do with his favors on the Hill for the Corps than his talent as a Marine. Some said his use to the Corps as a Marine ended the day he rescued the Marine company. Stahl seemed happy reunited with the force commander, Major General Vic Dumaine.

Susanna's boss, Lieutenant Colonel Steve Camden, warned his new intelligence deputy to stay far away from the headquarters as long as Stahl lurked in the building. Susanna understood, but Camden's suicide following the exposure of his elaborate larceny scheme put Marcasi and Stahl on their collision path.

Susanna had noticed suspicious activity from Stahl's computer. She had one of the public affairs Marines rig his office with a crude camera and recording equipment. Now in the top intel slot, she had unlimited access and used it. Hacking skills aside, between e-mails and stacks of paper on Stahl's desk, she squirreled away everything she could without detection. He had detailed his lucrative side business of ordering weapons and equipment for reserve units and then selling them to the highest bidder. Her in-depth report sat with the Department of Defense Inspector General, bypassing the Marine Corps she had learned to distrust.

Susanna did not understand that the inspector general owed his allegiance to his buddies first. DoD passed the investigation to the Marine Corps. Colonel Paul Railey, the Corps's IG and a Stahl friend from Vietnam, read Stahl excerpts of her report. Railey believed Susanna acted following a lover's quarrel with Fred and left the matter with the charismatic general.

Stahl closed the door to his office and rested his back against the wall. His selection for major general stood as a matter of tremendous, though understated, prestige with his Hill colleagues. His gun-running and military equipment empire netted more than $2 million a year. He saw that the bitch Marcasi threatened his future, his livelihood, and his reputation. She had made a mistake. No one other than he and Susanna knew of his activities, save for the IG oxygen bandits and that damn valor thief Dumaine, a man with the intellect of a goldfish who continued to milk the Blue Max, that, in truth, belonged to Stahl.

An enraged Manfred Stahl decided he had to deal with Marcasi himself.

Susanna Marcasi stayed in shape as a recreational runner. Far from fleet-footed, she became a "let's-see-what-color-that-house-is-this-week" type of jogger. Every Wednesday and Friday she would head straight out Dauphine Street toward the French Quarter. Antoine, the gate guard, always implored, "Captain M., ma'am, you be careful." She would nod and waive to him. The Ninth Ward had had its challenges since the bottom had fallen out of the oil market in the late 1980s. On some days, horrific childhood memories of moving from "uncle" to "uncle" with her mother sobered her view of the fanciful shotgun homes. At other times, she played guest on Ninth Ward turf.

Dauphine, like the other streets in the Bywater had its share of derelict structures. Family homes at one time, now they sat as empty shadows of what had been. Others loomed as predictors of things to come.

"Scuse. Scuse me, Miss. ExSCUSE me," called the little boy, tears streaming down his cheeks.

Susanna slowed her pace and turned back to look at him. The child, no more than six years old, motioned for her to return. She jogged toward him.

"Can you help me get my cat?" he asked.

"Your cat? You have a cat? What's your name?" Susanna knew just about every scheme run by kids in the city. This sounded like yet another, but the little boy seemed distraught and appeared honest.

She had no money on her, though she always wore the hunk of gold on her right hand that screamed, "I went to the Naval Academy."

"I'm Sam. My cat's Maxine and she went in there," he said.

He pointed at the dilapidated shell of a shotgun. "Blighted properties," the city called them.

He moved his hand to shake Susanna's. He had a firm grip, she thought.

"I'm Susanna. Can you show me where you think she might be?" she asked.

The boy hesitated, but slipped his tiny hand in hers. Sam led Susanna into the crumbling structure. "Maxine," called the boy. "Oh, Miss. I think I see her over there," he said pointing to the back of the building.

Susanna grew uneasy. "OK. OK, I'll look." She walked hunched over calling, "Maxine." She walked through one room then another calling the cat's name in her Neanderthal cat crouch, the universal position of all cat owners. She thought about how much she deplored cats as she entered the last room.

"Yeah, yeah, in there, Miss," said Sam.

Susanna stooped down lower to peer under a peeling painted dresser missing its bottom drawer. As she knelt, she felt something slam into the back of her head forcing her face into the urine-soaked concrete slab. She lay surrounded by used needles and condoms. Junk food wrappers dotted the landscape from her vantage.

Dazed, and unaware of what had happened, Susanna scraped her bare arms as she pulled them under her. She placed her palms in a foul-smelling slurry and pushed herself on her knees. Light made its way through the back window, which someone had covered in white latex, casting fanciful shadows. She lifted her head, this time feeling the full force of the large-gauge pipe against the back of her head. Again her face slammed the putrid surface beneath her. As Susanna tried to turn around she shouted, "Run," to the boy.

The boy, house, cat, pain?

Nothing made sense.

Manfred Stahl gave Sam $20 and the boy looked back at Susanna. He could see this was not the surprise the man had told him he had for his daughter. He took the money and ran.

Susanna rolled over and saw Brigadier General Stahl staring down at her.

Camden called it, she thought.

"Too fucking clever," muttered Stahl as he swung the pipe like a bat. Susanna had her arms up defending herself. He struck her braced forearms and beat them until they fell limp on her chest and slid to her sides. He stomped his right heel into her stomach and kicked her in the back when she rolled on her side to throw up. She prayed she would lose consciousness, but her request went unfulfilled.

Her mind cleared. God meant for her to fight. She had her legs. Stahl dragged her to a raised slab. *Another God damn altar*, she thought. She waited without a sound. As he reached to pull off her shorts, she kicked him in the chest. Stahl wanted her to fight. He wanted the Vietnamese and his wife to fight. He wanted them all to fight. Victory should be earned, like his medal. He lunged toward her again. She landed her right foot in the center of his groin. He stumbled back unable to breathe. She scrambled off the sacrificial altar and ran for the window. It would not budge. She tried to kick it out, not noticing the metal security bars outside. She shattered her ankle, but started to make a dash across the room. Her leg gave out in 15 feet. She crawled on her left hand and both knees toward the door, muffling her screams of pain as she dragged her ankle and a broken right arm toward freedom.

She felt her waist-length hair in his grasp. Stahl swung Susanna around and slapped her again and again. Blood seeped from the cuts to her lips as she balanced on her strong leg.

She had not said a word, but finally screamed, "Stop, you freak, just stop."

She stunned both of them. To her surprise, Stahl backed away, lowering the pipe.

Bloodied, but without fear, she looked at her attacker. Out of breath, she bent over, placed her hands on her knees, and studied Stahl.

"You make me sick," she spat as she grew light-headed.

He looked at her. Manfred Stahl reigned over all. But Susanna's stare made him feel less the rightful deity he had long fashioned himself. She took another deep breath and fell over onto the cracked concrete floor. Stahl looked at her and saw the form of an angel but with the powers of a demon. He loved her, but he felt certain she could read his thoughts. She had seen his dark soul. He needed a fearless equal like Marcasi, he thought. His own coward-of-a-son, Josef, remained of marginal use to him, but his whore from their academy days, Captain Susanna Marcasi, she possessed the qualities the child of Manfred Stahl would have.

Stahl had two problems: First, he had no choice but to finish what he had started or risk exposure. Second, as close as Marcasi had come to tricking him into believing her worthiness as his successor, no woman could stand as his equal.

Susanna opened her eyes and saw Stahl's face. She looked at him with an all-knowing stare.

He shuddered.

She could smell his fear.

Susanna had to finish him if she hoped to escape. As she reached for him, her attacker's image grew grainy. Her vision faded to black. Susanna Marcasi lost consciousness. Stahl held her fate in his hands. He pulled out his knife and approached the motionless girl, swinging the pipe.

***

Sam ran home to tell his brothers what had happened. "That white man is beating the nice white lady," he said.

"You gonna share that $20?" asked a disinterested Andrew.

"Won't the police help?" asked a worried Sam.

"No police gonna help three boys like us. You helped that man, Sam," said Aaron, the oldest.

The little boy began to cry again. Sam grabbed his Rottweiler, Marcus, and ran out the door. His brothers followed. An hour had passed since the child had left Susanna. Smoke rose in the distance. To their horror, the three boys saw flames had engulfed the house in which Susanna had tried to help find Maxine. They rushed closer, but the heat and smell of gasoline and the old lead-painted wood overpowered them. Sam looked at Marcus and the boy and his young Rottweiler disappeared into the smoke.

New Orleans Police Chief Roscoe Russell, who lived in the Bywater, pulled up in his unmarked vehicle. He radioed the fire department as he jumped out of his car.

"Boys, get back. What happened?" he asked, shielding himself from the heat.

"Mister, there's a lady in there who got hurt by some man. Our brother and dog are trying to get her out," said Aaron.

"Your brother?" he asked.

"Yeah, He's only six. Please help us, mister," pleaded Andrew.

Russell had heard most of the scams, but a boy and a girl, not to mention the dog, sounded outrageous but plausible to him. He soaked his shirt in water from a can in his trunk. He looked at the boys, "Where are they?"

The frantic boys shook their heads.

"Great," Russell said with characteristic frustration.

Russell sprinted. The towering police chief stayed as low as he could. He heard the dog barking. *Smart dog,* he thought. He went to the last room still untouched by flames and found the little boy on his knees tugging on Susanna, a blood stripe painted down the front of her, trying to drag her out. "C'mon, Miss. C'mon. We gotta go." He had not moved her an inch, but her blood covered the little boy. Russell grabbed Susanna from the blood pool beneath her and placed his arm around her chest. He snatched up with boy with his other arm. Marcus followed. Fire trucks outside had started to douse the flames and extinguished a pile of fiery debris blocking Russell's path.

Sam and the chief coughed and gagged from the smoke. Susanna had stopped breathing. Russell got a couple of breaths into her before he collapsed. Paramedics worked on Susanna, the police chief, and the tiny boy.

***

A decade later, it took Stahl's detailed dossier for Susanna to recall events surrounding the assault. This night she stood on the rich carpet facing her attacker. Now Stahl stood within her reach. She no longer lay on a urine-soaked slab, as she had years earlier. Her bones had healed, but other scars remained.

Few recover, but even fewer get a second chance.

She softened her stance and moved toward him. She pressed against him and ran her gloved hands up and over his shoulders pulling him closer to her. She feigned her attraction to him. It had always bothered Stahl that Susanna Marcasi never remembered his attack. To have survived him made her a legend to him on some level.

"You don't remember, do you Susanna?" He toyed with her like a cat with a mouse.

"How could I forget a disgraced general and Lori O'Reilly's murderer," she cooed still pressed against him, looking up at the 6-foot Stahl as she spoke.

Susanna felt him begin to shake with rage. He felt like a volcano ready to blow.

"I recall you met with an unfortunate accident that ended quite a promising career." He started to slip his tentacles around her, but pulled back.

"What a shame. Injuries like yours are difficult to survive. Odd, they were so similar to Lori's."

They stood toe-to-toe. She could feel the tension through his trousers. Susanna felt powerful. Stahl slipped his hand to the small of her back.

"Such a will to live is arousing." He pulled her closer into him. The smell of her hair intoxicated him. He moved his lips across the top of her head and down her dark waves. He pushed her hair back with his tongue and kissed her neck. She moaned and then turned. Her cheek met his. Her lips touched him. As she let out with a yell, Susanna grabbed his shoulders pulled him off balance. She dashed to find a better position. They were up too high for anyone below to have seen or heard the exchange.

Susanna found her spot, pulled her Luger from her handbag, and pivoted toward Stahl, pointing the relic pistol at his heart. "So let's talk, Fred. You'd be surprised what I remember." She paced back and forth, looked at the ceiling, and then fixed her gaze on Stahl.

"You were the reserve deputy commander in New Orleans. I'm surprised you only traffic weapons, equipment, and now men." She continued to pace move toward him, waving the loaded pistol.

"Ah, how could I forget? You like to beat women, if I recall. And, Fred, I know all about your little private army scheme. Like you said, just the two of us. I'm feeling really nostalgic." Susanna hissed the last word inches from his grasp.

"You ingrate. You and O'Reilly, both ungrateful women who don't know their place." His voice had jumped an octave. He targeted his unbridled anger at Susanna. He started toward her. Her aim remained fixed on him. He looked behind her surprised and saw Mike ready to fire.

"Well, I can see our evening together is coming to an unfortunate end. Ms. Marcasi, a pleasure as always, and I will see you soon."

He walked past Mike without acknowledgement.

They both shook their heads. Chief Russell had arrived and stood at the top of the stairs.

"She's crazier than you are Singleton," said Russell entertained by the pair.

Russell's men had started to secure the building. Mike took it as their cue to leave.

Russell called out, "I'll see everyone at the funeral tomorrow. I think St. Joseph's may become the OK Corral."

CHAPTER THIRTY-SIX

Mike and Susanna drove back across the river in silence. With Lori's two-day wake behind them, the funeral lay ahead. Mike stared at the road, blurred by the lights, mist, and his thoughts of Susanna. She rested her head against the passenger window. Within a few hours this chapter would close.

Then what, Susanna wondered? Lori had been her lifeline, though Susanna never shared that with her. With Lori a few miles away, Susanna had always had hope. Lori filled the roles of safe room and panic button. Lori equated, "Break in Case of Fire."

Terror engulfed her.

Mike pulled up in front of his apartment building. "I have to meet the admiral," he said.

Susanna nodded and exited without a word.

Mike laughed out loud when she accidentally shut Marcus's head in the door and then pulled him in for the night. He decided he preferred Marcus's company to that of Bartholomew's.

Mike drove double the speed limit, eager to get back to the grieving Susanna. He parked in his usual spot in the Pentagon's North Parking field of endless asphalt. He cut the lights and sat.

Another midnight meeting with Ken Bartholomew. *Had the office become the admiral's primary residence? Where did he sleep? When did he sleep?* The admiral's behavior seemed, well, odd, even for the chain-smoking Ken Bartholomew.

Mike approached Bartholomew's office. The admiral had his back to the door.

"Mike, come in," invited a curiously calm Bartholomew.

Did he have a camera in the office or low-tech eyes in the back of his head?

"Did the boys show to the party?" he asked.

How does he know?

Mike described his encounter with Joe Earhardt the first night and the earlier bizarre encounter with Manfred Stahl.

"Ken, shouldn't there be some federal investigative arm involved at this point? Stahl wants Marcasi, and I think he is going to kill her." Mike stood firm in front of Bartholomew's desk.

"Mike, I hear you, but let's see what Stahl does," said Bartholomew as he turned to face Mike.

What more do you want to see?

"We have worked on this off-the-books military machine too long. Just a little more time. Earhardt has confirmed more than we ever found watching him, but I'm not sure how reliable he is. He wasn't such a fucking mess at school." Bartholomew paused to take a couple of long drags from his cigarette. He had become a solid three-pack-a-day man.

"Jesus, Mike. He whines like a four-year-old and thinks his father is George fucking Washington. We have Earhardt, but we need Stahl. We can always put Stahl back on active duty and try him via court martial. I am not ready to pull the plug on this one yet," said Bartholomew.

So, this was not about Earhardt? Is it really about Stahl?

Bartholomew would not yield. He would get that third star and later reign as the youngest Chief of Naval Operations in modern Navy history. God damn the torpedoes and Manfred Stahl.

"Fine. The guy is going to get people killed, and it's on you when he does," declared an angry Mike Singleton, slamming his fist on the desk.

"I'm willing to take that risk," said Bartholomew, unmoved by Singleton's passion.

"Well, I'm not. I'm out. Find someone else, Ken."

Mike turned to leave.

"This is why we are like brothers, Mikey," the manipulative

Bartholomew called after him. "I know you won't leave Marcasi alone with that bastard. If you have to take out Stahl, do it, but try to bring him in alive. This mother fucker has done some horrific things. I know about the senator. I know about his wife. I've known Marcasi's story, and I've been watching your relationship with her."

Bartholomew had proved as kind as he was daring, but knowing he withheld information about Susanna felt like another betrayal. He recalled the lie as well as Susanna's read on the admiral. Mike eyed Bartholomew certain of the admiral's involvement but lacked proof.

Bartholomew read Mike's face.

Mike saw the admiral blink.

They both knew.

"Mike, if I had told you, Marcasi would have become your priority. We must stop Earhardt and Stahl. I know you and Susanna are close again, and, frankly, her restraint is vastly superior to yours ..." said Bartholomew working to repair the damage.

Mike heard these as words of manipulation. Disgusted, he shook his head side to side. He had no evidence of Bartholomew's activities, but he could ensure Susanna's safety. He turned to walk out a second time.

"Hold on, Singleton," said Bartholomew faced with the unexpected challenge. He thought sharing more information might sweeten their deal. He knew the funeral could be the final move in their two-year pitchers' duel. He needed Mike at the plate for the last at-bat.

"Mike, there have been other women. Rape. Same wounds," the admiral said. Anything alluding to Susanna gained Mike's attention, but he remained dubious.

"All have died except Marcasi and Stahl's ex-wife. No one has enough on this guy to do anything. You're the closest. Do what you have to do, but bring in Stahl," said Bartholomew.

For Mike that meant, "Shoot to kill."

"Got it, admiral." *I am your assassin. Yeah, I am your trident, Poseidon. Glad to help.*

CHAPTER THIRTY-SEVEN

Susanna lay in Mike's arms, staring at the ceiling. The clock read 7 a.m. The funeral would begin at 11 o'clock. Marcus lay on one side of her and rested his head on her bare thigh. She held her breath listening to the first quiet moment since she kicked the 18-year-old out of her bed almost a week earlier.

She thought about the funeral. She had pushed off the good-bye as long as she could. Planning the wake and funeral bought her precious time, but it would soon end. Mike would walk out of her life. She loved him. She knew the loneliness she would feel that evening and did not want to go back to a life of perpetual pain. The promise of emptiness overwhelmed her, and thoughts of her old panic button returned to the forefront. "Suicide" remained the perfect safe word, as long as no one else heard it. Since she played the Blessed Virgin for Mick O'Reilly, she had found comfort in her choice to live or die.

Plan B looked like a good option that morning to the grieving Susanna Marcasi.

"Are you OK?" asked Mike. He had just three hours' sleep following his tête-a-tête with the admiral. He caressed her shoulders. She did not flinch, but felt reassured. He did not see the smile of satisfaction that appeared across her lips. He did not sense the depth of emotion she had for him. She had hidden it well.

But he could feel something had changed.

"I'm fine. Why?" She turned toward him.

"You look sad. Actually, bewildered," he observed though he did not want to frighten her.

"Yeah, of course I'm sad," she said.

Her voice trailed off. Mike kissed her soft brown hair.

"Mike, I need you to help me through this," she said looking away.

"Of course," he said. How could she not know he was there for her until she told him to leave again, he wondered, frustrated.

"Susanna, I'll help you through today, tomorrow, and the day after that," he said.

She did not believe him.

At 10 o'clock, Susanna and Mike walked up the steps of St. Joseph's, her hand tucked into his arm. She wore a black vintage Chanel suit and a spring swing coat. Mike chose another dark Armani creation. They entered together. Susanna turned and looked at the Hart Building against a perfect blue spring sky. The temperature had passed 70 degrees, warm for April, and no one complained. The weather almost assured a standing room-only crowd. Susanna saw the visible support as good for the family.

Once inside, she turned and looked at him. "As we discussed?" she asked.

He nodded.

Susanna went to the left side of the church to check the lectern and then took her place with the O'Reillys in the first pew. She sat as far from Mick O'Reilly as possible. She passed Joe Earhardt to her right, resplendent in his Dress Blues, like the Joe she once knew. No sign of Stahl. Despite D.C.'s strict gun laws, she carried her Luger. Again.

As the priest said Mass, the closed, polished casket sat at the base of the altar surrounded by many of the flowers from the two previous days. After a brief homily, the priest nodded. Susanna rose and took her place at the lectern for the eulogy. She scanned the church.

Still no sign of Stahl.

"On behalf of Lori's family, I'd like to thank Lori's Washington, D.C., family as well as our friends who made the trip from New Orleans for coming. The O'Reillys have allowed me to say a few words about their daughter and sister. I owe a tremendous debt to the O'Reilly family. They saved me as a child, and Lori carried on that tradition years later when she gambled and made me a part of her congressional kin. She covered for my transgressions more often than I can recount. But I was not the only recipient of her kindness and generosity. Lori loved people and helped countless in need. It was who she was."

Susanna pushed the microphone to the side. She spoke with force, painting the final picture of the girl in red, the girl who worshipped Joe.

The woman who said, "No," to Manfred Stahl.

As she talked, she spotted a mysterious figure at the rear of the church. She looked again but it disappeared. She thought she hallucinated. A couple of minutes later it reappeared. Then it vanished. A male figure walked across the back of the church through the overflowing crowd gathered to say its final good-bye to Lori O'Reilly.

Susanna lost her concentration. She shunned notes and had none with her. She reverted to Lori stories and began to veer out of control. She started to tell the vehicular manslaughter story outside Tipitina's, but caught herself. She felt certain she saw Stahl lumbering between the crevices of the church like a rodent.

She stood alone, exposed on the altar.

At that moment she understood the meaning of "fish in a barrel."

"Lori O'Reilly died a hero. She isn't just my hero; she is a hero to all on the Hill. Lori died exposing a traitorous scheme of a former colleague."

She knew she could draw out the rat.

She stood in control.

Stahl had not expected the exposé. *Damn that Marcasi.* Had he not convinced her to shut up while in his grasp hours earlier? Her boldness distracted him. Her unabashed lunge for power made him want her. He found their confrontations erotic. Her challenge on the altar in her little frock like his first wife wore, more so. He wondered, *Kill her? Violate her?* Lie with her in his splendid Louis XIV bed?

Befuddled, he hesitated.

Manfred Stahl gathered his thoughts like he racked pool balls. He had to act. Susanna continued to confess his sins, though she had not named him. He found this a curious move and her, a formidable foe. He wanted credit for those marvelous deeds she described. He was Manfred Stahl; the rest in the church sat as bleating sheep.

When Stahl reappeared, he moved up the center aisle and wedged his way into a pew. Only she took notice of him, and he knew it. The police covered the church, but had not detected anything unusual. He saw this as just the two of them, as he remarked with her pressed against him the previous evening.

Susanna eyed Stahl and started to describe the attack on Lori. She detailed how the murderer had berated Lori in a Senate conference room, slapping her, but she refused to back down. She described the unfathomable things he did to her and revealed she suffocated on her own blood.

The mourners sat repulsed, yet riveted. They waited for more from Susanna. They had expected a funeral, but found first-rate theater.

Stahl gasped. Marcasi knew about the conference room. She knew everything. Susanna held back her sobs as she laid out the horrors Lori suffered. The packed church ached with her. Susanna had offered testimony more than eulogy and she knew it.

"I share these gruesome details with you because of her determination to stop a plan to …"

Stahl's chest tightened. Susanna had her memory back. Or she never lost it. She stood as the only one who could testify against him, save for his gutless son. He stood up from the pew and took his characteristic large steps down the aisle. Susanna brushed her hair back and reached into the lectern. Stahl moved closer, drew his pistol from his shoulder holster took aim on Susanna. He did not notice Joe to his right as he stormed past the pews. Through the sound of her breathing, she heard a roar, "No more!" Joe leaped from his seat tackling his father from behind. The shot from Mike and his rifle in the organist seat high in the back of the church rang out at the same time, piercing Joe. Susanna fumbled beneath the lectern. The mourners screamed. Some stood to run.

Manfred Stahl pushed Joe's motionless body off of him. He rose and took aim on Susanna 25 yards ahead. He closed to 20. To 15 yards. Susanna pulled her hands from the lectern. Two bullets in quick succession from her Luger struck him in the heart. A third in the head. Mike's single shot hit Stahl at the base of the skull. His lifeless corpse hit the floor.

The mourners froze. Had Susanna Marcasi just killed Manfred Stahl?

Susanna watched as Stahl collapsed. She had not killed anyone since the Persian Gulf War and did not see herself getting used to it. She looked up at Mike, waiting for him to exhale. He looked for a sign from her. Susanna opened her eyes wide then slowly closed her lids, drawing a shade between them. She opened them with characteristic grace exposing the soft, dark gaze he never tired of. She saw the air of concern that filled his lungs leave him.

They stood as one.

Susanna and Mike looked at the fallen foot soldiers on the cold stone floor. Blood began to pool.

My God! thought Susanna. *What have we done?*

Susanna ran through the week's sordid trail in her mind. *How did it come to this? Who are we to have placed ourselves in the middle of Stahl's cabal?* she wondered. *If not Stahl's scheme, then whose? Did it matter? Stahl,* she thought. *Fucking Stahl.* Hell, she did not think her God would mind some profanity directed at Manfred Stahl even on Catholic turf. Stahl, her tormentor and rapist. A traitor, though some will say patriot, she predicted.

It did matter. She and Mike had removed their sole buffer against the main backer of Stahl's scheme, maybe worse. If he or she could make Stahl his puppet, that person could prove capable of far worse than Manfred Stahl.

He would come for her, too.

She sighed, looking back up at Mike. He studied her face and he knew, but hoped she would change her mind.

Susanna looked at Russell and his men who had their weapons

drawn with mouths gaping. She nodded and Russell's team removed father and son.

Susanna closed her eulogy as she had penned in her head, "Goodbye, my dearest friend, my only friend, my truest friend. You saved my life many times over." She paused, her voice began to crack. "Though I can never repay you for your many sacrifices, I hope it is not too long before we laugh and hug again."

Susanna turned away and left the church.

CHAPTER THIRTY-EIGHT

The morning after the funeral, Susanna stood with Mick O'Reilly on the platform at Union Station, steps from the Capitol.

Susanna stared at him. The sick bastard was right. The fading of memories made loss more painful. She would close one of the most important chapters in her life. It did not seem possible. She threw her arms around him her old torturer and would not let him go. She sobbed.

"I know, Susanna. I know. Your home is always with us," he said.

She smiled and nodded. He disappeared onto the train. She assumed he disappeared from her life forever.

As Susanna turned to leave she peered down the platform. She craned her neck. She squinted her tear-filled eyes. She saw a man in black. Mike Singleton stood on the other end of the long, tiled walkway wearing the form-fitting black jeans that made her blush, his black boots, and buttery soft leather jacket. He added a black shirt and tie to complete her fantasy.

The sight of Mike made her weep. Lost years. Lost love. She blamed herself. *Too much loss,* she thought. She turned and walked away. He watched her leave as he had so long ago. Susanna hurried through the crowd of travelers. Above the noise of men and machines she heard his pitch-perfect whistle. She stopped but dared not look. She recalled the whine of his harmonica as he would entertain her and Joe in the room the boys shared. She waited. He saw she stood still. He offered his most mournful,

"You are my sunshine
My only sunshine ...
Please don't take my sunshine away."

She turned and faced him, murmuring the final line with him as he walked toward her. For Susanna, the sunshine was gone. The fire extinguished.

It was over.

Susanna Marcasi looked at Mike Singleton. He saw a faint smile of regret fading from her lips. She turned and disappeared into the crowd.

BLOOD STRIPE

ABOUT THE AUTHOR

GINA MARIA DINICOLO *is a military historian and award-winning journalist who has written on military topics for nearly two decades. She is a graduate of the U.S. Naval Academy and served as an officer in the Marine Corps.*

BLOOD STRIPE